USA TODAY Bestselling Author

Laura Scott
and
Heather Woodhaven

Guarding the Witness

Previously published as *Copycat Killer* and *Chasing Secrets*

LOVE INSPIRED
INSPIRATIONAL ROMANCE

LOVE INSPIRED®

INSPIRATIONAL ROMANCE

ISBN-13: 978-1-335-42457-0

Guarding the Witness

Copyright © 2021 by Harlequin Books S.A.

Copycat Killer
First published in 2020. This edition published in 2021.
Copyright © 2020 by Harlequin Books S.A.

Chasing Secrets
First published in 2020. This edition published in 2021.
Copyright © 2020 by Harlequin Books S.A.

Special thanks and acknowledgment are given to Laura Scott and Heather Woodhaven for their contribution to the True Blue K-9 Unit: Brooklyn miniseries.

This edition published by arrangement with Harlequin Books S.A.

For questions and comments about the quality of this book, please contact us at CustomerService@Harlequin.com.

Love Inspired
22 Adelaide St. West, 40th Floor
Toronto, Ontario M5H 4E3, Canada
www.Harlequin.com

Printed in U.S.A.

CONTENTS

Laura Scott is a nurse by day and an author by night. She has always loved romance and read faith-based books by Grace Livingston Hill in her teenage years. She's thrilled to have published over twenty-five books for Love Inspired Suspense. She has two adult children and lives in Milwaukee, Wisconsin, with her husband of over thirty years. Please visit Laura at laurascottbooks.com, as she loves to hear from her readers.

Books by Laura Scott

Love Inspired Suspense

True Blue K-9 Unit: Brooklyn

Copycat Killer

Justice Seekers

Soldier's Christmas Secrets

Callahan Confidential

Shielding His Christmas Witness
The Only Witness
Christmas Amnesia
Shattered Lullaby
Primary Suspect
Protecting His Secret Son

True Blue K-9 Unit

Blind Trust
True Blue K-9 Unit Christmas
"Holiday Emergency"

Visit the Author Profile page
at Harlequin.com for more titles.

COPYCAT KILLER

Laura Scott

Blessed is he whose transgression is forgiven,
whose sin is covered.
—*Psalm* 32:1

This book is dedicated to Lisa Collins,
who loves dogs as much as I do.
I'm so happy to have our families forever joined
by the marriage of our children.

ONE

Willow Emery approached her brother and sister-in-law's two-story home in Brooklyn, New York, with a deep sense of foreboding. The white paint on the front door of the yellow brick building was cracked and peeling, the windows covered with grime. A short decorative black iron fence surrounded the small front yard, revealing empty food wrappers and cigarette butts strewn across the tiny lawn. She swallowed hard, hating that her three-year-old niece, Lucy, lived in such deplorable conditions.

Steeling her resolve, she straightened her shoulders. This time, she wouldn't be dissuaded so easily. Her older brother, Alex, and his wife, Debra, had to agree that Lucy deserved better.

Squeak. Squeak. The rusty gate moving in the breeze caused a chill to ripple through her. Why was it open? She hurried forward and her stomach knotted when she found the front door hanging ajar. The tiny hairs on the back of her neck lifted in alarm and a shiver rippled down her spine.

Something was wrong. Very wrong.

Thunk. The loud sound startled her. Was that a door

closing? Or something worse? Her heart pounded in her chest and her mouth went dry. Following her gut instincts, Willow quickly pushed the front door open and crossed the threshold. The assault of sour milk mixed with awful bodily odors hit hard. Bile rose in her throat as she strained to listen. "Alex? Lucy?"

There was no answer, only the echo of soft, hiccuping sobs.

"Lucy!" Hurrying now, she followed the sound through the kitchen, briefly taking note of the dozens of empty liquor bottles and overflowing dirty dishes in the sink. Reaching the living room, she stumbled to an abrupt halt, her feet seemingly glued to the floor. Lucy was kneeling near her mother, crying. Alex and Debra were lying facedown, unmoving and not breathing, blood seeping out from beneath them.

Were those bullet holes between their shoulder blades? Her brother's head was turned to the side, his eyes vacant and staring. *No! Alex!* A wave of nausea had her placing a hand over her stomach.

She locked her gaze on her niece. "Lucy?"

The girl lifted her head. Her tearstained face tugged at her heart. "Aunt Willow, Mommy and Daddy won't wake up," she sobbed.

"Lucy, sweetie, it's okay. Come with me, baby." Hands shaking, Willow stepped carefully, avoiding the large pool of blood, until she was close enough to lift Lucy up and into her arms.

Lucy didn't stop crying, but curled her arms around her neck, clinging tightly. Willow pressed a hand to her niece's wavy blond hair, holding her close for a long moment. Then she shifted the girl to her hip, bent down and pressed her fingers against her brother's neck, searching for a pulse.

Nothing.

A sob rose in her throat, but she fought it back. With trembling fingers, she checked Debra, too. Still nothing. Should she try CPR?

Remembering the thud gave her pause. She glanced furtively over her shoulder toward the single bedroom on the main floor. The door was closed. What if the gunman was still here? Waiting? Hiding?

The terrifying possibility had her spinning away and retracing her steps through the disgusting kitchen and out the front door. She stumbled through the lawn, kicking something that crinkled beneath her foot out of the way, until she reached the sidewalk.

Fumbling for her phone with her right hand, she tried to understand what had just happened. Who had shot Alex and Debra? And why? What caused the thudding noise?

What had her older brother gotten himself into?

She pulled herself together, knowing she needed to call the police, to get help.

She dialed 911 and pressed the phone to her ear, one arm still securely wrapped around Lucy.

"This is the operator. What's the nature of your emergency?"

"My brother and his wife have been shot. Please send the police right away!"

"Are you safe, ma'am?"

Good question. The back of her neck tingled with fear and she whipped around, frantically searching for something, anything, out of place. She wished for a place to hide. There was a small tree nearby, and she instinctively made her way toward it, cowering beneath the branches that were just now budding leaves, pressing her back against the slim trunk. "I—I don't know."

"What's the address?"

She rattled off the number of the house on Thirty-Fifth Street. "It's off Linden Boulevard in East Flatbush. Please hurry!"

"I'm calling the closest officer to your location. Please stay on the line."

"Just get here, soon!" Willow didn't want to stay on the line; she needed both of her arms to hold Lucy. Leaving the phone on speaker, she tucked it into the back pocket of her jeans. She held her niece, stroking a soothing hand down Lucy's back, murmuring reassuringly in her ear. Vehicles moved up and down Linden Boulevard, yet Willow still felt vulnerable. Exposed. What if they were still in danger?

What if the gunman was out there, watching her?

She swept her gaze over the area again, but still didn't see anything suspicious. Yet she couldn't shake the itchy feeling of being watched. The narrow tree offered little protection. Where should she go? What should she do? She momentarily closed her eyes, fighting panic.

Dear Lord, keep us safe in Your care!

The whispered prayer helped to calm her irrational need to run far, far away. Her apartment was in Bay Ridge, too far to walk, let alone run. Not to mention the bloodstains on Lucy's clothes would draw attention to them. Willow took several deep breaths, knowing she needed to relax so Lucy wouldn't pick up on her fear.

"It's okay, Lucy. We're fine. We're going to be just fine."

Lucy's crying slowly quieted, but the little girl didn't release her deathlike grip, as if afraid of being left behind.

A white SUV with the blue NYPD K-9 logo along the side and a red flashing light on its dashboard came barreling down the street toward them, abruptly pulling over to the curb. A tall, lean blond officer dressed in a black uniform came out from behind the wheel, weapon held ready. Moving quickly, he opened his hatch, letting a beautiful yellow Lab wearing a K9 vest out of the back.

"Stay where you are," the officer said when she moved from the relative safety of the tree to head toward him. His gaze raked the area as he hurried over. His name tag identified his last name as Detective Slater. "What happened? Are you both okay?"

"Yes. But I found my brother and his wife d—" She glanced at Lucy and amended what she'd been about to say. "Um, hurt. Both the gate and the front door were hanging ajar when I arrived." She shivered, the reality of it all just starting to sink in. "The bedroom door was closed. I'm afraid someone is still inside."

He nodded but didn't move away. He spoke into his radio, asking for an ETA of his backup. She couldn't deny the overwhelming relief she and Lucy were no longer alone.

"I need you to both wait inside my SUV." He took her elbow and urged her toward the police vehicle just as his backup arrived. "Stay inside. I'll be back soon."

She didn't argue, feeling much safer inside the car. She continued to hold Lucy on her lap as she watched Detective Slater and two uniformed cops go inside the house with their weapons up in a two-handed grip.

The seconds went by with excruciating slowness and she buried her face against Lucy's hair, still grappling with what had happened.

A sharp rap against the window startled her. She relaxed when she saw Detective Slater standing there. He opened the door and she slid out, standing to face him. She had to look up at him, which was unusual as she was taller than most women. His expression was kind, but grim. "I'm sorry for your loss. The house is clear. There's no one inside."

Sorry for your loss. She momentarily closed her eyes and rested her cheek on Lucy's head. She'd known her brother and his wife were dead.

Murdered.

Why? She couldn't imagine anyone wanting to kill her brother and his wife. And what about Lucy?

Was the little girl in danger, too?

Nate Slater kept his gaze on the tall, pretty woman holding the cute little girl, fearing she might collapse under the weight of the bad news.

He tucked a hand beneath her elbow to hold her steady. "Are you sure you're okay?"

She shook her head, but then nodded. Shrugged. "I have to be."

He understood where she was coming from. The poor woman and the little girl had witnessed the result of violence that most only read about. Going through an ordeal like this couldn't be easy for either of them.

As part of the newly established Brooklyn K-9 Unit, an offshoot of the original NYC K-9 Command Unit that was still located in Queens, he and his four-legged partner, Murphy, had been dealing with another issue close by when he'd gotten the call to come to this location. The Brooklyn K-9 Unit responded to calls across all five boroughs of New York City, the canine partners' specializations aiding the officers in investigating crimes and tracking down perpetrators. Nate's dog was cross-trained in a variety of skills. "I need to ask a few questions, Ms.…"

"Willow. Willow Emery. This is my niece, Lucy Emery." She raised her chin and the stubborn flash in her light brown eyes was surprisingly reassuring. "I'll tell you whatever you need to know."

"You mentioned the front door wasn't closed all the way. Did your brother normally keep the place locked up?"

"Yes. Always. That's why the noise was so jarring."

"Noise?" His interest was piqued.

She nodded. "A thud, like a door banging closed."

"Or the sound of gunfire?"

Her eyes rounded in horror. "No!"

The timing seemed off, but he continued. "Okay, and normally the back door would also be locked?" He'd noticed the back door had been closed, but not locked. It appeared the intruder may have been let in from the front, maybe someone the victims had known. Something must have gone wrong, and they'd been shot in the back, the killer escaping out the back door.

"I think so, yes. Unless they were outside. The back patio has a little fence around it, similar to the one in the front."

Yeah, he'd noticed the fence, more for decoration than anything else, and not very high, so any able-bodied person could easily climb over.

He felt certain the perp had escaped that way and

itched to begin searching. But he needed more information, something to go on.

"Lucy?" He waited for the little girl to look up at him. "Did you see anything?"

She didn't answer, and Willow lightly stroked her hair.

"It's okay, tell the policeman what you saw."

"Bad clown."

Lucy's whisper gave him pause. Nate leaned closer, trying to appear nonthreatening. "What did you say?"

Lucy immediately ducked her head, hiding her face against Willow's neck.

He caught Willow's gaze, silently pleading. He needed to question the little girl further.

"Lucy, you're safe here with me and Detective Slater. But we really need to know, did you see someone hurt your mommy and daddy?" Willow's tone was soft, gentle.

There was a momentary hesitation, then the little girl gave a tentative nod.

Nate's pulse spiked with adrenaline. A possible witness, albeit a very young one. But maybe old enough to provide something for them to go on. "Can you tell me what you saw?"

Lucy hunched her shoulders without responding. Long seconds ticked by before the child finally said, "The bad clown weared black."

Bad clown wearing black? Nate still didn't quite get it, but now they had a description to go on. The two uniformed officers who'd helped him clear the house crossed over to join him, as another K-9 officer from his unit, Vivienne Armstrong, and her black-and-white border collie partner, Hank, arrived. Hank's specialty was search and rescue, and Nate was glad to have the excellent tracker on the hunt.

"Nate? What's going on?" Vivienne asked.

He stepped back from Willow and Lucy, instinctively taking charge of the scene. "Two DOAs inside, house has been cleared but it's possible the perp went out the back. I need one NYPD officer to stay here with Willow and Lucy. The rest of us need to fan out and search for the killer, likely dressed in black and possibly wearing a mask." He couldn't be certain what Lucy meant by clown and thought the perp could be wearing something plastic over his or her face.

"I'll stay," Officer Klein volunteered.

"Good. Murphy and I will go south. Vivienne, you and Hank head east. I need you, Officer Talbot, to head west," he directed. He didn't think anyone would have come north toward the front of the house. "Keep your radio frequency open and if you find someone suspicious, proceed with caution. Perp is likely armed with a gun."

"Got it," Vivienne said as the rest nodded in agreement.

The three of them split up, he and Murphy taking the path he thought was more likely the one the killer used as an escape route. The Holy Saints Cemetery was located a few blocks to the south of the Emery property, and he thought there was a good chance the "bad clown wearing black" had gone that way.

A quick glance at the crime scene hadn't revealed anything left behind by the perp. He wanted to stay to search more closely but couldn't deny a keen sense of urgency. How much time had passed since the emergency call Willow had made? Five minutes? Seven?

Too long.

He and Murphy reached the twin dark gray stone arches of the cemetery entrance in less than two minutes. Entering the cemetery grounds, he examined the soft earth around the tombstones searching for signs of footprints. After the April rainstorm late yesterday afternoon, which had softened the ground and eliminated most of the leftover remnants of winter snow, he was hopeful no one could cut through without leaving evidence behind.

A partial footprint in the mud caught his gaze. It was wide on top and deep, making him think it was made by a man, maybe even someone running. Expanding his search, he tried to find another one that looked similar, in an effort to provide a direction the perp may have taken. He wanted to use the footprint as a scent source for Murphy to follow, but knew that without a second footprint indicating evidence of running away, he couldn't be sure it was left by the killer. He didn't want Murphy to search for the wrong person.

He searched for another fifteen minutes but came up empty.

Either the guy had stayed to the paved walkway snaking around the grounds or he hadn't come this way at all.

Nate didn't want to give up, but after more fruitless searching, he cued his radio. "Any sign of the perp?"

A chorus of negatives echoed from the other officers.

"Let's call it off." He didn't want to but didn't see the point of continuing a random search. In his gut he felt the killer was long gone, but he'd hoped for something, anything, to go on. "Thanks for your help."

Several ten-fours echoed from the radio.

Nate and Murphy double-timed it back to the scene of the murders. He slowed to a walk when he came around the Emery house.

Willow was sitting crossways on the passenger seat of his SUV with the door open, still holding Lucy on her lap. He noticed she was wearing soft blue jeans and a thin pink hoodie in deference to the sixty-degree spring day. There were many vehicles parked on the street, so he wasn't sure if she'd driven over or if she'd arrived via subway or bus. The little girl was wearing a cheerful yellow top with a flared hem over yellow bloodstained leggings. Officer Klein, the uniform who'd stayed behind, remained standing nearby.

"Doggy," Lucy said, pointing at Murphy. "Big doggy."

He crossed over to where Willow and Lucy were, dropping to his knees so he was eye level with both Murphy and the little girl. He wondered why the child had been spared. Because she was in another room? Or because the perp drew some invisible line at shooting an innocent child?

"This is Murphy." He introduced the K-9 again. "Friend, Murphy." He touched both Willow and Lucy, while repeating, "Friend."

"Hold out your hand for the doggy to sniff," Willow encouraged.

Lucy held out her hand, smiling a bit when Murphy's nose touched her skin. "Nice doggy."

"Yes, Murphy is a nice dog. He won't hurt you."

Willow searched his gaze. "Find anything?"

He shook his head. "I'd like to ask Lucy a few more questions if that's okay."

Willow's light brown eyes looked concerned, but she nodded. "Can't hurt to try."

Nate waited until Lucy looked at him, with eyes that were mirror images of Willow's. If he didn't know any better, he'd think they were mother and daughter instead of aunt and niece. "Lucy, can you tell me more about the bad clown that wore black?"

Her tiny brow puckered with fear. "Scary," she whispered.

"I know it was scary," he agreed with a gentle smile. "But you're a brave girl, aren't you? I need you to tell me what the bad clown looked like."

"Big. Mean." Lucy scrunched up her face. "Clown face with blue hair on top." She lifted a hand to her own hair as if to describe what she meant.

Blue hair? His chest tightened at her description. Twenty years ago—today—there had been a double murder in Brooklyn. Two of his colleagues, a brother and a sister, Bradley and Penelope McGregor, then just kids, had lost their parents. Bradley, fourteen, had been at a friend's house, and four-year-old Penelope, left unharmed like Lucy, had been the only witness. She'd described the killer as a clown—with blue hair. He'd been thinking about the cold case today, as he knew the entire unit was, because of the anniversary. Twenty years unsolved. "You're sure the hair was blue?"

She bobbed her head. "Blue like my dolly."

Her dolly? He lifted a brow and glanced up at Willow, who nodded.

"Yes, she has a doll with bright blue hair."

"Okay, blue hair on the top of the clown face," he repeated. "Did you notice anything else about him?"

She shook her head. "Too scary."

He imagined she'd hid her face and hoped that she hadn't seen her parents being murdered in cold blood.

He thought again how odd it was they'd both been shot in the back. As if they'd been heading out of the kitchen, toward the living room. Is that where Lucy had been? Or were they going there for some other reason?

No way to know for sure. The place was a mess, but it was difficult to tell if it had been searched by the killer. After making a mental note to tell the crime scene techs to make the living room a priority when looking for evidence, he turned his attention to the little girl. "What else, Lucy? Were you in the house when he came inside?"

Lucy shook her head, reaching out to pet Murphy's sleek fur.

"No? Where were you?" Willow asked.

"Outside playing." Lucy looked over toward the front of the house. "Mommy and Daddy were inside."

Nate's gaze sharpened. "He came up the sidewalk and into the fenced-in front yard?"

"Yes. He gave me a toy and told me to stay outside." Her lower lip trembled, and Nate was concerned she might cry.

"It's okay, Lucy, you're safe with us," Willow said, gently hugging her. "What kind of toy?"

"A monkey." Lucy's face crumpled. "I don't want it anymore."

A monkey? He sucked in a breath. The McGregors' killer had also given Penelope a stuffed monkey. What was going on here?

"Are you sure?" he asked hoarsely. "Was it a stuffed monkey?"

Lucy bobbed her head up and down. "I left it outside when I heard the loud noise, but I don't want it anymore. I want my mommy!"

"Shh, it's okay. I'm here, Lucy." Willow cuddled her close.

Nate rocked back on his heels, stunned speechless. The clown face with blue hair on top, two bullet holes in Lucy's parents and a stuffed monkey.

The exact same MO as the twenty-year-old unsolved McGregor murders. The brutal slaying of the parents of fellow Brooklyn K-9 detective Bradley McGregor and his sister, desk clerk Penelope McGregor.

Down to the very last detail.

The idea that a killer from twenty years ago was still out there concerned him.

They needed to get this guy, and soon. Before anyone else ended up hurt, or worse, dead.

TWO

At first Willow thought Lucy was imagining things. Mean clown with blue hair? Wearing black? Giving her a stuffed monkey and telling her to stay outside? But she vaguely remembered her foot hitting something soft yet crinkly as she crossed the front lawn, and the shock that rippled over Nate Slater's face was all too real. "What's wrong? Do you know who did this?"

Nate shook his head, averting his gaze. "No, but we're going to do our best to find the person responsible." He turned and smiled gently at Lucy. "You're very brave, Lucy. Thank you for telling me what you saw." He stood. "Come, Murphy. Vivienne? Will you and Hank give me a moment?"

"Sure." The pretty, dark-haired, dark-eyed K-9 cop hurried over and followed as Nate and Murphy headed purposefully to the front of the house, no doubt searching for the stuffed monkey.

Lucy burrowed against Willow. She cuddled the little girl close, knowing her niece was traumatized, and silently promised to make sure Lucy was set up with a child psychologist as soon as possible.

She also hoped the little girl wasn't in any sort of ongoing danger. Granted, the mean clown had tried to hide his identity, but she couldn't afford to ignore the possibility that he might return to finish what he'd started.

Nate returned, a small stuffed animal enclosed in what appeared to be two evidence bags. "Lucy, is this the monkey? Did the bad clown give it to you in a bag?"

Lucy lifted her head from Willow's shoulder and nodded.

He glanced at Vivienne. "This guy is smart, knew enough to minimize the scent by wearing gloves and putting the toy in a bag. Murphy wasn't able to pick up the scent to track. We can hope to lift prints from the plastic bag surrounding the monkey, but I'm not holding my breath."

Vivienne grimaced. "Nate, you'd better call Sarge, give him the update."

"Yeah." He dropped his tone making it difficult to hear. "Gavin Sutherland is going to take this personally. You know how much he feels responsible for Bradley and Penny McGregor, especially today. It's not going to be easy to tell them their parents' killer may be back." Nate tucked the double-bagged monkey in his pocket and reached for his phone.

Her gaze clung to Nate Slater's tall, muscular figure as he contacted his boss. She couldn't help overhearing pieces of his conversation.

"Gavin? Slater here. Listen, this is big. I've got two dead victims, parents of a child who survived, and the perp's MO is exactly like the McGregor case from twenty years ago down to the last detail, including the stuffed monkey."

Nate fell silent as he listened to his boss.

"I agree, the murderer must have resurfaced again, but why? Where's he been all this time—"

"Is there anything I can get you?" Vivienne interrupted with a polite smile.

Willow flushed, wondering if the female K-9 officer knew she'd been eavesdropping.

"Yes, I—uh, would like to get some of Lucy's things, like her clothes and a few favorite toys."

Vivienne frowned. "I'm sorry, but I don't think you can take anything out until the crime scene has been processed." The officer's gaze sharpened at something over her head. "It appears the ME and crime scene techs are here now."

Willow turned in time to see two large vehicles. The dark van must belong to the coroner; the other was a white box truck with the NYPD logo that parked directly in front of Detective Slater's SUV. She watched as a petite blonde with dimples emerged from behind the wheel, crossing over to join them.

"Darcy, this is Willow and Lucy Emery," Vivienne said by way of introduction. "Darcy Fields is a forensic specialist with NYPD who often responds to our cases."

Willow nodded a greeting, the names already becoming a jumble in her mind.

Except for Nate Slater. And Murphy.

Nate disconnected from the call and crossed over to rejoin them. "Darcy, after you process the main crime scene, I want you to do a thorough sweep of the living room to see if you can find anything that may be hidden."

"Hidden in the living room?" Willow asked. "What makes you think that?"

The three of them glanced at her as if they'd forgotten she was there.

"No special reason," Nate hedged. "Just a hunch."

"Got it," Darcy agreed. The bright paisley scarf

around her throat was a burst of scarlet against the tan khaki slacks and white blouse. She hurried back to the van and began donning protective gear.

Hunch? About something hidden? Willow realized Nate and Vivienne weren't going to clue her in as to what their investigation was revealing; it must be against some sort of cop rules. She frowned, thinking over her brief foray into the house. The kitchen had been a disaster, but she'd seen it that way before. The living room had been unusually messy, as well. Two months ago, the last time she'd confronted her brother and his wife about Lucy's welfare, it had looked much the same.

It hurt to remember how she'd found Lucy hungry and wearing dirty clothes, with little food appropriate for a young child in the house. Alex had quickly sent Debra out to pick up some groceries, then told Willow to mind her own business.

She'd been tempted to report Alex and Debra to Child Protective Services, but decided to give them a chance to do better. To make things right. But as the weeks passed without a response to her many phone calls to Alex, she'd come to face off with them in person. To tell them to voluntarily give her temporary custody of Lucy or she'd notify CPS.

Now they were dead. *Dead!* It all seemed so surreal. As if this nightmare was happening to someone else, not to her.

Which brought her back to the present. Why was Nate focused on something being hidden in the living room? It didn't make sense.

As Lucy turned in her lap, reaching out to pet Murphy again, it hit her.

Alex and Debra had been shot in the back, lying

facedown just inside the living room. She could almost imagine the shooter being in the kitchen, firing as they were walking, or maybe even running, toward the living room.

Her stomach churned. Had they been trying to get to something they'd hidden for safekeeping? She was thankful that Lucy had been outside when the "bad clown" had killed her parents. But that didn't prevent her from wishing she had called CPS months ago.

If she had, maybe her brother and his wife would have pulled themselves together, doing the right thing to get Lucy back. Had they been involved in something shady that had gotten them killed? Or was it a random murder?

Anyway, now it was too late. They were gone. And she couldn't turn back the clock.

"Aunt Willow, I'm hungry." Lucy's plaintive tone made her realize how long they'd been outside.

"Okay, hang on, I have some animal crackers with me." She dug in her oversize shoulder bag, finding the animal-shaped vanilla crackers. She'd purposely brought them along in case there wasn't any food in the house like last time.

Lucy nibbled on a cracker, her attitude subdued rather than her usual playful self. Willow's heart ached for the little girl.

"Excuse me." Willow lifted her hand to get Nate's or Vivienne's attention. "How much longer do we need to stay? Am I able to take Lucy home with me?"

Nate and Vivienne exchanged a long glance before Nate nodded. "We need to contact Child Protective Services first to let them know the situation. Where do you live?"

"Bay Ridge."

His brow levered upward. "That's where our K-9 headquarters is located." He glanced at his watch. "Give us a few more minutes. Vivienne, will you get an okay from Child Protective Services on Willow taking Lucy home tonight? Once they approve, I'll drive Willow and Lucy there."

"Sure." Vivienne moved away to use her phone.

"Okay." Frankly, she wouldn't mind a ride; the idea of carrying Lucy through the subway wasn't appealing. She gazed wistfully at her brother's place. If only she could pick out a few things, like Lucy's stroller, her clothes and toys, it would be an easier transition for the little girl.

Lucy rested against her, eating another animal cracker. She pressed a kiss to the top of Lucy's wavy blond hair, reveling in the calming scent of baby shampoo.

Lucy was safe, and that was all that mattered. She had some money saved up. She could buy whatever Lucy needed.

Willow would do everything in her power to keep Lucy in a safe, warm, stable and loving home.

From this moment forward and for the rest of their lives.

Nate's phone vibrated with an incoming text message. He tore his gaze from Willow and Lucy, pulled the device from his pocket, and read Penelope McGregor's note.

Today is the 20th anniversary of my parents' murders. The same MO can't be a coincidence.

Nate shot a quick message back in return. Don't worry, we'll figure it out.

Still reeling from the similarities between the recent Emery double murder and the twenty-year-old McGregor cold case murder of Penny and Bradley's parents, he mentally reviewed the scene of the crime.

April 14, the exact same date with the same MO, all the way down to the clown face with blue hair and the cheap stuffed monkey. He shivered just thinking about the cold case. Forty-year-old Eddie and Anna McGregor had been killed in their Brooklyn home, each shot at close range. Their son, Bradley, just fourteen, had been at a sleepover at a friend's house. Daughter Penny, just four years old, had witnessed the murders. To make the case even more heartbreaking, Bradley had been considered a suspect for a long time. His parents had been neglectful, same as the Emerys, and Bradley had been known to fiercely argue with them, particularly as it concerned his little sister. There had been no evidence connecting Bradley to the murders, so he'd been dropped from the suspect list, but the taint had never quite left him. Bradley and Penny had been taken in by the lead detective on the case and his wife, and the dedicated cop had gone to his grave not knowing who'd killed the McGregors.

Nate knew that Bradley—and Penny—wanted to rectify that. Now, suddenly, there was movement on the case, a break. Because another set of parents had died with the remarkably same MO.

The murderer was back after twenty years. Why? And where had he been all this time?

"What did Gavin have to say?" Vivienne asked, interrupting his thoughts.

Gavin had been rattled by the report of the same MO; Nate had heard it in his voice, even if the sarge worked hard to hide it. "He's worried about how Bradley and Penny are handling the news. Once the media gets wind of it…" He shook his head.

"It won't be pretty," Vivienne agreed. She glanced around the crime scene, where a dozen cops and techs were busy processing the evidence. The two EMTs had finally left, with only the coroner's van and the white crime scene box truck remaining on scene. "CPS agreed to let Willow take temporary custody of Lucy. I'm heading out, unless you need something?"

He was about to say no, but then hesitated. There was one difference between the twenty-year-old case and this current one.

Half of a leather watch band had been found at the scene of the McGregor murders. The DNA had been tested from dead skin cells lifted from the inside of the band, but so far no match in the national crime DNA data bank had been found.

He wondered if there was anything left behind by the murderer in the Emery case, other than the stuffed monkey encased in plastic. He thought about the fenced-in backyard. He'd been so focused on finding the gunman and then the monkey that he hadn't searched closely for clues.

"Stay here next to Willow and Lucy for a few minutes, would you?" He shortened up Murphy's leash. "Come, Murphy."

"Where are you going?" Willow's terse question caught him off guard.

"I'll be back shortly." He flashed a reassuring grin. "I'll take you and Lucy home after I check something out."

Her smile was sad. "Okay."

He understood she wanted to get Lucy out of here, so he quickened his pace. When he'd rounded the backyard earlier in an effort to follow the path the perp may have taken, he hadn't bothered searching for clues. The crime scene techs would be very thorough, but he still wanted to go back to check the ground beyond the house for himself.

Retracing his steps, he closely examined the ground on the other side of the fence, searching for evidence. Footprints, or something the perp may have dropped.

Unfortunately, the backyard butted right up against the road, no soft ground to reveal a footprint similar to what he'd found in the cemetery. He broadened his search outside the property, but still came up empty-handed.

Unless the techs found some kind of DNA evidence inside, they'd have nothing to use as a match for what had been identified on the leather watch band.

Disappointed, he turned back to the Emery crime scene. "Murphy, heel."

The yellow Lab obediently sat at his left side.

"Good boy." He bent over to scratch Murphy behind the ears, then hurried back to where Willow and Lucy waited next to Vivienne.

"I was just explaining to Willow that a caseworker by the name of Jayne Hendricks will be following up either tomorrow or Tuesday." Vivienne smiled gently. "I'm sure everything will be fine."

Willow nodded. "Okay."

"Ready to go?" he asked.

"Yes, thank you." Willow glanced down at Lucy. "Except I just realized we'll need a child safety seat for your vehicle."

He frowned, understanding her concern. "I'll run and grab one. Vivienne, will you and Hank keep watch?"

"Sure."

As he ran the errand, he thought about Willow and Lucy. There was something vulnerable yet strong about them. As if it was the two of them against the world.

It reminded him of how close he and his mother once were. When he was younger, it had been the two of them against the world, too.

When he returned, he opened the box and pulled out the car seat. Willow took it from him and expertly placed it in the back seat of his SUV.

Nate looked at the petite little girl, noticing again that her yellow outfit carried several dark smears of blood. He'd need to take her clothing in as evidence, which meant she'd need replacements.

"Why don't we stop and pick up a few more things along the way?" he offered. With the traffic, the drive between East Flatbush and Bay Ridge would take a good forty-five minutes. "There's a department store not too far from here."

"Thank you. That would be great."

He wasn't sure why he'd offered to take her home; he wasn't exactly the family kind of guy. Yet it was on the way to the K-9 Unit headquarters, so he told himself it was the decent thing to do.

Willow gently set Lucy in the car seat, while he put Murphy in the back K-9 crate area. Using the rearview mirror, he kept an eye on Lucy as he navigated the traffic toward Bay Ridge.

"Detective Slater?"

He glanced at Willow. "Sounds so formal. Why don't you call me Nate?"

"Um, okay, Nate." She cleared her throat. "I know you can't give me details about the investigation, but I'd like to be kept informed of your progress. I—need to know the person who killed my brother will be punished. No matter what my brother did—" She stopped and swallowed hard before continuing. "He and Debra didn't deserve to be murdered in their home."

"I can't make any promises," he cautioned. "But I'll do my best to keep you updated on the case." Considering the similarities between the Emery murders and the twenty-year-old McGregor case, he felt certain Gavin would fight hard to keep the newly established Brooklyn K-9 Unit on the case.

He'd been the first officer on the scene and wanted, needed, to see it through to the end.

"Thank you." Willow ran her fingers through her long straight brown hair. "I still can't believe this happened."

"Was your brother expecting your visit?" He glanced at Willow.

She winced and shook her head. "No, unfortunately he was ignoring my calls. Debra, too. This was my first day off in two weeks, so I decided to confront them face-to-face."

"About what?"

She hesitated, then waved a hand. "You saw the place. Empty liquor bottles, dirty dishes piled up to the cabinets and hardly any decent food. Is that a good environment for a child? I knew Lucy wasn't exactly a planned addition to their family, but I thought they'd settle down, do the right thing." She let out a heavy sigh. "They didn't."

He nodded thoughtfully. Her brother's lifestyle may

have made it easier for a stranger to get into their house. Maybe someone who'd confronted them, then fired his weapon as they ran away. But why? That was the nagging question.

If the killer was the same murderer from twenty years ago, he couldn't figure out why they'd struck again, all these years later.

"Oh, there's the store." Willow gestured toward her side of the road.

He'd almost forgotten his promise. He quickly maneuvered over to the right lane, then pulled into the parking lot. The moment he stopped the car, Willow pushed out of her passenger seat and opened the back door to get Lucy from the car seat.

He fetched Murphy, unwilling to leave him in the car, and easily caught up to her. It felt strange to walk into the store with Willow and Lucy. He'd never dated a single mother, or any woman who wanted to settle down. He was keenly aware of the smiles aimed in their direction, as if they were a happy little family.

Maybe because his blond hair was similar to Lucy's, not to mention, Lucy had Willow's cinnamon-brown eyes.

He found himself putting distance between them, instinctively shying away from being associated with the role of husband and father. That was a path he'd never take.

Not with his history.

Willow lifted Lucy into the seat of a shopping cart, then whizzed through the aisles, picking out clothes, a stroller and toys. Then she added groceries before heading over to the checkout lane.

"I'm sure you'll be able to get some things from

the house once the scene has been processed," he re-minded her.

"I know, but these are essentials." The total was stag-gering, but she didn't blink as she paid the bill.

He stored most of the items in the back seat while Willow lifted Lucy up and buckled her in.

"Ready?" He glanced at Willow.

For the first time since he'd met her, she offered a genuine smile. The way her entire face brightened made his mouth go dry. Willow was incredibly beautiful, tall and slender like a model might be. "Yes, thank you."

Inwardly shaking his head at his foolishness, he started the SUV. Pulling back into traffic, he decided not to mention that he'd need Lucy's bloodstained clothes as evidence until after they'd reached her apart-ment. "What's your address?"

She rattled it off and he recognized it as a prewar redbrick apartment building, not far from where their headquarters was located.

"Nice," he said. "A two-bedroom place?"

"No, just one." She glanced back at Lucy and shrugged. "It will have to do for now."

He was curious as to what her job was that allowed her to afford even a one-bedroom in the nice neighbor-hood, but told himself it wasn't his business. His own single-bedroom apartment had been his mother's, one that he'd inherited after she died. Conveniently located on the ground floor, there was a small yard for Murphy.

Thinking about his mother, and how far they'd come after leaving his abusive father, wasn't helpful. He needed to stay focused on the case at hand, not the disturbing memories of his past.

When he reached her apartment building, she looked

at him with uncertainty in her gaze. "Thanks. The killer hid his identity. There's no reason for him to come after us, right? After all, Lucy can't identify him, and I never saw him at all."

He threw the gearshift in Park. "Yes, I wouldn't leave you otherwise. But I'll arrange for a squad car to drive by hourly, just to be extra cautious. Come on, I'll carry your things up for you."

She gave a nod, then slid out of the seat. She set Lucy on her feet, then grabbed the bag of new clothes with one hand and clung to Lucy's tiny fingers with the other. He let Murphy out of the back, then hauled everything else as he followed her and Lucy inside. There was no key to get into the lobby, making him frown. But the lobby was nice, newly renovated with black-and-white tile floors.

"I'm on the seventh floor." She pushed the elevator button and stepped back.

Lucy looked around with wide, curious eyes. Then she lightly stroked Murphy. "Can the doggy stay wif us?"

"No, sweetie, he lives with Detective Nate."

It was on the tip of his tongue to offer to bring Murphy for a visit, but he caught himself in the nick of time.

When the elevator opened, Willow led the way to her apartment, number 706. She had her key but didn't use it. She came to an abrupt stop, then gingerly pushed the door open. He heard her gasp. "Oh no!"

"What is it?" He peered over her shoulder and instantly saw what was wrong.

Willow's apartment had been thoroughly and completely ransacked.

THREE

Her mouth went desert dry and her heart thudded painfully in her chest. She stared at the horrific invasion of her privacy.

Never in her entire life had she felt so violated.

"Stay back—let me check it out." Nate hastily piled the items he'd carried in just outside her apartment door, then gently nudged her and Lucy aside and pulled his weapon. Watching as he and Murphy crossed the threshold had her sending up another silent, desperate prayer.

Please, Lord, keep us all safe!

"Aunt Willow, you're messy like Mommy and Daddy," Lucy said, breaking into her thoughts.

The reminder of how much worse things could be helped calm her racing heart. She forced a smile, relieved that Lucy hadn't picked up on the sinister nature of their situation. "Yes, it sure looks that way."

"I'm hungry," Lucy complained.

Food wasn't even close to the top of her list, but she knew Lucy needed to eat dinner, especially since she highly doubted the little girl had eaten anything substantial for lunch. The burn of resentment hit hard, but she pushed it away. Alex and Debra were gone. Dead.

Despite their neglect of Lucy, they certainly didn't deserve to be murdered.

Was it possible the same person who'd killed them had done this to her apartment? If so, why? Had they been searching for something? The same thing they hadn't found at Alex and Debra's?

She suppressed a shiver.

Glancing again at the mess, she swallowed hard. It was very tempting to ask Nate to drive her and Lucy to the nearest hotel. Especially considering the handle on her apartment door was broken.

"There's no one inside," Nate informed her. "I'll call for a team to respond, although it seems unlikely we'll be able to lift any fingerprints. Whoever did this was likely smart enough to wear gloves."

The idea of more strangers invading her small apartment was unsettling. "Okay."

Nate's expression softened. "I'm sorry. I know you've already been through a lot. Whoever did this made a huge mess, but thankfully there isn't a lot of actual damage." He looked at her thoughtfully for a moment. "It seems the person responsible spent a lot of time going through your closet and dresser drawers as if searching for something."

The chill returned. "You think this is related to what happened to Alex and Debra?"

"Maybe, but I'm not convinced. You said yourself, your brother and sister-in-law weren't expecting you to visit. Then again, the timing is a strange coincidence." He frowned, thinking it through, then glanced at his watch. "The patrol officers should be here soon. Oh, and I'm sorry, but I need Lucy's bloodstained clothes for evidence."

She nodded, suppressing a shiver. Borrowing gloves from Nate, she carefully took the little girl's yellow outfit off, gingerly handing it to Nate, who placed it in an evidence bag. Stripping the gloves off, she dressed Lucy in a new pink outfit she'd purchased from the store. Sitting back against the wall, she wished she'd bought more snacks for Lucy. At this rate, the poor child would never get her dinner. She felt bad, as if she were no better at caring for Lucy than Alex and Debra had been.

The two officers arrived five minutes later. They disappeared inside her apartment with Nate and Murphy. Frustrated and exhausted, Willow sat on the floor in the hallway just outside her apartment next to Lucy. She pulled the baby doll she'd purchased at the store out of one of the bags and gave it to her niece. Together, they played with the doll, Willow doing whatever she could think of to keep the little girl occupied.

But she couldn't forget how her apartment had been thoroughly searched. Or the way her brother and his wife had been brutally murdered.

The fingerprint crew showed up a few minutes later, and it took them over an hour to check the various surfaces for prints.

"Willow?" Nate came out and hunkered down beside her. "We'll need your prints so we can exclude them from anything we may have found. The place was really very clean. There weren't many prints at all."

"Okay." She shifted Lucy off her lap. As she was about to stand, Nate held out his hand to her. After a moment's hesitation, she put her hand in his and allowed him to draw her upright. His warm palm was strangely reassuring. She wanted to cling to his strength but forced herself to let go.

"Thanks." She inwardly grimaced at her breathless tone. She really needed to get a hold of herself. This weird attraction she felt toward the K-9 cop was not healthy. She didn't have time for such nonsense.

Lucy was the only thing that mattered right now. Not her dearth of a love life. The little girl deserved a stable, loving home and Willow planned to do whatever it took to provide that for her.

Once she'd been fingerprinted, the crime scene techs took off, leaving a mess of black fingerprint powder covering numerous surfaces behind.

Crazy to have spent the hour after Sunday services cleaning prior to heading over to confront her brother about Lucy. She'd need to clean, again.

"Here, let's get your stuff inside." Nate bent down to gather her bags. "We'll leave the car seat here for now. I'll need you to tell me if anything has been stolen."

Feeling nervous, she followed him into the apartment. The two officers who'd initially responded were standing off in the corner of her living room, speaking in low tones. Murphy brushed against her legs and she was oddly reassured when the animal stayed close.

She wiped the kitchen counter, then began unpacking the groceries. Nate went over to speak with the two officers. The task of putting her apartment back together seemed overwhelming, but what choice did she have? She was emotionally and physically exhausted. The last thing she wanted to do was pack up and move to a hotel. But staying here with a broken door handle wasn't a very good idea, either.

The two officers headed out of the apartment. She must have looked upset, because Nate crossed over to put a reassuring hand on her shoulder.

"They're not leaving, I just want them to check the video cameras for any footage of the person who did this."

"Oh." She tried to offer a smile. "That would be good, right? Then we'd know who murdered Alex and Debra."

"Only if these two crimes are linked," Nate cautioned. "Listen, I want to look around again and then will likely have some questions for you."

"Okay, but I need to feed Lucy something for dinner. She needs something more substantial than animal crackers in her belly."

"Understood." He gave her shoulder a reassuring squeeze, then moved away. She instantly missed the warmth of his touch.

She reminded herself that the men in her life didn't stick around. She'd dated a few, only to have them quickly disappear. Either because she wasn't very exciting or because she worked too many hours, or both.

Once the pizza was in the oven, she quickly wiped down the small kitchen table so Lucy would have a place to sit, then replaced her sofa cushions. She couldn't comprehend why anyone would be looking for something of Alex's in her apartment. Especially since she and Alex hadn't been close in a very long time.

Since before the death of their grandmother, three years ago, right after Lucy was born. They'd each received a modest inheritance; she'd invested hers in this apartment. When Alex and Debra had moved into their two-story, she'd praised him for putting his money to good use, only to have him laugh at her, carelessly announcing they were just renting the cheap place and living off the money and enjoying life. Despite having

Lucy, Debra made it clear she wasn't interested in settling down.

Watching as Lucy played with her new baby doll, Willow tried to find the forgiveness in her heart that she knew God expected of her. Alex and Debra had gone down a bad path and unfortunately had paid the ultimate price.

Deep down, she knew they hadn't intentionally neglected Lucy. Despite Alex's being two years her senior, he was immature and irresponsible.

"Willow?"

Nate's deep voice startled her. "Yes?"

"Do you have a minute?"

"Sure." She peeked at the pizza through the glass oven door before hurrying to her master bedroom. "What is it?"

He gestured to a small slip of paper lying on the floor tucked beneath the open closet door. "That appears to be a cash receipt for gas. Is it yours?"

"Gas?" She dropped to her knees to see the receipt more clearly. "No." She glanced up at him. "I don't own a car. Why would I buy gas?"

"Yeah, that's what I thought." He pulled an evidence bag from the pocket of his uniform and used the plastic bag to cover his fingers as he carefully picked the receipt off the floor. The gas had been paid for with cash, and the identifying number across the top was smudged, but he thought Eden might be able to find the station. Maybe they'd discover there were cameras nearby.

Then he had another idea. After he had the slip of paper tucked inside the evidence bag, he called Murphy over and opened the bag for the K-9. "Seek, Murphy."

The yellow Lab buried his nose in the evidence bag, sniffing for what seemed like an inordinate amount of time.

"Seek," Nate repeated in a commanding tone.

Murphy put his snout to the floor and sniffed, breaking into a lope as he tracked the scent across the hardwood floor of her bedroom, through the doorway into the open-concept kitchen and living area. Then the dog headed for the door.

"Wait. Are you leaving us here alone?" She couldn't hide the underlying panic in her tone.

"No. Heel, Murphy." He paused and used his radio to call the two officers. "I need one or both of you to return to the apartment."

"Ten-four. We're on our way. The video isn't helpful anyway."

Once again, she tried to tell herself that the two cops were just as capable of protecting her and Lucy as Nate and Murphy.

But when they arrived and Nate took off with Murphy, she couldn't help feeling starkly alone.

Pumped with adrenaline at finally having a solid clue, Nate followed Murphy as the dog tracked the scent of the intruder down the hall toward the elevator. His partner made several twists and turns, but then pressed his nose against the narrow crack between the floor and the closed elevator doors.

Murphy stayed there for a long moment, then made a circle in front of the elevator, returning to the closed doors for the second time. He sat, then gazed up at Nate with what he perceived as an imploring gaze.

"It's okay, boy. We're going to get him." Nate quickly clipped Murphy's leash to his collar, then pushed the button to summon the elevators. The one on the right opened first, and he held the door open. "Seek, Murphy."

The dog put his nose to the ground and took his time, but never alerted. Nate squelched a flash of concern. He decided since there were only two elevators, he'd head down to the lobby to see if Murphy could pick up the scent there.

Once they were in the lobby, it took another several minutes of sniffing and searching for Murphy to pick up the scent, near the second elevator. "Good boy," he praised, giving Murphy a good rub. "Seek!"

His partner gamely went back to work, sniffing and alerting again near the doorway heading outside. Nate knew that once they were out in the elements the scent may be more difficult to track. About a year and a half ago, the NYC K-9 Command Unit in Queens had been gifted a Labrador retriever named Stella from the Czech Republic. Stella had delivered eight puppies shortly upon her arrival to the US. Stella currently worked as a bomb-sniffing dog, and several of her puppies had turned into equally talented K-9 cops. Murphy was one of Stella's pups, earning a reputation for being one of the best trackers their Brooklyn unit had working for them. Still, there were a lot of people walking around, moving up and down the sidewalks, back and forth from subways and other buildings. Murphy was good, but it wouldn't be easy to pick out one specific scent against all others.

"Heel." He waited for Murphy to sit at his side before offering the evidence bag again. This time, he pulled out the orange ball he carried with him. Like most of their K-9s, Murphy was trained with a reward system that involved playing. Murphy's tail wagged with excitement when he saw the ball, and he quickly sniffed at the evidence bag, eager to get to work.

"Seek, Murphy." Nate slipped the ball back into his pocket.

Murphy put his nose to the ground, going back and forth as he searched for the scent. Nate stayed close, keeping the leash short so that they wouldn't trip any of the pedestrians passing by.

Murphy picked up the scent a few minutes later, alerting near the corner of the apartment building. Nate could imagine the guy pausing there for a moment, sweeping his gaze over the area to see if anyone noticed him.

"Good boy," he praised again. "Seek."

Murphy put his nose back to the sidewalk and took off in an eastern direction, which made sense as Bay Ridge overlooked the upper and lower bays of the Atlantic Ocean and connected to Staten Island via the Verrazzano-Narrows Bridge to the west.

Murphy took a winding path as he tracked the perp's scent. His K-9 paused at the intersection, then alerted again, staring north.

When the light changed, they crossed the street and Murphy picked up the scent once again. As they approached the entrance to the subway, Nate's hopes deflated. If the perp had taken one of the trains, they'd never find him. Sure, there were cameras, but he didn't have a clue who they were looking for or even a time frame of the vandalism.

Thankfully, Murphy alerted at the next intersection, too. Trying to quell the sense of excitement, Nate glanced around, taking note of their surroundings.

There was a single long building housing a few shops and small restaurants with apartments located up above.

Was Murphy still on point? He trusted his K-9, but the streets were busy, and he knew the endless multitude of scents, from people, food and the ocean, could be confusing.

His stomach rumbled with hunger as he caught a whiff of hamburger grease, followed closely by the scent of hot dogs. He and Murphy crossed the street, and soon his partner once again alerted, indicating he'd picked up the scent.

"Good boy!" Nate knew he'd have to throw the ball for a long time once they were finished. The K-9 deserved a nice reward.

His partner alerted again, and then kept going, making Nate break into a jog to keep up. For whatever reason, it seemed the scent Murphy was following was stronger here. They turned right at the next corner, then Murphy abruptly came to a halt right outside the door to a small restaurant. The animal stared straight ahead as if he could see through the glass door to the inside where his potential quarry may be hiding in wait.

Nate took a step back to get a better look at the building. The sign above the door was done in bright red against a white background.

The Burgerteria.

In smaller letters beneath were the words *Gourmet Burgers Served Daily.*

Unfortunately, the place was closed for the day. Peering at the sign, it appeared the burger place closed early on Sundays, at 5:00 p.m. rather than the usual 11 p.m. on weekdays and midnight on Fridays and Saturdays.

Murphy continued sitting and staring at the door,

his nostrils quivering. Nate stepped up beside him and cupped his hands around his face so he could see inside without the glare from the light.

The place was empty and amazingly clean. There were several small square tables surrounded by four chairs as well as a long counter against the farthest wall.

He tried to imagine why the perp had come here so soon after ransacking Willow's apartment. Simply because he was hungry?

No, more likely because he was meeting someone. Maybe the perp had been paid to do the job by someone else. Nate couldn't imagine why the same person who'd searched Willow's apartment would want her brother and sister-in-law dead. Murder was a far cry from simple burglary.

Other than the timing, there was nothing else to indicate the two crimes were related. Especially considering the Emery murders had followed the same MO as the twenty-year-old McGregor murders, which he knew had hung like a black cloud over Bradley and Penny McGregor.

His gut told him these two events couldn't possibly be connected. As he was about to turn away, he saw a flash of movement out of the corner of his eye.

Someone was still inside!

FOUR

"Hey!" Nate rapped on the door, trying to get the guy's attention. "Police!"

Nothing.

"Open up! I want to talk to you!"

Still nothing. Peering through the window, Nate couldn't see the person inside any longer. Had he gone out the back?

"Come, Murphy." Nate whirled away from the glass door and quickly walked along the sidewalk, looking for the quickest way to get to the back of the long building.

When he found a narrow walkway between the one structure and the next, he didn't hesitate to enter. There was just enough room for Murphy to walk alongside him. As they approached the back of the building, he slowed, straining to listen.

He didn't hear anything above the routine traffic, subway train and pedestrian noise.

Murphy stood beside him, nose in the air as if still seeking the scent from the gas receipt. His partner didn't alert, so Nate crept around the corner, keeping his back pressed against the wall.

The alley was long, stretching the entire length of the

building. Several dumpsters were stationed at intervals along the way. He moved from dumpster to dumpster, wrinkling his nose at the pungent scent, searching for signs of someone hiding out.

He found what appeared to be the back door to the Burgerteria, but it was locked. He looked down at Murphy. "What do you think?"

The K-9 gazed up at him, waiting for the next command.

Nate offered the evidence bag to Murphy. "Seek."

Murphy eagerly sniffed the inside of the bag, then went to work along the alley. Nate kept one eye on Murphy, the other sweeping the area for any sign of danger.

Murphy scouted the area for several long minutes, but never alerted. Fifteen minutes later, Nate called him off.

"Heel, Murphy. Good boy." He rubbed the Lab's sleek coat, smiling as Murphy wiggled with joy and reminded himself he needed to take time to throw the K-9's orange ball.

"Come." He shortened Murphy's leash and returned through the narrow walkway to the street where the dog had last alerted on the intruder's scent. The Burgerteria was the only clue he had so far, other than the gas receipt itself, and he didn't like the fact that so far, both had led to a dead end. Maybe Eden could get more info from the receipt.

He headed back toward Willow's apartment building, wondering again if the perp had gone to the restaurant for a meal or to meet someone?

And if it was the latter, why? What could they have possibly been looking for inside Willow's apartment?

Nate always liked a puzzle, but this one bothered him

more than most. Maybe because Willow was a beautiful woman alone caring for her young niece.

Before he reached Willow's apartment building, his phone rang. "Hey, Gavin, what's up?"

"Emergency staff meeting. Can you get here ASAP?"

He thought about the cops he had watching over Willow and Lucy. "Yeah, sure. I'm only a few minutes away."

The Brooklyn K-9 Unit headquarters was housed in a three-story limestone building that was a former police precinct until the unit merged with another precinct. Their new K-9 unit gladly took the abandoned space, making it their new home. A K-9 center with an outdoor training yard was located right next door, perfectly fitting in with room to grow.

Nate and Murphy made it to headquarters in record time. After entering the building, he nodded at Penelope McGregor, their desk clerk. Tall and slender with long red hair and dark brown eyes, Penny was only twenty-four, and the entire unit was protective of her. No one as much as her brother, Detective Bradley McGregor. "Hey, Penny, how are you holding up?"

She shrugged and grimaced. "It's been horrible. I'm still reeling from this latest murder. Sarge asked me to attend the staff meeting with the rest of you."

"Good." Nate waved his hand toward the hallway. "Let's go."

He placed Murphy in one of the kennels kept in the precinct for just this reason, then followed Penny into the large conference room. The rest of the team was already assembled. The four female K-9 officers—Lani Jameson, who'd transferred from the NYC K-9 Command Unit after Gavin's promotion, Belle Montera,

Vivienne Armstrong and their newest rookie, Noelle Orton—were seated in a cluster, leaving the guys, Ray Morrow, Jackson Davison, Tyler Walker, Maxwell Santelli, Henry Roarke and Bradley McGregor, to fill in the other seats. Nate slid in next to Henry, while Penny took a seat beside her brother.

"Thanks for coming together late in the day on short notice." Gavin Sutherland swept a serious gaze over his team. "As you may have heard, a married couple in East Flatbush, Alex and Debra Emery, were murdered earlier today. Thankfully, their three-year-old daughter, Lucy, a witness, was spared."

"Just like me," Penny whispered.

Gavin nodded. "Yes. The MO of the Emery murders is far too similar to your parents' case."

"The murderer, wearing a clown face with blue hair on top, entered the front yard, gave a stuffed monkey to Lucy, then shot both the Emerys in the back." Nate glanced at his colleagues. "Every detail the same as the McGregor murders twenty years ago, down to the exact same date."

"We've always known my parents' murderer is still out there, but why would he strike again now, after all these years?" Brad asked.

"We have to keep an open mind," Gavin cautioned. "But it's possible the perp was locked up at some point, for some other crime, and recently got out. Once the forensic specialist gets through the evidence, we may have more to go on." Gavin looked at his whole team. "I need all of you to work together on this. To back each other up in every way possible."

"We will." Nate infused confidence in his tone, and

several of the other team members nodded their heads in agreement.

"Any news on Liberty?" Noelle Orton was paired with the beautiful yellow Lab, who they recently learned had a ten grand price placed on her head from a high-ranking gun runner. Liberty had foiled two military weapon smuggling operations in the past two months, so the kingpin wanted her and her skills out of the police business. The talented Lab was costing the gun runners way too much. Unfortunately, the dark smudge on Liberty's left ear made her far too easy to spot, so Gavin asked them all to be vigilant about watching for any strike against the K-9.

"No, unfortunately Liberty remains a target with a bounty on her head," Gavin said grimly. "You and Liberty need to continue keeping a low profile."

"Yes, sir." Noelle tried to hide her dejection, but everyone knew the rookie couldn't very well prove herself if she and her K-9 partner weren't allowed to work big cases.

Nate subtly glanced at his watch. Willow would be wondering where he was if they didn't finish up soon.

As if on cue, Gavin waved a hand. "That's all I have for now. Just be careful out there, okay?"

A chorus of "We will" echoed from the team members around the room.

Normally Nate would have lingered to chat with the rest of the team, heading over to the 646 Diner where they often went for a quick meal after work. But he needed to get back to Willow and Lucy, so he released Murphy from his kennel and left.

As he entered Willow's apartment building, he thought about Gavin's staff meeting and what he'd seen at the Burgerteria. He made a silent promise to get to the bottom of what was going on with Willow, even while continuing to investigate the Emery murders and the obvious link to the twenty-year-old McGregor case.

Willow tried to ignore her discomfort with the two uniformed officers standing outside her broken apartment door as she watched Lucy eat.

Voices from the hallway caught her attention.

"Thanks for staying." Nate's deep tone rippled through her, instantly relaxing her tense muscles. "I'll take it from here."

"Call if you need anything. We'll be on duty until eleven."

"I will."

Turning toward the doorway, she met Nate's gaze. "Well? You were gone for a long time. Did you and Murphy find anything?"

"Maybe." He entered the apartment, two silver dog dishes tucked under one arm and a container of kibble in hand. He closed the door behind Murphy, even though it didn't latch because the handle was broken. The yellow Lab took a seat in the center of her small kitchen, waiting as Nate filled one of the bowls with water, the other with dog food.

Murphy lapped up the water, then began to eat.

Nate watched his partner for a few minutes before turning toward her. "Murphy followed the scent from here all the way to the Burgerteria restaurant. Could be a simple coincidence, but my gut tells me the person who did this—" he waved a hand to indicate the mostly cleaned-up apartment "—was meeting someone there."

"The Burgerteria?" She drew her gaze from Murphy,

grappling with the idea of the vandal going to the restaurant. "That's where I work as a line cook."

Nate's gaze sharpened. "For how long?"

"Three years, since I moved into this apartment." She thought it was strange that the vandal would go there. "Are you sure Murphy didn't follow my scent instead of the receipt?"

Nate's eyes darkened. "I'm positive. He's one of the best trackers we have."

She wanted to believe him, but it wasn't easy. Why would the vandal go there? Sure, the place was only a few blocks away, and served great food, if she said so herself, but still.

"Aunt Willow? Are we safe now?" Lucy's tone drew her from her thoughts.

She did not want Lucy listening to their conversation. "Of course. Everything is going to be fine now. Where's your dolly?"

"Baby!" Lucy ran over to pick up her baby doll from the sofa, clutching it to her chest. Nate took off Murphy's vest and leash, and the lab went over to sniff at Lucy, then licked her. Lucy giggled but held the doll out of Murphy's reach, as if the K-9 might steal her. "My baby."

"Yes, she's your baby. Why don't you play in my room?" Willow smiled at her niece. "Maybe your baby needs a bottle?"

"Yes! She must be hungry." Lucy disappeared into the bedroom. Murphy followed, but then turned around and stretched out in front of the bedroom doorway. She watched him, touched by the way he was clearly protecting the little girl.

"Is there any reason someone at the Burgerteria

would come here to search your place?" Nate's voice brought her back to the issue at hand. "Anyone carrying a grudge against you for some reason? Or have reason to believe you're hiding something?"

She let out an exasperated sigh. "Why would they? I make hundreds of gourmet burgers every day. I can't imagine why on earth that could possibly make someone upset with me. Or think that I would have something they'd want."

"Not sure." Nate glanced around, as if searching the apartment for answers. "It just seems like an odd coincidence that your place was tossed by someone who immediately left and went to the restaurant."

"A coincidence?" Her annoyance grew. "You mean like the fact that my apartment was broken into and searched the same day my brother and his wife were murdered? That kind of coincidence?"

"Easy, now. I told you, I'm not sure the two cases are related." Nate's attempt to calm her wasn't working.

"Well, it seems logical to me, that if anyone was looking for me, they'd know to come to the Burgerteria. They wouldn't have to come here to search my place. I don't have anything here." She was tired and cranky but knew it wasn't Nate's fault. He was only trying to help.

It was all just too much.

Her stomach rumbled, and she blew out a breath and gestured toward the pizza. "Are you hungry? We can share what's left."

"I could eat." Nate stepped toward her, his blue eyes searching hers. "Willow, I know you've had a long day. I'm just trying to understand what's going on."

"I know." His gentleness was nearly her undoing. Tears threatened, and she bit her lip and pinched the bridge of her nose to ward them off. She couldn't afford to break down. Not with Lucy in the next room. She drew in a deep breath. "I— Thank you, Nate. I appreciate everything you've done for us."

"Sit down." He put a hand on the small of her back and steered her toward a chair. "I'll dish up the pizza."

She dropped into the seat and sighed. "It's probably cold."

"I love cold pizza."

His comment made her smile. Talk about being willing to look on the bright side of things. She watched as he went to the counter and opened cupboards until he found plates and glasses. After piling two slices of pizza on each plate, he brought them over. "Milk? Or water?"

"Milk is fine. We may as well drink it up. I bought it for Lucy, but she doesn't seem to care for it much."

"Maybe she hasn't been exposed to it enough." Nate filled two glasses with milk and set them on the table. "Give her some time. She'll get used to it."

She thought about how her brother's kitchen had looked, with the dirty dishes, trash and empty liquor bottles strewn about. "You're probably right. I'm afraid that little girl is going to need a lot of time to adjust to her new life. And to the loss of her parents."

Nate reached over to squeeze her hand. "I'm glad she has you."

The stupid tears burned again, but she summoned a smile. "We have each other."

They finished the rest of their pizza in silence. She felt herself blush when Nate's gaze lingered on her features and she wondered if she had smears of pizza sauce on her face. She wiped at her mouth and pushed her plate away. "You can have the rest, if you like. I'm full."

"Sure?" Nate's gaze was hopeful.

"Yes. It's the least I can do." She frowned and glanced at her door. It bothered her that the door handle was still broken, but she didn't have a clue how to replace it. "Do you think we should move into a hotel for the night?"

Nate followed her gaze and she wondered what he was thinking. He cleared his throat. "I have a better idea. Murphy and I will bunk here for the night."

"Here?" Her voice squeaked. "There's not enough room."

He shrugged. "I'll sleep on the sofa. Murphy doesn't mind the floor."

"The sofa?" She knew she sounded like a parrot repeating everything back to him. She didn't want to be alone, but the idea of sharing her small apartment was a bit distracting. "Are you sure?"

"Absolutely." He smiled and she had to cross her arms over her chest to keep from hugging him.

She probably wouldn't sleep much anyway, but knowing Nate Slater and Murphy were here to protect them gave her the sense of peace she desperately needed.

As Willow spread a sheet over the sofa and added a blanket and pillow, he found himself wondering if he'd lost his mind.

Everything about Willow Emery screamed happy homemaker. She was a nurturer, a nester.

She was everything he knew he couldn't have.

"If you need anything else, just holler." Her smile was sweet. "Thanks again for doing this."

He cleared his throat, pulling himself together with

an effort. "You're welcome. Listen, I have to take Murphy outside one last time, but I won't go far. I'll keep my eye on the front of the building at all times."

A flash of alarm rippled across her features, but she nodded. "Okay."

He pulled out his cell phone and swiped at his screen, then met her gaze. "Tell me your number."

She recited the number. He punched it in, then he called her phone. The screen lit up and the phone chirped. "There, now you have my number, too. I promise, it won't take long."

She went over and scooped up her phone. "Thank you."

He nodded, then placed Murphy's vest on, and clipped the leash to his collar. "We'll be back soon."

He took Murphy down to the lobby. There was a small patch of grass that wasn't far from Willow's redbrick building. Once Murphy did his thing, Nate cleaned up after him, then tossed the orange ball, keeping his eye on the front door of Willow's building. Several people entered, but no one looked suspicious.

His phone remained reassuringly silent.

The puzzle pieces surrounding the case filtered through his mind. The perp had gone from Willow's apartment to the Burgerteria where she worked. To meet someone? It was the only thing that made sense.

Yet Willow had a point about how anyone looking for her would know when she was working. Why break into her apartment to search for something today, a day she had off work? Why not pick a day she was working late instead?

All good questions without the barest hint of an answer.

Ten minutes later, he bent over to rub Murphy, deciding he'd given the K-9 enough attention for now. He pocketed the orange ball and took Murphy back inside, riding the elevator to the seventh floor. He approached Willow's broken door, then dropped to one knee to examine the handle more closely. It would need to be replaced, something he could do for her in the morning.

After heading into the apartment, he closed the door and pressed one of the kitchen chairs firmly up against it. Murphy would let him know before anyone got close, but he figured the added barrier couldn't hurt.

Murphy lapped water from his bowl. As Nate went past the bedroom door, he heard Willow and Lucy talking.

"It's time to say our bedtime prayers," Willow said.

"What are bedtime prayers?"

"I'll show you. First you need to be tucked in underneath the covers." There was a rustle of sheets as Lucy complied. "Now put your hands together like this and close your eyes."

"Okay."

"Dear Lord, we ask You to bless Nate and Murphy, for everything they've done for us today. We also ask You to watch over us as we sleep, keeping us safe from harm. Amen."

There was a pause, before Willow added, "Lucy, you need to say amen, too."

"Oh. Amen."

"Good. Now we can go to sleep, knowing that we'll be safe in God's care."

Nate backed away from the door. The idea of praying like that was completely foreign to him.

For a moment he remembered the night his father had lost all semblance of control. The way the old man had lashed out, hitting his mother so hard she flew half-way across the room. The way he'd rushed his father, his skinny ten-year-old fists hitting his father's belly, bouncing off harmlessly as he begged him to stop.

The way his father had backhanded him, pain blooming in his head as he crashed into the wall, falling to the floor in a crumpled heap.

Sweat popped out on his forehead, the back of his throat burning from pent-up screams locked in his mind. With an effort, he forced the twenty-year-old images away. Turning away from the door, he went over to stretch out on the sofa. Murphy plopped on the floor next to him.

He reached down to rest his hand on Murphy's soft fur. His partner was real. Murphy would do whatever was necessary to protect him and the woman and child in the next room.

No, he didn't believe for one moment that God had ever watched over him.

FIVE

Lucy had woken up twice during the night, each time crying over the bad clown with blue hair. Willow's heart ached for the little girl and she had cuddled her close, rocking her back to sleep.

Finally, they'd both slept. When daylight filtered past the window shades, Willow awoke, staring at the ceiling fan overhead. She prayed that God would guide her in being a good aunt to Lucy, and for God to provide comfort to the little girl as she struggled through this difficult time.

Feeling at peace, she slid from bed, trying not to wake Lucy. But her niece must have sensed her absence, as she almost instantly opened her eyes. "Aunt Willow? Where are you going?"

"I'm not leaving, I'm just going to the kitchen to make breakfast. Are you hungry?"

Lucy rubbed her eyes and nodded. She pushed her hair from her face and popped up from the bed.

Willow led Lucy out to the kitchen. The little girl remained glued to her side, and she knew her niece was strongly feeling the impact of yesterday's events.

And likely would for a long time to come.

Murphy came over, his tail wagging in greeting.

"Hey, Murphy." Willow stroked his soft fur and scratched him behind the ears. "You're a good boy, aren't you?"

Murphy licked her, his entire body wiggling with happiness.

Lucy wrapped her arms around Murphy's neck, pressing her face to his fur. "I love Murphy."

"I know you do." It was clear that having Murphy around was good for Lucy's emotional well-being. She glanced at the living room sofa. Nate's lean body was still supine on the sofa, but he was awake, blinking sleep from his eyes, looking adorably rumpled with his bedhead and shadowed jaw. She felt her cheeks grow warm and hoped he didn't notice her embarrassment. "Good morning, Nate."

"Morning." He yawned and rolled into a sitting position, rubbing his hand against his jaw. "Did you sleep okay?"

"So-so." She didn't want to remind Lucy about the nightmares. She noticed the chair pushed up against the door, and was grateful Nate had agreed to stay.

As if he'd noticed her gaze, he gestured toward the door. "I need to take Murphy outside, but afterward, I'll work on replacing your door handle."

"Thanks. Lucy is hungry and so am I, so I'm going to make breakfast for all of us." She glanced down at Lucy. "Do you like scrambled eggs and toast?"

Lucy tipped her head to the side, her brow puckered in a frown. "I don't know."

Her heart ached for the little girl.

"I love scrambled eggs and toast." Nate's assertion caught Lucy's attention.

"You do?" Lucy looked up at him curiously.

"Absolutely. They're my favorite." Willow thought he might be exaggerating about that just a bit but appreciated his help.

"Will you give them a try?" Willow smiled down at Lucy.

"Okay."

"Would you like to help me cook the eggs, Lucy?"

Lucy nodded and she took the little girl over to the counter. She pulled over a chair and helped Lucy stand on the seat so she could reach. As Willow broke a half dozen eggs in a bowl and showed her niece how to whisk them together, Nate took Murphy outside.

When Nate and Murphy returned, the eggs and several slices of toast were finished. She set the plates on the table, bringing the chair back over for Lucy to sit in.

Lucy looked at the eggs with suspicion, but as Nate eagerly dived into his meal, she gamely tried hers. Her face broke into a grin. "These are yummy, Aunt Willow."

"Thank you." She was relieved Lucy liked them. "It was nice of you to help me make them."

"It was fun." Lucy ate another bite of her eggs.

"Thanks for breakfast. As soon as I'm finished here, I'll work on your door," Nate promised.

"That would be great." She knew, though, that just having a locked door wasn't going to make her feel safe. It was having Nate and Murphy here overnight that had given her peace of mind.

But she also knew they couldn't stay forever.

"Do you have to work today?" She glanced at Nate.

"Yes, but I can go in a little later than usual. I told Sarge I'll be a bit late, and he understood."

She remembered the conversation with his boss when they'd discussed Alex's and Debra's murders as potentially being committed by some sort of serial killer on the loose. But before she could ask him about it, Lucy spoke up.

"Are Mommy and Daddy coming to get me?"

She froze, giving Nate a panicked look. He frowned and offered a helpless shrug. She carefully set her fork down, searching for the best way to approach the subject of death and dying with her niece. Finally, she curled her arm around the little girl's shoulders. "No, sweetie, I'm afraid not."

She fully expected Lucy to ask more questions, but the little girl seemed to accept her answer.

For now.

Lucy pressed her face into Willow's chest. She held her niece for a long moment, silently praying for God to help the little girl get through this.

Nate's empathetic expression was touching. After a few moments, he cleared his throat. "Lucy, after you finish breakfast, would you mind playing with Murphy? I think he feels a little lonely."

Intrigued, Lucy lifted her head. "Really?"

"Really." Nate finished his toast and eggs, then stood to carry his plate to the kitchen sink. "Willow, do you have a screwdriver?"

"Yes." She went into her closet to pull out a small tool kit. "I have all the basics here."

"Nice. The handle is broken, so I'll need to find replacement parts or buy a new one."

Lucy finished her breakfast, then scampered down off the booster seat to play with Murphy. The yellow Lab was exceptionally patient with the little girl, as if sensing his role was not only to protect her, but to keep her occupied.

"I'll call a friend to pick up a new door handle."

Willow nodded, turning her attention to household chores. When Nate had the new handle, he went back to work on the door. She liked listening to him whistle under his breath as he worked. It was nice having him around, but she knew that once he'd finished his task, he and Murphy would need to leave.

Their boss was waiting for them.

Speaking of which, she abruptly glanced at the clock. Nine forty-five in the morning. Oops. She'd completely forgotten to call her boss to let him know she wouldn't be in. She originally had planned to use the Nanna's Nook Day Care for Lucy while she worked, if she'd been able to convince Alex and Debra to let her take Lucy, but after everything that had happened, she didn't want to leave the little girl alone.

The restaurant opened at ten thirty in the morning, but she normally arrived an hour before. She picked up her phone and called the Burgerteria. "Damon? It's Willow. I'm sorry, but I'm not going to make it in to work today."

"What?" The outrage in his voice made her wince. "I need you. You're supposed to be here right now prepping for the lunch crowd!"

"I know, I'm sorry. But my brother and his wife were murdered yesterday, and I have my three-year-old niece here. I can't leave her alone."

"I'm sorry about that, but I don't have anyone to replace you." The anger faded from his tone. "Isn't there any way you can make it in?"

She glanced at Nate, who was clearly listening to her

side of the conversation, a frown puckering his brow. "I'm sorry, but I can't leave Lucy. In fact, based on the long hours I normally have to work it may be better for me to give my notice."

"You're quitting?" Damon let out a harsh laugh. "Fine. Have it your way."

The connection went dead.

"Well. I guess that's that." Willow set her phone on the counter, a hollow feeling in her chest. While she knew that this was the best thing for Lucy right now, it didn't sit right to be completely out of a job.

She had some money saved up, but it wouldn't last forever. She'd need some sort of employment, something that would help support Lucy while offering some flexibility of hours.

Doing what, exactly? She had no clue.

Nate couldn't deny being relieved that Willow had quit her job at the Burgerteria, as he didn't like how Murphy had followed the intruder's scent to the place. Yet, the forlorn expression on her face bothered him.

"Are you okay?" Now that her apartment door handle was replaced, the lock secure, he moved closer to her. He rested a hand on her slim shoulder.

"I will be." She put on a brave smile. "Damon isn't happy with me, but I know it's the right thing to do, for Lucy's sake."

He searched her gaze. "And you're absolutely sure your boss doesn't have a reason to be upset with you?"

"You mean other than quitting my job?" There was a brittle edge to her tone.

The break-in had happened while she'd been in East

Flatbush. Before the murders? Or afterward? He wished he knew for certain.

"Yes, I mean prior to today. Was your boss unhappy with your work performance for any reason?"

"Not that I'm aware of. In fact, he'd just asked me to take photos for the new menu."

He raised a brow. "I'm surprised he didn't hire a professional photographer."

She snorted. "No way. Do you have any idea how much that would cost? I'm in a photography class, and did a decent job photographing the various types of gourmet burgers, if I say so myself."

"I'd like to see them." He didn't see how pictures of burgers could play into this, but the intruder *had* gone to the Burgerteria after ransacking her home, and there had to be some connection. Plus, maybe he was also just a little curious to see her work. For some strange reason, Willow Emery intrigued him. Not just because she'd taken her niece in without a moment's hesitation, but because she was beautiful and smart. Because of the way she'd kept her cool under pressure in the aftermath of violence, while displaying a softer, gentler side toward her niece.

She was a bit of an enigma, but he couldn't afford to get emotionally involved.

"My camera is in my bag. I tend to carry it wherever I go." Willow opened the oversize bag he recognized from the day before. She pulled out a midsize digital camera and turned it around so he could see the screen.

"That's a pretty nice camera." Nate looked impressed.

"Didn't cost as much as you might think. I bought it at the new discount store that opened recently, Basement Bargains." She tapped the screen. "See? Dozens of pictures of burgers."

He had to admit they were good photos. She'd done a good job of getting the correct angle, displaying the burger in a way that emphasized what toppings were included. Anything from the traditional mushroom and swiss cheese to avocado and alfalfa sprouts.

"Did you use these for your class?"

"Yes, among others." She took the camera and flipped through the photos. She hadn't been kidding—there were well over three dozen hamburger photos. "I added a few with people, too. A few at the restaurant but more at the park."

He recognized Owl's Head Park and appreciated how she'd chosen interesting people to photograph. An older woman sitting with a large bag at her feet, two young kids chasing each other, a young man resting with his head back, eyes closed. He went back to the photos at the Burgerteria and found one with two men talking to each other.

"Who are these guys?" He held the camera toward her.

She pointed toward the younger of the two men. "This one is Damon Berk, the restaurant manager. I don't know who the other man is. I only photographed him because of his craggy face. It was so unique, I wanted to capture it."

He couldn't deny she was right about Craggy Face. His cheeks were lined and loose, yet his cheekbones were prominent, reminding him of twin mountain peaks overlooking a crevasse.

He thought back to the shadow he'd noticed in the back of the restaurant last evening. Had Damon Berk been back there? As the manager it made sense, but he couldn't be sure.

"My photography instructor loved that one, asked me to print a copy for the rest of the class to see." Willow's voice brought him back to the present.

He jerked his gaze to hers. "You sent it via email? I'd like to see it up close."

"Of course." She went over and pulled a small notebook computer from her bag. "The battery is low. Give me a moment to power it up."

While she plugged in the computer, he noticed Lucy had tied her doll's bonnet on Murphy's head. It was a testament to his training that Murphy didn't go nuts trying to rip it off. Murphy thumped his tail, his large brown eyes looking up at Nate as if saying, *hey, whatever makes her happy.*

"You're a good boy," he praised.

Murphy came over, tail wagging. Lucy followed, clutching her baby doll to her chest. "Isn't Murphy cute?"

"He sure is." His lips twitched at Murphy's bonnet. "Willow, you should take a picture of this."

She turned from her computer and picked up the camera. As if sensing he was the subject of the photo, Murphy looked away.

It took several attempts, and Willow was chuckling by the time she was finished. "So typical, takes twenty attempts to get one decent shot."

He leaned forward to see the screen. "It's great."

Lucy went back to the sofa, still talking to her baby doll. It occurred to Nate that she needed more things to play with and he made a mental note to find out how soon the crime scene would be cleared so Willow could pick up more of Lucy's things.

"Okay, here's the picture of Damon with the man at Burgerteria." Willow turned the computer screen so he could see it better. "I did make a few changes, but this one was my favorite. Blurring out the background helped make his features stand out more."

"It sure does." He stared at the craggy face, committing it to memory. Then he was struck by an idea. "Hey, can you print this one for me? I might be able to put his face through our database to find his name."

"I don't have a printer here. I use the one at school. They let us print for free as long as we purchase the photo paper." She snapped her fingers and rose to her feet. "Wait, I printed extra copies for myself. I'm happy to give you one. The photograph will be better quality than via text message or email."

"Great, thanks. Although I wouldn't mind if you texted me the picture of Murphy."

She glanced at him in surprise, then nodded. "Of course."

Nate knew there was no proof that Craggy Face had anything to do with ransacking her home, but he figured it couldn't hurt to ID the guy. Especially since Murphy trailed the intruder's scent directly to the Burgerteria.

Willow opened several drawers of the narrow desk set in the corner of the living room. "I don't understand. I thought for sure I left the photos in here."

The back of his neck prickled in warning, and he shot to his feet. "Those drawers were open when you came in last night, weren't they?"

Willow straightened, her expression full of concern. "Yes." She glanced back down at the drawer. "I know for sure the photos were in a brown envelope tucked into this top wide drawer. They were too big to fit in the narrower ones along the side."

Nate crossed over to join her. In his mind's eye he remembered how the closet and bedroom drawers were opened and searched, along with the couch cushions being on the floor, and then this desk, with the drawer left open. The rest of the living room and kitchen had been basically untouched.

Because the intruder had found exactly what he'd been searching for.

Willow's photographs.

SIX

Her pictures had been stolen. Willow stared down at the empty drawer, trying to wrap her mind around what had happened. None of it made any sense. "They searched my apartment just for the photos?"

"Looks that way to me." Nate lightly rested his hand in the center of her back. "I have to believe the person who did this really wanted that photo of the craggy-faced man. Are you sure you don't know who he is?"

She lifted her shoulders in a helpless shrug. "I'm sure. Damon never introduced him to me, so he must not be involved in running the place."

Nate's blue eyes flashed with interest. "You've seen him before? He's a regular at the restaurant?"

Clearly this was important, so she tried to think back to the day she'd done the hamburger photos. Craggy Face had been there that day, but she hadn't really paid attention to him, or to Damon for that matter. Her focus was on getting the best pictures possible for the menu. The better the restaurant did, the more job security for her.

At least, that had been her thought at the time.

Had she seen Craggy Face before that day? Her mind

was nothing but a jumble of bits and pieces of memories. She honestly couldn't say.

"I'm sorry." She hated feeling as if she were letting Nate down. "I don't remember if he had been around the restaurant before or not. It's possible. The only thing I can say for certain is that he's not a regular."

Nate offered a crooked smile. "Don't apologize. It's my job to ask difficult questions. I guess it's good to know he isn't a regular. But I'd really like to know who he is. Seems like he must be a significant piece of the puzzle."

His words hit square in the gut, and she sank to the edge of her sofa. "You were right. This break-in wasn't related to Alex and Debra's murder."

"Yes, that's my take on the issue." His tone was gentle and he came over to sit beside her. His musky scent soothed her frayed nerves and she tried not to think about what it would be like to be in the apartment without him and Murphy standing guard. "Something is up with your boss and that guy in the photo. Bad enough to break into your house to get their hands on the picture. I'm sure they believe you deleted them from your camera, but regardless, I'm glad you quit your job, Willow. You need to stay far away from your boss and the restaurant."

She sighed. "I won't miss the long hours, especially now that I have Lucy, but the pay was decent. I'll need to find another job, hopefully one with flexibility."

His brow furrowed. "Do you need extra money? I can lend you some..."

"What? No!" She jumped up, horrified by his offer. "I'll be fine for a while. I just can't live off my savings forever."

"Okay, but don't hesitate to call me if you need something."

She wouldn't, but it was a kind gesture. She had to call Nanna's Nook to let them know she may not be bringing Lucy in for a few days. Maybe they'd let her postpone a week or so without charging her. Hopefully by then she'd have at least a part-time job.

She wished she could make a living as a photographer; the hours would be extremely flexible. Yet she knew that while it was a great hobby, she wasn't good enough to bring in a steady income.

Nate's phone chirped and he abruptly rose to his feet. "Excuse me." He moved toward the kitchen. "Hey, Sarge, I have a name I need you to run through the system. Damon Berk, manager of the Burgerteria."

As Nate moved into the corner of the room to discuss her current situation with his boss, she went over to her computer and went to a job search website. Since her recent experience was in the restaurant business, she narrowed her search to similar types of jobs within a five-mile radius.

She recognized the Sunshine Sidewalk Café, a small but nice place that happened to be located a couple of blocks from her apartment, in the opposite direction from the Burgerteria. The café was advertising for a server position, and while she would prefer to be a cook, the hours as a server at the café might be better for child care.

She glanced over at Lucy. Her niece was stretched out on the floor next to Murphy, talking to herself as she rested her head on his torso. Her blond tresses were nearly the same color as Murphy's silky coat. Seeing the two of them together had her reaching for her camera.

This time, Murphy didn't move from his position, almost as if he didn't want to disturb the little girl. She took several cute photos, wondering what steps she'd need to take in order to become Lucy's legal guardian. So much had happened yesterday that she hadn't given the legalities of her new situation much consideration.

She made a mental note to check in with Child Protective Services to find out. But then it occurred to her that not having even a part-time job may actually be a black mark against her.

Setting her camera aside, she went back to the job site and clicked the link to submit her résumé.

Nate returned and she caught the last part of his conversation. "Yes, Lucy is our only witness to the Emery murders. Staying here on protective detail for a bit is good, but I need to work the case, too. Finding and arresting this guy is important to me. Especially given the link to the McGregor murders."

She remembered he'd said something about her brother's murder being similar to a previous murder. Was that why he'd seemed so struck by Lucy's description? She couldn't help looking directly at Nate as he disconnected from the call.

"Any clues?"

"Not yet. Damon Berk is clean, no criminal record."

She wasn't surprised. "He's a very busy restaurant manager. I can't even imagine he'd have time to be involved with any criminal activity."

"You never know." Nate cleared his throat. "I hope you don't mind, Willow, but Murphy and I are going to stick around for a couple of days. I promise we won't be any trouble."

"Of course I don't mind. Having you and Murphy

stay is no problem at all." She hoped he didn't sense just how happy she was to hear the news.

As much as she knew she needed to be careful not to get too emotionally involved with the handsome K-9 cop, she couldn't deny the overwhelming wave of relief that he and Murphy weren't leaving anytime soon.

Frustrating that Damon Berk didn't have a rap sheet. The more Nate thought about it, the more he believed Craggy Face was the key.

"Listen, Sarge wants you and Lucy to come in for a formal interview."

Willow frowned, glancing at Lucy. "Today? I don't know...she woke twice last night with bad nightmares."

It was troubling to hear Lucy was suffering from nightmares, but she was their only witness to a crime that could help solve a twenty-year-old murder, as well as this current one. "I know. But I wouldn't ask if it wasn't important."

A resigned expression crossed her features. "Okay, fine. But I want to make a quick stop along the way."

He tensed. "What kind of stop?"

"The Sunshine Sidewalk Café has a job opening." She gestured toward her computer. "I want to check the place out."

He resisted the urge to yank at his hair and kept his tone even with an effort. "This isn't a good time to get a new job, Willow."

"It's not like I'm going to start a new job today." She closed her computer with a snap. "I'm sure I can start in a week or so, once the danger is over."

He didn't like it but figured a quick stop couldn't hurt. As Willow helped Lucy get ready to go, he thought about his conversation with Gavin. Damon Berk had been a dead end, but they had a new line to tug on. Gavin had told him how neighborhood interviews revealed the Emerys weren't well-liked because of their party lifestyle, their messy home and the way they often ignored Lucy. Apparently, several neighbors had been concerned about the girl playing outside alone. Even more importantly, they hadn't paid their rent for the past five months. Late notices and potential eviction warnings had been ignored. The owners of the duplex were a married couple by the name of Mike and Liz O'Malley. Gavin had put their tech guru, Eden Chang, on task to track them down.

It seemed extreme to believe a property landlord would stoop to murder—and borrow from the MO of a cold case—in order to get rid of a couple of deadbeat tenants, but stranger things had happened, and he knew every possibility, no matter how remote, couldn't be ignored. They'd need to verify the O'Malleys' alibi, if they had one, in order to cross them off the suspect list.

He kept coming back to the similarities between the Emery murders and the twenty-year-old cold case. The exact same day, clown mask with blue hair, dressed in black and the stuffed monkey.

Leaving a small child alive, despite being a potential witness.

Why use the same MO? What did it mean?

"I think we're finally ready."

Willow's voice cut into his thoughts. He turned to find Lucy strapped into a lightweight stroller, clutching her baby doll. They were so cute, his heart gave a betraying thump of awareness in his chest.

"Guess I'm lagging behind. Come, Murphy." His

partner came to his side. He pulled Murphy's vest on, then clipped a leash to his collar. Murphy instantly straightened, his nose working as he understood he was now on duty. "Do you have everything you need?"

Willow looped her bag over her shoulder. "I think so."

"All right, let's go."

"I hope you don't mind walking to the café." Willow pushed Lucy's stroller into the hallway, then locked the apartment door, stuffing the key into her large bag. "It's only three blocks away."

Murphy needed exercise, so he nodded. "Not a problem. But we'll need to take the SUV to headquarters."

She stopped in front of the elevator. "Good thing we left Lucy's car seat in your vehicle."

He smiled and nodded. "I know."

The elevator doors opened. Willow pushed Lucy's stroller inside, turning around so she faced front. He and Murphy crowded in beside her, the scent of lilac teasing his nose.

When they reached the lobby and stepped outside, the bright sunlight was blinding. Nate pulled on his sunglasses and tightened Murphy's leash.

"Look! Another doggy!" Lucy was gazing around as if she hadn't spent much time out in the general public. Remembering the disastrous state of the Emery household made him scowl. Was it possible Lucy had lived her entire life either inside the squalor of the place or outside in the littered yard?

He fought back a flash of temper, reminding himself that Lucy would be fine now that she was with Willow.

And watching the two of them together was just more proof that he couldn't afford to let his defenses down.

Being a part of a family wasn't his thing. He didn't want that, and worse, didn't trust himself to have it.

He had no idea how to be a good husband and father. It was too late for him, but not for Willow and Lucy. When the time was right, they'd find someone to complete their little family.

"Can we have a hot dog, Aunt Willow?" Lucy's head was moving back and forth as she took in the sights and smells of Brooklyn from her stroller.

"Are you hungry already?" Willow's brow furrowed in concern. "We just finished breakfast two hours ago."

Lucy bobbed her head up and down. "I wanna hot dog!"

He quickly intervened. "How about we get a hot dog when it's lunchtime?" When Willow frowned, he added, "My treat."

"Okay." Lucy was satisfied with his response, but Willow couldn't help thinking like a parent.

She leaned in to whisper, "She's been through a lot. But we shouldn't give her everything she wants."

"Oh, sorry." He felt the tips of his ears burn with embarrassment. "I didn't think about that. I just wanted to make her happy. A hot dog seemed like a small price to pay."

Her expression softened. "I know. But part of being a good guardian means setting limits."

We shouldn't give her everything she wants. We? For a moment he lost the ability to think. There was no *we.* There was Willow and Lucy, end of story.

"Nate?"

"Yeah, okay. Got it." He forced the words past his tight throat and changed the subject. "Where is this café of yours anyway?"

"We're going to turn right at the next block. The café should be about halfway down."

Murphy was having a great time. After they turned the corner, he saw the sign of the Sunshine Sidewalk Café. The sidewalk in front of the restaurant wasn't very wide, but there were four small tables crowded in front of the building. People were sitting outside, enjoying the sixty-degree April weather. Less than a week ago, they'd experienced an unexpected snowstorm, two inches covering the grass and trees, and now it was practically summer. That was spring in New York. Completely unpredictable.

"Would you like a table inside or outside?" A petite woman with short dark hair greeted them.

"Actually, I'm here about the server position." Willow looked nervous. "Have you already filled it?"

"Not yet." The woman thrust out her hand. "I'm Angela Rivera."

"Willow Emery. Are you the manager?"

Angela laughed. "Owner, manager, server, hostess, accountant, you name it."

"It's great to meet you. I'm really interested in the position. As you can see I have a young girl to support. I have a lot of restaurant experience, too."

Nate suddenly heard a panicked shout. "Help! Police! Help!"

What in the world? He turned to look over his shoulder. A young man in a baseball cap and a Yankees jersey was waving his arms in a frantic attempt to get his attention.

"Help! Someone is being attacked!"

He hesitated, unwilling to leave Willow and Lucy there alone. Willow was still chatting with Angela, the two women cooing over Lucy, so he made a split-second decision to respond. "Willow? Stay here. I'll be right back. Come, Murphy."

"This way!" The Yankees fan turned and disappeared around the corner, clearly expecting Nate and Murphy to follow.

Nate broke into a jog, dodging pedestrians while keeping Murphy close to his side. He listened intently but didn't hear any sounds indicating an attack. He hoped he wasn't going to be too late. As they turned the corner, he raked his gaze over the area, searching for anything suspicious.

There was no obvious sign of an attack, but the Yankees fan was still several paces ahead. "Hurry! Over here! In the alley!"

Nate darted around a group of tourists. He came to the spot where the Yankees fan had been, in front of a long narrow alley, but the guy was gone. He'd vanished like some sort of magician's trick.

There was no attack.

His gut clenched with fear. *Willow! Lucy!*

He whirled around and instantly ran back to the café. The sidewalk seemed to stretch forever. He'd followed the stupid Yankees fan farther than he'd realized.

And it had been nothing but a clever ploy to get him and Murphy out of the way.

No! How could he have been so gullible? He quickened his pace, unable to bear the thought of something happening to Willow and Lucy.

He wheeled around the corner, his heart lodged in his throat. Even more people crowded the sidewalks now.

Lucy was crying, loud screeching sobs. "Aunt Willow! Aunt Willow! Come back!"

A pedestrian got in his way and he nearly plowed the guy over in his haste to reach Willow and Lucy.

"No! Stop!" Willow's voice was muffled. He caught a glimpse of someone dressed in black with a hat pulled low over his forehead dragging her toward a black sedan double-parked a few spots up from the café.

"Stop! Police!" He shouted as loud as he could to be heard above the din. Realizing he might be too late, he reached down and released Murphy's leash. "Get him, Murphy. Get him!"

Murphy took off running. Like a racehorse, he closed the gap between him and Willow faster than Nate ever could.

The man with the hat must have realized the same thing, because he abruptly pushed Willow toward Murphy, then spun and took off running in the opposite direction.

It all happened like a scene unfolding in slow motion. Willow tripped over Murphy. His partner yelped as the two of them tangled together. Then Willow hit the pavement with a *thud*. Lucy was still crying, her stroller several feet away from Willow and Murphy.

"Willow! Are you okay?" He finally caught up to them, crouching down to check Willow and his partner. Murphy had managed to free himself from Willow. He was up on his feet, staring in the direction the intruder had gone.

"Get him," Nate repeated. He didn't like sending his partner off alone, but he couldn't leave Willow and Lucy.

The yellow Lab took off, trotting fast, his nose periodically going to the ground.

Murphy could track just about anything, but he

wasn't trained to go into subway stations without Nate. A fact he hoped the assailant didn't know, as there was a subway entrance at the opposite end of the block.

"What happened?" He helped Willow to her feet.

"He—came out of nowhere." Her voice was shaky, her hands trembling. Her palms were scraped and bleeding, but she didn't seem to care. "I didn't notice until he grabbed me."

"Shh, it's okay." He caught her in his arms for a quick hug, then turned toward Lucy. Some instinct had him lifting the girl from her stroller and handing her over to Willow. They clung to each other, much the way they had outside the scene of the Emery murders.

His gaze fell on the license plate of the black sedan abandoned by the would-be kidnapper. He quickly memorized the plate number, hoping it would be a clue as to who'd attacked Willow.

A sharp dog bark caught his attention. His heart was hammering, and he desperately wanted to go after Murphy. What if the assailant tried to hurt him? Nate took one step forward, then another, but stopped.

He couldn't leave Willow. He had to trust in his partner's training. The K-9 would soon return.

Murphy came running through the crowd of onlookers, returning to Nate's side.

"Murph!" He went down to his knee and wrapped his arms around his partner. From what he could tell, Murphy wasn't hurt.

Unfortunately, the assailant had gotten away.

SEVEN

Willow clutched Lucy close, unable to stop trembling. Her shoulders were sore from where the guy had roughly grabbed her, trying to force her into the vehicle. Everything had happened so fast. She'd tried to crane her neck to get a better look at his face, but his arms were like steel bands around her. She'd barely caught a glimpse before Nate had shouted, causing him to roughly shove her toward Murphy.

The only reassuring part of the whole incident was that the attacker hadn't bothered to go after Lucy. Her niece was safe, for now. But glancing back at the Sidewalk Sunshine Café, she was sad to understand there was no way she could work there anytime soon.

Maybe never. The owner, Angela Rivera, had sounded positive, but had needed someone immediately, not in two weeks or longer.

"Are you okay?" Angela had come over to check on her. "What happened?"

"It's nothing." She tried to smile. "A misunderstanding."

"Are you sure?" Angela's doubt was clearly reflected

in her gaze. "When I came out of the kitchen, it looked like that guy was trying to force you into his car."

"I'm safe now, and so is Lucy. Thanks for coming to check on us."

"Sure." Angela gave her one last look, as if sensing Willow was downplaying the event, then hurried back to her customers. For a moment Willow envied her ability to run her own little café, with no worries other than offering good food.

"Run this license plate for me." Nate was kneeling beside Murphy, speaking into the radio on his collar. It took a moment for her to realize he was reciting the plate number belonging to the black sedan. When finished, Nate rose to his feet and turned toward her. "We need to get you and Lucy away from here."

Rattled by the near miss, she could only nod.

Nate spoke into his cell phone. "Eden? Sorry, I also need you to check video footage from the Bay Ridge Avenue subway station. Perp dressed in black with a black cap pulled over his forehead left less than five minutes ago. I need Belle Montera to call me, ASAP."

She shivered again and glanced over her shoulder. Pedestrians had originally stopped to gawk at the commotion but were now moving on with their busy lives. It struck her then, her life may not return to normal anytime soon.

No matter how much she wanted it to.

Nate's phone rang, and he stayed close to her side as he answered. "Belle, thanks for calling me back. I need you and your K-9 to keep a lookout for a man dressed in black with a hat pulled down over his forehead. He just disappeared through the Bay Ridge Avenue station." There was a pause before he added, "I know it's not much, but do your best, okay? Get Max to help, too. I'm working with Eden to get a photo and I'll shoot it your way as soon as I get it."

It bothered her to know the guy who'd tried to abduct her had gotten away. She sent up a quick prayer, thanking God for sending Nate back in the nick of time to save her.

"I think I've covered all bases for now." Nate slipped his phone back into his pocket.

"Thanks, Nate." She managed a smile over Lucy's head. "Your timing was perfect. If not for you and Murphy, he may have gotten away with me."

He scowled. "Don't thank me, Willow. This is all my fault. I shouldn't have left you in the first place. I should have realized that the fake cry for help was nothing more than a ploy to get you alone."

"Really?" She tilted her head to the side, regarding him thoughtfully. "How could you possibly know that?"

He stared at her for a moment, then looked away. "I just should have."

"And ignore the possibility an innocent person was in trouble?" She shook her head. "No way. You never could have stayed here, doing nothing. It's not in your nature, Nate. You're a cop. I'm sure you've responded to other ridiculous calls, too."

He let out a heavy sigh. "Maybe you're right. Still, it burns to know that he almost succeeded."

"But he didn't." Willow didn't want Nate to feel guilty about this when it was her decision to come here about the job in the first place.

"Nate?" The sound of a female voice caused Nate to glance over his shoulder. A pretty female K-9 officer with shoulder-length dark hair was coming toward them, accompanied by a large German shepherd. "No sign of him yet, but I let Max know, too."

"Belle, this is Willow Emery. Willow, K-9 officer Belle Montera and her K-9 partner, Justice."

"It's nice to meet you." Willow smiled but felt like a giraffe towering over the petite woman. There weren't too many men who made her feel less conspicuous, but Nate had several inches on her.

More to like about him. Not that it mattered.

"Thanks, Belle. As soon as I get something from Eden, I'll let you know." Nate moved closer to Willow's side and she was touched by his protective stance. "We'll be at the precinct if you need me."

"Sounds good." Belle turned toward the black sedan. "Did you call for a tow truck? We may be able to get a DNA hit from the interior."

"Not yet, but that's a good idea. Will you take care of it?"

"Of course." Belle grinned. "I can tell you want to get out of here."

Nate didn't disagree. "Thanks again." He turned to Willow. "Come on, my SUV is parked near your apartment building."

She buckled Lucy into her stroller. They'd barely gone a block when his phone pinged. He glanced down at the screen, then turned the device so she could see the image. "Recognize him?"

She cupped her hand over the phone to cut down the glare from the sun. The photo was a bit blurred, showing a man wearing all black, a black cap pulled low over his forehead, rushing into the subway station, his head slightly turned to the side.

A chill rippled over her, lifting the hairs on her arms. "Craggy Face."

"Yeah. I think he was the one who ransacked your place." Nate's expression was grim. He worked the phone, no doubt sending the photo to Belle as she was responsible for patrolling the subway stations. She leaned over with a frown. "Hey, is that my photograph of him that you're sending?"

He nodded and glanced up. "Yes, why? It's the one you sent me."

The clarity wasn't great, but she figured it would work well enough for what he needed. "No reason, glad to have something to help your team find him."

"We will. And I'll start with your former boss, Damon. He was photographed talking to the guy, so he must know who he is. We'll catch him, Willow. I promise."

Nate's tone oozed confidence and she wondered if he was putting on a brave act for her benefit. Having her apartment broken into was one thing; being grabbed by Craggy Face and nearly forced into a vehicle was something very different. The moment she'd felt him grab her flashed in her mind's eye. An overwhelming burst of fear had momentarily paralyzed her.

She made a silent promise not to let that happen again. Next time, she needed to keep her wits about her. To fight, with every ounce of strength she possessed, the instant she felt something was wrong.

Lucy needed her, now more than ever.

"Willow, I want you to know, I'll never leave you and Lucy alone like that again."

"I know." His promise touched her heart. "I guess I shouldn't have asked to go to the café."

Nate unlocked his SUV, then turned toward her. "You can't take the job at the café, Willow. Not until we have this guy in custody."

Her shoulders slumped. "I know."

His clear blue eyes burned into hers, seeing too much. "I can help get you whatever you need, including cash. Just trust me, okay?"

She wouldn't take his money—she'd use her savings—but she did trust him. More than she'd ever trusted anyone else.

Maybe she trusted him a little too much. Once she and Lucy were safe, he'd be assigned another case. Moving on in his career, leaving her to focus on raising Lucy.

She needed to remember that this…closeness between them wasn't real. It was temporary. In her experience, men didn't stick around for long.

Despite how much she liked and admired him, there was no possibility of a future with Nate.

The near abduction still had Nate's pulse in the triple digits. And he feared it wouldn't return to normal anytime soon. He hated knowing Willow was in danger.

Nate forced himself to keep his hands at his sides, when all he wanted to do was draw Willow into his arms, holding her and Lucy close.

Why this sudden attachment to a woman he was assigned to protect? He'd never mixed his professional role as cop with his personal life before.

No reason to start now. Yet as he watched Willow buckle Lucy into her car seat, he couldn't help but notice how amazing they were together.

He shook off the unusually tender feelings, forcing

himself to concentrate on finding and arresting Craggy Face. He and Murphy had to find him, and soon.

Before he tried again.

When Willow finished with Lucy, she opened the passenger door and slid inside. He put Murphy in the back, then went around to the driver's side, still thinking about their next move. Interviewing Lucy and Willow again wouldn't likely give them too much more to go on, yet it was important to try. He itched to start searching for the owner of the black sedan, but hadn't heard from Eden yet.

He'd been right about the fact that whatever was going on with Willow wasn't connected to the Emery murders. He pulled into traffic, mentally reviewing the similarities between the cold case and this one. Same MO, but what about motive? What did the Emerys have in common with the McGregors?

Other than both sets of victims being Brooklyn residents and lousy parents neglecting their children, what else connected them?

The date. The Emerys were killed on the twentieth anniversary of the McGregors' murders.

But why? What was the missing link? Why had the killer struck again all these years later? Why single out the Emerys as potential victims?

Again, lots of questions and no answers. Yet.

Once Willow and Lucy were safely at the police station, he'd head to the Burgerteria to interview Damon about Craggy Face. But for now, that conversation would have to wait. There was no way the guy who'd just tried to abduct Willow would be hanging around the restaurant with its connection to her. Still, maybe

Nate would get something out of the Burgerteria's manager to go on.

The drive to headquarters didn't take long. There was one parking spot left, so he quickly pulled in. His phone rang, and he was relieved to see the K-9 unit's tech guru's name on the screen. "Eden, please tell me you have something on the car."

"It was reported stolen earlier this morning."

He sighed and glanced at Willow. "That figures. Where was it taken from?"

"That's the interesting part. It was stolen from a driveway in Windsor Terrace at zero three hundred hours. The guy apparently came home late, leaving his car in the driveway. He didn't realize the vehicle was missing for several hours."

"How does that help us?"

"It's a crime of opportunity. I'm doing a search on other similar stolen car cases now, to see if I can find a pattern. This may not be the first time these guys have used a stolen car to do their dirty work."

The idea of a connection brought a flash of hope. "That's good stuff, Eden. Thanks."

"I aim to please, Slater." Her airy response made him smile.

He slid the phone back into his pocket and glanced at Willow. "Ready?"

She nodded, but her light brown eyes were clouded with apprehension. Not for her, he knew, but for Lucy. "Sounds like you have a lead."

"We do." He couldn't share all the details of their investigation but wanted to reassure her. "Our K-9 unit is a great team. We'll get this guy soon."

"I'm sure you will. I'll keep praying for God's strength and guidance. I know God is looking out for us."

He was humbled by her faith and wondered once again if he was missing out on something special. Gavin was a believer, as were several other members of the team.

The painful memory of his father screaming curses and smashing his fist into his mother brought him back to reality. He was happy for Willow, but that kind of thing wasn't for him. He and his mother had barely escaped with their lives, and he didn't see how God had anything to do with that.

He took care of Murphy as Willow strapped Lucy into the stroller. Willow glanced at the building in awe, and he understood how she felt. Their new Brooklyn K-9 Unit was housed in an attractive three-story limestone building that had been used as a police precinct many years ago, until that department had merged with another one, moving into a much larger building. It was perfect for their smaller unit and even had diagonal parking along the front of the building, a rarity in New York. A K-9 center was adjacent to the building, housing impressive indoor and outdoor training facilities.

It was an honor to be here, working for Gavin Sutherland and the rest of the team. Nate liked being a K-9 cop. He'd come a long way from the scared kid who'd escaped with his mother from his abusive father all those years ago.

His gaze rested on Willow, her tall, lean frame bent over Lucy. She straightened, her eyes clashing with his. Awareness shimmered between them, so powerful he almost put out a hand to push it away.

"Looks like a nice place to work." Willow's comment cut through the tension.

"Yeah." He took Murphy off the leash, tucking it in his pocket before heading over to join her on the sidewalk. "I'll carry the stroller inside."

She stepped back, giving him room to maneuver. There were three concrete steps leading inside and he easily carried the stroller up and into the building with Murphy on his heels.

Penelope McGregor was working the front desk when they entered. Nate kept his expression neutral, but his heart went out to Penny. The whole unit knew she had to be thinking of her parents' *unsolved* murders. Penny—and her brother—had to be reeling from the news. Especially because, once again, there was very little evidence. And no leads on the killer.

Penny's eyes widened in surprise when she saw them. She quickly jumped out of her seat and came around to meet them, immediately holding her hand out to Willow. "Hi! I'm Penny McGregor. You must be Willow Emery."

"Yes, and this is Lucy." Willow smiled at her niece.

Penny's expression softened as she crouched down beside the little girl. "Hi, Lucy, how are you?"

Lucy didn't seem intimidated by meeting so many strangers, but didn't exactly answer Penny, either. "Doggy." She buried her tiny fingers in Murphy's pale yellow fur. "Nice doggy."

"Yes, Murphy is a good dog." Penny's brown eyes were concerned when they met his. "Might be best to take Lucy into one of the interview rooms. She probably needs some time to relax before we begin."

"Agreed." Penny wasn't a cop, but considering she

was the sole witness of her parents' murders, including seeing the perp who'd worn black and a clown face with blue hair, and had also been given the stuffed monkey, he thought it might be a good idea for her to gently question Lucy. "Room A appears to be open. Why don't you get her settled in there?" Willow looked as if she might argue, but he sent a reassuring smile. "It's okay. Penny is good with kids."

"All right." Willow rubbed her hands up and down her arms. "Thanks."

He watched them disappear into the interview room, then took Murphy back past the coffee station to the cubicle area. He crossed over to his desk and booted up his computer, hoping to find Craggy Face's photo in their mug shot files.

Gavin Sutherland poked his head around the edge of his cubicle. "Hey, I heard what happened."

"Yeah." He turned to face his boss, a tall man in his early thirties with dark hair and eyes. Gavin could intimidate the best of them, but the guy had a huge heart. "I don't think this thing going on with Willow Emery is linked to her brother's and sister-in-law's murders, though."

"It doesn't seem likely, since the MO mirrors the McGregor case and the incidents involving Willow are all connected to those photos the perp stole." Gavin frowned. "You might want to keep *two* eyes on her."

"I plan to. Anything new on Liberty?"

"No, and it's bugging me. That highly skilled Lab is cross-trained in all specialties and we could really use her services."

"I know. She's tops and we need her out there. Instead, a criminal is keeping her from being able to do what she does best: find smuggled contraband." Nate glanced down at Murphy, stretched out at his feet. A flash of anger burned deep in his belly. He wasn't sure what he'd do if someone had put a bounty on his partner's head—and Liberty was one of Murphy's littermates. "Let me know if you need me to do something more."

Gavin touched his shoulder. "I will, Slater. Thanks."

Nate was still thinking of the bounty on Liberty's head when his phone rang. He quickly answered, hoping for good news. "Slater."

"Nate? It's Belle. With Eden's help we tracked down the subway stop where the perp who tried to abduct Willow exited the train."

"Great." He surged to his feet.

"Hang on," she cautioned. "The guy immediately slid into a car—the driver was obviously waiting for him—and disappeared."

"Disappeared? Did Eden get a plate number?" He tightened his grip on the phone, holding his breath. Eden Chang was their tech guru and if anyone could get something from nothing, she could. At just twenty-seven, she was a master at searching through police and public databases, cross-referencing, and homing in on helpful information.

"No. Unfortunately the plate was obscured with mud and the camera angle was bad. She's playing with the video some more, but so far doesn't have a single letter or digit to use as a possible reference point."

"You've got to be kidding me." He jammed his fingers through his hair, battling a wave of frustration. "So you're telling me this is nothing more than another dead end."

"I'm afraid so." Belle's tone held regret. "Still, we might get some DNA from the car that Craggy Face used in his attempt to kidnap Willow. I have the forensic team working on that right now."

"Thanks." Nate tossed his phone on his desk. First Eden had been unable to trace the cash-paid gas receipt found in Willow's apartment, and now this.

Willow had nearly been kidnapped right in front of his eyes, and he'd have absolutely nothing to go on unless he could get Willow's ex-boss, Damon Berk, to talk.

Not likely, but he'd do his best to make that happen.

EIGHT

Lucy didn't seem too intimidated to be seated beside Penny McGregor, maybe because Penny had started off asking questions about her favorite things, like colors and TV shows.

"You're a very brave girl." Penny placed her arm around Lucy's shoulders, radiating compassion. "And I want you to know you're safe with your aunt Willow."

Lucy nodded, taking a sip from the container of chocolate milk that Penny had given her. Her niece obviously preferred chocolate milk over plain, and Willow made a mental note to stop and pick some up on their way home.

"Lucy, can you tell me again about the bad clown you saw yesterday?" Penny's gaze was kindly sympathetic.

The little girl tensed and shook her head. "Too scary."

"I know, but remember how brave you were to talk to Detective Nate?" Penny gently reminded her. "Can you tell me what happened?"

Willow didn't like the look of distress on Lucy's face. "Maybe it's too soon."

Penny nodded and turned her attention back to Lucy. "I was scared by a mean clown, too, when I was your age."

Lucy's eyes widened. "You were?"

Penny nodded. "A scary, mean clown hurt my mommy and daddy, too. If you can tell me what happened, it will help the police find him and throw him in jail where he belongs."

Lucy glanced at Willow, then back to Penny. "Okay."

"Where were you when he came?"

"I was playing outside when he came into the yard." Lucy's voice had dropped so low it was difficult for Willow to hear her.

Penny nodded encouragingly. "Then what happened?"

"He gave me a bag with a stuffed monkey and told me to stay outside." Lucy's eyes welled with tears. "I don't like monkeys anymore."

"I know. I don't like them, either." Penny gave the little girl another hug. "What did he look like?"

"Blue hair like my dolly."

"Anything else?" Penny gently prodded. "Do you remember what color his eyes were?"

Lucy scrunched up her forehead. "Bad clown with mean eyes."

"Did you stay outside like he told you?"

Lucy nodded, then shook her head. "I heared loud noises. *Bang! Bang!* So I went inside."

Willow wanted to stop her niece there, unwilling to have her relive the moment Lucy hadn't been able to wake up her mommy and daddy, but Penny went on.

"What did you see?"

Lucy's eyes welled with tears. "Mommy and Daddy were on the floor. They wouldn't wake up when I shaked them."

"Okay, that's good, Lucy. You're so brave." Penny stroked her hand over Lucy's wavy hair.

Lucy looked at Willow and Willow's heart squeezed painfully in her chest. "I love you, Lucy."

"I love you, too." Lucy sniffed and swiped at her face.

"Would you like more chocolate milk?" Penny asked.

"Yes." Momentarily distracted by what appeared to be her new favorite drink, Lucy took the carton of milk and sucked what was left through the straw, making a loud noise as she drained every drop from the container.

"I'll be right back." Penny squeezed Lucy's hand, then left the interview room to get the promised chocolate milk.

"We'll go home soon, Lucy, okay?" Willow smiled reassuringly. "Thanks for being so brave."

"Will Murphy stay with us again?"

Uh-oh, the little girl was becoming too attached to Murphy. "We'll see." She couldn't deny she wanted Nate and Murphy there but wasn't sure if Nate's plan to stay had changed.

And she refused to make promises she couldn't keep.

When Penny returned, she brought Nate with her. "Willow, Nate would like you to look at a few photographs if you have a minute."

"Oh, um, now?" She didn't hide her lack of enthusiasm. The last thing she wanted was to keep Lucy here at the precinct longer than necessary.

"It won't take long," Nate assured her. "And it may help us catch the guy who tried to grab you."

"All right." She stood, then bent to press a kiss to the top of Lucy's head. "I'll be back soon, okay?"

"Okay." Lucy didn't seem to mind, her attention centered on Penny as the desk clerk opened another container of chocolate milk.

Nate stood, holding the door open for her, with Murphy standing patiently at his side. She followed him past a coffee stand, taking note of the large map of Brooklyn hanging on the wall, until they reached his work station. Murphy dropped down beside the desk, as if he were used to this.

"We have computer-generated mug shots." Nate gestured to his chair. "Have a seat. I entered the hard copy and facial features that match your Craggy Face guy into the database."

She took his chair, keenly aware of his woodsy scent as he leaned over her shoulder to work the mouse. This ridiculous awareness of him had to stop. She was sure he wasn't interested in her and even if he was, she had to focus on adopting and raising her orphaned niece and finding a job that would still allow her a lot of time with Lucy.

"There are six images on a page," Nate was saying. "Could be that Craggy Face was picked up for a crime at some point when he was younger. You have a good eye—let me know if any of these guys look familiar."

His offhand compliment shouldn't have made her feel good, but it did. She turned her attention to the screen, rejecting the first page of images, then the second. She tried not to rush through them, but as she clicked through page after page, she knew in her gut that Craggy Face wasn't any of these men, now or when he was younger.

"I'm sorry, Nate." She sat back in the chair with a sigh, turning to glance up at him. "I don't think he's in your system."

"Yeah, I'm getting that impression, as well." He had to be as frustrated as she was, but he didn't show it. His phone rang and he reached around her to snag the receiver. "Slater."

There was a pause as he listened to whoever was on the other end of the line. She clicked through a few more images for something to do but couldn't help but listen to his side of the conversation. He was clearly talking to someone who'd been working on a lead.

"Thanks, Darcy. I appreciate you letting me know."

"No prints on the black sedan?" It was a logical assumption.

"Darcy's still working on evidence from your brother's house, but she asked another tech to put a rush on the black sedan for me. No match in the system." He shrugged. "At least there's a print. Could belong to the owner, too. They have someone heading out to get his prints to compare against now."

She didn't understand why he looked so dejected. "But a fingerprint is a good thing, right?" She thought back to those terrifying moments when she struggled with Craggy Face, then frowned. "No, it's not a good thing. I'm pretty sure he was wearing gloves."

"When he grabbed you?" When she nodded, Nate sighed again. "Well, it's possible he wasn't wearing gloves when he stole the vehicle. Or maybe Craggy Face had someone stealing the car for him, and that guy didn't wear gloves. Criminals aren't always as smart as they think they are."

She liked how he turned a negative into a potential positive. "Let's hope the print leads to something good." She rose from his desk chair. "Is it okay if I take Lucy home now?"

"Would you mind hanging out here for a while longer?" He walked beside her as they made their way back to the interview rooms. "I need to take Murphy back to the Burgerteria to question Damon Berk, your former boss. It shouldn't take me too long."

She didn't like the idea of staying in the police station, but it was probably better to wait for Nate to take her and Lucy home. "I guess, but it's a nice day out and it would be good for Lucy to play outside. I'm worried she'll get bored sitting around in my apartment."

Nate nodded. "I get it." He opened the door to the interview room. "Penny? I'd like to take Willow and Lucy on a quick tour of the station, introduce them to the crew, and I'm wondering if you'd mind arranging for Willow and Lucy to have a tour of the K-9 training center afterward?"

"Of course." Penny grinned at Lucy. "Would you like to see more doggies?"

"Yes!" Lucy jumped off her seat. "I love doggies."

Willow reluctantly smiled. "Sounds like fun."

Nate nodded. "Our tour begins, then," he said, gallantly sweeping his hand forward. "Follow me, ladies."

Lucy giggled, and Willow and the little girl trailed behind Nate around the front of the main desk where Penny had been sitting when they'd arrived.

"This is everyone's first stop," Nate said. "Need to talk to an officer, report a crime, offer a tip? You speak to Penny McGregor. She's very important to the team."

Lucy's eyes widened with admiration at Penny, who'd returned to her seat.

"And behind Penny's desk is where all the police work happens," Nate added.

Willow took in the many desks, officers hunched

over computers and phones, typing, taking notes, talking, comparing information, dashing from one desk to another and to the back offices. And a lot of sipping from take-out coffee cups. The big room was hopping with activity. Last night, Nate had told her about his unit and his colleagues, and it was clear from the warm way he'd described them, sharing a bit about why each had become a cop, that they were already close, despite being a new unit operating for only a few months. As she glanced around the big room, she recognized some of the team based on his descriptions.

Tall, lanky Raymond Morrow, a narcotics K-9 officer who'd been poring over reports for evidence in a drug case he was working on, stood up and came around his desk. He smiled at Willow, then knelt in front of Lucy and extended his hand. "You must be Lucy. It's very nice to meet you. I'm Ray. My partner, a furry springer spaniel named Abby, is in the kennel right now, but she'd love to meet you when you head over."

"I'd like that," Lucy said shyly.

Willow watched Nate send Ray an appreciative nod. Nate had mentioned he didn't know too much about Raymond's past, but he knew the dedicated officer had a difficult family background related to why he became a narcotics cop. His kindness to Lucy was touching.

Next they ran into bomb detection K-9 detective Henry Roarke, who at six foot four towered over Lucy to the point that she had to tip her head way back. Henry was African American and wore his curly black hair military short, but despite his height, he laughed and knelt down, too. He told Lucy a cute knock-knock joke and Lucy giggled. A warm, funny guy, Henry seemed a natural around kids, probably due to having raised his teenage sister after the loss of their parents. Willow was surprised she could remember so much about what Nate had shared.

Nate glanced around and reminded her she'd already met K-9 transit officer Belle Montera and her German shepherd partner, Justice. Willow recognized officer Vivienne Armstrong, with her short dark hair, on the phone at her desk and taking furious notes.

Willow couldn't recall what Nate had told her about the tall, dark-haired, green-eyed officer walking toward them. He introduced himself as Jackson Davison, who also worked in Emergency Services, and shared a cute story about his chocolate Lab partner, Smokey.

"Hi, Lucy!" said blond K-9 detective Tyler Walker once he got off the phone. He spun around his desk chair. "Want to see a photo of my partner, Dusty? She's a golden retriever and a great finder." Willow remembered Nate mentioning that Tyler was the single parent of a toddler daughter.

"I'm good at hide-and-seek, too," Lucy said, her shyness evaporating.

Tyler grinned, and his phone rang, so he grabbed it.

Nate glanced around again, and Willow had the feeling he was looking for K-9 detective Bradley McGregor, Penny's brother. From what Nate had shared, Bradley had been through so much as a teen when he and Penny's parents were killed. Willow didn't see anyone matching his description. Bradley must be out on a case.

Penny stood up and let them know the training center next door was all set for Willow and Lucy's tour.

Nate thanked Penny, then turned to Willow. "I'll be back as soon as possible." He lightly squeezed her shoulder before turning away. "Come, Murphy."

Willow watched as Nate left the precinct with Murphy. She found it hard to believe Damon had anything to do with ransacking her home, but the man *had* been photographed with the guy who'd tried to wrestle her into the black car. Maybe Damon had nothing to do with it, and Craggy Face had simply noticed her taking pictures, realized she must have gotten one of him and panicked. Why, she had no idea. Hopefully Nate would get some information about the guy out of Damon. He wasn't the nicest person but he'd always been reasonably fair.

This weird loneliness she felt watching Nate go had to be related to the danger surrounding her.

It was nothing personal. She knew from past experience with men, including her father, who'd walked out when she was only two years old, that once Nate had Craggy Face in custody, she wouldn't see him again.

Nate couldn't believe how difficult it was to walk away from Willow, feeling her gaze on his back. It was strange how close they'd gotten in such a short period of time. Even from this distance, he could pick up the lilac scent of her.

Or maybe it was all in his head.

He shook off the strange and unwelcome sensation and focused on what was important. He couldn't afford to get emotionally involved with Willow or her adorable niece. She and Lucy deserved to be safe, and that meant he needed to remain professional. Getting emotionally involved increased the chance of making a mistake. He needed to focus on the two cases. The Emery murders and the attempted abduction of Willow.

He knew better than to hope for success on the fingerprint found on the sedan, but he'd try to get a name out of Damon Berk, the manager of the Burgerteria.

Outside, he glanced up, taking note of clouds gathering overhead. Spring could be dicey, the temperature rising like the sun, then falling like a rock. He quickened his pace, knowing that a rainstorm could easily wash away any remaining scent left behind by Craggy Face.

"Up, Murphy." He lifted the back hatch for his partner. Murphy jumped gracefully inside the crated area.

The drive to the Burgerteria didn't take nearly as long as it took to find a parking spot. He would have walked, if not for the impending storm. When he found a spot, he let Murphy out.

They were still fifty yards from the restaurant, which was fine with him. He once again opened the evidence bag containing the gas receipt. "Seek, Murphy. Seek!"

It only took Murphy a moment to pick up the scent. His partner followed the same path he had the evening before, the scent trail leading to the doorway of the restaurant where Willow once worked.

"Good boy." He leaned down to give Murphy a brisk rub. Then he opened the door to the restaurant. "Seek!"

Murphy eagerly complied, nose to the ground as he crossed the threshold.

"Hey! We don't allow dogs in here!"

Nate glanced up from Murphy to find Damon Berk scowling at him from across the room. He held up his badge. "Police business."

"Wh-what?" Damon sputtered. "It doesn't matter if you're a cop. I run a restaurant. Having an animal in here violates all kinds of health codes."

Nate ignored Damon's mini rant, his gaze centered

on Murphy. His partner had followed the scent to a vacant table near the door and sat, waiting expectantly for his praise.

"Good boy, Murph." He again rubbed the animal's silky coat. This time, he walked the animal farther inside the restaurant. "Seek, Murphy."

Murphy put his nose to the ground, sniffing around the area. They were garnering attention from the other customers, but Nate didn't care. Despite his attempt to widen the search area, Murphy eventually ended up back at the entrance to the restaurant. Within minutes, his partner quickly returned to the same spot as before, sitting right in front of a high-top table with two seats.

"Good boy." He gave Murphy a final pat, then straightened. He caught the manager's attention by raising his voice. "Damon Berk? I have a few questions for you. We can talk here or outside, your choice."

"What is this about?" Damon was clearly put off by his arrival. "I have a business to run."

"This shouldn't take too long." Nate gestured to the vacant high-top table. "Here? Or outside?"

Berk glanced over his shoulder, taking note of how many of his customers were watching them with frank curiosity. "Outside."

"Fine with me." Nate opened the door and waited for Berk to pass through first. He followed with Murphy at his side. "Heel."

Murphy sat.

Damon Berk didn't seem impressed. "What do you want?"

Nate raised a brow at his curt tone. "My name is Detective Slater and I have a few questions. What is your role here and how long have you been employed?"

"I'm the manager and have been since we opened."

"And when was that?"

"Three years ago." Despite how the air had cooled beneath the gathering storm clouds, Nate noticed a bead of sweat forming at Berk's temple.

"Is that how long Willow Emery was working here before you fired her?"

Damon blanched. "Yes. Is that what this is about? Listen, I didn't fire her, she quit."

Nate wanted to badger him more about that, but decided it was better to get to the point about Craggy Face. "Okay, now I'd like to ask about one of your customers." He pulled out his phone and tapped on the screen, bringing up the photo Willow had taken of Craggy Face. "I need to know this man's name."

Damon barely looked at the screen. "I don't know him."

"Really?" Nate glanced at the photo again, then captured Damon's gaze. "Because you're talking to him here in what appears to be more than a casual conversation. Take a closer look."

Damon shifted his feet nervously, a bead of sweat rolling slowly down the side of his face. But he obeyed Nate's request, leaning over to peer intently at the screen. Damon's brow was furrowed with what was supposed to look like concentration. Nate wasn't buying it; he felt sure the manager knew the guy who'd tried to abduct Willow, but wasn't surprised when he once again repeated, "Sorry. I don't know him."

"You don't remember what you were discussing with him?"

Damon's gaze darted right and left, as if fearing they were being watched. "I talk to a lot of my customers, but it doesn't mean anything. Schmoozing is part of the hospitality business. I'm always hoping they return to the restaurant again—that's part of keeping this place afloat. But I don't ask their names or get any other personal information from them. That would be crossing the line."

"Funny, but this doesn't look like schmoozing to me." Nate tapped his index finger on the phone screen. "Looks like an intense conversation, maybe even an argument."

Another bead of sweat rolled down Damon's face. "Maybe he was upset by the food. I often reassure customers that if they don't like their meal I'll give them a discount to return." Berk brightened. "Yes, now I remember! This man requested to speak to me about a problem with his burger. He'd cracked his tooth on something hard inside the beef and was demanding I do something about it."

"Did you pay for his tooth?" Nate planned to ask for proof of payment, even though he didn't really believe him.

"I—uh, well, no." Damon didn't fall for his trap. "I didn't charge him for his meal and told him he could return anytime for a free lunch or dinner on me."

"And you didn't get his name?"

Berk spread his hands wide. "Why would I? I wasn't even sure he'd take me up on my offer. He was pretty upset about his tooth."

"Right. When was this broken tooth incident, exactly?"

Damon waved a hand. "I don't know, not recently."

"That's interesting, because Murphy picked up his scent at the high-top table near the door." He wasn't about to let Berk know that Willow's photo was stamped with a date and time.

Damon paled, then backpedaled. "Well, it could have been the past week or so, I didn't exactly take the time to write the complaint down on my calendar. Now if you'll excuse me, I have a lot of work to do. With Willow gone, I have a trainee in the kitchen."

"Just one more question," Nate said. "Where were you on Sunday evening?"

"Here at the restaurant, then at home." Another bead of sweat rolled down his face. "Why? Are you accusing me of something?"

"Just curious. But I do need something else from you."

Berk looked impatient. "Now what?"

"If this man shows up again, I'd like you to call me." Nate fished out a business card and held it out for him. Damon stared at it as if it might bite him before he reluctantly took it.

"Fine. But I doubt he'll be back anytime soon. It's not like he's one of my regular customers."

"Still, I'd appreciate a call when he does return."

Damon shoved the card into his pocket, then hurried back inside the restaurant. Nate watched through the window as Berk quickly wove his way toward the back of the restaurant.

To check on his trainee cook? No, he felt certain Damon had gone straight back to call Craggy Face. Too bad he didn't have enough evidence to request a search warrant for Berk's phone records. The photo alone wasn't enough; Berk claimed he was a disgruntled customer, and he didn't have any way to dispute his claim.

Nate wasn't sure what business the two of them had together, but sensed it was illegal.

Why else were they so desperate to get their hands on Willow's photograph?

NINE

The K-9 training center was an impressive facility, but Willow couldn't help glancing at her watch every few minutes, wondering when Nate would return.

This strange attachment she was feeling toward him bothered her. She and Lucy were safer here, surrounded by two-legged and four-legged cops, than anywhere else.

Still, she felt oddly vulnerable without him. Which wasn't good. She really needed to find a way to put distance between them.

At least Lucy was enjoying herself. Penny had given them a tour of the kennels and the indoor training yard, and now they were in the outdoor yard, which was fully fenced in. The little girl had managed to shake off the effects of the interview and had run through the K-9 obstacle course pretending to be Murphy.

"I'm a doggy, woof woof!" Lucy went down on her hands and knees and crawled through a colorful flexible tunnel.

She couldn't help but smile at her niece's antics. The little girl displayed an incredible imagination and she couldn't help wondering if that was related to how much time Lucy spent alone without parental supervision.

Just remembering how Lucy had been outside by herself when the killer had approached was horrifying.

Her smile faded as the reality of her situation hit hard, stealing her breath. When exactly would the woman from Child Protective Services, Jayne Hendricks, show up for a surprise visit? What if Ms. Hendricks learned about her close call with Craggy Face? Would she decide that leaving Lucy in Willow's care would be too dangerous? Would she demand the little girl be placed into foster care until the threat against Willow was gone?

As much as she couldn't bear the idea of Lucy being in danger, she felt strongly her niece needed to be with someone familiar, not a houseful of strangers.

She closed her eyes for a moment, silently praying that God would continue to look over them, keeping them safe in His care, and allow Lucy to remain in her custody.

"Lucy, sweetie, that hurdle is only for furry friends, not humans."

Penny's voice caught her attention. She glanced over to see Lucy reaching up to grab on to a small hurdle that was used for the dogs to jump over. Willow pulled herself together and hurried to her niece, sweeping Lucy into her arms, trying to make a game out of it.

"I've got you!" She twirled in a circle before setting Lucy back on her feet. "We have to be careful, Lucy, these are set up for the doggies, not for kids to play on."

"I'm a doggy, woof!"

She stifled a sigh, startling when her phone rang. When she pulled the device from the pocket of her pink hoodie, her heart gave a betraying thump when she recognized Nate's number.

"Hello?"

"Hi, Willow, I just wanted to let you know Murphy and I are on the way back to the precinct. How are things going?"

"We're fine. Lucy is pretending to be a dog. Can't you hear her barking?"

"Woof! Woof!" Lucy shouted.

Nate's low chuckle sent shivers of awareness down her spine. "Cute. I should be there in ten minutes, maybe less depending on traffic. I thought we might want to make good on our promise to have hot dogs for lunch."

"Fine with me. Thanks."

"See you soon." Nate disconnected from the call.

Penny crossed over to stand next to Willow and gave her an assuring smile. "Well, Lucy," she called, "it's time to go back to the station. I hope you can come visit the doggies again."

"I hope so, too!" Lucy said with a grin, taking one last look around at her new furry friends as she crawled over on her hands and knees, still in her doggy persona. Willow smiled and decided to let her continue at least until they were outside the building.

Penny led the way and when they reached the concrete sidewalk, Lucy must have decided the cement hurt her knees because she scrambled to her feet. "Aunt Willow, I'm hungry."

"I know. Don't worry, Detective Nate will be here soon. Do you remember what he promised you could have for lunch?"

Lucy scrunched up her face, thinking. "Hot dogs?"

"That's right. We're having hot dogs for lunch."

Penny glanced at her with a warm smile. "Sweet of Nate to take you and Lucy out for lunch."

Willow felt her cheeks burn and quickly shook her

head. "It's nothing, really. He's just being nice while protecting us."

"Hmm." Penny's knowing expression indicated otherwise, but Willow sensed arguing further would only reinforce her beliefs. Better not to bring that on.

Back inside the precinct, Penny gestured toward the interview room they'd used earlier. "Why don't you and Lucy wait in there? Your stroller is still inside, too." She knelt down in front of Lucy. "Thanks for talking to me today, Lucy. I had fun showing you the dogs."

Lucy grinned and said, "Me, too," and Penny returned to her seat behind the front desk. The officer who'd taken over in her absence left with a smile at the three of them.

"Sounds good. And thanks for the tour. It was nice that you let Lucy play outside for a while." Willow was truly grateful for Penny's assistance with Lucy.

"It's the least I could do." Penny's gaze dropped to Lucy, who was occupied a few feet away by the basket of toys and stuffed animals Nate had told her the unit kept for little visitors "I know only too well what your niece is going through. As you know, I was Lucy's age the night my parents were murdered. My older brother, Bradley, was spending the night at a friend's house. A man dressed in black, wearing a clown mask with blue hair, came in through our backyard, where I was playing. He gave me a stuffed monkey, then went inside the house. I heard the gunshots, but was too little to understand what had happened."

"I'm so sorry." Willow knew that Penny had suffered through a murder that was exactly like Lucy's, but she shivered at the similarities between the two cases.

"I'm grateful that I have my brother. It's nice that

Lucy has you, Willow." Penny flashed a sad smile, then quickly picked up the phone when it rang, understandably relieved for a reprieve from the harrowing conversation.

Willow wondered about the terrifying similarities. The same killer was back? Why? Could there be a connection between Penny's parents and Alex and Debra? Something they had in common? Twenty years ago, Willow's brother had been nine years old. It seemed so strange to think that the same killer had targeted Alex and his wife all these years later.

It didn't make any sense.

Willow ushered Lucy into the interrogation room, and the little girl went straight to a book and doll that Penny must have put on the table before the tour. The door opened, revealing Nate and Murphy. She had to tamp down the urge to greet him with a hug as if he'd been gone for days rather than a couple of hours. "Hey, are you two ready to go?"

"Yes." She rose to her feet and reached for the stroller, searching his gaze. "How was the interview?"

He shrugged. "Berk denied knowing the guy, claimed their conversation was related to an 'anonymous customer' being upset that he'd cracked a tooth on a burger."

"What? No way. I would have remembered something like a chipped tooth. I can't imagine Damon wouldn't have told me about that, considering I make the burgers. He never hesitated to tell me about food complaints."

"I know. I'm pretty sure he wasn't being honest with me."

It bothered her to know that Damon Berk had lied to the police. What sort of shady dealings had her former boss gotten involved in? Something bad enough to send someone to break into her apartment to find the photographs, and to risk attempting to kidnap her right off the street.

"Willow?"

"Yes?" She met his gaze, realizing she'd been lost in her thoughts. "Sorry, what did you say?"

"Are you and Lucy ready to head out?"

She nodded. "Of course. Come on, Lucy, time to get back in the stroller."

She half expected an argument, but Lucy willingly came over. After buckling Lucy into the stroller, she pushed it through the doorway.

"I'll carry her down the stairs." The muscles in Nate's arms bulged as he lifted the stroller and carried it down the few steps leading to the sidewalk. He gestured toward the parking spaces. "I'm at the end of the row."

She pushed Lucy's stroller down the sidewalk. "Where would you like to get our hot dogs? There's a vendor that usually sits a few blocks down from my apartment."

Nate opened the back passenger door, so Willow could place Lucy in her car seat. "I was thinking it might be nice to eat at Owl's Head Park." He glanced up at the overcast sky. "According to my weather app we have a few hours before the rain hits."

"That sounds nice." Willow hoped he didn't notice her pink cheeks. She knew better than to treat this little outing as a date, as she knew full well that Nate was only looking out for her and Lucy's welfare.

"They have hot dog stands around the park, so we'll pick up something there." He took the stroller, folded it up and slipped it on the floor of the back seats. Then he let Murphy in the back. "This helps me, too," he confided, once they were both buckled in. "I need to spend some time playing with Murphy. He worked hard again today."

There, see? Not a date. "He's so smart." Willow glanced over her shoulder, watching as Murphy pressed his nose against the wire crate near Lucy. Even with the barrier between them, she sensed that his intent was to protect the little girl.

Willow settled back in her seat, reminding herself that she needed to be thankful for Nate and Murphy's presence. For their protection and dedication to finding the man who'd killed her brother and his wife, and the guy who'd tried to kidnap her.

It would be selfish and wrong to wish for anything more.

Nate told himself that the main reason he was taking Willow and Lucy to the park was because he needed to reward Murphy. And because he'd promised Lucy a hot dog.

But deep down, he knew that wasn't the entire truth.

No, this little trip to the park was his attempt to make Willow happy.

For being a guy who didn't intend to have a family of his own, he couldn't deny how he'd grown attached to Willow and her niece. He'd laughed upon hearing Lucy barking like a dog and it occurred to him that he hadn't laughed like that in a long time.

He'd always been focused on work, on taking criminals off the streets. His personal life was always secondary, not deemed a priority.

So why was he making Willow and Lucy a priority now?

Sure, his job was to keep them safe, and that might be easier to do while being in her apartment rather than out in the park.

Not that he was really worried about their safety. He trusted Murphy to alert them to any potential danger, especially since he had Craggy Face's scent.

It took a while for him to find a parking spot, but he managed to snag one that wasn't far from the park entrance. He kept a wary eye on the cloudy sky as he followed Willow, who pushed Lucy's stroller along the sidewalk.

Murphy's nose worked as he took in the new scents surrounding them. Willow headed straight for one of the hot dog stands.

"We'll take two hot dogs," Willow said, digging in her purse for her wallet.

"Make it three, my treat." He nudged her aside so he could pay for their meal. "And make mine a chili dog." He turned to Lucy. "What would you like on yours?"

"I just like plain hot dogs!" Lucy said.

Willow smiled. "I'll take mine with mustard and sauerkraut."

"And now what to drink?" Nate asked.

"Chocolate milk!" Lucy said, kicking her heels with excitement.

"Add a chocolate milk, and—" He turned to Willow. "What would you like to drink?"

"Water is fine." She looked nonplussed at his taking over the food ordering.

"Add one root beer and one water," he told the vendor. "Thanks."

"No problem." The woman handed over a cardboard tray loaded with the hot dogs. He passed it to Willow so he could take the drinks.

"You didn't have to pay for our lunch. I'm not destitute." Willow's voice was quiet as they headed toward the closest picnic table. He pushed the stroller, as Willow's hands were full.

"I never said you were. But this was my idea, remember?" He set the drinks down, then took the hot dogs and napkins from her. "Playing is an important reward for K-9 training, so it really is critical that I spend some time throwing the ball for Murphy."

"I guess I didn't realize it was such a big deal." She released Lucy from the stroller and set her on the bench of the picnic table. She quickly unpacked the food, giving Lucy the milk first, before opening the wrapper around the hot dog.

Willow watched Lucy eat with gusto before taking a tentative bite of her own hot dog. "Delicious."

"Of course. All New York City hot dogs are delicious." Nate grinned as he quickly ate his chili dog. "I may have seconds."

Willow smiled and he was struck again by her beauty. When he'd finished his hot dog, he wiped his hands and took Murphy off his leash.

"Sit." Murphy sat, his gaze going from Nate's pocket back up to his face. He waited a long moment before reaching in and pulling out the bright orange ball.

Murphy strained forward, his gaze locked on the orange ball.

"Get it!" Nate threw the ball and Murphy took off like a rocket after it, capturing the ball in his mouth and then rushing back to him.

They repeated the sequence several more times, Murphy loping back and forth, ears flopping as he gamely fetched the ball. Lucy came running over.

"Can I throw the ball?"

It wasn't part of the training, but he couldn't stand the idea of disappointing the little girl. "Sure." He crouched beside her, then looked at Murphy. "Sit. Stay."

Murphy sat, tongue lolling, sides heaving from exertion. Still, his gaze didn't waver from the ball.

Lucy threw the ball, but it only went a foot. Murphy cocked his head to the side, as if confused, but then went over to pick up the ball. He dropped it in front of Lucy, then sat.

"I'll help you," Nate offered. He picked up the ball and helped Lucy throw it a little farther this time. Murphy didn't hesitate to chase after it.

"I want to throw it far like you." Lucy gazed up at him with her wide cinnamon eyes.

His heart squeezed and for a moment he imagined what it would be like to be a father to a little girl just like Lucy. Then as quickly as the thought formed, he shoved it away.

"You'll be able to throw it farther when you grow up to be big and strong." Nate picked up the orange ball and stood. He tossed it again for Murphy, watching his partner gallop across the grassy area to fetch it.

A few minutes later, he tucked the ball away and bent to give Murphy a rub. "Good boy, yes, you're such a good boy."

"I have water left, if he needs it." Willow lifted her water bottle toward him.

"It's okay, there's actually water in the back of my SUV." He glanced at the picnic table; the waste from their meal was cleared away. "Ready to return to your place?"

"Of course. I know you have things to do."

He lifted a brow. "I'm planning to camp out on your sofa again, if you don't mind."

"Oh, um, sure. If you think that's necessary." She looked flustered and he wondered what she was thinking. Had she expected him to drop her and Lucy off and head back to work?

Gavin had given him permission to work from Willow's place, so he could keep an eye on her. But maybe she didn't want him and Murphy invading her personal space.

"Just a couple more nights," he assured her. "I'm sure we'll get this guy soon."

"I know you will. It's truly not a problem." Willow put Lucy in the stroller. "Thanks for the picnic. This was really nice."

The clouds overhead were growing darker and he realized they'd stayed out longer than he'd intended. "We better hurry, or we might get drenched."

He connected Murphy to his leash, then followed Willow toward the park entrance. The low rumble of thunder reached his ears, so he quickened his pace.

Murphy began to growl low in his throat. Nate glanced at his partner in surprise. Normally Murphy didn't react like this to bad weather.

"What is it, boy?" He glanced around the area, searching for something that may have caught his K-9's attention. There weren't many people in the park, and those who were there were scurrying toward the exits as well in an effort to beat the rain.

More growling, then Murphy abruptly put his nose

to the ground. Nate frowned. Was it possible Murphy had picked up Craggy Face's scent?

He reached for the evidence bag. "Seek, Murphy. Seek!"

Murphy took in the scent and quickly alerted along the edge of the sidewalk.

Craggy Face was here? Nate's heart thudded in his chest. "Willow? We need to hurry."

As much as he wanted to keep Murphy on the scent, he didn't like having Willow and Lucy out in the open. He huddled behind her, protecting her with his body as much as possible as he urged her toward his SUV.

It wasn't far, but the ten feet stretched for what seemed like ten miles. He quickly opened the rear passenger door. Before Willow could get Lucy out of her stroller, a sharp retort echoed through the air.

"Get down!" Nate curled his body over Willow and Lucy, the open door offering some protection from the right. Lucy began to cry, and he could hear Willow softly praying.

He grabbed his radio. "Shots fired at Owl's Head Park! Officer requesting backup. Hurry!"

Murphy continued to growl low in his throat. Nate couldn't move; he needed to protect Willow and Lucy.

He kept himself positioned so that he was a human wall in front of Willow, Lucy and Murphy, braced for the inevitable impact from a bullet.

TEN

Dear Lord, keep us safe in Your care!

Willow repeated the prayer over and over as she clutched Lucy close, reassured by how Nate covered her back. Lucy's tears ripped at Willow's heart and she would have done anything to prevent her niece from reliving the sound of gunfire, a horrifying reminder of her parents' murders. Murphy crowded close, his low growls seeming nonstop.

Craggy Face wouldn't stop until he had her—or the camera with the digital proof of him at the Burgerteria. Why was the photo so important? Because it put him with Damon? Because it placed him in the restaurant? She had no idea and could not figure out what was behind all this. He had to figure that she'd shared the photo with police, so what was the point of coming after her?

She strained to listen, fearing more gunfire, but all she could hear was the roll of thunder, the air thick with humidity.

"Are you okay?" Nate's voice was low and husky near her ear. "You and Lucy weren't hit?"

"No physical injuries." She didn't add that she and Lucy couldn't possibly be all right, now knowing someone had actually aimed a gun and fired at them. But she tried to reassure her niece. "Shh, Lucy, it's okay. Detective Nate and Murphy will keep us safe."

"I want my Mommy." Lucy's wail stabbed deep. It was the one thing Willow couldn't do for the little girl. She couldn't bring back her mommy or her daddy.

"I know, baby, but I'm here. I love you, Lucy. We're going to be okay." Willow wondered if she repeated that often enough, she and Lucy might actually come to believe it.

The faint sound of police sirens grew louder as Nate's backup came rushing to the scene. Willow tentatively lifted her head, her gaze finding the reassuring red-and-blue swirling lights. They'd arrived quickly, but those tense moments had stretched endlessly.

Fat drops of rain splattered against her, and she had the ridiculous hope that the storm may chase away the gunman.

Nate didn't move away from her and Lucy until a member of his team arrived. When he stepped back, a cool breeze made her shiver. Willow lifted Lucy and placed her in the car seat, so she would be protected from the rain. Turning, she recognized dark-haired Vivienne and her K-9, Hank, from the station tour earlier and also the previous day.

Was it really only twenty-four hours ago?

"How many shots were fired?" Vivienne asked.

"Just one, came from the east." Nate's expression was grim. "Murphy picked up the scent just before the gunfire, but I had to get Willow and Lucy out of harm's way. I need to go back and see if Murphy can find it again, before the rain washes the scent away."

"Go. I'll stay here." Vivienne smiled sweetly at Lucy,

then gestured to the vehicle. "Willow, you should get inside. I won't let you two out of my sight, promise."

She wasn't going to argue. She decided to sit beside Lucy's car seat in the back, rather than up front. The little girl had stopped crying, but her tear-streaked expression was forlorn. Willow bent close to kiss her forehead.

"Where's Murphy?" Lucy rubbed at her eyes, looking exhausted. Willow wondered if her niece needed a nap.

"He's with Detective Nate. They'll be back soon." At least, she hoped so. Gazing over Lucy's head through the window, she could see Nate and Murphy making their way along the sidewalk not far from where they'd been just a few minutes earlier.

Knowing that Murphy had picked up the scent gave her a flare of hope. Maybe the K-9 would find Craggy Face so Nate could arrest him, putting an end to this nightmare once and for all.

Nate and Murphy headed east, toward a cluster of trees. Her heart thudded painfully as Nate held his weapon ready, clearly expecting the worst.

The inside of the car window grew foggy with their breath, so she reached over to lower the window just enough so she could see. The minutes dragged before Nate and Murphy returned.

"Find something?" Vivienne walked toward him.

"This." Nate held up a plastic evidence bag. She squinted trying to see what was inside, swallowing hard when she caught a glimpse of brass. A bullet? Her stomach knotted, then she realized that wasn't right. It was a shell casing from a bullet. "I'm hoping the forensic team can come up with a match in the system."

"Good work," Vivienne said.

"It was all Murphy." Nate bent and rubbed his K-9, who immediately shook his body to get rid of the rain-water. "We need to spread out in a half circle, see if we can find the bullet."

"Let's go." Ignoring the weather, Vivienne and Hank went one way as Nate and Murphy went the other. More K-9 cops joined them and together they widened their search area, wiping the rain from their eyes as they scoured the ground.

After roughly twenty minutes, they returned to the SUV. Nate scowled. "Nothing."

Vivienne shrugged. "Likely his aim was off."

If that was the case, Willow was thankful for it. She felt blessed. God had truly been watching over them.

Nate brought Murphy toward the car, trailed by the additional K-9 cops. "Willow, this is Officer Max Santelli, his K-9, Sam, and you met Tyler Walker and his K-9, Dusty, earlier today."

She nodded. "Thanks for your help."

"We're a team," Max said with a shrug. "We always have each other's backs."

"I'm going to take Willow and Lucy home." Nate glanced back at them. "I'll follow up with Sarge later."

"Okay. Thanks for the backup, Max and Ty." Vivienne waved at the two K-9 officers as she and Hank headed for her vehicle.

"Anytime." The taller of the two, Max had dark hair and eyes; his K-9, Sam, was an intimidating-looking rottweiler. Ty Walker's K-9, Dusty, was a pretty golden retriever. She was impressed with how well they all worked together as a team.

Nate opened the back to let Murphy jump in, then came around to slide in behind the wheel.

She glanced at Lucy, relieved to find that the little girl had fallen asleep. All the playing and crying had worn her out to the point that the car doors closing didn't wake her up.

Nate's gaze met hers in the rearview mirror. "I'm sorry." The words were quiet in deference to Lucy's sleeping.

"For what? This wasn't your fault. Thanks to Murphy and your quick thinking, we weren't hurt. God was watching over all of us today."

Nate's self-recriminating expression indicated he felt otherwise. But he didn't say anything more as he pulled away from the curb, his attention now on the rain-washed road in front of him. It troubled her that he didn't lean on God or his faith. Because he hadn't grown up hearing God's word? Or because he'd lost it along the way?

Something never learned could be taught and something lost could be found.

If the will was strong enough.

She wanted, needed to help Nate find his way, to learn to accept God's strength and support.

The pelting rain didn't let up until they neared her apartment. Nate found a parking spot that wasn't too far and pulled in. He glanced back at her. "You want me to carry Lucy?"

She felt physically and emotionally exhausted. "Yes, please."

He nodded, sliding out from behind the wheel. She pushed out of the seat as he let Murphy out, standing back as the dog once again shook off the dampness. She joined Nate on the other side of the vehicle, waiting as he gently lifted Lucy from the car seat and cradled her against his chest.

The sight of him holding Lucy as if she were something precious made her throat swell with emotion. Alex had once carried Lucy like that, until he allowed himself to get swept away with Debra's desire for a good time.

Nate would be a wonderful father someday.

They walked down the sidewalk toward her apartment building, Murphy on alert. Willow didn't relax until they were inside her unit with the door securely locked behind them.

"Put her on my bed," she whispered, leading Nate through to her room. Nate gently settled Lucy on the mattress, then stepped back. She drew the sheet up over her, then followed Nate back to the living room. Murphy was stretched out on the floor, resting his head between his paws. He looked content, as if he liked being there with her and Nate.

"Thank you." Tears pricked her eyes, the events of the day abruptly overwhelming now that they were home.

"I shouldn't have suggested going to the park." Nate's blue eyes were dark with regret. "My carelessness exposed you and Lucy to danger."

"No, Nate. You saved us." She took a step closer, aching to reach out to him. "You put yourself at risk to shelter us."

"Willow." Her name was nothing more than a whisper, his blue gaze clinging to hers. They were both soaking wet from the storm, but that didn't matter.

She took another step forward and suddenly he pulled her into a crushing hug, burying his face against her damp hair.

His woodsy scent filled her with a mixture of peace and joy. Safety and excitement. From the moment they'd first met she'd longed for this. To feel his strong arms around her.

The cadence of his heartbeat matching hers.

Time hung suspended between them, enclosing them in a cocoon of warmth, until his phone rang. Nate sighed, then released her.

He glanced at the screen and grimaced. "My boss. I have to take this."

She nodded, unable to speak. Nate lifted the phone to his ear.

He ran a hand over his damp hair, his expression serious. She knew in that moment she was in trouble. Deep, deep trouble.

Because she cared about Nate Slater far more than she should. And knew, deep down, he'd only break her heart.

"A dead body?" Nate repeated, gathering his scattered thoughts. Making the leap from Willow's comforting embrace to yet another crime wasn't easy.

"Yeah, found in the alley behind the Burgerteria." Gavin's voice held a note of urgency. "There's a possibility this latest murder is related to whatever is going on with Willow Emery."

"Yeah." Nate glanced at Willow, still reeling from the near miss at the park. He found it incredible that she didn't blame him for what had happened. That she'd actually thanked him. "Was any evidence found at the scene?"

"Yep, a shell casing."

That pricked Nate's interest. He pulled the evidence

bag from his pocket, looking at the one he'd picked up from the area where Murphy had alerted on Craggy Face's scent. "I have one from the park shooting, too."

"Good. We also have a witness." His boss had saved the best news for last. "I'd like you to get over there to interview him. Show him the guy in Willow's photo, see if he can ID him as the shooter."

Leave Willow and Lucy? Every cell in his body wanted to stay. But he couldn't ignore this potential link to finding Craggy Face. "Okay, but I need you to send someone here to watch over Willow and Lucy. It's clear they're still in grave danger. That gunshot was far too close."

"Yeah, okay. I'll send Vivienne and Hank. I have Ray and Abby on scene in the alley. They're waiting for you."

"Ray?" Nate was good friends with the narcotics officer and knew his springer spaniel was a great drug-sniffing dog. "Why send him to a homicide?"

"There's a possible drug connection. You'll find out more when you get there. Vivienne and Hank should be there in less than five minutes."

"Got it." He disconnected from the call and looked at Willow. Her apprehensive gaze made him feel bad. Was she upset about their embrace? Or because she knew he and Murphy had to leave for a while? He updated her on the situation.

"You really think this new murder is connected to me?"

He wasn't sure how to respond. "I don't know, but the location suggests a connection to the Burgerteria."

"Craggy Face." Her face went pale. "It all comes

back to the stupid photo I took of Damon and Craggy Face."

There had to be more behind this than a simple photograph, but he didn't want to add to her concern. "Their involvement in something criminal isn't your fault, Willow. You just happened to be in the wrong place at the wrong time, with a camera."

"I don't understand. Is he coming after me because he thinks I have the camera on me?" Willow had given the camera to Nate as evidence in the case. "Or does he just want me out of the way because I can ID him?"

"I wish I knew." The escalating threats against her had to be related to something more than the photograph or camera. But what? "Listen, Vivienne and Hank will be here soon. I want you to think back to your time at the Burgerteria. The day you saw Craggy Face talking to your boss. Was there anything else going on that you can remember? Anything that may have seemed out of the ordinary?"

She shook her head, but then sighed. "I'll try, but nothing comes to mind."

"All I can ask is that you try." He smiled and moved toward the door. "I'll wait downstairs for Vivienne so the buzzer doesn't wake Lucy. Come, Murphy." The dog stretched, then joined him.

"Okay." Willow didn't move as he and Murphy crossed the apartment. There was no reason to feel as if he were abandoning her, yet it was difficult to keep walking, carrying her lilac scent.

He and Murphy took the elevator down to the lobby. They emerged just as Vivienne and her black-and-white border collie, Hank, arrived.

"Thanks for coming. I won't be long." He brushed

past her, heading outside. The rain had stopped, but the air was thick with moisture, gray clouds hanging low.

He and Murphy walked the short distance, rather than risk losing his primo parking spot. As he approached the alley, he caught sight of a police SUV similar to his, parked so that the entryway to the back alley behind the building was blocked.

Edging past it, he and Murphy made their way to the crime scene. Murphy was on alert, his partner no doubt remembering they'd been this way before.

Ray Morrow and Abby were standing several feet from the dead body, next to a young kid wearing a bright yellow hoodie and carrying a skateboard. Probably their witness. As Nate approached, he could see the victim was lying facedown, his head turned to the side, a bullet hole in his back, in an eerie replica of how he'd found Willow's brother, Alex and his wife, Debra.

"Hey, Nate." Ray moved away from the guy in the yellow hoodie to meet him. He gestured to the dead man. "Vic's name is Paulie White."

Nate's gaze sharpened. "You know him?"

Ray nodded. "He's a low-level drug dealer. We've popped him a couple of times for intent to sell, but he never had more than a few grams of coke on him. He didn't play in the big leagues."

Nate crouched down to see the victim's face. The guy didn't look at all familiar to him. He glanced back up at Ray. "You don't think his murder is drug-related?"

"Maybe, but since we found the body here, Sarge wanted me to bring you in." Ray knelt beside him. "Interestingly enough, we found a brand-new top-of-the-line phone in his pocket. It's odd, because drug dealers lean toward using throwaway devices. Even better, we found a slip of paper in his pocket with a name and phone number."

A name and number! Nate felt a surge of adrenaline and rose to his feet. He and Ray took a few steps away from the victim. "I'd like to see it."

Ray handed him an evidence bag. The paper looked like it had been ripped from the bottom corner of a spiral notebook. The name *Carl Dower* was scribbled across the top, with a phone number written beneath.

"Did you run the name?" He looked at Ray.

"Not yet. I think that's why Sarge wanted you here. We also found this." Ray lifted an evidence bag holding a shell casing.

Nate pulled his shell casing out, too, comparing the two side by side. They looked identical, but he knew that alone didn't mean anything. They'd need the forensic team to prove they came from the same weapon. He handed the evidence bag to Ray. "Would you make sure the crime scene techs process both of these?"

"Absolutely." Ray took the bagged shell casing.

"What's the story with the witness?" He looked to where the kid was shifting his weight from side to side as if anxious to get out of there.

"Claims he was about to take a shortcut through here on his skateboard when he heard the shot." Ray gestured with his hand. "His name is Aaron Kramer and he just turned eighteen, so no need to wait for his parents to question him."

"Good. Come, Murphy." Nate strode to where Aaron waited.

"I already told the other cop everything I know. Can I go home now?"

"Just need a few more minutes of your time, and I

appreciate your help." Nate smiled to put the kid at ease. "Would you mind starting again from the beginning?"

Aaron sighed heavily. "Like I told the other cop, I'd just turned the corner to cut through here on my skateboard when I saw this old geezer pull out a gun and shoot the skinny dude in the back."

"You saw the gunman's face?"

Aaron bobbed his head. "Yeah, man, it was freaky. Although I only saw him from the side, not directly."

A profile view was better than nothing. "Did he see you?"

"I don't think so. I immediately jumped off the board and ducked down behind that green dumpster back there." Aaron screwed up his face, then shook his head. "He didn't look in my direction, just took off that way," he added, pointing away from the dumpster. "I heard the sound of a car engine and assumed he had someone waiting for him. Man, he was in and out of here in less than a minute."

Less than a minute to kill a man in cold blood.

"Can you describe the guy?" Nate asked as he pulled out his phone.

"He was old and kind of heavyset."

Nate glanced at Aaron. "About how old?"

The kid shrugged. "I don't know. He had like wrinkles and stuff. Gray hair. You know, old."

The kid's description was far from helpful. He used his phone to call Eden, the unit's tech guru. "Hey, can you pull together a quick six-pack of mug shots for me to show our witness? Make sure they are all the same age and similar characteristics of Craggy Face and include his photo, too."

"Sure thing." Eden's fingers tapped on the keyboard of her computer. "Sending it now."

He heard the ping on his phone and pulled up the six-pack. Using a small phone screen wasn't ideal, but it would work in a pinch. He held the device toward Aaron. "There are six men here. Any of them look familiar to you?"

Aaron took the phone and used his fingers to enlarge each picture. To the kid's credit, he took his time. Then he nodded. "Yeah, man, this guy. He's the old geezer who killed the skinny dude."

Nate sucked in his breath. The witness had identified Craggy Face as the killer.

ELEVEN

Lucy awoke from her nap asking for her dolly. Willow gladly played with her niece, hoping the early-afternoon gunfire was long forgotten.

Vivienne and Hank helped keep Lucy occupied and for that Willow was grateful. When Vivienne's phone rang, Willow glanced over, wondering if the caller was Nate.

"Really?" Vivienne's eyes widened in surprise. "That's great news. Now we just need to find out the guy's name."

There was a brief pause as Vivienne listened, then the cop's knowing gaze met hers.

"Yes, I'll let her know. Thanks, Nate." Vivienne tucked the phone back in her pocket. "Nate stopped at his place to pick up a few things, but he and Murphy are on their way here now."

"What's the good news?" Willow unfurled herself from her seat on the floor.

Vivienne hesitated. "It's best if I let Nate fill you in."

Willow tamped down a flash of impatience. "I understand that there's only so much you can share about an ongoing investigation, but my life is in danger." She glanced down at Lucy, who was still seated on the floor with her doll. "Lucy's, too."

Vivienne nodded, her gaze solemn. "I know, but this is Nate's case. Sarge is letting him take the lead."

Her stomach clenched at the thought that Nate and Murphy would soon leave her in the care of other officers. Not that she could blame him. He'd been with her for well over twenty-four hours now. She was grateful for his protection and support, but sensed Nate wouldn't be happy unless he was in the center of an investigation, rather than watching from the sidelines.

"Sure." She forced a smile, then startled when there was a knock on the door. She moved forward to answer, but Vivienne was faster.

"Let me." The K-9 officer peered through the peephole, then stepped aside, glancing at Willow with a frown. "Are you expecting a visitor?"

"No." Her stomach clenched with fear and she swiftly picked up Lucy from the floor. "Who is it?"

"I'll find out." Vivienne waited until she took Lucy into the bedroom.

Several tense seconds went by before Vivienne opened the door with a sheepish expression on her face. "It's Jayne Hendricks, Lucy's caseworker."

"Oh." Her shoulders slumped in relief, but then tensed again. This woman would be key in deciding whether or not she was an appropriate guardian for Lucy. She straightened her shoulders and followed Vivienne into the living area.

"Ms. Emery?" Jayne Hendricks looked to be in her late forties, with dark hair and glasses. Her deep brown eyes reflected a keen intelligence that made Willow believe she wouldn't be a pushover when it came to doing whatever was best for Lucy.

"Yes, I'm Willow, Lucy's aunt." She shifted the little girl in her arms so she could take Ms. Hendricks's outstretched hand. "It's nice to meet you."

"Likewise. And this must be Lucy." Ms. Hendricks's expression softened as she looked at her niece. "How are you, Lucy?"

Shy with strangers, Lucy hid her face against Willow's neck without answering.

"She's doing very well, considering." Willow forced a smile, wondering if she was required to tell the social worker about the recent gunfire at the park or the failed kidnapping attempt.

"I'm sure." Jayne Hendricks's gaze was compassionate. Then she glanced around the apartment. "You have a nice place here. Two bedrooms?"

Her stomach knotted again. "Just one. But I'm hoping to upgrade to a two-bedroom as soon as possible." She needed to get a decent price for her current apartment, but would that be enough to afford something larger? She tried not to panic.

"Hmm." The noncommittal response wasn't reassuring. Ms. Hendricks crossed the apartment, poking her head into the bedroom and then the bathroom.

Willow wondered if she'd get extra points for being a clean freak or if only having a one-bedroom apartment would be enough for this woman to decide to take Lucy away.

She tightened her grip on Lucy, who still hadn't said anything. No way was she letting this little girl go.

"How's Lucy coping?"

The question caught her off guard. "She had nightmares last night but calmed down when I held her in my arms."

"I'm sure it's a comfort to her to have you with her."

For the first time since the woman had entered her apartment, Willow felt herself relax. "Yes, I believe it's best for Lucy to be with someone she knows and loves. I promise I will do whatever it takes to care for my niece."

Ms. Hendricks opened her fridge, hopefully taking note of the chicken breasts and fresh broccoli she'd purchased the other day to make for dinner. Surely the healthy food had to be another point in her favor.

"I agree." Ms. Hendricks shut the fridge and turned to face her. "I think you're doing a wonderful job with Lucy and it's clear she trusts you."

"Thank you." Willow pressed a kiss against Lucy's temple, fighting tears of relief.

"Are you planning to adopt her?"

"Absolutely." She didn't hesitate. "I—just haven't had time to figure out how to go about doing that. I'm sure there's paperwork involved, right?"

"Yes. Our website contains all the information you'll need." Ms. Hendricks's gaze was warm now, and Willow felt certain that the paperwork would be little more than a formality. Her brother didn't have a will as far as she knew, but she was Lucy's only living relative. Ms. Hendricks held out a business card. "Call me if you have questions."

Willow took the card, tucking it in the front pocket of her jeans. "Thank you."

Ms. Hendricks glanced at Vivienne and Hank, who were standing off in the corner. "I assume you're here to protect them from the person responsible for murdering the Emerys?"

Willow froze. This was it. The moment of truth. Ms. Hendricks might decide to take Lucy away if she knew Willow was in danger from someone unrelated to her brother's murder.

"Yes, ma'am." Vivienne glanced at the doorway as Nate and Murphy entered the apartment. "There's Detective Slater now. Members of our team are alternating the duty of watching over Ms. Emery and Lucy."

Nate looked surprised to see the newcomer but quickly picked up on the fact that Lucy's caseworker was doing a surprise home visit. He set a small duffel in the corner, then straightened. "Is there a problem?"

"No problem." Willow's voice was faint. She cleared her throat and injected confidence in her tone. "Detective Slater, this is Ms. Jayne Hendricks from Child Protective Services. She wanted to make sure Lucy was doing okay being here with me."

"Understandable. The little girl has been through a lot." He shook the caseworker's hand. "Nice to meet you. I want you to know, we're keeping a close eye on Willow and Lucy to keep them safe."

"I can see that." If Ms. Hendricks thought that having two sets of K-9 officers in her apartment was unusual, she didn't let on. "Well, that's all I need for now, but I'll be in touch."

Willow knew that meant she could expect another visit in the near future. Swallowing hard, she escorted Ms. Hendricks to the door. Even after the caseworker left, she couldn't entirely relax.

"I feel guilty." She looked at Nate. "I should have told her about the recent threats targeting me. Maybe Lucy is better off with a foster family."

"Do you really believe that?" Nate's tone was soft, gentle.

She instantly shook her head, resting her cheek against Lucy's wavy hair, breathing in the comforting scent of baby shampoo. "No. I'm afraid sending Lucy off with strangers would cause more harm than good."

"There's your answer." Nate turned toward Vivienne. "Thanks for your help. I'll take over from here."

"No problem. Come, Hank." Vivienne led Hank out of the apartment. Nate locked the door behind her.

"Doggy!" Lucy reached a hand toward Murphy. Now that the strangers were gone, she'd reverted back to her old self.

Willow set her on the floor, watching as her niece made a beeline for Murphy. Clearly, Lucy wasn't shy around Nate.

As Lucy gazed up at Nate in adoration, Willow realized her niece was growing emotionally attached to Nate.

And feared that his leaving once the danger was over would break the little girl's heart.

Nate quickly filled Willow in on the latest news on Craggy Face being identified as the shooter in the alleyway homicide case. "We're going to find him very soon." He opened his laptop and took a seat at the kitchen table. "I just need the guy's name."

"That is good news." Willow's smile was strained and he knew that being under the scrutiny of CPS had to be stressful. "I'm—uh, going to start dinner in about an hour or so. Are you planning to stay?"

He was surprised by her question. "Yes, unless this is your way of kicking me out?"

"No, of course not." She flushed and avoided his gaze. "I wasn't sure what your plans were."

His primary goal was to link Carl Dower—the name on the piece of paper found on the victim—to Craggy Face, so they could issue a BOLO for the guy. His secondary and no less important goal was to keep Willow and Lucy safe. He gestured toward his duffel bag. "I'm here until we find and arrest the man responsible for trying to hurt you."

"Thanks." Her smile was fleeting, and he frowned at the hint of sadness in her expression.

She put on some cartoons for Lucy, who enjoyed sitting beside Murphy while Nate searched for information on Carl Dower. He found a listing for the guy, and quickly dialed the number, only to discover there was no answer and no way to leave a message.

Drumming his fingers on the table, he tried to think of other ways to get a photograph of Carl Dower. He'd searched on social media to no avail. Was the eyewitness testimony against Craggy Face enough to get a search warrant for Damon Berk's records? He didn't think a simple photo of the two men together would be enough, especially since Berk claimed the guy had complained about a burger causing a cracked tooth.

In his gut he felt certain Carl Dower *was* Craggy Face. Too bad he couldn't find the evidence he needed to prove it.

Turning to the McGregor cold case helped distract him from failing to identify Craggy Face. He reviewed the notes, struck again at the similarities between the two cases.

His gaze lingered on photos of the brown watch band that was found at the scene of the McGregor case. The

DNA hadn't belonged to either of the victims. How good was the DNA testing twenty years ago? Certainly not as meticulous and thorough as it was now. Surely it had been tested again more recently.

Or had it?

Reaching for his phone, he called Gavin. "Sarge, when was the last time we had the watch band retested for DNA?"

He could hear the shuffling of papers on the other end of the line. "Five years ago, but you raise a good point. Could be someone has been arrested in the years since. I'll get the forensic team on it."

"Sounds good. Let me know if you get a hit."

"You and the entire team will know the minute I do," Gavin promised.

"Still nothing from the Emery crime scene?"

"Nothing outside the parents. Their DNA is all over the place."

"Yeah." He sighed. "Okay, thanks." Setting his phone aside, Nate thought about how impossible it seemed that the McGregor killer hadn't struck again in the five years since they'd had the DNA tested, or if he had, had been smart enough not to leave one iota of DNA behind.

As the evening wore on, Willow busied herself in the kitchen cooking dinner. He tried to ignore her, but the simple fact was that no woman had ever cooked for him.

Not him, he swiftly corrected himself. Willow was cooking for Lucy. He and Murphy didn't belong here.

Yet somehow, he felt more comfortable sleeping on Willow's sofa than he did in his own place. Shaking his head at his foolishness, he startled when his phone rang.

"Slater."

"Nate? It's Darcy from the forensic team. I have good news."

"I'll take it." At this point any evidence would be welcome. "What did you find?"

"The two bullet casings Ray dropped off from the attempt at Owl's Head Park and Paulie White's murder in the alley at Burgerteria are a match. They're the same make and caliber and have the same markings indicating they are from one gun, a thirty-eight to be exact."

One gun. He turned the information over in his mind. He had to believe that Craggy Face had shot and killed Paulie White after the attempt on Willow at the park. Or was it possible he'd used the weapon at the park, then handed the gun to an associate who'd gone after Paulie? The timing seemed almost too close.

"Do we have a time of death on Paulie White?"

"Not yet. ME's not doing the autopsy until the morning, but the tox screen will take several days. At least we know the same gun was used on both crimes."

"Yeah, but within a narrow time frame." He tried to estimate how much time he and Vivienne had spent at the crime scene at the park. Ninety minutes? Was that enough time for Craggy Face to hightail it back to the Burgerteria to nail Paulie? And if so, why had he killed a low-level drug dealer? That piece of the puzzle really didn't make any sense.

"Hey, are you still there?"

He pulled his thoughts together. "Yeah, thanks, Darcy. Appreciate the heads-up."

"I'll let you know if I come up with anything else."

"Thanks. Oh, do you know when Willow can have access to her brother's place? She still needs to pick up Lucy's things."

"Maybe tomorrow. I'll check with my boss and let you know when we're ready to release the scene."

"Thanks." He set his phone aside, still grappling with the timeline between the shootings.

"Dinner's ready."

He hastily put his computer away to make room at the small table for the meal. The scent of Italian seasoning made his mouth water. Willow put Lucy in her booster seat, then set the baked chicken, marinara sauce, noodles and cheesy broccoli on the table.

"What's that?" Lucy pointed at the cheesy broccoli.

"Little trees and cheese. They're yummy." Willow's tone was encouraging.

"Little trees are my favorite," he declared, helping himself to the broccoli. Lucy had tried the scrambled eggs when he'd said that, so he was hoping she'd do that again.

"Just a small bite," Willow cajoled.

Lucy obliged, then smiled. "Little trees are my favorite, too."

"The cheese helps," he whispered as Willow cut the chicken into bite-size pieces.

"Exactly." Willow smiled wryly. "Not sure she's had much exposure to veggies. I appreciate your help encouraging her to try the broccoli."

"Hey, it is my favorite." He tried to keep his tone light, even though this sharing a meal together felt too cozy for his peace of mind.

This—being together—couldn't amount to anything. He wasn't father material and refused to be tempted by something he couldn't have. In fact, he wanted to spend more time on the Emery murders. The minute they had Craggy Face in custody, he'd have to move on. The Mc-

Gregors had waited twenty years without answers; this new murder with the same MO had to be investigated for a potential link. Besides, Willow and Lucy deserved justice for the loss of Alex and Debra.

His life revolved around putting bad guys in jail. Not playing happy homemaker with Willow and Lucy.

As soon as they'd finished eating, he went back to work on his laptop. Willow cleaned up the kitchen, gave Lucy a bath, then tucked her into bed. He found himself listening as they said their nightly prayers.

"God bless Aunt Willow, Detective Nate and Murphy," Lucy said. "Amen."

"Amen," Willow echoed. "Good night, Lucy. I love you."

"I love you, too."

His throat closed with pent-up emotion. Listening to them only reinforced his role of being on the outside, looking in. He shut his laptop with a sigh. Carl Dower was nowhere to be found, and the phone number remained a dead end, too. He stood, stretched, intending to lie down on the sofa, when Willow emerged from the bedroom.

"Hey." She offered a wan smile. "I'm too keyed up to sleep. Thought I'd make some chamomile tea."

"I'm not much of a tea person. Does it help?"

She lifted a shoulder. "Sometimes." After filling the teakettle, she placed it on the stove. "It can't hurt."

Silence engulfed them as she waited for the water to boil. When she'd filled a mug with steaming water, she came into the living room to sit beside him on the sofa.

"What made you choose to become a K-9 cop?" She cradled the mug in her hands as if absorbing the warmth. She'd asked that question the first night he'd stayed over, and he'd found himself talking more about his colleagues' reasons—only the ones who were open about it—than his own.

"Oh, well, that's kind of a long story." One he normally didn't talk about.

Willow looked embarrassed. "Sorry, I didn't mean to pry into your personal life. I get it's none of my business."

"No, really, it's okay." He felt bad for making her feel guilty. If anyone deserved to know about his past, Willow did. They'd grown close over the past thirty-six hours, and he thought telling her about his past might help her understand him better. "There was a cop, a guy named Geoff Cally, who came to our rescue the night my mom and I managed to escape my dad."

"Escape?" Her brow furrowed, her cinnamon gaze searching his. "He hurt you?"

"Yeah." He instinctively reached up to massage the collarbone his dad had cracked that night. The bone had healed, but the pain lingered in his mind. The shock of being hit hard enough to slam into the wall, to break a bone. "My father drank a lot and took his anger out on my mom. I was a skinny kid, ten years old, when I decided to fight back."

"Ten." Her voice was a horrified whisper. "Oh, Nate."

He shrugged off her sympathy. "That's all in the past now, but that night Officer Geoff Cally came to our aid, arrested my dad and had us taken to the hospital, then a shelter." He thought back to the horror of that night, going to the hospital, then being moved to a shelter. "He didn't just drop us off and forget about us. He returned to check up on us, to make sure we were okay. He eventually helped us find an apartment of our own." The place had been a dump, but he'd felt safer there than he ever had in the house they'd lived in with his dad. "He was truly an amazing guy."

"A role model that made you want to become a cop, just like him."

He couldn't deny it. "I went to the academy and placed in the top of my class. I worked the beat for a couple of years, then heard about an opening in the K-9 unit." He reached down to stroke Murphy's soft coat. "I'd always wanted a dog, but, well…" He shrugged. "The competition is stiff. I wasn't sure I'd be chosen, but thankfully I was accepted into the program. I worked in another unit for a few years, and was recruited for the new Brooklyn team. I like working for Gavin Suther-land, and with the rest of the crew." He hesitated, then added, "They're the only family I'll ever have now that my mother is gone."

"What do you mean?" Willow frowned.

He shook his head. "I haven't lost my temper yet, and I don't drink, but there are times I feel the anger simmering deep inside." He forced himself to meet her gaze. "I can't risk having a family of my own, Willow."

"Oh, Nate." Her compassion was nearly his undo-ing. "You're nothing like your father. You've been noth-ing but sweet and kind to Lucy, and I think you'd be a wonderful dad. And don't forget, God is watching out for you."

She didn't know what she was talking about, but he couldn't find the words to correct her.

Willow scooted over to him, placed her hand on his arm, heat radiating from her fingertips. Then she bent over to kiss him. He was sure she'd meant it to be a chaste, healing kiss, but that wasn't the case. Their lips clung, then meshed. He drew her into his arms, deepening their kiss.

"Aunt Willow!" Lucy's plaintive cry had them springing apart. "The mean clown is back."

"Excuse me." Willow hurried into the bedroom to comfort Lucy from her nightmare, leaving him gasping for breath, wrestling with the realization that his feelings for Willow were not that of a cop whose duty was to protect her, or even that of a friend.

No, he cared about Willow on a personal level, far more than he had a right to.

TWELVE

The impact of Nate's kiss made it difficult to sleep. Willow had stared blindly up at the ceiling for an hour, emotions spinning in turmoil. Her heart ached for the young boy who'd been beaten by his father, who'd escaped with his mother to live in shelters. She thanked God for watching over them, and for bringing a man like Geoff Cally into Nate's life. The cop had not only helped keep Nate and his mother safe but had been a wonderful role model for Nate.

Yet Nate didn't think he deserved a family of his own. And hadn't mentioned God or faith. Because he didn't believe? The thought made her sad. And avoiding a family wasn't the right path; he would make a wonderful husband and father.

But not for her and Lucy. That much had been made clear.

After a restless night, she slid from the bed early, doing her best not to wake Lucy. But by the time she'd finished in the bathroom, Lucy was sitting in the middle of the bed, sleepily rubbing her eyes.

"Good morning, Lucy." Willow crossed over to give her niece a hug.

Lucy hugged her back, more clingy than usual. "I hav'ta go to the bathroom."

"This way, remember?" Willow took her into the bathroom, grabbing a new outfit for her to wear so she could change out of her jammies. When Lucy was set, they returned to the kitchen.

"Are you hungry? I'm making French toast for breakfast."

Lucy frowned. "I like regular toast."

"Do you like maple syrup?" When Lucy nodded, she smiled. "Then trust me, you'll like French toast, too. Come on, you can help."

"Is Murphy here?" Lucy looked up at her with wide, hopeful eyes.

Hearing his name, Murphy got up from his position on the floor next to the sofa where Nate was stretched out and came over to greet Lucy, tail wagging, licking her face. She giggled and threw her arms around his neck.

"I love Murphy."

"I know, baby." She glanced over at Nate, who was wearing sweatpants and a T-shirt, his blond hair mussed from sleep. Gold whiskers dusted his cheeks, making him look rugged and somehow even more attractive.

Do. Not. Remember. His. Kiss.

"French toast for breakfast." She cleared her throat and headed into the kitchen. When she lived alone she'd never cooked this much, especially since she spent her days making gourmet burgers in her job. But now she knew Lucy needed structure, to know when her next meal would be.

No more living with uncertainty. Bad enough that her niece was haunted by nightmares. As she whipped up the egg mixture for French toast, it occurred to her she should have asked Ms. Hendricks to recommend a child psychologist. She made a mental note to call her later.

Nate took Murphy outside, returning after a few minutes. "Lucy, will you play with Murphy while I take a shower?"

"Yes." Lucy looked thrilled with the idea.

By the time Nate returned, the French toast was finished. She put out a plate for Lucy, cutting the toast in bite-size pieces.

"Thanks, Willow, this is great." Nate's praise made her cheeks go pink.

"You're welcome, but it's truly not a big deal." She took a sip of her coffee. "Have you learned anything new about Craggy Face?"

"Not yet." Nate glanced at her. "But I do need to head out for a while. I'd like you and Lucy to stay inside with the door locked."

She paled at the thought of being here without Nate and Murphy watching over them. "Alone?"

"I've arranged for someone to hang out here for a bit." He avoided her gaze and she wondered if he'd made these so-called arrangements after their kiss.

The one she was not going to remember.

"Vivienne?" She didn't mind having female company but wondered how the officer felt about being assigned to babysitting duty.

"No, another colleague of mine, Noelle Orton." He glanced at his watch. "She's a rookie, but a very good one, and our boss is keeping her off the streets for a while since her K-9 partner has a bounty on her head for being too good at her job. Noelle should be here within the hour."

"Okay." She told herself to get over it. So what if they would be stuck inside for a few hours? Keeping Lucy safe was all that mattered. She forced a smile. "We'll find something fun to do."

"Listen, Willow. Darcy, the forensic tech assigned to your case, is checking with her boss to see if they'll release your brother's place sometime later today." His gaze was full of compassion. "I know you're anxious to get more of Lucy's things. When I get the okay, I'll take you over there to pick out what you'd like."

"I would love that and I'm sure Lucy will be glad to have more toys to play with, too." She was touched he'd thought of it. "Thanks, Nate."

He nodded and quickly finished his breakfast. She wanted to ask what he was planning to do, but doubted he'd be able to tell her.

All she could do was pray that he and Murphy would be safe.

"I'm full," Lucy announced. "Can I watch cartoons?"

"Yes, but only until I'm finished with the dishes." She wiped the sticky syrup off Lucy's hands and face, then took her into the living room to turn on the promised cartoons.

"I like this one." Lucy plopped in front of the television.

"That's fine." At least the show would keep her niece mesmerized for a while.

She returned to the kitchen to find Nate had already cleared the table. "I'll help with the dishes."

"There's no need. I can handle it."

"I don't mind." He filled the sink with sudsy water. "You keep feeding me, so it's the least I can do."

She decided there was no sense in arguing. They worked side by side in silence for several minutes, listening to the cartoons in the background. Murphy stretched out on the floor in front of Lucy.

"Lucy is going to miss Murphy when you're gone." She glanced at him as she dried a plate. "I'm going to miss both of you."

Nate's hands went still in the water for the space of a heartbeat. "Willow, I feel like I need to apologize for kissing you last night."

She lifted a brow. "I'm fairly certain I was the one who kissed you."

The tips of his ears turned red. "Regardless, I should have stopped you. I told you about my father, Willow. As much as I care about your safety, there can't be anything more between us."

In other words, no more kissing. It wasn't anything she hadn't already told herself but hearing him say the words caused a pang in the region of her heart. "I understand, but I believe God is watching over you, Nate. He'll always be there for you, no matter what."

"I'm not sure I believe that." His words sounded guttural, almost harsh. "God wasn't there when my father slammed me into the wall or punched my mother in the face."

She sucked in a harsh breath. "Oh, Nate. I know how horrifying that must have been for you, but don't you think that God had a hand in sending Geoff Cally to save you and your mom that night? That God asked Geoff to look out for you, to keep you both safe?"

He shook his head, but she saw a flash of uncertainty in his eyes. "Maybe."

She wanted to say more but decided to let it go for now. When Nate finished washing the dishes, he turned to her. "You could be right."

Her heart soared with hope. "You're always welcome to attend church services with us next weekend."

She expected an instant refusal, but he slowly nodded. "Maybe. Depends on what's happening with the case."

No point in pushing, because she knew that for cops, firefighters, nurses and doctors, sometimes church services had to be skipped while on duty.

But as Nate went over to put Murphy on his leash, she hoped and prayed that he'd find a way to attend church with her.

If there couldn't be anything personal between them, she'd find a way to live with that. But she refused to accept the idea of Nate living his life without God's strength and support.

Where in the world was Noelle? Nate desperately needed to get out of the apartment, to get some distance from Willow and Lucy.

The moment he'd woken up to see Willow standing there, he'd wanted to pull her into his arms and kiss her again. To breathe in her calming lilac scent.

Now she was talking about God and asking him to go to church with her and Lucy. And he'd practically agreed.

What was wrong with him?

He headed for the door. "I'll be right outside. I'm sure Noelle will be here soon."

She nodded and he quickly stepped into the hall before he could do something he'd regret.

Like kiss her goodbye.

His phone rang and he pounced as if it were a lifeline. But the caller wasn't Noelle, it was fellow K-9 officer Lani Jameson. Lani was married to Noah Jameson, the current chief over the NYC K-9 Command Unit in Queens. With a protective brother on the team and her husband running it, Lani had transferred to the Brooklyn K-9 Unit the moment she heard about recruitment efforts. Nate had met Lani a few times on the job and had always considered her to be a good cop.

"What's up, Lani?"

"I need your help. I just saw a skinny stray dog that looks a little like Snapper—she definitely has some shepherd in her—and I think she's recently given birth. I'm worried about her puppies and where they might be. Can you spare some time right now?"

The entire NYPD knew about Snapper's history. The beautiful German shepherd had once been partner to Jordan Jameson, Noah's older brother and the former chief of the NYC K-9 Command Unit. The dog had gone missing after the chief was murdered, and when they'd finally found the K-9, he was partnered with Lani, particularly to keep Snapper in the Jameson family. In Nate's humble opinion, the two of them made a great team.

"Sure, I'll help," Nate said. "But I need to stop at the Burgerteria after. I have more questions for the manager. Where are you now?"

"I'm in Sunset Park." She gave her exact location. "Where are you?"

"Bay Ridge. I'll meet you in twenty minutes." A

beep indicated he had a second call. "See you soon." He switched over to the new call. "Noelle?"

"I'm here in the lobby." The rookie officer sounded cheerful.

"Thanks, Noelle. I really appreciate this. Come on up to apartment 706."

"Got it." The call ended.

When Noelle arrived, he introduced the petite, dark-haired officer to Willow and Lucy, trying not to squirm beneath Willow's all-too-knowing gaze. She seemed well aware that Nate really needed some space.

After leaving Willow in Noelle's care, it didn't take long for him to meet up with Lani in Sunset Park, a neighborhood that offered a nice view of the Statue of Liberty.

"This is where I saw the stray last," Lani explained, gesturing to a wooded area of the park. "I think she's hiding her pups somewhere close by. I'm worried she'll be picked up by the humane society or that the puppies will die."

He had to admit, he didn't like the sound of that, either. "Okay, let's spread out a bit, see if one of our K-9s can flush her out."

Only a few minutes went by when he heard Lani's urgent call. "Nate! Over here!"

He broke into a run, catching a quick glimpse of the skinny shepherd trotting past about twenty yards away. Lani had her phone out to snap a picture before she headed toward the stay. "Here, girl."

The skinny shepherd glanced at them, then began to run.

"Hurry, we're going to lose her! I need to find those puppies!" Lani and Snapper ran faster.

He and Murphy tried to close the gap, but as they came out from beneath a large tree, he abruptly stopped. "Where did she go?"

Lani stopped, too, breathing hard as she scanned the area. "I don't know. She was right there!"

He turned in a circle, noting they were in the corner of the park where it butted up against two other neighborhoods: Borough Park and Windsor Terrace. "Do you think she crossed the street? There's nothing but residential housing on the other side."

"I hope not. What if she gets hit by a car?" Lani sounded worried.

"Maybe she's just hiding."

"I shouldn't have stopped for a picture, but I was hoping to share this with the rest of the team, so we could all be on the lookout for her." She sighed. "Poor dog. I just hope her puppies are okay."

"I'm sure they will be. Listen, we can try looking for her again later, but I have to go. There's some legwork yet I need to do on my case."

"I get it." Lani sounded dejected. "Next time, I'm coming out here with a small steak."

That made him smile. "Should do the trick."

Lani shared the dog's photo with Nate and sent one to Eden Chang as well to be dispatched to the rest of the team. She also texted the Brooklyn Animal Care Center to be alerted to check for puppies in the park if the stray was brought in. "I'm calling her Brooke, short for Brooklyn."

"I like it."

They made their way back to where they'd left their respective vehicles. Nate fought stop-and-go traffic heading back to Bay Ridge. He wanted to push Damon

Berk a bit more about Craggy Face. Maybe once Berk knew the guy was wanted for murder, he'd change his tune about the guy complaining about a cracked tooth.

Nate wanted to know the true nature of their conversation.

When he finally reached Bay Ridge, he circled around several blocks before he found a parking spot. He let Murphy out of the back and clipped his leash before walking down toward the Burgerteria.

The restaurant had just opened for business and the early lunch crowd was seated on the various tables inside. Several of the patrons eyed Murphy curiously as he scanned the interior searching for Damon Berk.

One of the servers, wearing a name tag that identified her as Salina Alden, finally approached. "I'm sorry, but we don't allow dogs in here. It's a health hazard."

"I need to speak to Damon Berk."

"He's not here. He left me in charge." Salina frowned. "Why do you want to talk to Damon? Is this about the guy who was found dead in the alley behind the restaurant yesterday? Everyone has been talking about it all day."

Good guess. He wasn't surprised the news had spread like wildfire. "You're positive he's not here? Maybe you could check his office to make sure."

Salina rolled her eyes. "I'm telling you, he's not here and hasn't been all morning."

Nate wondered if Berk was avoiding the place because of the recent murder. Without a search warrant, he couldn't poke around, looking for something, anything, that may explain why Willow had become a target and Paulie White had been murdered. He pulled out a business card. "Will you call me when Damon returns?"

Salina reluctantly took the card. "I guess so. But Damon doesn't know anything about that murder. None of us do."

"Paulie White didn't work here?"

"No!" Her eyes widened in horror. "Of course not."

"You didn't notice anything out of the ordinary yesterday?" He figured the uniforms had already canvassed the area, but was stalling for time, hoping Damon might show.

"Nothing. We were super busy, running around like chickens when we heard the shot. Even then, we thought maybe it was a car muffler or something."

Brooklyn was noisy, but he felt certain the shot would have sounded loud even in here. "I'd like to talk to the staff working in the kitchen. They may have noticed something prior to the shooting."

Salina didn't look happy but did as he requested, bringing the kitchen workers out to talk to him. He performed quick interviews of the dishwasher and the cook who'd replaced Willow, but they both claimed they didn't see or hear anything.

By the time he was finished, Damon still hadn't shown. And for all he knew, Damon had taken off somewhere with Craggy Face. Or maybe he was hiding from the guy. Nate decided to pick up something for lunch on his way back to Willow and Lucy when his phone rang.

"Hey, Sarge," he greeted his boss. "Tell me you have good news."

"We finally located the O'Malleys."

It took a moment for Nate to place the name. "The landlords who own the home Alex and Debra Emery rented, correct?"

"Yeah. Apparently, Belle tracked them on vacation

in Florida. They acknowledged that the Emerys were five months overdue in their rent, and claim they were going to put them on eviction notice when they returned but deny having anything to do with the murder." There was a pause before he added, "Their alibi is rock solid, Nate. They're in the clear."

He'd run out of leads to follow in both of his cases, leaving him cranky and frustrated.

How much longer before Craggy Face struck again?

THIRTEEN

Willow enjoyed playing with Lucy, but she couldn't deny feeling on edge, even with the female officer there, as she waited for Nate and Murphy to return. When her phone rang, she eagerly grabbed the device, her heart thudding when she saw Nate's name on the screen.

"Hi, Nate."

"Hey, Willow. I'm on my way back with a basket of chicken for lunch. Hope that's okay."

She was pleased he'd thought of the little girl. "Thanks."

"My boss also confirmed he released the scene at your brother's house. He gave us the okay to head out to pick up what you need for Lucy."

"That's wonderful news." Lucy was already getting bored with her doll, and she would be glad to have more of Lucy's things to help the little girl feel at home.

"See you soon."

"Okay." She disconnected from the call and set her phone on the table, glancing over to where Noelle Orton was seated on the far end of the sofa. "Nate's on his way back. I'm sure you're getting sick of sitting around doing nothing."

The petite rookie officer looked surprised. "Protection detail is part of my job and I'm happy to be here."

For the first time, she realized how seriously Nate's team was taking the threat against her. She suppressed a shiver and strove for a light tone. "Well, thanks for spending your morning with us." She glanced at Lucy, who was playing with some blocks on the rug. "Time to wash our hands, Lucy. Detective Nate will be here soon."

"Yay! I miss Murphy," Lucy said, and followed her aunt to the bathroom.

Just as Lucy was drying her hands, Willow heard footsteps outside the apartment door and then Noelle opening the door for Nate. The little girl rushed out to say hi.

"Hi, Pipsqueak." Nate's welcoming smile and cute nickname warmed her heart. "I brought chicken for lunch." He glanced at Noelle. "For you, too."

"Thanks." Noelle joined them at the table. Willow put Lucy in her booster seat while Nate unpacked the chicken.

"What did Damon have to say about Craggy Face?" Willow asked as they all began eating.

"Damon didn't go in to the restaurant today, so I didn't get a chance to talk to him." He glanced at his watch. "I've located his home address. I'm planning to head over there later. But first, we can take a trip to East Flatbush to pick up Lucy's things."

Willow wanted to protest. The idea of Nate going to confront Damon at his home worried her. Sure, he was a trained cop and had a great partner in Murphy. But still, she didn't like it.

"Maybe Noelle should go with you." The words popped out of her mouth before she could think about them.

The two cops exchanged a look. "I'll be fine," Nate said. "Noelle has other duties, I'm sure."

Noelle finished her chicken, balled up the wrapper

and stashed it in the bag. "I need to get back to Liberty, but if you need me, let me know."

Nate scowled. "I won't."

Willow grimaced. She shouldn't have overstepped. "Thanks again for coming over to sit with me, Noelle."

"Not a problem." Noelle waved her gratitude. "Thanks for lunch, Nate, but I gotta run." The officer said goodbye to Lucy and then left the apartment.

"You don't have faith in my ability to manage Berk?" Nate asked with a frown.

"I do. I just…" She hesitated, unwilling to say too much. "I don't want you to get hurt." *Or killed.* The image of her brother and his wife lying dead on the living room floor flashed in her mind.

"I'm done!" Lucy's voice was a welcome intrusion. "I wanna get down."

Willow dabbed the girl's face with a napkin before lifting Lucy out of the booster seat.

"Ready to head out?" Nate asked as he helped her clean up the table.

"Sure." She glanced down at Lucy, wondering how her niece would take this. Maybe she could ask Nate to stay with Lucy in the car while she went in to get what she needed.

She helped Lucy wiggle into a light jacket, then the little girl got into the stroller.

Outside, the air was cool after the rainstorm the day before. She kept a tight grip on Lucy's stroller.

"My SUV is this way." Nate walked beside her, his body placed in a way that protected her from anyone driving past on the street. Murphy kept pace beside him, his nose sniffing the air.

When they reached Nate's police vehicle, she was

secretly glad when he stood protectively behind her as she placed Lucy in the car seat. Only after they were both settled safely inside did he put Murphy in the back and slide in behind the wheel.

"Do you really think Damon will talk to you?" She couldn't help ruminating on his plan to confront her former boss.

Nate shrugged, his gaze focused on the traffic. "It can't hurt to try. For all we know, he's hiding from Craggy Face."

"Maybe." She thought back to the day she'd taken photos of her gourmet burgers. It seemed like eons ago instead of mere weeks. Had the conversation between Damon and Craggy Face held a note of animosity? She didn't think so. But then again, she hadn't paid close attention to the conversation, her eyes on the lens.

As they drove, she fell silent, dread forming in her gut as Nate brought them closer to her brother's home. Like scenes from a movie, she remembered hearing the squeaky black iron gate swing open, seeing the front door hanging ajar, hearing the sounds of Lucy's sobs.

Finding her brother and his wife, dead.

Nate pulled up to the curb and she forced herself back to the present. The house looked just as forlorn and unkempt as before—worse now, maybe, because of what had transpired within the four walls.

Before Nate could speak, she looked at him. "I think you should stay in the car with Lucy while I go inside to get Lucy's things."

He frowned. "No way. You stay here while I go."

"But I know where everything is." She didn't really want to go inside, but felt as if it was her duty to pick out the things Lucy needed.

"Is her room on the second floor?" She nodded. "I'm sure I can find Lucy's clothes and toys. Stay here, please." His blue eyes were mesmerizing as they pleaded with her. "Maybe you can play a game to keep Lucy occupied."

She twisted in her seat, looking at Lucy, who was putting her fingers up to the crate and giggling as Murphy licked them. She nodded, deciding it was best for the little girl. "Okay."

Nate reached over to gently squeeze her hand before he got out of the car. He let Murphy out of the back and approached the house.

Her hand tingled from where he'd touched it. She told herself to stop being foolish. Nate had made his stance perfectly clear. There couldn't be anything between them.

Other than friendship.

Nate carefully moved through the crime scene, heading up the stairs to the second floor with Murphy at his side.

His partner sniffed around the room, no doubt recognizing Lucy's scent. Nate tried to think like Willow, choosing outfits that matched, then poking through her toys. He found another doll and some large pink, orange and white Legos. He stuffed as many items as he could fit inside a large plastic bag before making his way back down to the main level.

The crime scene was still marked with dried blood, but the rest of the house remained the same. He thought again about the mess, wondering if the killer had been searching for something. If Darcy or anyone on the team had found anything suspicious, like drugs or money hidden someplace inside, they'd have let him know. Either the killer had found it, or the items had been hidden somewhere else.

He knew the crime scene techs had taken dozens of samples to test, a task that would likely take weeks to complete. And what they had tested so far had come up with a big fat nothing.

Tamping down a stab of frustration, he reminded himself that the forensic team members were excellent at their job and would eventually find something that would help them solve the case.

He hauled the bag outside, glancing up and down the street as he made his way toward the SUV. A black sedan, looking much like the one that had been stolen and used in Willow's kidnapping attempt by Craggy Face, was coming toward them, driving much slower than the rest of the traffic.

His pulse spiked and he quickened his pace, closing the gap between him and the car. "Willow, get down!"

Willow's pale face stared blankly at him for a moment, then she unlatched her seat belt and climbed over the console into the back seat. She curled her body protectively around Lucy in her car seat.

He understood her need to protect the little girl, but he hated knowing they were both in danger yet again.

Nate pulled his weapon, pointing it at the black sedan, tracking it as it crawled forward. He caught a glimpse of a deeply lined face behind the wheel, but then the driver pulled a cap down low and abruptly stomped on the gas.

The black sedan lurched forward.

"Stop! Police!" Nate's shout caused several other drivers to look around as if trying to figure out who he was talking to.

The black sedan rolled past. He wanted to shoot at the tires, but there were people crossing and so he held back for their safety.

He stared at the license plate, which was covered in mud. Despite the dark smears, he could just make out the last two letters, *EM*.

He opened the back hatch. "Jump, Murphy."

His partner leaped inside the crated area. He slammed the back shut, then rounded the vehicle to get into the driver's seat, taking a moment to toss the plastic bag of Lucy's things in the passenger seat. He gunned the engine, flipped on the red-and-blue lights, and pulled into traffic.

It was illegal to have your license plate obscured, unable to be clearly seen, an offense he could use to pull the driver over and issue a citation. If it was Craggy Face, all the better. He didn't like following the guy with Lucy and Willow in the back seat, so he quickly keyed his radio.

"This is Unit Ten requesting backup. I'm heading southwest on Linden Boulevard following a black Lincoln sedan, license plate mostly covered with mud, the last two letters Edward Mary."

"Ten-four," the dispatcher responded. "There's a patrol located about a mile east. I've directed them to your location."

"Copy." Nate kept his gaze on the sedan. The driver ignored his lights, darting the Lincoln among cars to put more distance between them. Nate did his best to keep up, not wanting to lose him, yet unwilling to engage in a full-out chase with Willow and Lucy riding in the back seat.

"Hurry. He's getting away." Willow's voice was low and intense.

He briefly met her gaze in the rearview mirror. "I can still see him. Backup will be here shortly."

"But I think it's Craggy Face! And he's getting away." Willow looked distraught over the possibility.

The black sedan made another cut over to the left lane, the driver he'd cut off punching the horn in a display of irritation. Nate did his best to keep pace without putting them in danger, desperate not to lose him.

"He's turned!" Willow's voice rose in panic.

Nate pushed his foot harder on the accelerator, cars moving out of his way as they realized he wasn't interested in pulling them over, but in following someone else.

Seconds later, he reached the same intersection, turning left. But when he looked up ahead, he didn't see the black sedan.

No! He couldn't have lost him!

"Look right, tell me if you see him." Nate kept his gaze on the streets off to the left. There were several black cars, but no Lincoln sedan.

"He's not this way from what I can tell." Willow's voice was low and hoarse, as if she were fighting tears. "But there are lots of places to hide."

He couldn't disagree. Still, he kept going straight, hoping he'd find the sedan. He reached for his radio. "Subject turned off the boulevard, and I haven't been able to pick him up. Any hits on a black Lincoln with a license plate ending in Edward Mary?"

"Let me send you to Eden, she's searching for a possible match."

"Thanks." He ground his teeth together, vying for patience.

"Nate? I have a report of another stolen vehicle, a

2013 black Lincoln sedan." She read him the license plate, ending with *EM.*

"Stolen?" He couldn't believe it. "When?"

"Earlier this morning, same MO as the previous theft. Owner is Joe Keene. He works for Keene, Carmel and Banks, a law firm. He claims he came home just after midnight and didn't realize his car was gone until late the following morning." Eden's voice held remorse.

"Get a BOLO out for the vehicle. I want every cop in the entire borough looking for it."

"Understood." He heard Eden's fingers tapping on her computer keyboard. "I'm bringing up all cameras in the Linden Boulevard area. Maybe we'll find him."

"Yeah. Call me if you do." Nate dropped his hand from the radio, resisting the urge to slam his fist against the steering wheel.

He couldn't believe he lost him. That his backup hadn't arrived in time. Sure, Eden might be able to pick him up, but he knew it was likely that the driver, if it was Craggy Face, would ditch the stolen vehicle as soon as possible.

"We lost him." Willow's voice was little more than a pained whisper.

Her disappointment stabbed deep. Remorse burned hot, churning in his belly. This was the second time he'd failed her. First when he'd been lured away by a fake crime, barely returning in time to prevent Craggy Face from kidnapping her, and now this.

He couldn't allow a mistake like this to happen again.

FOURTEEN

Lucy's sobbing had eventually eased, but knowing her niece was calm didn't make her feel any better. Willow knew that the black sedan with the muddy license plate had been there because of them. A close call that could have ended much worse if Nate hadn't shown up when he did. Despite how much she'd wanted clothes and toys for Lucy, it wasn't worth the risk.

She wished she understood why Craggy Face was after her. None of it made any sense and she was growing weary of constantly being under surveillance and protection.

The sooner Nate and his team found and arrested Craggy Face, the better.

Nate's grim expression held a note of self-recrimination. As if this was his fault, when she'd been the one to ask to come back for Lucy's things.

From now on, she knew she needed to stay inside the apartment with Lucy. No more outings, no matter how stir-crazy they became from being cooped up inside.

"I'm taking you and Lucy home," Nate said, interrupting her thoughts. "I never should have allowed you to come along."

"None of this is your fault, Nate. God was watching over all of us, and thanks to you and Murphy, you scared him off."

Nate gave a sharp shake of his head in a frustrated gesture but didn't argue. They rode in silence back to her apartment building in Bay Ridge. Ironically, the black sedan had taken them in the direction of her home.

And the Burgerteria.

It seemed all roads led back to the restaurant where she'd worked for three years. Three years! And never a hint of anything illegal going on related to Damon Berk, or anyone else for that matter.

She rested her head against Lucy's car seat, battling a wave of exhaustion. Logically she knew her fatigue was just the aftermath of the adrenaline rush, but she also hadn't been sleeping well.

Mostly because Lucy had been plagued by nightmares of her parents' murders. The little girl often moaned about the mean clown and repeated over and over again she didn't want the monkey.

Willow wasn't sure how to reassure Lucy that taking the stuffed monkey from the bad clown didn't mean she was responsible for the death of her parents. She thought again about Penny McGregor and the rapport she'd established with her niece. Maybe she could get Penny to come back to talk to the little girl again.

Nate pulled into a parking spot and shut down the engine. He turned in his seat to look at her. "Murphy and I are going to escort you and Lucy inside first. I'll bring up your things later."

"Okay." She took Lucy out of the car seat, holding her close as she slid out of the vehicle. Nate's strong arms surrounded her and his woodsy scent helped calm her nerves.

The trip to her apartment was uneventful. Nate left Murphy on guard as he retrieved the plastic bag, along with his computer.

As she unpacked, putting Lucy's things into dresser drawers, Nate remained hunched over his computer. When she'd finished creating a toy corner for Lucy, she crossed over to see what he was doing.

"That's a nice building," she said, looking at the elegant apartment building on the screen. The building looked new.

"Yeah, the real question is how does Damon Berk afford to live there?"

Good point, although her building was nice. Not new and fancy, but decent. "Maybe, like me, he had money from an inheritance."

"Maybe." Nate didn't sound convinced. He continued various searches. "Check this out. The owner of the new apartment building Damon lives in is a guy by the name of Oscar Banjo. Banjo also owns the building that houses the Burgerteria and that new place you were talking about the other day, the Basement Bargains store."

A shiver snaked down her spine.

Nate's gaze was fixated on the screen as he continued to search. "Banjo isn't our Craggy Face, though. Here's a photo of him at the ribbon-cutting ceremony. That's him, standing beside Theresa Gray, deputy mayor of housing and economic development."

She bent over his shoulder to see the screen more clearly. Oscar Banjo was young, in his thirties. Younger than she'd thought to have amassed such a fortune. "Definitely not our Craggy Face."

Nate pulled a chair over and gestured toward it. "No, but it is interesting that he owns the building the restaurant is in. Sit down, Willow. I need you to think hard about whether or not you remember seeing this man in the restaurant, maybe before you took those photos."

She dropped into the chair, her gaze fixated on the screen. There was something familiar about his features, but she couldn't place where she'd seen him. "I can't say for sure, but he may have been in the restaurant."

"Take your time," Nate urged. "You have a photographer's eye. Think back to those weeks leading up to the day you took the photos of your gourmet burgers."

She didn't want to disappoint him, and she really, really wanted to help put Craggy Face behind bars. But as she stared at Oscar Banjo's face, she simply couldn't say for certain when he'd been in the restaurant. His features were ordinary, nothing that would have captured her artist eye.

"I'm sorry, but I can't say for sure." Her shoulders slumped. "I wish I could, but I can't. There's nothing about this guy that would have captured my attention. He could be one of hundreds of customers that came in and out of the restaurant each day."

"That's okay. Thanks for trying." If Nate was frustrated, he didn't show it. "Interesting that he's so young. This guy is being touted as one of New York's up-and-coming real estate moguls. He just turned thirty-six last month."

"Yeah, but again, that doesn't prove anything." She wasn't sure where Nate was going with his comments.

"I'm sure he made a couple of investments that happened to pay off."

"Or he has someone backing him up," Nate countered.

She swiveled in her seat to stare at him. "Are you insinuating he's part of the mob?"

He lifted his hands in a gesture of surrender. "I'm not insinuating anything. It's just a theory." His gaze returned to the screen. "I'm going to keep digging for a while, see if I can find anything that links Banjo to Craggy Face, aka Carl Dower—or at least I'm pretty sure that's his name. It was written on a slip of paper found on the drug dealer Craggy Face killed."

She nodded and rose to her feet. She trusted Nate to find Craggy Face. More, she trusted Nate with her life and Lucy's.

When Nate's phone rang, she jumped, looking over at him expectantly. His expression was serious as he listened. "Okay, thanks, Eden."

"What?"

"They found the stolen Lincoln, abandoned not far from Prospect Park. They're checking for prints, but…" He shrugged.

Disappointed, she sighed. Craggy Face was too smart to leave fingerprints behind.

Although she wished she knew why he was so intent on causing her harm.

The rest of the evening passed by uneventfully. Lucy was happy to have her princess pajamas that Nate had brought from her brother's house.

Willow lay beside Lucy to tell her a story but felt herself dozing off, her niece snuggled against her.

"I'll kill you and the brat, too!"

"No! Please, Lord, save us!" Willow ran and ran, through the alley, dodging around dumpsters, her breath heaving from her lungs, her pulse thundering in her ears.

Nooo.

She awoke with a jolt, her face wet with tears, hardly able to breathe from the tightness of her lungs. She swiped at her face, reminding herself it was only a dream.

A terrible, horrible dream.

Taking care not to wake Lucy, she slipped from the bed and made her way to the bathroom. She splashed cold water on her face, trying to erase the images in her mind.

"Willow? Are you all right?"

She dried her hands and face and opened the bathroom door. Nate stood there, looking rumpled from sleep, yet still far too attractive for her peace of mind. Murphy stood beside him, looking up at her as if he were worried about her, too. "Yes. I'm sorry I woke you."

"I heard muffled crying, thought it was Lucy." His gaze was dark with concern.

"It was me. I—had a nightmare." She shivered. "But I'm fine. Thankfully I didn't wake Lucy."

"Come here, sit down for a minute." Nate took her hand and led her to the sofa. Murphy flopped on the floor at their feet. "Do you want something? Water? Tea?"

His offer was sweet, but she shook her head. "No, thanks. I'm fine."

He sank down beside her. "You want to talk about it?"

She blew out a breath. "It was just Craggy Face chasing me, telling me he was going to kill me and Lucy." The images her mind had conjured up had been all too real.

Nate put his arm around her shoulders and drew her close. She reveled in his warmth. "I won't let anything happen to you, Willow. You and Lucy are safe with me and Murphy."

"I know. God is watching over all of us." She leaned against him, burying her face against his T-shirt. He was a rock in an otherwise stormy sea. "I just want this to be over. For Lucy to be safe."

"I know." He brushed a kiss to her temple.

Nestled against him, she didn't want to move. Somehow, in the short time she'd known him, Nate had become important to her. More than a friend, despite her best efforts to hold him at arm's length. He was so wonderful to her and to Lucy, she just knew he'd make a wonderful husband and father.

After several long moments she lifted her head, searching his gaze in the dim light from the city flowing through the living room window. "You're a good man, Nate Slater," she whispered.

He shook his head, but his gaze clung to hers. "You don't know how often I wrestle with my anger."

She tipped her head to the side. "Don't we all wrestle with our flaws? Mine happens to be impatience, in case you haven't noticed. None of us is perfect, Nate, but God loves us anyway."

He didn't say anything, his gaze thoughtful. She leaned up to kiss him on the cheek, even though she'd rather have a real kiss from him.

He flashed a wry smile and hugged her. For a moment she clung to him, wishing for something more.

As she pulled away, his mouth captured hers and she couldn't stop from kissing him the way she'd wanted to.

But then she forced herself to pull away, knowing that this was the path to heartbreak. Her breathing was ragged, but she managed to pull herself together. "Good night, Nate."

He released her and she thought she could feel his gaze boring into her back as she moved toward the bedroom.

As she slipped back inside the bedroom she shared with Lucy, she heard his whisper.

"Good night, Willow."

No surprise that Nate didn't sleep well after Willow's mind-blowing kiss. The words she'd told him had echoed over and over in his head.

He'd found himself wondering if God had been looking out for him and his mother, bringing Geoff Cally into their lives to help save them.

That God was actually helping him to keep a tight rein on his temper. To be fair, he'd never lost it, but he'd always assumed it was a matter of time.

He'd caught a few hours of rest until Willow and Lucy had gotten up. He took care of Murphy first, then when they were finished in the bathroom, he took his turn.

Willow was making scrambled eggs when he emerged. Lucy had her doll sitting on the chair beside her and was trying to convince her aunt to give her dolly some breakfast, too.

"She can share some of yours, Lucy." Willow glanced at him with a smile. "Good morning, Nate."

"Morning." He cleared his throat and took the seat

across from Lucy. "I'm going to head out for a while today, but I'll arrange someone to come and stay with you."

The light in Willow's cinnamon eyes dimmed but she nodded. "Okay. Breakfast will be ready in a jiffy."

"Thanks." He was humbled by how easily she included him in meals, so he made an effort to keep Lucy entertained as she cooked.

"Who's coming to babysit this time?" She placed a plate with eggs and toast in front of Lucy, then brought him a larger serving.

"I'm waiting to hear back." He'd made the call while outside with Murphy. He didn't want to leave her alone, but knew his preoccupation with Willow and Lucy had to stop. "The team is busy this morning, and if one of them can't come, then I'll get someone from the closest precinct to come over."

"Okay." Willow joined them at the table.

When they'd finished eating, Nate helped clean up the dishes, then made another call to his unit. There was still no one available for protection duty, so he made the call to the nearest precinct. Their boss had to talk to Gavin before they agreed to send a female cop, Kathleen Kuhn, over.

She arrived almost thirty minutes later. She didn't look happy about the assignment, but he didn't care. Finding Damon Berk and/or Craggy Face was his top priority.

And he couldn't do that while sitting here in Willow's apartment. As it was, he was getting a later start than he would have liked. Still, he forced a smile. "Thanks for coming, I really appreciate it."

"Yeah, sure." He didn't let her lack of enthusiasm

gct to him. "What's your phone number, in case I need to reach you?"

He rattled it off, then entered her cell number into his phone, too. He put Murphy's vest on, then straightened. "I'll be on the radio, too." He turned and headed to the door. "Come, Murphy."

Murphy was on alert as they left Willow and Lucy with Kathleen. Despite her attitude, he felt certain the cop would take protecting Willow and Lucy seriously.

Willow's apartment wasn't far from the Burgerteria, so he headed there first. He wasn't leaving until he'd confronted Damon Berk about Craggy Face and the murder of Paulie White.

The restaurant was supposed to be open by ten thirty in the morning, according to the hours posted on the door, but as he and Murphy approached, the interior was dark, no sign of customers seated inside. He tried the door, but it was locked.

He frowned, a sliver of apprehension snaking down his spine. Were the employees running late? Or was something deeper amiss?

He leaned in close, cupping his hands around his face so he could see better. At first there was nothing, then a dark shadow of movement. The figure turned and he instantly recognized Damon Berk.

"Hey! Berk! Open up! Police!" He rapped sharply on the door, holding his badge up so that Damon could see it. The manager looked indecisive for a moment, as if he wanted to run, then reluctantly approached.

He opened the door just enough to talk. "Now what do you want?"

"Why are you closed?"

Damon scowled, sending a furtive glance over his

shoulder as if seeking reinforcement. "My delivery truck is late. Can't make burgers without ground beef. I'll be opening soon. Why does it matter to you?"

It didn't but he'd wanted to get the guy talking. "Listen, your buddy Carl Dower is wanted for murder." His blunt statement seemed to catch Berk off guard.

"What? Wait a minute, he's not my buddy." Panic flared in Damon's eyes.

"How did you know who I was talking about, then?" Nate challenged. "The guy who you were talking to in the photograph Willow took was Carl Dower, right?"

"No, I—uh, well, I may have remembered his name from when he complained about his food, but that doesn't make him a friend." Sweat beaded along Berk's hairline again. Nate couldn't contain a surge of satisfaction that he had Berk right where he wanted him.

"If you don't want to be arrested for aiding and abetting a known felon, you'll tell me where to find him."

"I don't know." Berk's denial sounded weak.

A flash of movement from behind Berk caught his eye. "Who's back there? Is that him? Dower?"

"No!" Berk blocked the doorway with his body, closing the door even further. "It's the cook. I told you my food shipment is late."

Nate didn't believe him. Murphy growled low in his throat, his nose working as he sniffed the air, and that was enough to convince him. He whirled away from the restaurant door, instinctively knowing Dower had headed out the back. "Come!"

He raced down the road, around the corner leading to the back alley running the length of the building. Murphy kept pace, although he knew his partner could easily outrun him.

As he headed down the alley, he could make out a figure dressed in black up ahead. It wasn't easy to tell from the back, but Nate felt certain it was Carl Dower. "Get him, Murphy!"

Murphy put on a burst of speed, easily closing in on the guy.

The perp suddenly stopped and turned. A gun! No! Dower was pointing the weapon at Murphy!

"Heel, Murphy! *Heel!*" Nate reached for his weapon, hoping, praying that he could stop Dower from shooting his partner.

The command caused Murphy to stop on a dime. His partner turned and came back toward him. The sound of a gunshot echoed sharply, ricocheting off the buildings surrounding them.

"No!" His voice was hoarse as he returned fire. "Murphy!"

He was so focused on his partner that he didn't realize that Dower had fled the scene. He dropped to his knees, gathering Murphy close, feeling for any sign of an injury.

No blood, thankfully. Nate sent up a quick prayer of thanks to God for watching over his partner.

He rose to his feet and ran to the end of the alley. But it was too late.

Dower was gone.

FIFTEEN

Nate called for backup, frustrated with himself for letting Carl Dower escape. While he waited for someone from his team to arrive, he ran around to the front of the restaurant and pounded on the glass door. "Berk! Open up!"

The manager didn't answer. Nate wondered if the manager had taken off once he and Murphy had gone around back, or if he was hiding inside. His gut leaned toward hiding. He yanked on the door, but it was still locked.

"Berk!" He shouted and pounded again, but there was still no response. Reeling in his temper, he spun away from the door and reached for his phone.

"Roarke? It's Slater. I need your help." Henry Roarke was a K-9 detective who was stuck on modified desk duty while IAB investigated an excessive use of force allegation, a claim no one believed for one minute. Roarke wasn't happy about the situation, annoyed with how long it was taking the IAB to clear his name, but being on desk duty meant Henry was in a good position to do the paperwork he desperately needed in order to get a search warrant for the Burgerteria.

After explaining to Henry what he needed, the K-9 detective sounded hesitant. "I don't know, Nate. Dower isn't in the restaurant now. He took off. I'm not convinced a judge will approve this. After all, you don't know for sure that Dower was inside the restaurant, right? You didn't see his face until he was in the alley. All we can say is that Dower may have been in the restaurant but was for sure in the alley."

"I know it was him." He scowled and rubbed his jaw, replaying those tense minutes when he'd caught the flash of movement. He let out a heavy breath, knowing he couldn't lie. "But you're right, I didn't get a good look at him inside the restaurant."

"Listen, I'll do my best," Henry promised. "I'll call you back as soon as I hear something, okay?"

"Yeah, thanks." He disconnected from the call and returned to the alley just as Vivienne and her K-9 partner, Hank, approached.

Nate jogged over to meet them. "Carl Dower was here—around back. He fired a gun at Murphy and took off on foot. We need to find him!"

"Did you call Eden to look for camera footage? He may have gotten on the subway or at least close enough to be picked up on the subway cameras."

Good point. He reached for his radio. "Dispatch, I need to talk to Eden." He waited for the dispatcher to transfer the call, scanning the alley. "Vivienne, call the crime scene techs. If possible, I'd like Darcy to come look for the brass left behind from Dower's weapon."

"Will do." Vivienne reached for her phone.

"Chang," Eden answered through the radio.

"It's Nate. I need you to look at the cameras near the Burgerteria restaurant, see if you can pick up Carl

Dower, aka Craggy Face, you know, the guy you found on video before. He took a shot at Murphy."

"Oh no! Is Murphy okay?"

Nate glanced down at his partner. "Yeah, he's not hurt. Thankfully Dower missed."

"Okay, let's see. I have five cameras up around the area you've mentioned. Here!" Her voice lifted in excitement. "I found him! He's still on foot, about seven blocks from you, heading east. You better hurry, the camera on the next block is broken. He's heading into a video dead zone."

"I'm going. Come, Murphy!" Nate broke into a run, envisioning the streets in his head so he could find the shortest route. His police SUV was located in the opposite direction, so he didn't bother to go back for it.

"I'll try to head him off at the pass in my vehicle." Vivienne shouted from the driver's seat. "Stay on your radio!"

He barely spared her a glance as he ran for all he was worth. He knew Dower was armed but couldn't tolerate the idea he might actually get away.

Nate wanted, needed to find him. To toss him behind bars where he belonged.

He made good time, but as he reached the intersection, there was no sign of Dower. He called Eden, breathing hard. "Do you have him on video?"

"No. I'm sorry, but he's gone." Eden's voice echoed with regret. "He never showed up on any of the other cameras after heading into the radius of the broken one. I have to assume he once again was picked up in a vehicle."

"How is that possible?" Nate bent over to brace his hands on his knees. Murphy nudged him with his nose, then licked his face. He slowly straightened, raking his gaze over the area. "Do you think he knew this particular camera was broken?"

"Maybe, but I'm not sure how. It's not general knowledge available to the public, but who knows if he has friends in high places? I'm sorry, Nate. I feel terrible that I lost him."

"It's okay." He sighed. The broken camera was hardly her fault; in a city the size of New York, there was no way to avoid the occasional broken camera. Still, it nagged at him that Dower had managed to disappear in the black void.

"I'll keep scanning for him. Maybe I'll be able to pick him up again."

"I hope so." Nate disconnected, then turned to retrace his steps to go back to the Burgerteria, Murphy keeping pace beside him.

His phone rang and he quickly picked it up. "Slater."

"It's Vivienne. I'm stuck in traffic. Have you found him?"

"No. Eden lost him, too. Broken camera." He tried not to sound as disappointed and upset as he felt. "I'm heading back to the Burgerteria. Hopefully Henry can get the search warrant I requested."

"Nate, Sarge wants us to report to headquarters. He wants an update on this case ASAP. He didn't like hearing Murphy was almost hit by a bullet."

The last thing he wanted to do was to leave the scene of the crime. But if their boss wanted an update, he didn't have any choice but to comply. "Okay, fine. I'll be there soon."

"Later." Vivienne ended the call.

Nate broke into a light jog. Instead of going to the

restaurant, he went to where he'd left his SUV. Murphy needed water, and the backs of all their K-9 vehicles were equipped with a fresh water system, a key component in taking good care of their four-legged partners.

He had to trust that Darcy would find the brass left behind by Dower's gun.

Once they found the guy, he planned to charge him with attempted murder of a police officer, adding to the long list of crimes the guy was guilty of perpetrating.

Additional crimes they no doubt had yet to uncover.

What had Dower been doing with Damon Berk in the back of the restaurant? Was it possible he'd threatened Berk? If so, with what? Did Dower have something to hold over Berk's head? Was the sweat beading on Berk's face more of an indication of fear, rather than nervousness at getting caught doing something illegal?

He didn't know and that bothered him. The only clue they had to why Willow and Lucy were in danger was related to the stupid photograph. Unless…he straightened in his seat. Unless Dower and Berk thought she knew more than just what she'd captured on film.

Like what? He had no clue.

But the possibility wouldn't leave him alone.

Willow tried to ignore Officer Kuhn as she played with Lucy. The female officer was nice enough, but not nearly as friendly as Vivienne, Noelle and the other members of the K-9 unit.

The ones she knew were more like family to Nate and Murphy.

Not that being nice and friendly really mattered as long as she and Lucy were safe.

As the hour approached noon, Willow pushed herself

to her feet. "I'm making grilled ham and cheese sandwiches for Lucy's lunch. Would you like one?"

"No, thank you." Officer Kuhn's tone was polite, yet distant. "I'm vegan, so I ordered online from a local vegan restaurant that delivers."

"Okay."

"Aunt Willow, I hav'ta go to the bathroom!" Lucy suddenly jumped up from the floor, so Willow led her into the bathroom.

She heard a thudding noise from the apartment and thought it was likely that Officer Kuhn's vegan lunch had arrived.

"I'm hungry," Lucy said as Willow helped her wash her hands.

"Lunch will be ready soon, honey." Willow used the towel to dry Lucy's hands. "You need to clean up your toys while I grill our sandwiches."

The door to the bathroom abruptly opened, hitting her sharply in the elbow. "Hey!" She turned toward the doorway, annoyed that Officer Kuhn had barged in. But it wasn't the female officer at all.

Craggy Face stood in the doorway, his expression grim with a mixture of anger and satisfaction. She noticed his face was flushed and sweaty, his overall appearance disheveled. Had the man run here from somewhere? He held a gun in his hand, the muzzle pointed at her chest. "Don't move or I'll shoot."

Her pulse spiked, her mouth desert dry with fear and loathing. How had he gotten in her apartment? Where was Officer Kuhn? She felt trapped in the tiny bathroom yet managed to find her voice. "What do you want?"

Lucy began to wail. "Bad man with a gun!"

"Shh, it's okay." Willow didn't take her gaze off

Craggy Face but reached down to pull Lucy up and into her arms, cuddling the little girl close and smoothing a shaky hand over her hair. "Stop it! You're scaring her."

"You should be scared. Move it." Craggy Face stepped back, waving his gun in a way that indicated she needed to come out of the bathroom. Dressed in black from head to toe, baseball cap on his head, he looked menacing and all too capable of carrying out his threat. Willow didn't want to leave the sanctuary of her apartment, but what could she do? There was no way to outrun a bullet.

If it were only her being held captive, she might have taken the risk. But she couldn't put Lucy in danger.

It was her duty to keep the little girl safe.

Dear Lord, help us! Please, keep us safe in Your care!

The prayer helped calm her nerves. Nate and Murphy were out there. They'd figure out that she and Lucy were missing and would do everything in their power to find her.

Craggy Face locked a hand on her arm, squeezing so tight she winced. The cold barrel of the gun pressed into her side. "We're walking out of here nice and easy, understand? If you say or do anything to get someone's attention, I'll shoot you and deal with the consequences."

"Wh-why?" She forced the words past the tightness of her throat. "Y-you have the photographs. What more do you want?"

"It's not what *I* want." His breath was hot against the side of her face and reeked of onion. She tried not to gag. "It's what the boss wants. Let's go."

He shoved her hard and she stumbled, nearly losing her grip on Lucy. As much as she didn't want to leave the child alone, she couldn't bear bringing her into the center of danger. "Hold on, Lucy will slow us down. Let me leave her here."

Craggy Face sneered then shrugged. "Hurry!"

"Stay here, Lucy, okay? You'll be safe." She put Lucy down. It wrenched her heart to listen to Lucy's sobs as she closed the bathroom door to keep the little girl inside, but knew it was for the best.

She gasped when her desperate gaze landed on the prone figure of Officer Kuhn, lying in an unconscious heap on the floor, blood seeping from a wound on her temple.

"Wait! She needs medical attention!" Willow dug in her heels, trying to stall for time. Maybe Nate would contact Officer Kuhn, and then rush over here when she didn't answer her phone. "We need an ambulance."

"No." Craggy Face dug the gun barrel into her side, making her suck in a breath as pain shot through her midsection. She tried to shrink away from the gun barrel but couldn't. "Move it! Or you'll be sorry."

She moved as instructed. Craggy Face pushed her into the hallway and closed the door behind them. He didn't take her onto the elevator, though, shoving her instead toward the stairwell.

"Not a word," he warned.

She swallowed hard and nodded. She continued repeating her silent prayer, hoping someone else would come upon them in the stairwell. That someone would notice there was something wrong and call the police.

But as they went down one set of stairs after another, taking all seven floors down, they didn't see anyone. And when they reached the lobby, Craggy Face wrapped his arm around her shoulders, as if he were comforting her, while the barrel of the gun pressed painfully in the soft tissue beneath her rib cage.

Remembering the cameras in the lobby, she glanced upward, attempting to telegraph her fear with her eyes without raising Craggy Face's suspicions. Yet even as she did her best, she knew it may be hours until anyone watched the video footage.

At which point it may very well be too late.

When they stepped outside, her hope of being discovered evaporated into a fine mist. Pedestrian traffic was brisk; summer tourists crowded the streets. Everyone was in a hurry, no one paying attention to the woman being ushered down the street by a man old enough to be her father.

Maybe they assumed Craggy Face *was* her father.

She glanced from person to person, trying to make eye contact in an effort to let someone know there was something wrong.

But no one appeared to notice.

"Wh-where are we going?" Her voice was hoarse with fear.

"I told you." The onion breath was strong, and she couldn't help wrinkling her nose beneath the assault to her senses. "To meet the boss."

The boss? She frowned. "Damon?"

Craggy Face let out a harsh laugh. "Not hardly. This is all his fault in the first place. If that idiot doesn't watch out, he'll be dead meat, too. This is his last chance to make things right."

Dead meat, too. The boss. Not Damon Berk. Willow managed to put one foot in front of the other, following Craggy Face's orders with a sick sense of dread. She felt as if she were walking toward her execution and didn't know how to stop it.

She truly didn't understand what was going on. Something criminal, clearly, but what? The photograph had been of Craggy Face. What about that had gotten her to this point? To the assault on a police officer? To being dragged out of her apartment at gunpoint?

To this man being so willing to shoot her in cold blood?

SIXTEEN

"I really want to get inside that restaurant." Nate looked at his boss, Sergeant Gavin Sutherland, seated across the table. "All roads lead to the Burgerteria."

Gavin nodded. "Henry's working on the search warrant...but I haven't heard back yet."

They'd gathered in the large conference room located on the second floor of their precinct. He'd only been there for thirty minutes and was itching to get back out to the alley. Darcy hadn't found the bullet casing yet, but he knew it had to be there somewhere.

Although getting the casing and matching it to the others they'd found wouldn't necessarily convince a judge to sign off on the search warrant. They needed more.

He put his hand down to stroke Murphy's soft fur, forgetting they'd all kenneled their partners for the meeting. Gavin had requested a rundown, which he'd given as succinctly as possible.

"Anything else?" Gavin asked.

"No. That's it." Nate hesitated for a moment, then added, "Listen, I need to go." He couldn't ignore the itchy feeling crawling up his spine. "I want to get back to the Burgerteria in case the search warrant comes through. And if it doesn't, I still might be able to convince Damon Berk to cooperate."

Gavin leveled a steady glare at him, as if silently warning him not to go off the rails. "Fine. But keep me updated on what you're working on. I don't want to hear about an officer nearly being shot from the dispatcher."

He couldn't stop in the middle of a pursuit to contact his boss, but he understood Gavin was more upset about Murphy's close call than angry with him.

"I will." He surged to his feet and left the conference room. Down on the main level, he freed Murphy from his crate and headed back outside. He drove straight to the Burgerteria, intent on getting through to Damon Berk.

He knew, deep down, that somehow the restaurant was the key to cracking the case.

His phone rang. Officer Kuhn.

He pulled over to the curb, double-parking in a spot near the entrance to the alley. His heart thudded painfully in his chest as Kathleen said in a groggy voice, "Willow is gone. I— He hit me. I lost consciousness but when I came to, she was gone and the kid was closed up in the bathroom. I'm sorry."

Who had grabbed Willow? Even as the question formed in his mind, he knew it was Craggy Face. Carl Dower. "Stay with Lucy, will you? I'll call for an ambulance and backup." He disconnected from the call, quickly called dispatch and jumped out of the SUV. After taking Murphy out of the back, he ran to the back side of the restaurant.

Rounding the corner, he caught a glimpse of Willow being pushed in the rear door of the restaurant by Dower.

No! His chest was so tight it hurt to breathe. He reached for his radio. "I need backup in the alley behind the Burgerteria! My prime suspect, who I believe is Carl Dower, has kidnapped Willow."

"Ten-four. Backup on the way."

He and Murphy ran down the length of the alley, his mind grappling with the fact that Willow was inside with Dower. He couldn't wait; he needed to go after her right now. There was no need for a search warrant; these were exigent circumstances. A crime in progress.

Weapon in hand, he paused at the door, taking a deep breath to steady his nerves before easing it open.

Please, Lord, keep Willow safe!

The prayer rose from his heart, reaching for the sky as he entered the building with Murphy at his side. The idea of Willow being harmed made it difficult to concentrate. He kept his partner off leash, knowing that they would need every advantage in order to get Willow out of there, alive and unharmed.

Inside the building, he noted a steep staircase leading down into a basement storage area. Terse voices echoed off the concrete, but the words weren't easy to understand.

Holding his breath, he eased down on the first step, expecting a loud creak or groan of the wood to give him away. Hearing nothing but the staccato beat of his heart, he eased down a second step. Then a third, hugging the wall and holding his weapon ready.

Using hand signals, he instructed Murphy to stay at his side. As he drew closer to the bottom of the stairs, the words from the men below became clear.

"Why is this my fault?" Damon Berk's nasal voice was distinctly familiar. "You're the stupid idiot who shot Paulie right behind the restaurant over a stupid phone. What did you think would happen? Of course the cops came here looking for you."

"Paulie was threatening to talk! And it's your fault because of her!" The lower, husky voice had to be that of Carl Dower. "You encouraged her to take those pictures! Now the boss wants our heads on a platter!"

"She was supposed to take pictures of burgers, not people!" Damon's nasal voice turned whiny. "How was I to know she was some sort of amateur photographer? And would find your ugly mug interesting!"

"That photo is on the wall of the community college for everyone to see!" Dower's low voice rose with anger. "I grabbed it, but not until it had been posted for days. All because of you!"

"You need to convince the boss it was her fault, not mine," Damon whined.

Nate wondered if Damon and Carl were the only two men down there, or if there were others, possibly someone standing guard over Willow. He took another step. The wood beneath his boot creaked and he froze, his heart lodged in his throat. He signaled for Murphy to stay and leveled his weapon, prepared for the worst.

The seconds ticked by slowly. Eventually, he let out his breath in a soundless sigh. The two men were arguing loud enough that they must not have heard him.

Every cell in his body wanted to rush to Willow. But he forced himself to remain calm. Nate took another step and noticed there were several large boxes piled along the wall in front of him. He thought they must contain food or other restaurant supplies, but then he caught a glimpse of a popular phone logo along the side.

What in the world? He frowned, trying to understand why the basement of the Burgerteria would contain boxes of expensive phones, when it clicked. The expensive new phone that Paulie White had.

This wasn't about drugs, as he'd originally suspected, but about stolen goods.

Involving enough money to kill for.

Willow huddled as far from Craggy Face and Damon Berk as she could get within the confines of the small space. The entire basement was filled with boxes of various sizes and shapes, containing items like high-end televisions, laptop computers and phones.

There was even a box of cameras just like hers.

She tried not to worry about Lucy, hoping the little girl was safe in the apartment. She backed up to a stack of boxes and leaned against them for a few moments. She knew Craggy Face had brought her here to face their boss, but he hadn't let a name slip.

While the men had argued, she tried to reach for her phone again. She pushed the buttons on the screen without looking, estimating the numbers 911, but without success. The call didn't connect. She tried again, and when that didn't work, she edged the phone out further and glanced down at the screen.

No service.

Swallowing hard against a shaft of disappointment, she slipped the phone back in her pocket. Being surrounded by concrete must have made it impossible to get a cell signal.

The stairs were to her left and a little behind her.

Maybe if she could get to the staircase leading up to the main level, she could make a run for it.

Maybe.

The image of being shot in the back caused a shudder to ripple through her. But what option did she have? She couldn't just stand here waiting for the boss to arrive.

For all she knew, the boss planned on killing her anyway. Might as well try to escape before that happened. Especially since the two guys were intent on their argument.

Willow sent up a silent prayer, asking for God to give her the strength she needed to get out. Feeling calmer, Willow eased away from the boxes and took a tiny and silent step to the side, toward the stairs.

She thought about what Nate had said about his childhood. She understood his perspective a little better now. Being in danger like this, knowing Craggy Face was armed with a gun, made it difficult to believe. But she refused to give up hope. Deep down, she knew God was watching over her, and that He would send Nate, or another cop, to save her, too.

"I'm going upstairs to wait." Damon's statement caused her heart to sink in her chest. She didn't want to be left alone down here with Craggy Face.

In her heart she didn't believe Damon was a killer, but there wasn't a single doubt in her mind that Craggy Face could pull the trigger, shooting her in the blink of an eye.

"You're not going anywhere." Craggy Face took a menacing step toward Damon. "We're waiting right here, understand?"

Damon shrank from the older man. "Yeah, uh, sure, Carl."

Willow took another step, her gaze glued to Craggy Face. Had he noticed her movement? He continued threatening Damon Berk until the man was practically cowering in the corner, his face buried in his hands.

Now! She turned and ran toward the stairs.

"Hey! Stop or I'll shoot!" Craggy Face's voice held a note of panic.

She didn't stop. She hunched her shoulders, expecting to feel the sharp impact of a bullet at any moment.

A dark shadow moved from the landing of the stairway, and she feared she was too late. That their boss, whoever he was, had come down without her hearing him.

But then she recognized Nate and Murphy. She knew it! Her heart soared in her chest. She knew he'd come!

"Get behind me." Nate grabbed her arm and quickly shoved her behind him. She heard a sharp retort ring out, followed by a second gunshot.

No! She stumbled, almost going down to the concrete floor at the thought of Nate being hit. She tried to turn back, to see what had happened.

Nate lowered his weapon, his expression grim. Damon was on the floor, curled in a ball, his arms covering his head. "Don't shoot, I'm not armed, don't shoot!" The sobs came from deep within, and she almost felt sorry for her old boss, even though she knew he was complicit in the crimes Craggy Face had committed.

Craggy Face swayed, his hand pressed to his bleeding chest, a look of surprise on his face. As if in slow motion, the gun in his hand fell from his grip, clattering loudly against the cement floor. "You shot me."

The words came out in a surprised tone as he slowly sank to the floor.

"Stop! Police!" The shout came from up above and suddenly there were several cops thundering down the stairs to the basement. She had to move out of the way to give them room to get by.

"Nate? Are you hurt?" She raked her gaze over him, searching for injuries.

"I'm fine, but the box of phones isn't." He gestured toward the bullet hole that had gone into a box mere inches from where he stood. She understood he'd had no choice but to shoot Craggy Face in self-defense. Nate abruptly stepped forward, pulling her into his arms. "Are you all right?"

Her knees went weak as the initial rush of adrenaline began to fade. "I—think so. Scared, but not hurt. But I had to leave Lucy in the bathroom…" She swallowed a sob.

"Lucy's okay. Officer Kuhn has her."

She closed her eyes on a wave of relief. "Leaving her behind was the hardest thing I've ever done. I need to call Officer Kuhn."

"Of course."

She reached for her phone but once again, there was no service. She'd need to wait until they were up in the alley.

One of the cops pressed a towel to the bleeding wound in Craggy Face's chest while another cuffed him just in case. The officer then handcuffed Damon Berk, as well. Damon didn't protest; in fact, he almost seemed grateful to be with the police, his eyes red and puffy from crying.

It was over.

"Let's get out of here." Nate's voice was low and husky in her ear.

She nodded, forcing herself to step away from the warmth of his arms. Without hesitation, she headed up the stairs.

In the alley, she was about to pull out her phone, but then saw Office Kuhn and Lucy standing near several police officers.

"Lucy!" She rushed forward to take her niece into her arms. "I'm so happy you're okay." She lifted her gaze to the injured officer. "Thank you so much."

"I'm the one who owes you an apology." Kuhn's expression was contrite. "She kept crying and the ambulance crew felt we were both fine, so I thought it best to bring her to you."

"Thank you." Tears pricked Willow's eyes.

Nate came over to join them, his expression mirroring her relief. He reached out to stroke the little girl's back, his touch so gentle it made her heart ache. Lucy went from her arms to his, as if needing Nate's strength. He held her close, his low voice and strong arms offering Lucy a solid male reassurance she didn't possess.

He'd be such a good father, if only he'd let himself believe in God's strength and endurance.

She summoned a shaky smile. "I knew you'd come for us."

His blue eyes were dark with concern. "I was almost too late."

She shook her head. "No, you were right on time."

He wrapped one arm around her shoulders, bringing her in for a three-way hug. "I put my faith in God and prayed. He showed me the way."

Her heart melted at his profession of faith. "I'm so glad to hear you say that."

Nate pressed a kiss to her temple. "I couldn't believe it when you turned to run toward me. Did you hear the stairs creaking?"

She shook her head, resting against him, breathing in his woodsy scent. She always felt safe and secure in Nate's arms. But then she lifted her head to look up at him. "No, I didn't hear the stairs creak at all, I just decided to run. Figured it was better than waiting to be— you know." She didn't want to use the words *shot and killed* in front of Lucy.

Murphy nudged Lucy's foot, causing the little girl to shift in Nate's arms to look down at him. "Good doggy," she whispered.

"Yes, Murphy is a good doggy." Willow was surprised at how silent the yellow Lab had been despite all the activity going on in the basement.

"You need to get home." Nate's voice held a note of remorse. "But I can't go with you. I need to stay here."

She felt herself tense. "Why? Because you fired in self-defense?"

He nodded. "Yes, and this means I'm on desk duty until the investigation is complete."

Desk duty? A frisson of fear streaked through her. "But I need you, Nate. What about the boss? Craggy Face told me his boss wanted to deal with me personally."

Nate's brow furrowed. "I heard them talking about some boss. I still don't understand why they want you, specifically."

"I don't know." She shivered and cast a worried

glance over her shoulder. Even standing beside Nate in the alley, with cops surrounding them, didn't feel safe.

Was the guy in charge of this whole mess out there right now, watching them? Waiting for his chance to strike?

She instinctively moved closer to Nate, putting her hand over his where it rested on Lucy's back.

"It's obvious they're selling stolen goods," Nate continued. "There has to be hundreds of thousands of dollars' worth of merchandise down there. And clearly Damon Berk doesn't have the guts or the brains to be in charge of something this big."

"Please, Nate." She couldn't ignore the deep need to keep him close. "Don't leave us."

Nate hesitated, and glanced around. "Okay, listen, I don't want to leave you, Willow, but I have to stay at least for a while yet. Don't worry, I'll find someone to take you home and this time, I'll keep a K-9 team with you."

She tried to think of a way to change his mind. "What about the photograph?"

He glanced at her in confusion. "What about it? We already know Carl Dower was upset about you capturing his face."

"No, I think there's something more." She thought back to the way she'd edited the picture, blurring the background to bring the craggy features into sharper contrast. "I think I may have captured something else in the image."

"Like what?" There was an underlying urgency in his tone.

"I don't know. But Craggy Face made a comment that the boss was upset about the photograph being displayed at the community college. I didn't consider the photo being on display as a problem, but it doesn't matter because I think there's something else, too." She met his gaze. "I need to find the original digital file, see if I can bring the background into sharper focus. It may give us a clue as to who the big boss is."

Nate hesitated, and she could tell by the anguished expression on his face that his duty warred with the need to uncover the truth.

"Okay, we can check it out," he finally relented. "Shouldn't take too long to get the camera from the evidence room."

"Thanks, but I have all the originals on my computer at home, too." She released her breath in a soundless sigh of relief.

The photograph was the key; she just needed to figure out how to unlock the secrets buried within.

And maybe once they found the guy in charge, she and Lucy would be safe at last.

SEVENTEEN

Nate cuddled Lucy close, breathing in the calming scent of baby shampoo. He silently thanked God for giving him the strength he'd needed to save them.

The idea of losing Lucy or Willow was too much to bear.

He looked at his SUV parked at the end of the alley, knowing full well he shouldn't leave the scene of an officer-involved shooting. Yet he desperately wanted to take Willow and Lucy home. He told himself he was working the case, following a new lead, but he felt certain Sarge wouldn't see it that way.

Before he could so much as take a step toward his SUV, though, Vivienne and her border collie partner caught up to him. She scowled, glancing between him and Willow. "Slater, where are you going?"

"I need to take Willow and Lucy home." Even as he said the words, Vivienne's eyes widened and she quickly shook her head.

"You can't do that. You know the protocol." Vivienne glanced at Willow, who had taken Lucy from Nate's arms. Her expression softened. "I know you've been through a lot, Willow, and I know you're scared. But if you care about Nate at all, you won't let him risk his job for you."

"Now hold on," Nate began, but Vivienne cut him off.

"You can't leave. End of story."

"She's right." Willow's voice was low, soft and full of remorse. "I'm being selfish. You absolutely need to stay here and do your job, clear your name." Her smile looked wan. "We'll be okay. I'm sure one of the officers will escort us home."

He pushed down a surge of anger. No, they wouldn't be okay until they identified and arrested the big boss. The man who'd ordered Carl Dower to kidnap Willow and Lucy. The man in charge of this criminal endeavor, who ordered men, women and even a child to be killed without hesitation.

Leaving an officer on guard at her apartment hadn't prevented Willow from being taken against her will. From being threatened and almost killed.

No matter what happened to him, he couldn't bear the thought of failing to protect her again.

"I'll look at the original digital images and let you know what I find," Willow added.

"Digital images?" Vivienne raised a brow. "The ones you took of Carl Dower?"

"Yes." Willow looked tired but still wore the familiar stubborn expression on her face, the one that refused to quit, no matter what. "I want to examine it more closely."

Nate abruptly straightened. "I have an idea. My laptop is in my SUV, we'll pull up the photos on my computer and enlarge the image so we can see if there's anything in the background. We can also call Eden

Chang for help. She's a genius when it comes to uncovering hidden secrets."

Vivienne didn't look entirely convinced but nodded. "Fine, but don't leave the scene. Sarge is on his way and will want to talk to you."

"Understood." He put his hand beneath Willow's elbow. "Let's go. My SUV is at the end of the alley."

He led Willow through the mass of officers and crime scene techs to where he'd left his SUV only a short time ago, but it seemed like hours.

It was easy to remember the bitter taste of fear that had clogged his throat when he'd witnessed Dower dragging Willow into the back of the restaurant at gunpoint.

Thankfully, he'd gotten there in time. It had been the first time he'd ever shot a man in the course of duty, but looking back, he didn't see that he'd had an alternative.

Carl Dower had fired first, leaving him no choice but to take out the threat.

Still, he knew that while he had Willow as a witness, the evidence would have to be carefully examined in order to prove his side of the story.

Especially if Dower didn't survive his injury.

Shaking off the depressing thought, he opened the front driver's-side door, leaving it ajar to help air out the vehicle. Willow placed Lucy in the car seat from the other side of the SUV as he booted up the computer and then linked his phone to access the internet.

"We'll use the back. Murphy needs some water anyway." He carried the laptop around to the back of the SUV, opened the hatch and set the laptop down. Murphy gracefully leaped into the back, drank some water, then jumped back down.

"Let me access all my photos." Willow gestured to

the screen. "Especially the one I took before I did the editing."

"Have at it." He watched over her shoulder as she logged in and pulled up the message and attached photo she'd sent to her photography instructor just ten days ago.

"This is the finished photo, after I blurred the background." Willow minimized the photograph and went back in her files. "The original one is here, somewhere."

"If you don't find it, I'll get an officer to pick up your laptop and bring it here." Nate was anxious to see the original photograph on a large screen. There had to be something important that she'd unwittingly caught in the picture.

Something he should have thought about days ago, when she'd first shown him the photo on her digital camera. Had he let his emotional response to Willow and Lucy cloud his judgment?

As Willow worked, he stepped to the side and scanned the alley. Dower was hoisted into the back of an ambulance, the drivers no doubt rushing to take him to the closest hospital. Berk was still handcuffed and tucked in the back of a squad car. The crime scene techs were hard at work preserving evidence, but the number of cops that were around the area had dwindled.

The threat had been minimized and there were no doubt other calls coming in.

"I found it!" Willow's excited voice drew his attention back to her. "I think I see someone in the background but I can't make out the facial features."

"Send it to me, so I can forward the original to Eden."

"Okay." Seconds later, his phone pinged with a text message. He relayed it to Eden, then called her. "This is the original photograph that Willow took. Can you sharpen the background?"

"I'm putting together a digital timeline of Dower taking Willow and Lucy to the alley behind the restaurant. Sarge wants it ASAP."

"Okay, but this photo is important, too."

She sighed. "Okay, fine. I'll do my best and will call when I have something, okay?" Eden didn't wait for his response before disconnecting from the call.

"I'm getting it." Willow glanced up at him. "Eden probably has better skills, but it almost looks like a woman in the background."

"A woman?" He frowned, peering over her shoulder. The figure way in the back of the room did seem to have long blond hair. For a moment a flash of recognition flickered. "Deputy Mayor Theresa Gray."

"I knew you'd figure it out eventually." The scathing tone caused him to glance up in shocked surprise. The woman in the photograph was standing off to the side. In her hand she held a small yet lethal gun pointed directly at them. "Don't move, or I won't hesitate to shoot." She lifted the gun a little higher and pointed it first at Murphy, then back at Willow. "At this range, I won't miss."

Nate's heart thudded painfully in his chest. He'd found the true perpetrator a little too late.

"You're going to get into the SUV, slowly," Theresa Gray said. "Secure the dog in the back. Willow will slide in beside the brat, and you, Detective Slater, will get behind the wheel. We're going to take a little drive. Trust me, no one will stop a police car."

He glanced at Lucy, tucked into her car seat. She hadn't noticed the danger yet. He needed to find a way to neutralize the threat before Lucy had to suffer yet another traumatic event.

He faced the deputy mayor, hoping, praying someone would notice what was going on. But they were mostly hidden behind the SUV. And everyone assumed the danger was over.

If only he'd taken Willow and Lucy back to their apartment as he'd originally planned! Too late, now. He'd protect them both with his life, if he had to. He gathered his scattered thoughts together and cleared his throat, stalling for time. "This won't work. The original digital file has already been sent to our tech specialist. Killing us now will only make it worse. They'll easily figure out that you are the one behind all of this."

Instead of alarm, a slow, evil smile creased her features. "I've already thought of that. I always have a plan, unlike Dower, who's an incompetent idiot. It will be easy enough to pin this entire mess on Carl and Oscar Banjo."

His heart quickened. "How?"

"I'll claim I caught Dower in the restaurant talking to Berk as evidenced in the photo and suspected they were planning something. That I tried to figure out what it was, and soon realized Oscar Banjo was involved in something illegal."

"Selling stolen goods in the Basement Bargains store owned by Oscar Banjo," he said, finally putting the pieces together.

"Yes." Theresa's smile was smug. "My story will be that before I could go to the police, Dower kidnapped the woman." She waved a hand at the alley. "The rest happened because of Dower, and Banjo panicked. Once you're both gone and Banjo is arrested, there won't be anyone who can claim anything different. It will be my word against Oscar's, and, well, I'm the deputy mayor."

He didn't want to admit that she just might be able to pull it off.

"What about Berk?" Willow asked. "He knows the truth."

The deputy mayor lifted a thin shoulder. "Don't you know that accidents happen in jail all the time? Tsk, tsk." Her gaze hardened. "Now move!"

Nate lifted his hands in a gesture of surrender. The last thing he wanted to do was make the trigger-happy woman angry. Yet he knew there had to be a way out of this.

One that wouldn't cause any harm to come to Willow or Lucy.

Willow stepped around to the side of the vehicle. He took a step to follow her, glancing down at Murphy. They'd have to make their move soon.

Before it was too late.

Willow couldn't believe everyone around them was completely oblivious to what was going on. Granted there were fewer cops milling about, but several were standing and chatting nearby, unaware that they were being kidnapped by a crazy woman with a gun.

"Get in!" The terse order startled her.

"O-okay." Willow glanced at Nate and knew by the intensity of his gaze that he was going to risk his life to save them.

No! It couldn't end like this. She refused to let it end like this!

She abruptly leaped forward to the front seat of the vehicle, slamming her fist onto the center of the steering wheel. The horn blared loudly, echoing off the brick buildings on either side of them.

In the same moment, Nate launched himself at the deputy mayor. "Get her, Murphy!"

The sharp retort of a gunshot could be heard above the sound of the horn. Finally, the officers who'd been standing just thirty feet away came running toward them.

"Nate! Nate!" He'd pinned Theresa Gray against the asphalt, his hands fighting for control of the weapon. Willow didn't see any blood, but feared the worst. "Someone please help him!"

After barking loudly in Theresa's face, Murphy shifted and grabbed her ankle in his teeth, clamping down tight enough to make her scream in outrage.

"Get him off me!"

That was all the advantage Nate needed. He yanked the gun from her grip and tossed it out of reach just as two officers joined the fray, surrounding them and helping Nate up and off Gray. In seconds they had the deputy mayor handcuffed.

Willow let out a ragged sigh of relief. This time, it was finally over.

Then she frowned. Bright crimson drops stained the white paint of the police SUV. What in the world? "Nate? Are you hurt?"

He stared at her blankly for a moment before glancing down at himself. Slowly, he put a hand up to the upper part of his left arm. The blue uniform was dark and when he pulled his palm away, it was covered in blood.

She gasped in horror. "She shot you!"

"Yeah." He looked surprised. "I hadn't noticed until now."

Tears pricked her eyes, but she quickly brushed them away. "We need an ambulance!" Feeling desperate, she turned to the front seat of the SUV. There had to be something she could use to help stop the bleeding.

"The glove box." Nate's voice was calm and sturdy despite the fact that he'd been shot. "And don't panic, it's just a flesh wound."

A flesh wound that was bleeding like a sieve. Opening the glove compartment, she found a first aid kit. Pulling out some gauze, she turned toward him and placed several white squares against the opening in the ripped sleeve of his shirt.

Seeing the wound up close, she realized he was right. The injury didn't look too serious, but was bad enough to need at least two layers of stitches. The amount of blood made her think an artery might have been hit.

"I knew you were going to jump toward her." She kept pressure against the pack of gauze. "I just knew it."

"Is that why you hit the horn?"

"Yes. I was hoping to get someone to pay attention." The corner of his mouth quirked up in a lopsided grin. "Smart move. It startled her and caused her aim to go high and to the side. Probably saved my life."

Her eyes misted again. "I didn't know what else to do. I absolutely didn't want to get into the car with her."

"Shh, it's okay." As if he wasn't injured, he pulled her close for a moment, brushing a kiss over her forehead. "It's over now for good."

She savored his embrace for a moment before pulling away, making room for the paramedics to move in. Feeling helpless to do anything more, she turned to

Lucy, who had started to cry when the gun went off. Reaching into the back of the SUV, she gently pried her niece out of the car seat and into her arms.

"Shh, Lucy, it's okay. We're fine. Everything is going to be just fine."

Lucy gripped her tightly around the neck, buried her face in Willow's shoulder. It occurred to Willow that she'd said those same reassurances to Lucy several times now, but things hadn't been fine.

Just the opposite. They'd been in danger ever since the moment she'd brought Lucy home to live with her.

And as far as she knew, the police were no closer to finding the mean clown with blue hair that had killed Lucy's parents. She knew the Brooklyn K-9 Unit was working hard on the case, though.

"I'm sorry, baby. I'm so sorry." She rested her cheek on Lucy's wavy hair. "You've been so brave."

"I wanna go home." Lucy's words were muffled against her neck.

Willow helplessly wondered if Lucy meant her apartment or her real home, the house she'd once shared with her parents.

"I know, baby. I know."

She hugged Lucy close, grateful the threat against them was over.

"I can walk." Ignoring Nate's protests, the paramedics assisted him onto the gurney. "It's not that bad."

"I think it's better to let the doctor decide that. You may need minor surgery to repair that wound." The paramedic near the head of the gurney rolled his eyes. "Why do our patients always think they know more than we do?"

"No clue," the paramedic at the foot responded.

"Hey, stop talking about me as if I'm not here." Nate scowled and winced as they tightened the straps around him. "It's just a flesh wound, and I'm not leaving without my partner. Murphy, come!"

The paramedics exchanged a long look. "Listen, buddy, your dog can't come with us."

"I can't leave him here." Nate levered himself upright. "I'll refuse to go with you. You can't force me."

"Nate, please." She reached out to lightly touch his uninjured arm. Her heart ached for him, and she realized how much she cared for this man she'd only known a short time. "Do as they say, okay? I'll take care of Murphy for you."

He shook his head. "I don't think Sarge will let you do that. Murphy is a cop. He'll have to go back to the precinct."

Vivienne stepped forward, her gaze full of concern. "I'll smooth things over with Sarge. We can let Willow take Murphy for now. I can always pick him up later."

Willow wanted to weep with relief when Nate stopped fighting and nodded. "Okay, fine."

"We'll take good care of him." She forced a reassuring smile. "And we'll see you soon."

"No." The word came out so harsh she reared back as if he'd slapped her. "Listen, Willow, do me a favor and take Lucy and Murphy home, okay? You have both been through a lot, but you're safe now. There's no reason for you to come to the hospital. I'll be fine."

"Why not? I don't understand…" Her voice trailed off as the paramedic team began wheeling him toward the waiting rig.

She stared after them in shocked surprise. What was going on? Why didn't he want her to come to the hospital, to be there for him? Was this Nate's way of telling her their time together was over?

The thought of never seeing him again made her blood run cold. She'd hoped things would turn out differently once she and Lucy were safe. That maybe Nate would decide to give a relationship a try. Hadn't Nate admitted to putting his faith in God?

Then again, he'd made it clear he wasn't the kind of guy who wanted a family. Maybe he'd only used his father's anger and physical abuse as an excuse.

Maybe this was much more personal. That it was just Willow and Lucy he didn't want.

Nate and Murphy had saved their lives. It was more than anyone had ever done for her. She loved Nate, but would have to find a way to get over it. Time to stop wishing for things she couldn't have, to focus on the blessings God had granted.

She reached down to stroke Murphy's pale fur.

They were alive, and relatively unharmed, at least physically. Emotionally? Well, she knew Lucy would carry the psychological scars for a long time to come.

The best thing she could do for Nate was to support his decision. Despite the fact that every cell in her body wanted to scream in protest, she told herself to move on.

Nate had sacrificed himself for them.

The least she could do was let him go without a fuss.

EIGHTEEN

Considering he hadn't realized that he'd been shot, it was amazing that now that he was aware of the injury, his left arm throbbed worse than a sore tooth. Nate hated being in the ambulance and in the Emergency Department; playing the role of helpless victim wasn't his thing. He was relieved when the doctor had announced that once the wound was cleaned and stitched and he'd been given antibiotics, as bullets were obviously considered to be a source of infection, he was free to go.

As he waited for the antibiotic to drip through his IV, he tried to forget the wounded expression in Willow's eyes when he'd told her not to come see him. He closed his eyes against the harsh overhead lights, telling himself he'd done the right thing. Better to have a clean break.

The danger was over. She didn't need him anymore.

But the idea of not seeing her and Lucy again hurt at a visceral level, far worse than the physical discomfort in his upper arm.

The events outside the SUV replayed over and over in his head like a stuck video loop. The moment of searing anger that had hit him seconds before he'd launched himself at the deputy mayor at the exact same time Willow had hit the horn.

Taking her down to the asphalt and fighting for the gun.

He'd managed to hold his anger in check as the officers had pulled him off the woman who'd tried to kill him and Willow, but he'd been secretly horrified at his reaction.

The idea that he might be more like his father than he realized wouldn't leave him alone.

And it had forced him to realize Willow and Lucy were better off without him. He may have fallen for Willow and the adorable Lucy, but they would be fine. Better, probably, without him.

"Detective Slater?" He opened his eyes when a nurse lightly touched his arm. "There's someone here to see you."

Willow? His heart soared with anticipation, but when he turned to look at the person standing in the doorway, a K-9 at her side, disappointment stabbed deep. Still, he forced a smile. "Vivienne, what are you doing here?"

"Checking in." Her brow furrowed with concern. "Sarge wants an update on your condition."

"I'm fine." He didn't want or need sympathy from his team. Bad enough that he hadn't figured out what was going on until it was too late.

Until he'd almost lost the woman and little girl he cared about more than anything.

More than himself.

"Hmm." She stared at the IV. "Are you sure about that?"

"Yeah." He shifted on the gurney. "They're letting me out of here as soon as the meds are in. It's just a flesh wound, only needed about a dozen stitches. Nothing bad enough to keep me off duty for very long."

"It sure bled enough." Vivienne stepped closer, her expression full of concern. "I'm sorry I stopped you from taking Willow and Lucy home. If I had let you go…" Her voice trailed off.

"Not your fault. You were right about sticking to protocol." Granted, the same thought had filtered through his mind, but it was ridiculous to play the what-if game. For all he knew, the deputy mayor might have followed them to Willow's, where the outcome could have been much worse. "Besides, I have a feeling she was hanging around there for a while, waiting for us. Leaving earlier likely wouldn't have changed anything."

"Maybe not," Vivienne conceded. "Listen, I have to head back to the station. Gavin called another staff meeting, wants us there in an hour."

He glanced up at the IV that was still dripping. "The antibiotic is almost finished. Do you mind giving me a ride? I'd like to be there."

"Sure, why not? Your SUV is being processed as part of the crime scene, anyway."

"Great." He couldn't deny being anxious to get out of here. "All this fuss over a flesh wound."

"I'm pretty sure that even a flesh wound can get infected." Vivienne tipped her head to the side, her expression turning thoughtful. "Why did you tell Willow not to visit?"

He glanced away, unable to maintain eye contact. "I won't be here long enough to warrant a visit. Besides, it's better for her and Lucy."

"Yeah, but why? It's obvious she cares about you, and I'm fairly certain the feeling is mutual."

No way was he revealing the truth about his father's abuse. Willow was the only one he'd told, and he planned to keep it that way.

"Never mind, I shouldn't have asked." She glanced up at the IV. "I'm going to call Sarge, tell him we'll be there shortly."

As she stepped away to use her phone, he realized Vivienne didn't have Murphy with her, which meant he'd have to pick up his partner himself. Despite the fact that he had tried to make a clean break with Willow, for her sake and Lucy's, it appeared he'd be seeing her again soon.

Probably for the last time.

It was pathetic how grateful he was to have one more chance to see her prior to saying goodbye. Before he walked away, leaving his heart behind.

When he and Vivienne arrived at the station, the rest of the team was already gathered around the large oval table.

Gavin raised a brow when he saw Nate. "You sure you're okay?"

"Doc said I'm fine, just a minor lifting restriction for a couple of days." He took a seat between Max Santelli, one of the newer members of the Brooklyn K-9 Unit, and his buddy, Officer Ray Morrow.

"You're on modified until the investigation into the shooting of Carl Dower has been completed anyway, so it's no problem." Gavin swept his gaze over the rest of the team. "There are a few things I wanted to let you all know about. You may have noticed that the media has caught wind of the Emery murders having a similar MO to the McGregor case."

K-9 detective Bradley McGregor scowled. Nate knew how hard all this had to be on him—his parents killed twenty years ago. The killer suddenly back, committing a very similar double homicide. Nate froze. Was it the same killer? Or could it be a copycat?

"Noticed? Penny and I have been dodging reporters for the past twenty-four hours."

"Sorry about that." Gavin spread his hands. "At least this time, they seem to have focused on the fact that you were working during the time frame of the murders, so you're not a suspect."

"Yeah, sure." Bradley looked glum. "I never should have been a suspect in the first place."

"I know." Gavin smiled reassuringly. "I also want to congratulate Ray Morrow and his K-9 partner, Abby, for stopping a drug runner who was delivering two large suitcases of prescription opioids through the subway."

Ray shifted, looking uncomfortable with the praise. "Thanks, but Abby's nose gets the credit."

"Nice job." Nate grinned. "Did you get the guy in charge?"

"Not yet." Ray shrugged. "Idiot is refusing to talk, other than making stupid threats."

Gavin's gaze narrowed. "What kind of threats?"

"You know, things like, 'Watch your back' and 'The boss is gonna get you for this.' The usual garbage."

"Two suitcases full of dope is a lot," Gavin pointed out. "You need to take those threats seriously. Back off the case for a while, until things cool off."

"Sure," Ray agreed, but as soon as Gavin changed topics, he leaned toward Nate. "I'm not backing off," he whispered. "I won't stop pulling deliverymen off the streets until I catch the kingpin in charge of bringing drugs through Brooklyn."

"Just be careful, okay?" Nate knew that once Ray put his mind to something, there was no changing it. "Keep your head down."

"I will." Ray straightened, a fierce determination in his eyes.

"Okay, that's it for now." Gavin slowly rose to his feet. "You're all dismissed. Oh, and Nate?"

He paused, turned back to his boss. "Yeah?"

"Where's Murphy?"

"I'm picking him up right now." Nate gave Gavin a nod and headed out of the precinct.

As he made his way to Willow's apartment, he hoped and prayed he'd have the strength of will to ignore his desire to continue seeing her on a personal level. To hold back from telling her how much he'd come to care about her and Lucy.

For her sake and his own sanity. No sense in longing for something he couldn't have.

A family.

Her apartment seemed incredibly lonely without Nate's presence. Murphy helped, but she knew the K-9's visit was temporary.

After she'd cleaned up Officer Kuhn's blood from the floor, spoke to Jayne Hendricks about a child psychologist for Lucy and made an early dinner for her niece, she stared blindly out the window at the city streets below, wondering how Nate was doing.

In hindsight, she shouldn't have been surprised by Nate's refusal to have her come visit. Hadn't she tried to mentally prepare herself for this? She knew from personal experience that men didn't stick around.

They didn't want the same things she did, like a home, a family.

Maybe his concern over turning out like his father was nothing more than an excuse to avoid becoming emotionally involved. After all, her father had been nonexistent, disappearing when she was two years old, Alex only four. Then after their mother died, they'd been raised by their grandparents.

Maybe Nate was right, that it was better to avoid becoming entangled in something that you knew you couldn't handle long term.

Yet as soon as the theory formed in her mind, she rejected it. Nate had held her in his arms, had kissed her, twice. He'd held and kissed Lucy, too, caring for her the way a father would.

It was irritating how Nate was selling himself short; he had a great capacity for love and caring.

But maybe not with her and Lucy.

Well. Enough with the pity party already. She'd just have to remember she'd played a role in helping Nate find his way to faith and God. Wasn't that more important?

A knock at the door startled her. Murphy scrambled to his feet, going on alert. For a moment a frisson of fear snaked down her spine, but she told herself the danger was over. Besides, she felt certain Murphy would alert her to danger, but he was staring at the door, his tail wagging with anticipation.

Still, she checked the peephole to see who was out there.

Nate?

Her pulse spiked, then beat so erratically she had to take a moment to calm herself before opening the door. "Hi. Have you been released from the hospital already?"

"Yep." Murphy rushed over to greet Nate as if the K-9 hadn't seen him in days instead of a couple of hours. She couldn't help smiling at how the two of them looked together. After giving Murphy a good rub, Nate rose to his feet. "Told you it was just a flesh wound. I never should have gotten in the stupid ambulance."

"I'm just glad you're okay." She wanted to throw herself into his arms but forced herself to stay back. "I suppose you're here for Murphy?"

"Yes, I need to take him home."

"I'm sure Murphy missed you." *I missed you.*

"No! I don't want Murphy to go!" Lucy's plaintive tone made her wince. The little girl threw her arms around Murphy's neck, burying her face against his fur. "I want him to stay!"

"I know, baby, but Murphy and Nate work together as a team. They're both police officers." She gently extricated the animal from Lucy's grip and pulled her up and into her arms.

Nate put Murphy on his leash. "Well, I guess this is it."

She didn't want to agree with him, but she wouldn't force him to stay, either. "I guess so. Take care of yourself."

"I will." Nate stared at her for a long moment, as if there was so much more he wanted to say. Or maybe it was just that her heart wanted him to say something more.

"Bye, Willow, Lucy." His smile didn't quite reach his eyes as he opened the door.

"Nate, please don't go." The words escaped before she could stop them.

He stood for a long moment, then glanced at her over his shoulder. The stark longing on his face ripped at her heart. "I have to."

"No, you don't." She set Lucy on her feet and moved toward him. She couldn't just let him walk away without even trying to reach him. "I—have something to tell you."

"Willow, you don't have to…"

"I love you." She practically flung the words at him. "I love you, Nate Slater! You can go ahead and walk out that door, but it won't stop me from loving you."

This time, his mouth gaped comically, as if she'd said something he didn't understand. "What? No, you don't."

"Yes, I do." She took another step toward him. "I understand you don't feel the same way about me, but I wanted, needed you to know the truth."

"But—" He shook his head. "It can't work, Willow. You don't know the real me, the person deep inside."

His words offered a glimmer of hope. "I do know the person you are deep inside. You're kind, loyal, brave, smart and so much more."

"Angry." He said the word with a bitterness that made her wince. "You forgot about angry."

She threw up her hands in exasperation. "What are you talking about? Everyone gets mad, and sad, and frustrated and annoyed—none of that means you're a bad person."

A flicker of uncertainty passed over his face. "But my father…"

"Was a mean and abusive man." She took another step, close enough now that she could place her hand on his uninjured shoulder. "Did you know that most abuse is more about power and control than anger? Sure, sometimes people get mad enough to lash out, but you've never done that, have you?"

A look of anguish filled his eyes. "I want to say no, but I was furious at the deputy mayor when I tackled her to the pavement."

Really? That's what this was about? "Nate, your action saved our lives. Not because you were mad at her, but to get the gun away from her." Now she found herself growing irritated. "You can't possibly equate that action to what your father did to you and your mother."

"Maybe not, but the flash of anger I felt inside…" He shrugged. "I was afraid there was more of my father in me than I realized."

"Nate, you're not your father. And you'll never be your father." She pressed her hand firmly against him, turning him so that he faced her. "And you know why? Because God will never let you be that man. God will guide you, and protect you, and cherish you. As long as you believe in Him, you'll never fall into the depths your father sank to."

He reached up and covered her hand with his, searching her gaze. "You really believe that?"

"Absolutely."

"Willow." He slowly but firmly drew her into his arms. "I want more than anything to kiss you."

That made her smile. "I'm not stopping you."

His warm embrace and possessive kiss filled her with hope and anticipation. But the kiss didn't last long, as Lucy came over to tug on the hem of her hoodie.

"Aunt Willow, I wanna hug, too."

Nate lifted his head and chuckled. He readily bent

down and picked Lucy up, then pulled Willow in close. "Okay, now we're all hugging together."

Tears blurred her vision at how easily he accepted Lucy into their embrace. This was exactly how she imagined her life to be.

His gaze met hers over Lucy's head. "I love you, too, Willow. I don't know why it's taken me so long to realize the importance of focusing on the good things in my life, like you and Lucy."

Her breath caught in her throat. "Are you sure?"

"Yes. I'm sure." He kissed her again, then kissed Lucy's cheek. "I love both of you."

"I love you," Lucy said. "And Murphy, too."

That made her laugh. "I guess it's unanimous."

"Yes." Nate's gaze lingered on hers. "I promise that I won't stop searching for the man responsible for stealing the lives of your brother and his wife."

"I know." While a part of her worried about Nate's safety, she understood that this was part of being in a relationship with a cop.

And she'd gladly take him as is.

"Are we a family?"

Lucy's innocent question caught her off guard. She glanced at Nate, unsure how to answer. But then Lucy pointed at the dog. "I wanna hug Murphy." Lucy wiggled in Nate's arms until he set her on her feet. She ran over to the yellow Lab and wrapped her arms around his neck.

The two of them were adorable together.

Nate cleared his throat. "I know you're just getting used to having Lucy around, but I need to ask you something."

Her heart raced. "Ask me what?"

He stared deep into her eyes. "Willow, will you do me the honor of becoming my wife?"

She blinked, fearing she'd misunderstood. Hearing he loved her was one thing, but she hadn't expected this. "You…want to get married?"

"Yes, I want to marry you." Love shimmered in his gaze, and as he tugged her close, he glanced down at Lucy and Murphy. "I'd like to make you and Lucy a part of my family. Lucy deserves a father, a family. If you'll have me."

"Oh, Nate. That's exactly what I want, too." She rested her head on Nate's shoulder. "You'll be a great father and husband. I hope I can be just as good of a mother and wife."

"I love you, Willow. And we'll do this together, with God's blessing." He kissed her again and Willow knew that she'd cherish this moment, forever.

* * * * *

Heather Woodhaven earned her pilot's license, rode a hot-air balloon over the safari lands of Kenya, parasailed over Caribbean seas, lived through an accidental detour onto a black-diamond ski trail in Aspen, and snorkeled among stingrays before becoming a mother of three and wife of one. She channels her love for adventure into writing characters who find themselves in extraordinary circumstances.

Books by Heather Woodhaven

Love Inspired Suspense

True Blue K-9 Unit: Brooklyn

Chasing Secrets

Twins Separated at Birth

Undercover Twin
Covert Christmas Twin

Calculated Risk
Surviving the Storm
Code of Silence
Countdown
Texas Takedown
Tracking Secrets
Credible Threat
Protected Secrets

Visit the Author Profile page
at Harlequin.com for more titles.

CHASING SECRETS

Heather Woodhaven

A man's heart deviseth his way:
but the Lord directeth his steps.
—*Proverbs* 16:9

To my editor, Emily Rodmell,
and my fellow LIS authors. Thank you
for sharing your encouragement and wisdom!

ONE

Karenna Pressley searched the area, ignoring her gut feeling that this was a waste of time. So far, there was no sign of Sarah.

She hated walking alone, even in Prospect Park—her favorite place in Brooklyn. She tugged her jacket zipper higher. At the rusted lamppost, she turned onto a less traveled path that led to the south side of the lake.

The park provided a nature haven in the city with almost six hundred acres of beauty, but even on a crowded day, she could find isolated spots. This evening the crowds weren't a problem thanks to the rainstorm that had passed through an hour ago. The sun still shone but wouldn't stay in the sky for more than a couple more hours, and the May breeze held a cold bite, despite being in the sixties.

Karenna would've preferred to meet up at a restaurant after work, but Sarah Mayfair had insisted upon "their bench," a place they used to meet after high school to discuss whatever drama the day had given. A lot had changed over the past decade, but she would always consider Sarah her best friend forever, even if they no longer wore the tarnished necklaces as proof.

She ducked underneath a low-hanging branch. A few rain droplets managed to hit the back of her neck, the cold moisture sending a shiver down her spine. The thick foliage above filtered out the majority of sunshine, casting shadows across the walkway. Her hearing heightened at the sudden change in lighting. She squinted up the path, hoping to see Sarah already at the bench ahead.

Empty.

If Sarah stood her up yet again, they would have words. Karenna hadn't seen her in months. Sarah's go-to excuse lately was "unexpected plans" with her mysterious boyfriend, a guy named Marcus. Clearly, Sarah had given up their pact of sisters before misters. Karenna was finally supposed to meet the mystery man tonight, so she forced herself to keep an open mind. Maybe she'd like him in person.

A couple argued in the distance, out of sight, past the tree line. One of the voices sort of sounded like Sarah's. Birds squawked, as if scolding them for disrupting the peace. Karenna reached the bench and attempted to brush off the raindrops. The arguing stopped but a splash followed.

Keeping her flats more on the grass than the mud proved a balancing act as she ducked through the branches to get to the bank.

A man, tall, well-dressed, with perfectly coiffed hair and black sunglasses stood in an awkward posture on the slanted bank leading to the water with his left foot on—

"Sarah!" The scream tore from Karenna's lungs.

Even though she couldn't see the face underneath the water, she recognized the red boots her friend always wore on special outings. His foot held down her chest, Sarah's entire head submerged in the water, her arms and legs flailing uselessly. The man's face turned her direction.

"Get off!" Karenna rushed at him, whipping her purse his direction. She aimed for his head, but the bag bounced off his back and hit the ground. She shoved him with both hands and he stumbled backward.

Karenna turned and grabbed one of Sarah's flailing arms and tugged, pulling her up. Sarah gasped and coughs racked her body, mud and water dripping from the back of her head and shoulders.

A force like a wrecking ball slammed Karenna sideways into a tree trunk. Waves of pain rushed across her ribs and down her spine. Her heart raced as her chest seized, unable to take a breath momentarily. Her eyes stung with tears at the realization he'd knocked the wind out of her until finally, mercifully, she could breathe again.

"No! Not her!" Sarah stumbled her way. The man spun, placed his hand on the side of her face and propelled her backward. She hit the ground with such force, her body went limp.

Karenna pulled in another breath to scream but his hand clamped over her mouth. She fought to get her bearings, but he dragged her with his other impossibly strong arm toward the water. With one shove, he slammed her back against the mud, the sharp angle of the bank allowing gravity to do the rest of the work. She forced herself to gasp before he slammed his shoe on her chest.

Cold water rushed over her forehead and then her entire face. She fought to raise her head but couldn't lift it far enough to break the surface. The little breath left in her lungs tried fighting its way out of her mouth from the pressure his foot placed on her lungs.

Karenna knew not to thrash against him—she'd run out of oxygen faster if she did—but instinct refused to cooperate with logic as she twisted and kicked against him. She tried to reach his foot with her left hand.

Her lungs burned and her neck began to spasm, begging for her mouth to open. Her right hand reached out desperately, sand and pebbles digging under her fingertips. She grabbed blindly at a handful and tossed it wildly, hoping it would go in his direction. The instant the mass left her hand, she grabbed more and threw again.

The pressure on her chest increased. She grabbed again and flung a handful of pebbled mud. Her other hand found a larger rock and she pulled against the suction of the wet earth to loosen it and threw as hard as she could.

The weight left Karenna's chest. Her stomach groaned from the exertion as she lifted her head out of the water and drew in a giant breath. Coughs racked her body and sparks of red-hot pain shot through her temples, promising a future headache.

He still stood over her, as he threw off his sunglasses and wiped at his forehead and eyes.

Her left hand reached for something to help pull her fully upright, but she could only grab more of the mixture of mud, sand and pebbles. "Help!" Her scream came out in a desperate screech followed by another sharp inhale. She couldn't gulp enough air to satisfy her stinging lungs.

The man's chin had bright red streaks mixed with

mud dripping on his chest. One of the rocks she'd thrown had done the job, but he was still standing. He bared his teeth and rushed at her, both fists out, aiming for her shoulders.

She screamed as loud and hard as she could, scooting backward into the water. If she could get past his reach fast enough, she might be able to swim away.

Approaching voices grew louder. People! The man froze, only inches from the waterline, but his murderous glare never wavered. He spun, grabbed the sunglasses off the bank, and bolted, running through a grouping of trees and away from the oncoming group of loud park-goers.

Karenna's entire body began to shake, even as she strained to flip over to her hands and knees. She crawled across the mud. People had heard her. Help was coming.

Her teeth chattered, water rushing down the sides of her face. She reached the sparse grass, looking up expectantly for her rescuers to burst through the trees.

Nothing.

She crawled toward Sarah, still limp on the ground. Her hand reached her friend's arm, cold and clammy. Where was the help?

The pounding in her head started. She fought to focus and think straight, but the ground kept moving. Had anyone heard her? Were they ignoring her, thinking she was playing a game?

"Help!" The attempt to scream again was somewhere between a squeak and a whisper. Her heart stopped beating for half a second. Their attacker might realize no one had paid attention and come back to finish the job.

Her cross-body purse, covered in mud, lay next to a

puddle five feet away. Her shaking fingers fought with the zipper pull until it finally gave way. She shoved her hand into the damp bag. *Please still work.* Her hand wrapped around the phone, mercifully dry but sporting a cracked screen. She tapped the emergency call feature.

Seconds seemed to pass before the ringing started. Karenna leaned over Sarah's face. She couldn't tell for sure that she was breathing until she noted a small rise and fall of her chest. "Wake up, please," she croaked.

Karenna's eyes burned as she heard a voice come through the phone.

"Nine-one-one. What's your emergency?"

"My friend is unconscious. Someone tried to kill us." The tree branches to her right moved, despite the still air. "I think he's coming back to finish the job."

Officer Raymond Morrow grabbed his K-9 partner's favorite toy, a rope with a ball on the end, swung it, and tossed it as far as he could. Abby, an English springer spaniel, rocketed through the tall grass. He marveled at her speed. As the field variety of the breed, her legs worked much like the bow of an arrow. With every leap, they pulled inward with tension and then released with power, shooting her across the grass of Prospect Park. Her semi-docked tail had white fringe on the end and re-sembled a waving flag, making it easy to keep his eyes trained on her. Abby deserved a play break between patrolling for narcotics before they finished their long shift, and the respite served as the only time Ray could allow his mind to drift and process cases.

Recently, a double murder had brought a cold case back to the forefront for the Brooklyn K-9 Unit. Last month, a three-year-old girl's parents had been killed at their home while she'd played outside, and the MO was remarkably similar to a twenty-year-old unsolved case involving two of Ray's coworkers. Siblings Penelope and Bradley McGregor worked for the unit, Penny as a records clerk and Bradley as a detective. Their parents' killer had left no leads except some DNA collected from a watchband. The NYPD had run the DNA dozens of times through the years. All attempts came up empty. No matches in the databases.

Something had been nagging at the back of Ray's mind, though, something he couldn't latch onto, frustrating him to no end. He felt certain one of the true crime shows he'd watched in past years held the key, but he couldn't remember which one. To be fair, he'd consumed copious amounts of crime stories, paying particular attention to mistakes other cops made so he wouldn't follow suit.

Golden light filtered through the trees surrounding the grassy field. Abby swiftly grabbed the ball, the rope hanging from her soft mouth as she bounced back toward him. Bits of mud left over from the rain peppered the tops of her paws. She'd need a bath.

His radio sounded. "Attempted homicide. Prospect Park—"

Rapid-fire responses burst through the speaker. Ray was on the Windsor Terrace side of the park, but he'd left his patrol car on the Park Slope side and could get there within minutes. He chimed in that he'd assist.

"Time to go to work," he told Abby. The spaniel dropped the ball at his feet and waited for him to hook the leash back on her harness. In the distance, the Peristyle, a park shelter that looked transplanted from Ancient Greece, held a group of picnicking park-goers.

Abby didn't so much as give them a second glance. Her bubbly demeanor changed as they rounded the corner. The earlier rain had heightened her tracking skills. Instead of washing scents away, the high moisture actually trapped and held scents closer to the ground. While she wasn't quite alerting, she seemed to be heading toward a less-traveled trail that disappeared through the bushes.

A quick burst of sirens in that direction confirmed Abby's instincts. They split off the path and spotted an ambulance parked next to a bench. Abby pointed after them. Were there drugs involved in the attempted homicide? Knowing Abby's narcotics specialty, he had to wonder. He strode ahead and followed after the paramedics through a tight grouping of bushes and trees.

They surrounded a woman, seemingly unconscious on the ground. She looked vaguely familiar. Abby did a little dance, her nose forward, and then sat, which meant she'd caught the scent of a narcotic. Before he could acknowledge her passive alert, his eyes drifted to the other woman being interviewed by a patrol officer who'd beat him there.

Ray's mouth went dry. Five years had passed since he'd last held her in his arms. Her soaked blond hair, dripping onto the yellow emergency blanket wrapped around her shoulders, looked darker, but he'd recognize those pale blue eyes even if ten or twenty years had gone by.

Karenna Pressley—the woman he'd once thought he'd marry—shivered in place, her hands rubbing her bare forearms. The patrol officer looked over his shoulder and acknowledged him with a nod, and Karenna followed his gaze. Her mouth opened in recognition, but she said nothing.

What had happened here? His gut turned hot as he remembered it was an attempted homicide. His breath grew shallow. If anyone had hurt her—

The other officer, with the last name Holloway on his uniform, approached Ray.

"I found her guarding her friend with a rock and a stick," Holloway said in a hushed tone. He relayed a horrific story about a man attempting to drown her friend and then, in turn, trying to drown Karenna instead. Ray glanced over at the unconscious woman again. Now he knew why she'd seemed vaguely familiar. She was Karenna's best friend.

Holloway gestured toward the grouping of bushes and trees surrounding them. "Ms. Pressley had the feeling the guy would want to come back and finish the job. She had barely survived his attempt to kill her when loud park-goers startled him and he fled. Whoever attacked her and the friend, a Sarah—"

"Mayfair," Ray finished for him through gritted teeth. Barely survived?

"You know her?"

"Acquaintance. I know Karenna." Every muscle tensed as he thought about what would've happened if the attacker had succeeded.

Holloway studied his face for a minute before he nodded.

A wiry paramedic leaning over Sarah's form looked up at Karenna. "Did she have drugs in her system?" the man asked.

"What?" Karenna rushed toward them. "No, I told you. He was trying to drown her when I found them.

I went after him and he pulled her out and threw her down."

"You said she was breathing when he pulled her out?"

"Yes. She was fully conscious, but he threw her down hard. She went limp."

The other paramedic frowned. "Verbal and motor are no response. Pupils pinpointed. Blood oxygen level, heart rate and breathing abnormal…" Her words were meant for her partner, but, given the look they shared, the paramedics thought there was more to the story. Maybe Sarah had overdosed before the attack.

Once again Abby did her little front paw dance and strained her nose at a purse five feet away. "Is that Sarah's purse?" Ray asked her.

Karenna jolted slightly, as if she'd forgotten Ray was there for a second. "Yes. I mean I think so."

The other officer gave an almost indistinguishable nod for Ray to take over.

"Find," Ray said softly. Abby took one bound to the purse, touched her nose to it and sat back, her tail wagging and her mouth seemingly in a smile.

"Good girl." He pulled out the special toy he only used as a specific reward for a find. Abby popped it in her mouth and flopped down, happy. Ray slipped on gloves to protect himself from potential harmful substances and picked up the purse.

Inside was an empty prescription bottle without a label. He lifted it for further examination. "It's possible she had a dangerous level of narcotics in her system."

The paramedic eyed the bottle for half a second while he continued to prep Sarah to be moved to the backboard.

"You don't know that." Karenna pointed at Abby. "It could be a prescription medicine your dog alerted on. It could've been her boyfriend's—"

"Boyfriend?"

"Yes, I was supposed to meet Sarah's boyfriend today."

"Is he the one who attacked you, then?" Ray took a wallet out of the purse and opened it. "What's his name?"

"Marcus. I—I already told the other officer I don't know for sure if it was him. I've never met Marcus before, but I was supposed to today." She closed her eyes tight and bit her lip for a second. "His last name is escaping me."

"Don't worry," Ray said softly. He continued down his mental checklist of items in the purse. "No phone."

"I couldn't find her phone, either," Karenna said. "I looked while waiting for help to arrive. I thought maybe she'd have a photo of him on it and then I'd know for sure. I think the attacker took the phone with him."

Sounded more and more like the boyfriend was the attacker, but Ray didn't want to make assumptions. "No medical alert listed." Ray scanned the driver's license. "ID confirmed as Sarah Mayfair." He returned the wallet to the purse, zipped it up and set it on the edge of the stretcher. "Why do you think the bottle could've been the boyfriend's?"

"Because Sarah's *never* been a user. She wouldn't. Maybe she confronted him before I got here. We were supposed to meet at that bench." She pointed through the trees. "But instead—" Her mouth pursed, and her forehead creased as her gaze flicked to the lake.

The male paramedic injected Sarah with something, perhaps naloxone, the overdose medicine many responders carried, though sometimes was too late for it to work.

The female paramedic approached Karenna and began asking her questions, trying to assess her well-being. Karenna shook her head. "I'm fine, I'm fine. Just get her to the hospital."

"Ma'am, we're doing that. I need to make sure you're okay, too. You said he stepped hard on your chest to keep you under water?"

Ray's ears roared. He had no right to feel so protective, especially after all the years apart, but the surge in his adrenaline didn't seem to care. Sure, her wealthy father had said Ray's career wasn't a fit for her future and that a cop could never give her the lifestyle to which she was accustomed. The man had even insinuated he would be forced to disown his daughter if Ray didn't back off.

Her father wasn't the main reason for the breakup, though Ray had never told Karenna about the threat. It was simply a wake-up call to all the other problems they'd been up against. First and foremost, she'd never understood his intense dedication to his job, but *her* father hadn't died from an oxycodone overdose like his had.

Abby whined, staring at him, concerned at the change in his demeanor. He leaned down and patted the spaniel's head. Maybe if he and Karenna had still been together, he would've figured out Sarah's boyfriend was a potential dealer and caught him before Sarah or Karenna had been hurt.

Karenna waved away medical treatment, promising

she'd go to a doctor if she had new symptoms. "But I'd like to ride with Sarah to the hospital."

The paramedic shook her head in reply. "You'll have to drive yourself since you refused treatment. They also might not let you see her without a family member's permission until she's conscious."

"Ready," the other paramedic called. They moved as one, rushing Sarah toward the ambulance—a challenge considering the bushes.

"I've got her statement," Officer Holloway said to Ray. "I also requested a team to search the park. There's not too much to go on, though. Tall, well-dressed, with sunglasses." The guy pointed at Abby. "If you think this is drug-related, you want to take it from here?"

In other words, Holloway was all too happy to not have to be the one to write the report. Ray was grateful, though. He needed to see the case through if he was going to sleep at night.

"I need to contact her parents." Karenna said it so softly Ray almost missed it.

"Yeah, I'll take it from here," Ray said.

The officer nodded and followed the paramedics, leaving them alone. They were silent at first, staring at each other.

"Why'd you think the attacker would come back?" he finally asked.

Karenna's eyes glistened and she tilted her head to the sky. "I don't…" Her voice faltered for a second and she exhaled before trying again. "While I waited for help, I realized the attack on Sarah didn't seem planned. I mean if a person wanted to murder—"

Ray couldn't keep asking her to relive the moment,

but he thought he could catch her train of thought. "You think it was a heat of the moment crime."

Karenna nodded.

"So when he attacked you…"

Her eyelashes fluttered as she wrapped the blanket tighter around her frame. "I think he was angry I stopped him from killing Sarah, but more important, I saw his face. And if that was the case…"

She didn't need to say it. The man would want to clean up his mistake, finish the job. A promise rose to Ray's lips in a heartbeat. "I'll find him and make sure that never happens. You're safe with me now."

TWO

Safe with Raymond Morrow? The same guy who'd ripped her heart out five years ago by breaking up with her wanted to keep her safe? The promise sounded more dangerous than helpful.

After a year of dating him, she'd really thought they had a future, but after they'd gone to the next level of meeting each other's families, he'd simply said it was obvious they weren't going to work out. That was the last time she'd heard from or seen him in five years.

The lack of closure had almost turned her into a needy mess at first. Only her pride had kept her from seeking him out and begging for specific reasons. Instead, after a few weeks of daily visits to get a brownie from The Chocolate Room, she'd rallied and focused on what kind of person she wanted to be and the kind of life she wanted to live.

That painful time of reflection had emboldened her enough to step out from under her father's influence and make her own way in the world. So far it'd been a hard but worthwhile transition. She'd changed a lot since she and Ray had broken up, but one thought still stung. If Ray had ever really loved her, wouldn't he have stuck around long enough to explain his concerns, to give them a fighting chance?

Karenna couldn't voice her thoughts aloud, though, or he might assume she wasn't over him. His declaration, however, helped jolt her out of reliving the attack on an endless loop. She self-consciously glanced down at the yellow blanket draped over her before returning his gaze. "I never thought we'd run into each other like this."

His hair, wavy and thick on top but curled on the sides, was on the verge of being too long for the job. Ray always waited to schedule a trim until the last minute, but she'd never complained because she loved trailing her fingers through his hair while they talked or watched television together. Take-out and relaxing after work had been a favorite way to spend time together. He'd always fidget with his dad's army challenge coin, rolling and flipping it back and forth over his knuckles. After a while he'd unwind enough to talk about their day, their hopes and dreams...

She blinked the thoughts away. The dark blue uniform complemented his eyes, a dark brown that reminded her of chocolate. He'd only grown more handsome with age.

Figured.

Meanwhile, her mascara—since she hated the waterproof type—had likely created dark circles under her eyes, and she didn't even want to think about the state of her hair. Shallow thoughts—especially given the would-be killer on the loose—but she couldn't help it. In daydreams, she'd always looked attractive and happy when she bumped into Ray after so many years. Reality wasn't as kind.

His expression, much like his posture, looked hard

and unmoving as he hitched a thumb over his shoulder. "Can I give you a ride somewhere?"

She hesitated. Her pride wanted to prove that she didn't need his help at all, but the sun dipped dangerously close to the horizon. Either she waited alone for a ride she couldn't afford, walked home while constantly looking over her shoulder, or accepted his offer. "Yes, please."

He gestured to the opening in the trees closest to her. The cute dog at his side, with fluffy ears, moved to Ray's left as if knowing exactly how he would command, and they walked side by side on the path. Parkgoers in every direction seemed to be paying attention to her now. Perhaps it was the combination of dog, officer and yellow blanket that did the trick, but in any case, she only felt more self-conscious and scanned the surroundings for his squad car.

"I need to track down this boyfriend. Marcus," he said. "Has a last name come to mind yet? Did Sarah ever send you a photo of him or them?"

"Only once, after I teased her that he was an imaginary boyfriend because I still hadn't met him. She insists on using the Now You See app—you know, the one that shows texts or pictures only for a minute before it disappears. So annoying because you can't go back and reread what was discussed. I only have the app because of her."

He nodded and made a note on his phone. "So if you saw a photo of him… *Was* the boyfriend the same one who attacked you?"

That seemed like an easy question, but she couldn't answer with certainty. "It was back when they first started dating. The photo was far away and, if I'm being honest, I didn't really care what he looked like at the time so I wasn't paying much attention. He might not have even known Sarah took it."

"Anything else you can tell me? Identifying details?"

"He seemed to have money. I can't explain it, but I know he was wearing high-end stuff."

He shrugged. "Well, I'm sure you would know."

She stiffened at his comment. His tone was congenial and light, but something felt off.

"After a harrowing experience," he continued, "the mind takes a while to calm down. So if you think of anything else in the next couple of days, let me know."

The sounds of birds and nearby traffic didn't overcome the awkwardness of walking together. She gestured at his dog, a breed that looked like a cross between a collie and a poodle. "I always thought K-9 dogs were German shepherds or Labrador retrievers."

"Often, they are, but English springer spaniels have an incredible sense of smell. Police in the UK use them often."

"Congratulations, then. A K-9 team was always your goal, right? Narcotics division, I assume."

His expression hardened, maybe because of the implication that she used to know him so well. "Yes. Thank you." They walked in silence a few more steps. "I was offered the job when more positions opened up in preparation for a new K-9 Unit in Brooklyn. I got assigned my furry partner several months ago." He flashed a genuine smile. "We clicked instantly, and Abby and I have been inseparable ever since."

The cute dog glanced up at Karenna and tilted her head down in a fast nod as if to say, "You've got that right."

"Here we are." Even Ray's squad car had changed, now an SUV model. A sticker on the back door read Police Dog Keep Back.

Karenna took a step away from Abby and pointed. "Is she that dangerous?"

His eyebrows rose. "Abby?" He laughed. "No. She's a soft-mouth dog, but all K-9 vehicles have the warning. We need the public to stay back, no matter the breed, when we get the dogs out. Especially if we need our partner to get right to work."

He opened the backseat and Abby jumped in before he moved to open the passenger door for her. "I… Uh, I didn't realize officers called the dogs their partners," she said.

He helped her into the vehicle and closed the door behind her. She'd been in a patrol car before, as a ride-along once when Ray had worked in the traffic division. The computer system above the console seemed pretty similar. He quickly got in behind the wheel.

"I call her my partner because Abby *is* my partner." He stared out the windshield. "She risks her life for me and the public. Referring to her as my partner reminds me of that." He offered a slight smile and turned on the car. "I assume you still live in Park Slope?" His vowels grew longer when he was annoyed.

She glanced at him. True, there were swanky portions of the neighborhood, like her father's company apartment she used to live in, but there were also apartments that were bare bones—still ridiculously expensive, but she managed to scrape by to make ends meet. "Yes, I live in Park Slope, but not at the same place I used to."

He smirked slightly, but she didn't owe him any explanations. Even though she had walked away from her father's company and the cushy job and apartment it had provided, she didn't want Ray to think it was because of him.

"Where to?" he asked.

She took a deep breath and tried to refocus. All that mattered right now was Sarah. Even if she came out of her coma, that man who'd tried to kill them was still out there. Karenna grabbed her purse and searched for her keys in the small zippered pocket. Sure enough, she still had Sarah's spare key on the ring.

For the past few years she'd lived on her own but still wasn't able to make ends meet without pulling from her trust fund. Her job focused on working with nonprofits, and she'd felt like a fraud whenever campaign budgets were discussed when she couldn't even make her finances work without dipping into her father's money.

So six months ago she'd made a drastic decision and moved into the smallest place yet. Sarah had taken one look and insisted on giving her a key to her bigger and nicer apartment, telling Karenna she could crash whenever she wanted.

Sarah was the closest thing she had to a sister, but Karenna had still been too proud to accept. She had used the key to take in Sarah's mail and water her plants when her friend was out of town. Sarah hadn't gone away lately, though, since Marcus had come into her life.

The thought of him made up her mind. "I want to go to Sarah's place. She probably has a photo of her boyfriend in the apartment. I can confirm whether it's the same guy and you can put an alert out on him. Right?"

"Theoretically, yes. But I don't have a search—"

"No, I'm not asking you to. I've got her key and she said I could consider myself an unofficial roommate. I'm going to look for a photo and make sure this guy can't hurt her again." She rattled off Sarah's address.

He frowned. "If the boyfriend is the attacker, it's possible he has access to Sarah's apartment, too. I can't stop you from going, of course, but…"

"If it's going to cause you problems, just drop me off. I feel like I'm failing her by not knowing whether the attacker is the same guy or not."

He sighed. "Technically my shift is over. And since he could be there getting rid of evidence himself, I'd feel better if I went in with you. In an unofficial capacity. As a friend."

She almost flinched at those last words. They were not friends, and the last thing she wanted was more time alone with Ray. Even the smell of his aftershave, like the smell of a forest after a rain, taunted her with memories. The fastest way to get him out of her life was to confirm the identity of the attacker. "Fair enough. I mean… I'd appreciate that."

His left eyebrow raised but he didn't reply.

Ten minutes later, they pulled up in front of Sarah's brownstone. Karenna left the emergency blanket and her damp jacket in the vehicle when Ray opened the doors for her and Abby.

Past the wrought iron front gate, she ran up the stairs to the front door and used the silver key. Once inside the building, they took the elevator to the third floor. Sarah's apartment was the first one on the left.

Ray touched her shoulder gently. "Please let Abby and me go in first as a precaution."

She gave Ray the key to the apartment. He unlocked

the door then stepped inside and poked his head in the two rooms before waving her in. "All clear. We'll wait while you look."

Every piece of furniture looked brand-new, including the leather couch. Sarah had no qualms about using her modest trust fund to supplement her freelance art income. Although, Karenna wouldn't have thought her friend could afford high-end new furniture, either.

She moved to the bedroom. While her clothes were mostly dry, her shoulders and arms were freezing. She grabbed a blue cardigan—one she'd actually loaned to Sarah ages ago—from the closet and slipped it over her arms.

The pink and orange shades from the sunset shone through the open blinds as Ray entered the bedroom with Abby. "Any success?"

His K-9 partner strained toward the nightstand and did a little dance before she sat down, her nose pushing against the drawer.

On the nightstand there was a photo of Sarah and her parents in front of the Eiffel Tower.

"Karenna?" Ray pointed to the drawer but made no move to open it. "I know you want to protect Sarah, but whatever is in there might help the doctors treat her."

Her heart raced. She wanted to help Sarah, but what if whatever was in that drawer would actually ruin Sarah's life if in the hands of a cop?

Ray saw the fear in Karenna's eyes at his request. Despite her ruffled appearance, she had an ethereal beauty that had only magnified over the years. And right now she looked in desperate need of warm, comforting arms around her. If only he didn't know how right it felt to hold her close.

She looked between Abby and Ray. "I told you I wasn't expecting you to do a search. I had no intention to give consent. I agreed you could come because I was worried—"

"That the boyfriend might show up." Ray blew out a breath. "You're right. This isn't an official search. Obviously, you have a key, but you're not a regular resident. Even if I wanted to, claiming consent to search wouldn't hold up in court." He pointed to the drawer again. "Nevertheless, what's in there could help Sarah get the right treatment, but as you said, you're the unofficial roommate. It's up to you."

She crossed the room to get to the nightstand. "Or, whatever is in there might point to her boyfriend."

Ray didn't argue. Denial that friends and family had a drug problem proved hard to overcome, even with evidence.

Abby placed one paw out in front of Karenna's path as if to say, "Wait your turn." Ray almost laughed at the gesture.

Karenna hesitated then reached past and opened the drawer. Another pill bottle, mostly full, without a label, rested on its side next to discarded bobby pins, a bottle of hand lotion, a pair of sunglasses and a few pens.

"Please allow me, Karenna. We don't know what's in there yet." Raymond had dealt with his fair share of illegal drugs and depending on the dose and chemical variations, the stuff could be lethal by touch or smell. "Just last month an officer searched a car that had cotton balls soaked in fentanyl. He passed out and hit his head."

He held up the bottle to the light. The pills inside were stamped with a well-known antianxiety brand name, but the letters were crooked and some of the pills looked cracked and flaky. Lots of narcotics were made to look like legal prescriptions, though, and he knew this particular one like the back of his hand. Definitely a fake. "Either Sarah is messing with oxycodone. Or this mysterious boyfriend is."

Karenna's face fell and she crossed the room to the window. "No. I'm telling you, Ray, she wouldn't." Her voice shook. "I shared with her what happened with your dad and made her promise she would never touch the stuff."

Something unfurled in his chest, but he didn't take time to analyze it. "Why would you go so far as making her promise that to you?"

She slumped onto the edge of a pink wingback chair next to the other nightstand. She stared out the window and shook her head. "She was hanging out with some acquaintances from school who used to be into that sort of stuff and I was worried. I know people can grow up and change but…"

Unlikely. But he didn't want to cause her more grief. "Let's say you're right and the pills belong to the boyfriend. She found his stash, took the bottle away and chucked it in here with the intention of flushing the pills later. If she confronted him at the park about it, then we would have a motive." And if the drugs turned out to be Sarah's, then there were a couple of other motives he could think of, too.

Her face paled, and she pulled back into the chair as far as she could. "Ray," she whispered. "He's here.

Down there. Outside. Across the street." Her entire body looked rigid, her fingers gripping both armrests.

"What?" He strode over and looked out. The sky had dimmed to the darkest blue shade right before the colors on the horizon disappeared and the moon took over the shift. Ray didn't see anyone out there, but he didn't hesitate to grab his radio and call in for backup.

Ray grabbed the cord and lowered the blinds. His radio crackled with confirmation backup was on the way. He turned to Karenna. "Tell me what you saw. Was it the man who tried to kill you? Describe him. What was he wearing?"

"Yes, yes. It was him. He had those horrible sunglasses on. Dark hair. Black jacket for spring but it looked kind of tailored to him. Crisp. Dark shirt, dark pants, but with dress shoes that looked expensive."

That description probably fit half of professional New Yorkers. His frustration was probably evident.

"I'm not good at fashion like Sarah. I don't know."

"Did he see you? Did it look like he was leaving or coming?"

She threw her hands up. "I don't know!"

He held his hands out. "It's okay. We're going to get away from the windows and stay inside until backup arrives. Officers are going to check the perimeter and make sure he's not out there. If he is, we'll get him. This will all be over with, and I'll take you home."

Her face looked paler than the eggshell-colored wall behind her. She pulled her shoulders back and attempted to smile. "That sounds easy enough. Thank you."

His stomach flipped at her attempt to sound tough. She didn't move from the chair, though. Her fingertips turned white and they pressed as far into the padding as possible. He fought the impulse again to hold her hand and pull her in for a hug.

She never did like asking for help, which was probably why he was so surprised after a year of dating to find out that she'd been raised by a wealthy investment banker who ran the biggest conglomerate on the east coast. Karenna was nothing like the stereotypes of rich girls. "Hey," he said. "Let's try to find a photo of the boyfriend while we're waiting here for the officers to finish looking around outside."

Her eyes shifted to the walls, a new hopeful gaze to them.

He reached over and rested his hand on hers. He tried to ignore the electric heat rushing up his arm. "Today's been too much, right?"

She closed her eyes and exhaled before letting them flutter open again. "I'll be fine, Ray." Her voice had regained its business-like tone. She glanced at his hand with one eyebrow raised.

He removed it instantly and stood. "Sorry," he muttered. "I'll close the rest of the blinds. I'd like you to wait in the living room, away from the windows."

His radio squawked and Ray answered, relaying what little detail he knew about the man they were looking for to the responding officers. The fact the attacker was at the apartment building seemed a strong indicator they were dealing with Sarah's boyfriend. He hoped they could interview some of the neighbors to see if anyone had a better description of the guy.

Abby stayed at his side as he made the rounds, closing the blinds. He was in the small bathroom when she began to whine. Odd. He stopped for a second and watched her. Had she found more drugs?

She barked, looking straight at Ray then bouncing as if wanting him to follow her. He let the leash loose. She barked again and headed for the living room.

A faint beeping reached his ears. He followed Abby into the living room only to find Karenna, arms wrapped around herself, staring at the back of the kitchen wall.

The paint began to blister and pop with brown spots. "Ray? What do we do?" Her voice cracked with uncertainty. She held up a shaking finger. "I think the apartment next door is on fire."

As if agreeing, the smoke alarm closest to them went off. A hiss from the ceiling immediately followed. Sprinklers descended and sprayed freezing water over their heads. For half a second, Ray's muscles were paralyzed with indecision. A fire coming from the apartment next door had to be a trap, a way of forcing Karenna into the open. So the question remained.

Did they face death inside or outside?

THREE

Karenna hunched over as the cold water from the sprinklers pelted the top of her head.

Ray bolted for Sarah's room and returned with a New York Mets cap and jacket. "Throw this on. We can't stay here, but we can try to disguise you."

She didn't hesitate, even though she would normally never betray the Yankees. Ray's radio burst with voice after voice giving out updates. Ray pressed the side button and asked for officers to meet them at the apartment door. Two seconds later, a knock sounded.

Ray reached for the doorknob but it wouldn't budge. He tugged harder, almost flying backward from the effort.

A male voice shouted from the other side of the door. "A key was put in the door and broken off. The lock is completely frozen. Stay back. We'll need to break the door."

The doorknob had been sabotaged?

Abby barked again. "You've got to be kidding me," Ray muttered.

Karenna followed his gaze, squinting through the water dripping from the bill of her cap, to the blistering kitchen wall. Flames began to flicker between the stovetop and oven hood. The sprinklers didn't seem to have an effect on the fire.

Abby shook her fur wildly, pelting Karenna's feet with an added deluge.

A thud hit the front door and the bottom half vibrated but didn't budge from the frame.

"Step back. They're trying to kick the door down. It's faster than waiting for a battering ram. But…" He gestured for Karenna to keep stepping back. She followed him inside Sarah's room.

He flattened his back against the wall and peeked out the window. "Fire escape starts here. If they aren't able to get us out in the next minute, we need to consider taking our chances out there. Though I fear that's what he wants."

Her mouth dropped and the scent of charred wood assaulted her. She cringed. "You think we'd be easy targets?"

His eyes met hers. "You'd stay behind me the whole time. I wouldn't let him get you."

Her breath caught at his intensity. Unlike the patrol officers she sometimes saw, she didn't see a bulletproof vest over Ray's shirt. "No." Her heart pounded at the implications, at his willingness to sacrifice his safety for hers. She couldn't let him do that when it had been her idea in the first place to come to Sarah's apartment.

A snap and deafening crack filled the apartment. She spun toward the noise as the front door splintered apart from the frame at the hinges. An involuntary scream escaped her as she flinched.

Rivulets of water fell from the hats of the two officers who ran into the apartment.

Ray placed a hand on her back. "Let's get you out of here."

The officers flanked all sides of her and rushed her down the hallway to the stairs.

"So far, all clear," the officer to her right said. "Property manager said the fire next door to you was an empty apartment, in the process of a remodel."

"Good to know. Stay on guard," Ray answered on her left, with Abby at his heel.

They reached the front door and Ray made a signal to wait. He took a step outside, tentatively. Three radios sounded at the same time on their shoulders.

"Possible arson suspect spotted running from the scene," the radio voice crackled. "Lost visual at crowd letting out of a movie theater."

Ray groaned. "So while I waited for backup we gave him time to start the fire and leave. Great."

Karenna whipped her head around to look at him. His eyes widened, as if he hadn't meant to say it aloud. Was his comment a dig about when they were dating? He had a tendency to rush into situations without waiting for backup as protocol dictated. It had been a sticking point between them that his supervisors happened to agree with her on.

In fact, the way he'd run into danger unnecessarily had been her biggest struggle when they were dating. He couldn't stand to wait for backup if he thought his actions would pull another drug dealer off the streets. It had begun to seem like his entire career was solely based on revenge, and that he was unconcerned whether he lived or died in the process.

She'd told him her concerns a few weeks before the end of their relationship. Surely, that wasn't why he'd broken up with her. She'd wondered about it back then, as well, but it hadn't made sense. Their conversation had never become heated and she'd felt heard by him. He'd said he would consider her thoughts.

The topic hadn't come up at all in the couple weeks preceding the break-up. So that couldn't have been why'd he called it quits.

Not that it mattered anymore.

A fire truck honked nearby. Ray leaned over so he could speak above the noise into her ear. "We need to get to the car and give the firemen room to do their job. Are you okay? Do you need a medic?"

"I'm fine," she hollered over the clatter, unwilling to turn her face any closer to him.

The officers didn't give her a spare inch of space to move until she was inside the police vehicle again while Ray secured Abby in the back. Smoke billowed out of a window on the left side of the building. Residents gathered in a cluster on the sidewalk half a block down, looking up.

She couldn't stop staring at them, even as she coughed the remainder of the foul smoke from her lungs. If she hadn't gone to look for that man's photo, would all those people still have had to leave their homes tonight?

Ray hopped in and glanced behind him, checking on Abby before he faced forward. "Can I have your address?"

Her cheeks heated. "What will happen to the residents?" The attacker had endangered all their lives.

"The responders will give them contact information for some organizations that might be able to help them, but if they didn't have renter's insurance, it's going to be expensive." Ray's voice had a silky quality whenever he spoke in low tones. "Let me take you home, Karenna."

She closed her eyes and gave him her address. A few minutes later they were parked in front of her brownstone.

Ray hesitated at the wheel after he shut off the vehicle. "Our shift has been over for a while, and Abby doesn't eat while she works. Do you mind if I feed her while I make sure your place is secure?"

"Of course not."

Something had shifted in Ray's demeanor. He seemed more like the charming man she'd met at the police ball all those years ago when her father had asked her to go in his stead for the fund-raiser event. Ray had asked her to dance and they'd ended up being the last ones to leave. She blinked away the memories.

Ray followed her through the gate with Abby and a backpack that she assumed held the dog supplies.

Instead of going up the building's front stairs, she sidestepped around. Ray froze for a minute. "You live in the basement?"

"I believe they refer to it as the garden level." On the left side of the stairs, the door was hidden from street view. "With a private entrance."

He laughed. "Garden level does sound more sophisticated. I have one of those, as well."

"A garden level?" She inserted the key to unlock the dead bolt before moving to the doorknob. "Does that mean you're not living with your mom anymore?" Keeping the surprise from her question was harder than it should've been. Ray had been taking care of his mom since high school, after his father had died. Any money he'd made from that point on went to help his mom pay the rent so she and his little sister wouldn't have to move.

"My mom decided to move in with my aunt a few years ago. My sister is actually staying with me right now while she tries to find her own place."

That had to be a relief for him, but they weren't friends who shared feelings anymore so she let his comment go.

Ray wanted to be the first inside the apartment again.

His silence felt heavy as he examined her humble studio apartment with its miniature fridge and stove, the love seat that doubled as her bed, and end tables that worked as both dining room tables and nightstands. Thankfully, she had put away her laundry from last night.

"You…" He turned around to face her. His eyes had never been wider all night, not even when they'd run out of a burning building. "You live here?" The positive lilt to his question was obviously forced.

Her neck burned with the scrutiny. This was exactly the conversation she'd wanted to avoid. "Yes." The place was small, but it was all she could afford while still being in the neighborhood she wanted.

He strode into the bathroom, peeked behind the shower curtain and came back into the living room. "I'll just check the windows and locks."

The towels were in the armoire, so she grabbed a few. "It might not help at this stage, but here."

He smiled and their hands brushed as she handed him one. The hairs on her arm seemed to stand on their ends from the electricity.

She spun away, quickly pulling out a T-shirt and jeans from her drawer and pointing to the bathroom.

"I'll just be a second. Feel free to help yourself to whatever you need for Abby."

As she feared, the bathroom mirror didn't pull any punches. She looked like a raccoon wearing a bad wig. Her professional attire of black-knit shirt and wide-leg trousers was wrinkled and appeared more like a bad set of pajamas.

She glanced at the bathtub and an involuntary shiver went down her spine at the thought of lying in water again. The man's sunglasses and sneer came to mind once more.

Nope. No more baths, no more sinking her head underneath the water. She breathed deeply, filling her lungs repeatedly while reminding herself it was over. She could breathe normally. In fact, showers only from now on…speed showers. Would dry shampoo get the job done?

After removing the two remaining bobby pins, the few strands of hair left in the twist dropped to her shoulders. She combed it as best as she could, wiped a washrag underneath her eyes, and applied some lip balm. In dry, soft clothes, she felt ready to face Ray with a little more of her dignity intact. She also felt more like herself. At work, she stuck to a minimalist professional wardrobe of whites and blacks, but at home she preferred pastel colors even though they probably made her pale skin look washed out.

She stepped into the room and Ray turned to face her, two dog bowls in his hands, one filled with kibble, the other with water. He set them down and Abby ate, then lapped up the water.

Ray crossed the room and held his hands out. "Look. I know we have a complicated history, but I'm determined to see this case through. So we're going to be seeing each other until I get the guy behind bars. Maybe we should clear the air and discuss our breakup."

Her stomach clenched so tightly she fought against nausea. While she desperately wanted to know what exactly had caused him to call it quits in the first place, the day's drama made her bones feel heavy. She wasn't sure she could handle reliving all the feelings of getting dumped and rejected all over again. "It's been a really long day, Ray," she said instead. "Do you mind if we table this for now?" Or maybe forever. The bottom line was he'd dumped her and she'd moved on.

"Fair enough. I guess I just wanted you to know that when I look back…" He sighed and placed his hands on his waist. "I realize I could've handled, or communicated, things better. I still had a lot of growing up to do back then." He turned to see Abby was done with her bowls. "We're good?"

She wouldn't go that far, but she nodded to prevent further discussion.

He gathered Abby's things but stopped abruptly at Karenna's desk and fingered something on the top of her stack of papers. "You're working for a nonprofit?"

She fought against the weariness. Might as well put everything on the table. "I work in donor development for a marketing agency specializing in nonprofits."

His eyebrows rose up and down as if processing the new information. "You don't work for your father anymore?"

"I've been on my own for the past five years."

"Because of what happened with us?" He looked shaken. "I didn't want—"

"I wanted a job I earned on my own merit." Her

throat was so tight with raw emotion she was on the verge of crying. "If you don't mind, I really am tired."

"Of course." He grabbed the doorknob and looked over his shoulder at her. "I'll make sure there's a patrol car making the rounds by here tonight. You should be safe. Lock up after me."

"Do you think the fire was his way of trying to finish the job tonight?"

He worried his lip as if debating how to answer. "The important thing is no one was hurt. While you were freshening up, they let me know the fire was started with a flare and a container of grease right against the adjoining wall to Sarah's apartment. I guess it's a type of fire that's a challenge to put out. Maybe he hoped the fire would ruin any possible evidence he might've left behind in that apartment. Whatever his motive, don't worry. Oh, and, Karenna? Did Sarah have a spare key for your apartment?"

Karenna shook her head. "No." She didn't feel the need to explain her apartment wasn't worth having a key for.

"Try to get some sleep. We'll find him before he gets another chance..."

He didn't need to finish the statement. Her lungs tightened at the thought, remembering all too well what that man was capable of.

Ray filled his fourth cup of coffee for the morning, having hardly slept. The paperwork alone had kept him at the station for hours before he could call it a night. But then thinking about Karenna... Well, he needed more coffee than usual.

He relayed the previous night's events to a few of

the other officers who'd just arrived at the limestone building in Bay Ridge dedicated to the Brooklyn K-9 Unit. "And the witness, a victim herself, happens to be my ex-girlfriend."

Henry Roarke, a fellow K-9 handler with biceps that seemed to get bigger if the guy even thought about going to the gym, quirked an eyebrow. "You had a girlfriend once?"

Ray's spine straightened, even though he'd noted the teasing tone. "What's that supposed to mean?"

"Not, like, a couple of dates?" Henry held both hands out as if physically examining his statement. "This was a person that you actually referred to as your girlfriend and she reciprocated by calling you a boyfriend?"

K-9 detectives Nate Slater and Bradley McGregor both chuckled at the interrogation as they filled their own coffee mugs. Their canine partners were currently waiting at the training center next door while the officers attended the shift briefing.

"Yes, a girlfriend." Ray looked around as if someone would appear to back him up. "Why is that so hard to believe?"

Henry crossed his arms over his chest and pursed his lips for half a second. "I've known you for the past few years, and you, my friend, are married to the job. I've never seen someone so determined to get the most collars—"

"Not just any collars—" Ray held up a finger, ready to argue his point. His dad's old army challenge coin rested in his shirt pocket at all times, a reminder of who and what he was fighting for.

"Yeah, I don't think the kind of collar matters when you miss every dinner," Nate interjected. "Henry might have a point. I've never seen someone try to get over-time as much as you…and not for the pay."

"Before calling me out maybe you should look in the mirror yourself—"

"I'm about to be a family man now. I've seen the light." Nate smiled and slapped him on the shoulder. Nate was engaged to marry Willow Emery and to-gether they were adopting her three-year-old niece, Lucy Emery. Lucy's parents had been the victims of what might be the copycat murder of the twenty-year-old McGregor double homicide.

If the unit could find a lead on the cold case then maybe they'd finally get somewhere on the recent Emery murder, too. His brain still teased him that there was something about the true crime shows he'd watched that could help. If only he could remember what.

He shook his head at Nate. "So I'm driven. Everyone on this team is. It's the nature of the job."

"Yeah, we are." Henry lifted his chin as if pointing at him. "But you take it to a whole other level. I'm just pleased you used to have a life."

Nate and Bradley laughed and walked ahead of them toward the meeting room, following their unit com-mander, Sergeant Gavin Sutherland, and the other K-9 officers for their morning briefing. Giving each other grief was par for the course, and Ray gave as good as he got, so he shook the teasing off and took his last sip of coffee.

"You ever think about getting her back?" Henry asked.

"It was five years ago, Henry. Ancient history."

"Ah, I get it." He sighed with compassion. Henry was known for speaking his mind, even if it wasn't his business. He'd recently been placed on modified desk duty for claims of excessive force, even though he insisted he'd followed protocol when the suspect went for Henry's gun. Internal Affairs was investigating, and the wait was tough on everyone.

They walked together into the room. "I ended the relationship," Ray said. "But now I'm the lead officer on her case."

He had ended it—and questioned the wisdom of that decision multiple times. Last night's conversation with Karenna had played on a loop, the main reason he couldn't sleep. Everything looked less clear in the morning light, but he wasn't about to start analyzing his feelings now. The past was the past.

"Good luck with that," Henry teased.

Ray mock rolled his eyes then looked across the table. "Are we getting started, Sarge?"

Gavin glanced at the clock in the room over Eden Chang's shoulder. As their resident tech guru, she wasn't normally part of the meeting, but she was explaining something about a fix to the sergeant's tablet. Gavin nodded and excused her with a thumbs-up. "Thanks. Glad we hired an expert who's a true tech genius in all regards."

"Hired an expert." Ray repeated the words aloud. Something clicked in his mind and he slapped his thigh in vindication. "We need to hire an expert, a genealogy expert, a geneticist. Something from a true crime TV show I saw a while back has been driving me crazy. Remember that serial killer in Wisconsin, back in the eighties?"

Officer Belle Montera's eyebrow rose. "Hate to break it to you, but someone already solved that case."

He ignored the laughter that followed. "It's *how* they got him that's been driving me crazy." He glanced at Bradley, feeling a little awkward about sharing his unorthodox idea on how they might catch the man who murdered his fellow officer's parents. At least Bradley's sister wasn't in the room. He didn't want to raise false hope that they might bring their parents' killer to justice.

Gavin turned to face him. "It was DNA, wasn't it? We've already checked the databases dozens of times, Morrow. It's a dead end."

"No." He shook his head. "We haven't checked genealogy. You know how people send DNA in to find out their ancestry?"

"After a decade, my cousin finally found her birth father using one of those sites," Henry said with a frown. "But those are private companies that aren't open for us to use."

"I know that. Hear me out. People can upload their encrypted findings to a public database to help them find other relatives."

"That way people don't all have to use the same service to locate relatives," Eden, still standing next to Gavin, said with a nod.

"Law enforcement can access CODIS, the FBI's combined DNA index system database," Ray added. "And, if they find a match, they can issue a warrant to the private DNA sequencing firm that comes up. In the Wisconsin case, they contacted a geneticist that helped fill in the gaps of their collected DNA sample to help them find the closest relative in the database. Once they narrowed down the family group, they were able to pinpoint the suspect."

"So you need a sleuthing geneticist willing to look at the DNA from the McGregor case and examine the public database."

"Basically." Ray nodded.

Eden crossed her arms. "I've got a connection to a geneticist we've been using in the NYPD off and on. She's got a stack of cases ahead of us, but I think she might be willing to do us a favor and bump this up. I can contact her to come work with our forensics team, but I think she would tell you not to get your hopes up."

Gavin nodded. "Nevertheless, this case is personal to the team, and I would think, with the media attention to the two murders, the higher-ups would have no problem bumping this up the forensic ladder. No stone unturned. Contact her."

Ray blew out a breath. Maybe God would finally listen to his prayers now and at least bring one murderer to justice. His phone vibrated. He normally had his phone muted during a meeting but contacts underneath his favorites tab still got through. Other than his mom and his sister, he only had one other person in that category, the one he'd added last night. A quick glance at the screen showed Karenna's name.

I have news. Can we talk soon?

The text made his heart race even though there was nothing there to cause alarm. Still, he stood. "New development on the case I told you about, Sarge."

Gavin nodded and Ray walked out the door to call her.

Penny McGregor, their records clerk and Bradley's sister, waved him down. Penny was only twenty-three and, like everyone in the unit, Ray always felt protective toward her. "We got the results on those pills you wanted tested."

Ray studied the report she handed him. He hadn't wanted to be right. The results confirmed his suspicions, though. This was now a drug-related case, which meant there was a dealer he needed to hunt down before anyone else got hurt. Especially Karenna.

FOUR

Karenna wobbled slightly in her heels but offered a smile to her coworkers as she made her way to her desk. They answered phones, joked, typed and clicked away like usual.

It was the same feeling as visiting a foreign country where she didn't speak the language but could survive with a translator and a guidebook. She'd often battled the sensation of being a misfit no matter the world she lived in, however this was a whole new level. She was wounded and scared, though none of that was visible. Not that she wanted them to know or ask what was happening in her personal life, but the sensation still felt odd.

Three people separately asked, "How's it going?" Their strides never slowed as they passed her in the hall so she didn't bother trying to answer.

The gray panels surrounding her uncluttered desk suddenly bothered her. Some employees had photos or flowers or knickknacks to offer their space some unique personality. She'd never taken the time or made the effort because she was there to work. Now it seemed like a poor decision. Something to make her smile or feel comforted would've been nice. The stack of work she'd left last night still waited for her.

Her phone buzzed. She took a seat and read Ray's name on the screen before she hurriedly answered. "I sort of thought you would text back. It wasn't that urgent." The last thing she needed was to owe Ray any more favors. He'd already gone above and beyond what a typical officer would do.

"I like to strike while the iron is hot. You said you had news."

"Yes. Sarah's parents texted me to let me know Sarah is in stable condition but still unconscious. They are on their way back from a business trip to Hong Kong so I'll get to see her after they sign some papers."

"That's good. Did you ask if they had any photos of the boyfriend?"

"They weren't that close. They didn't even know Sarah had a boyfriend. So no." Karenna looked around to make sure no one was listening. "But the reason I messaged you was because I remembered how Sarah met Marcus. It was through another high school friend, Zoe Keller. I found her number this morning and texted her. I'm meeting her at her place during my lunch hour. If she doesn't know where Marcus is, she should at least know his last name."

"Zoe Keller, you said? Give me her address, I'm happy to go talk to her."

Karenna waited a beat. Either he hadn't heard the part where she was going to talk to her, or he wanted to be the one to do it. She wasn't sure how she felt about the latter. "Aren't you working a shift? If you show up like that, Zoe is not the type of person who will talk to you unless you have a warrant."

"Why not? I can be pretty persuasive."

Yeah, like a steamroller, but Karenna moved past the comment. "Remember when I talked about the different crowd? Well, Zoe was part of that. I really don't think she'll talk to you. Besides, I'd like to be the one to break it to her about what happened to Sarah. They had stayed close after high school."

"Okay, then we go together. I'll pick you up at work—your agency doesn't look too far from my unit—and we'll both go."

"That's really not—"

"Look, Karenna. I didn't want to tell you this over the phone, but that pill bottle in Sarah's nightstand?"

The little bit of oatmeal she'd forced herself to eat for breakfast threatened to revolt. It wasn't illegal drugs. Sarah couldn't have gotten addicted. She'd promised.

"I had them tested. Not on the record but as a favor. They were oxycodone pills laced with fentanyl. That stuff is fifty times as addictive as heroin and—"

"I know." Her bones felt hot with the type of weariness she'd only felt when her mom had died, Ray had broken up with her, and the worst case of flu had brought her down. She closed her eyes and breathed slowly in and out, and the feeling, thankfully, dissipated slightly.

When she'd dated Ray and heard how driven he was to stop opioid dealers in the area, she'd started researching the problem on the side. Years later, the body of information was growing, but the takeaway was that dealers would keep growing if prevention and harm reduction weren't also utilized at the same time. The cause had grabbed hold of her heart, despite Ray not being in the picture.

In fact, her biggest client through the agency was the Opioid Crisis Foundation, so she knew all about the dangers of fentanyl. "I understand what you're saying, Ray, but you still don't know if those were Sarah's pills." Her voice rose in volume and the indignation somehow cleared her mind. "Hold on, please."

She held up a finger out of habit, even though Ray wasn't physically there. She tried to grasp the thread of memory slipping away. She imagined reading Sarah's texts in that Now You See app. She'd been at home, after Sarah had stood her up at the St. Patrick's Day parade, in her pajamas and consoling herself with a mint-chocolate sundae. Sarah had just met Marcus and was texting her...

"I think... I think Marcus worked as a chemist for some big pharmaceutical company. She was gushing that he was a genius."

"Good! That gives me something to go on before I pick you up."

The effort of trying to remember such a detail that had seemed insignificant at the time was exhausting. "You still haven't explained why you have to see Zoe with me. I'm not sure it's necessary." The less time she spent with him the better.

"These are highly dangerous, illegal drugs we're talking about, Karenna. My gut tells me a dealer tried to kill you and Sarah. So if Marcus isn't the dealer, he's working with one. You've seen his face and are about to go to a known acquaintance of his. Either give me Zoe's address or we go together."

Karenna took a second to answer, momentarily surprised she hadn't thought of Zoe in that way. Still, Ray would definitely be wasting his time if he went without her. "Fine. See you at noon."

With the small ray of hope they were getting closer to finding Marcus, her morning stayed mercifully busy with meetings and focused proposals for various non-profits needing help with their donor development. Lindsey, her closest friend at work, always sporting a bright smile, stopped midstride and leaned over the top of the cubicle wall surrounding Karenna's desk. "Good work on convincing that CFO not to mail out nickels in their fund-raisers."

"Or socks," Karenna added with a laugh that quickly fell from her face. She couldn't laugh while Sarah was in a coma, but she also wasn't ready to share with anyone at work what had happened.

As a whole, charities struggled with dwindling donations, more so in the past few years. Some organizations experimented with gimmicks, mailing odd things in hopes of increasing donor response. Karenna thrived on the challenge to come up with timely marketing materials that made economic sense to keep causes at the forefront of the public's mind without being intrusive or obnoxious.

"So there's a very handsome cop at the front waiting for you, with lunch," Lindsey said nonchalantly then clapped her hands together and flashed a smile big enough to show almost all of her teeth.

Karenna glanced down at the time on her phone. "He's early." She blinked. "Wait. Did you say with lunch?"

Lindsey waggled her eyebrows. "I mentioned the handsome part, right? I didn't know you were dating anyone, but I always imagined you would end up with someone like him."

"What do you mean?" Karenna pulled her chin back, wondering what would make her think that. "And, no, we're not dating."

Lindsey shrugged and turned to walk away. "I don't know. Seems like a servant-hearted, tough guy would complement your servant-hearted, compassionate personality. And the cute dog… I mean, come on, complete package." She laughed at herself and waved a hand as she walked away. "Have fun!"

Karenna's shoes almost flipped off her heels as she did her best speed-walk to the lobby. Why on earth would Lindsey think they were dating? What had Ray told them?

She found him in the lobby with Abby at his side, surrounded by three other female staff. Had he been talking about her? He held a take-out bag in his right hand. He beamed when he spotted her. "If you'll excuse me, I believe the lunch hour has started." He deftly stepped away from Maggie in mid-question and opened the front door, gesturing for Karenna to precede him and Abby.

She nodded goodbye at her coworkers. The moment the door closed behind them, Ray's smile widened while hers disappeared.

"What did you say to them?"

"Thought you might like some lunch." He frowned as he replayed the question she'd asked at the same time. "Nothing. I said I was a friend bringing you lunch. They were more interested in Abby."

"You didn't mention our history? Sarah? My father?"

They'd reached his SUV and Abby once again

jumped in first. Karenna hadn't noticed the built-in water bowl as part of the kennel the last time she'd looked inside. He waited until they were in the vehicle before he answered. "No, but I don't know why you would hide who your father is. I would think his connections might help your line of work."

"You don't know what it's like to have people you *thought* were friends try to use you to take advantage of your father's money or influence."

He handed her a burger, the grease already seeping through the wrapper. "It's from the 646 Diner. You've got to try this."

The abrupt change of topic took her a second to register what he was offering. She didn't feel like eating when she was annoyed. Her stomach overruled her intended refusal, though, the moment the delicious smell overpowered her. "Thank you." She took a bite and chewed slowly. Ray practically inhaled his burger, took a sip from his water bottle and turned the signal on to merge back into traffic. "Where to?"

"Head in the direction of Sarah's. Zoe's place is only a couple blocks from there."

He shook his head. "I didn't mean to bring your father up again. It's your business. But I didn't tell anyone in the office anything. Like every case, I exercise discretion."

"Thank you," she said softly. She weighed her next words carefully. "I really appreciated what you did yesterday and this extra precautionary measure as we go to see Zoe, but... Well, the point is, you're not acting like this is a normal case. So I think it'd be best after Zoe opens up and tells me where this guy is and you arrest him, you can feel your duty is done and move on."

* * *

Ray kept his eyes on the road, but his peripheral vision caught Karenna's hands tucked underneath her legs, her torso rigid, the half-eaten burger on the wrapper on her lap. Maybe she was right, and he was treating her too much like a former girlfriend.

It had felt so natural bringing her lunch and picking her up, so much so that until she'd said that last thing, he almost asked if he could eat the rest of her burger. But that kind of question was only appropriate if they were in a relationship, right?

"Take a right up ahead," she said.

He sighed inwardly. He still cared greatly for Karenna, but since she'd made it clear last night that she didn't want to discuss their breakup, they couldn't really clear the air. "I want this guy behind bars more than you know. The faster we get him, the faster I can move on to clean up this city one dealer at a time."

It might have been his imagination, but it almost seemed like she was trying not to roll her eyes. That attitude was the main reason they never would've worked. He opened his mouth to search for a tactful way to bring it up, but she pointed ahead. "Third building on the right."

After parking, they approached the landing of the brownstone. Two planters filled with flowers and greenery Ray couldn't name made an impressive display on either side of the door. He glanced at the labels for the apartments. "Zoe has an entire floor?" He didn't even want to think about how much an apartment in the building cost.

"Her parents own the building. They rent out the first three floors. Zoe and her sister get the fourth floor and her parents have the top floor. They're out of town most of the time, though. Zoe comes from a long line of trust funds." Karenna pressed the button for the fourth floor, labeled simply "Keller." The button for the fifth floor had no label.

Static filled the speaker. "Why is a cop with you?"

Karenna's glance screamed *I told you so* but she smiled. "He's my ride. My ex-boyfriend, actually."

Zoe's dramatic sigh through the speakers caused feedback. "All right. Be right down."

"Charming," Ray muttered.

"I'm sure she didn't want to buzz me up because you're here." She waved up and down in his direction. "Very intimidating."

He couldn't help but smile. "I'll take that as a compliment." The way she'd looked at him and the way her voice had lightened did something to his insides.

The front door opened. Zoe stood holding the door but still firmly in the lobby area, clearly not willing to let them inside. She specifically looked only at Karenna. "You said you needed to talk to me?"

Abby strained against the short leash and lifted her nose. Her front paws danced in rhythm before she sat down and looked up at Ray with a grin. The signals Abby gave meant Zoe had drugs on her person or had recently used drugs, but standing on a landing wasn't considered consent to search. Abby would be disappointed he couldn't reward her just yet. Instead he patted Abby's head so she'd know she was acknowledged and needed to stand down. If he didn't give her some signal, she'd start barking soon to make sure he understood.

Karenna reached forward, hugged the stiffened Zoe

and pulled back with a warm smile despite the woman's harsh demeanor. "I have some bad news. Sarah—"

"In a coma, right?" Zoe crossed her arms over her chest. "I heard she overdosed and probably wouldn't make it."

Karenna took a step backward. Ray instinctively placed a hand on her back to prevent her from losing her footing off the top step and felt her tremble with either shock or anger. "How…? Who told you that?"

Zoe shrugged. "I'm not sure where I heard it."

Ray didn't need a lie detector to know that was a blatant fib. He needed to alert hospital staff to tighten security of Sarah's hospital room. Enough time tiptoeing around. "Do you know a man named Marcus?" he asked.

Zoe's eyes darted to him and down to Abby. "For real, Karenna, why is he here?"

"He's trying to help me find Marcus. I need to talk to him. And since you introduced Sarah to him, I thought—"

"I have no idea where he is." Zoe's face paled. "I only bump into him randomly in public sometimes. It's been ages."

"Okay," Karenna said gently. Her kind, quiet voice put anyone she met at ease. "Well, maybe you can remember his last name. It's on the tip of my tongue, but I can't quite place it."

Zoe shook her head vigorously. "I'm not sure I ever knew it. No idea. Look, I've got to go."

The hinge of the gate at the sidewalk behind them sounded. A female in her late teens ascended the stairs. Her frown morphed to a wide-eyed grin. "Karenna?" She practically vaulted to the top of the landing. Abby barked a warning that the teen ignored as she wrapped a shocked Karenna in a bear hug. The woman pulled back only slightly before hugging her again. "I didn't think I'd see *you* again!"

Karenna's initial alarm was replaced with wonder. "Haley?" Karenna held the girl at arm's length for a second, searching her face. "You're so grown up, I almost didn't recognize you!" She turned to Ray for a moment. "Haley is Zoe's younger sister."

Haley beamed. "And you haven't changed at all. You dressed like an adult even when you were my age."

"I think you were only seven or eight the last time I saw you."

"Six." Haley beamed. "I'll never forget because no one else was willing to take me to the school carnival. Everyone was busy." She held up air quotes for emphasis.

Karenna laughed. "I was glad you were willing to let me take you. I was so jealous of my friends with siblings and wanted to find out what it would be like. It was a happy memory."

Ray marveled at the way Karenna's face lit up. For half a second, he imagined her as his wife, in his apartment, waiting for him when he walked in the door, ready to hug him. She'd be full of questions about his day, always with an emphasis on his feelings. But the place would feel like a home and less like an extended-stay hotel for sleep and TV before another shift. Except, Karenna wouldn't want him to go on another shift. She hated his job, and he needed to remember that.

Haley hugged Karenna again with a little jut of her chin at Zoe who waited impatiently at the front door. "See? This is what a big sister is supposed to be like."

Zoe responded with a dismissive shrug. Haley's expression sobered and she stepped back, looking between Karenna and Ray. "Why are you here, anyway?"

"They're trying to find Sarah's boyfriend. That's all." Zoe emphasized the last word, but her voice remained monotone. "I couldn't help them."

Haley's face fell. "Oh." She knew something, too. "Well, I just came to grab a different outfit. I've got to get going."

Ray pulled out his business card and gestured to Zoe. "If you or your sister remembers or hears anything about Marcus that could help us locate him, please give us a call."

Karenna reached for his hand and a shot of electricity ran down his arm at the touch. "Sorry. May I?"

He nodded. She took the business card from him and, after grabbing a pen from the front pocket of her purse, jotted down her name and number on the back. "And here's my number. You can text me. Anytime." She offered it to Zoe. "For Sarah."

The plea in Karenna's voice visibly affected both sisters. Their shoulders sagged and they averted their eyes as Zoe accepted the card, nodded and disappeared behind the closing glass door.

Karenna spun and raced down the stairs. Ray and Abby hustled to keep up with her.

"Please call the hospital," Karenna said. "It had to be Marcus who told her that bit about Sarah overdosing and probably not making it. That's a threat, if I've ever heard one. We need to make sure she's okay." She pulled out her phone and her thumb raced across the screen. "In fact I'm going to encourage Sarah's parents to hire some private security until we can apprehend him."

Ray didn't argue as he'd thought the same thing. It only took a minute for him to notify hospital security to beef up their watch. "They're going to pay close attention to Sarah's room until her parents arrive or send extra security."

He reached to open the back door for Abby when she stiffened. The hair the groomer kept short rose on the back of her neck and she uttered a small growl.

"What? What is it?" Karenna asked.

He watched Abby closely for a second and searched for what might have caught her attention. She looked around and slowly relaxed, her tail wagging again. "Sometimes she does that if she smells a rat close by."

Karenna laughed. "She must do that a lot, then!"

"Thankfully, not very often at all." Back in the SUV, he rolled his head side to side before putting it into Drive.

"A little tense?"

"Sorry." The sound of his neck cracking and popping just meant the stretches worked. "It's always frustrating to follow a lead to a dead end." Ray turned the wheel to reenter the street. A streak of fur rushed past. His eyes followed the trotting dog, a scrawny, thin, yet still beautiful German shepherd mix.

He grabbed his phone and pulled up the photo of the dog the team had been looking for the past few weeks. Officer Lani Jameson, the first to spot the dog, had said she was sure the dog had recently given birth. Thus far, no one had been able to locate any puppies—or find the stray.

He looked back and forth at the photo and at the dog trotting along the empty sidewalk. Sure looked like a match. Ray checked his mirrors and made a sudden U-turn.

Karenna shot a hand out toward the dashboard for balance. "What's going on?"

"Sorry. Do you mind if we take a detour on the way back to work? See that dog? The team has taken an interest. They've named her Brooke, short for Brooklyn." He clicked his radio and let the team know his location in case anyone else in the area wanted to tag team. "I'd like to see where she goes to see if she leads us to her puppies."

Karenna scrunched up her nose. "Part of a case?"

"No," he admitted. "She caught the attention of one of our handlers. The dog reminds Lani—Officer Jameson—of her own K-9, Snapper, who was lost for a while. Lani's sure the dog gave birth recently and we'd like to find the puppies to make sure they're well taken care of. Some of our best K-9s got their start being adopted by the city. The whole unit has been hoping to spot Brooke again."

"That's sweet. I'm pretty sure I remember seeing news reports and flyers for a missing police dog named Snapper. I'm glad he was found." She returned her focus to her phone. "I'm trying to spend some more time on this Now You See message app. Maybe there's some setting or something that would let me go back to see Sarah's messages again."

"I'm pretty sure the point of that app is that you can't."

"You're probably right, but I know she told me Marcus's last name once." She sucked in a sharp breath, seemingly fascinated by something in the distance.

Ray pulled over. "What? What is it?"

"I just… I remember getting the text and looking down and reading his name. Willington?"

His heart returned to its normal rhythm now that he realized she hadn't gasped because she'd seen Marcus up ahead. "That's great, Karenna. A solid lead." One quick look back to the sidewalk revealed Brooke had disappeared. He clicked his radio. "Lost sight of the dog."

The radio responded with Detective Nate Slater's voice. "She got the best of you, huh, Morrow? I like this dog more and more. I'm in the area. I'll keep an eye out."

Karenna cringed. "Sorry I made you lose the dog. Marcus Willington. Yes, that sounds right. I think his last name is Willington."

He ignored the apology because he had every confidence someone on the team would see the dog soon. He texted Eden, requesting the tech guru start the search for Marcus Willington.

Karenna turned to him, her eyebrows drawn tightly together. "What if I'm remembering wrong? It wasn't as if I heard it a bunch of times."

"Stop doubting yourself and go with your gut. Let me see if it gets us a lead. If we find him, then we can make sure we have the right guy." He offered her a smile, knowing she always worried about doing the right thing, paying close attention to how her actions affected other people's feelings. He loved that about her but also knew it could be a weakness. Right now, he really wanted her to worry more about her own safety.

She exhaled. "You're right. Thanks. I feel better."

He shifted the SUV into gear and drove her back to work, not able to say the same thing. His own thoughts had betrayed him. He *had* loved Karenna Pressley and the same feelings that left him gutted for months after he'd broken things off were beginning to resurface.

He needed to catch this guy before his heart was the one in danger.

FIVE

Karenna ignored the smiles, winks and stares at work when she returned to her cubicle. So everyone thought she was dating Ray. Great. She needed to nip those assumptions in the bud. So when Lindsey walked past, she was ready to share. A little. Maybe she would pass on that her interaction with Ray wasn't worth any winks.

"Hey, I don't want to make a big deal about it, but that cop you thought I would be good with? Well, I didn't have time to explain earlier, but the thing is we were a couple—pretty seriously—five years ago."

Lindsey's eyebrows rose but she quickly returned to the soft smile she most often wore. "Can I ask why you broke up?"

Something inside Karenna refused to open up about anything that was causing her pain or distress or worry. She wanted to bury those feelings so deep that they stopped using any emotional energy. "It's a long story," she said instead. "But the bottom line is there really isn't potential for a relationship with him. Ever."

Lindsey's hand covered hers. "And I made a big deal about you being good together. I'm so sorry. If he's back in your life, it's got to be hard, or at least awkward, right?"

"Something like that." She was proud of her self-restraint. Really she wanted to shout, *Yes! Lindsey, you have no idea. It's been absolutely ridiculous and I need him to get out of my life before I lose my mind and heart all over again.* But saying even that much would've meant an hour's worth of backstory to follow so Karenna left it at her simple statement.

"I'll be praying."

"Thank you."

Karenna had first started going to church with Ray and his mom and sister when they were dating, but after they'd broken up, she'd floundered until she'd met Lindsey. Now they attended the same church. Karenna still wrestled with lifting up any prayer requests for herself, knowing how fortunate she had been to be raised by a loving father in a wealthy home.

Lindsey, however, seemed to think God preferred to hear about everything from everyone. Karenna wasn't ready to go that far, but knowing Lindsey prayed on her behalf brought comfort.

Her phone buzzed.

"I'll let you get that." Lindsey continued down the hall.

The Now You See Me app flashed a "Message from Sarah" notification at the top of her screen.

Karenna's heart rate tripled. Sarah was awake? She'd gotten back her phone? Her shaking finger clicked on the app and the message popped up.

People who see my face either prove they're friends or are dead. Which are you?

She dropped the phone like it had a virus and let it fall to her lap. Marcus had Sarah's phone. Indecision paralyzed her for half a second. She probably should take a screenshot but the app would notify him if she did. Not a good option. It also would have notified him that she'd read the message. Her fingers hovered over the phone. She had to do something. Ray needed to know.

The phone buzzed again. An icon appeared underneath the message "Sarah is sharing her location with you."

Karenna reached for the phone and pulled back, scared to touch it. He wanted her to know where he was? Was it a trap? It had to be, but she needed to know. She finally tapped the icon. A map opened with a little red dot focused on a familiar building.

She grabbed the company phone with her shaking hands and dialed Ray's number. He picked up on the third ring. "He… Marcus…he has Sarah's phone. He's at Zoe's apartment. But he sent me the location on purpose, Ray. The app notifies him I've seen the message. I think Zoe is in danger, but it might be a test to see if anyone shows up or it might be a hostage situation or—"

"Karenna, slow down. We're trained to handle any possible scenario. We'll go check on her. Text me if you get any more messages. For now, stay put."

"Should I text Zoe to see if she's okay or would that cause her more danger?"

"Don't interact with him or her. If the phone does anything else, let me know. Otherwise, I'll be in touch as soon as I have news."

Karenna stared at the still untouched cell phone in her lap. Minutes ticked by until she finally moved the phone to the desk and stared at the little red dot on Zoe's building, even as the phone screen went dark. Her computer monitor turned to the screensaver, as well. Still she remained unmoving, waiting, as her heart refused to slow down.

If she'd never gone to Zoe's, then Zoe would've never been in danger. And what about Haley? Hopefully she was still out and about.

Coworkers waved goodbye as they began to leave. She stood and paced within her cubicle area. Hours had passed. Still no word. Karenna was no good to anyone in this state, unable to focus on work. That meant a late night of catch-up on some client accounts once she'd heard Zoe was okay.

Why hadn't she heard anything? She picked up her phone to make sure it still had battery and a signal.

The sound of panting drew her attention down the hall. Ray walked toward her with Abby at his side. The closer he got, the more grim his face appeared. He stopped at the entrance to her cubicle. "I'd like to take you home."

That was it? All he could say? She grabbed her purse. "Please tell me there's news."

"I thought you wouldn't want to talk about it here."

She exhaled. He was right, she had said that, but she couldn't stand to wait another second. She looked around. Nearby cubicle mates had already left anyway. "Please tell me."

"I'm sorry." His eyes dropped and he shook his head. "Zoe died of an apparent overdose."

Karenna couldn't breathe. "Apparent overdose? That's ridiculous. He killed her. You know he did."

"You're probably right, but we have to investigate all options. Sarah's phone was found beside Zoe. He's baiting us like it's a game."

"Or a test," she whispered. "He knew I wouldn't stay quiet and this was a warning."

"Either way, I'm making sure you get home safely." He gently touched her arm. Abby took the gesture as a signal that it was okay to nuzzle her leg. Ray grinned. "She knows you're trying to blame yourself for this, and she's trying to let you know that you shouldn't."

"If I hadn't suggested going to visit Zoe, she'd still be alive, Ray. We didn't even get anything useful from talking to her that would help us catch him."

"Abby alerted on that porch, Karenna. She was already—" He glanced down and must have noticed how she was fighting back tears because he pressed his lips together. "Well, we should go."

She nodded, relieved. Another second and she would lose the battle against crying. She pulled her shoulders back and walked out the door.

They drove in silence until he pulled up to her brownstone. As he let her out of the vehicle, Ray looked over his shoulder at the older gentleman approaching.

She returned the man's wave. "Don't worry. He's my landlord."

"Good. I'd like to ask him about the security of the building. And have him keep a lookout."

"If you don't mind, I don't feel up to talking to anyone right now."

"Why don't you give me a second and let me check your place first?"

"Marcus doesn't know where I live. I'll just step inside and leave the door open while you talk. You'll be able to hear me if I scream."

She could tell he wasn't pleased with her compromise, but she was desperate to get a moment alone.

She unlocked the door and searched her apartment for something to focus on, something that would engage her mind until Ray left for the night and she could properly cry in peace. Sarah was barely clinging to life and now Zoe was dead. Her throat ached from the willpower of holding back the sorrow.

The fridge had some sandwich fixings and the freezer held a few microwavable meals. Nothing appealed and at the moment she couldn't imagine her appetite ever returning. She filled the electric kettle and put the tea in the mug for something to calm her nerves. Thirty seconds later, she poured the water and let it steep.

Ray knocked on the open door before the pair stepped inside. "I'd like to go over your privacy settings on your phone before we look deeper at your social media."

"I've always been pretty strict on my privacy and location settings, but you're more than welcome to check. You're trying to make sure Marcus doesn't know where I live, aren't you?" Karenna nodded to where she'd left the phone on her desk, next to her purse, and rattled off her four-digit code as she picked up her mug and crossed the room to the couch. "And, thankfully, I don't use social media except when I'm working behind-the-scenes, but that shows up as different nonprofit logos, so he wouldn't be able to figure out where I work very easily."

The steam from the tea held hints of vanilla and chamomile, though the liquid smelled a bit off. The emotions of the day had probably dulled her senses.

Abby whined and danced.

Ray frowned. "When she gets off work, like when I go home, she can't relax until she searches the place like we did last night. Do you mind if we do a quick—?"

Karenna sat. "Sure. Be my guest, Abby."

Ray loosened her lead and they stepped into the kitchen area. "At home she's always so disappointed when she doesn't find drugs."

Karenna smiled and took a sip of the tea.

Her lungs and throat reacted and closed tighter than a drum. Her chest seized as she reached her hands out for anything to assist. She needed something to help her, but she couldn't call out.

Ray stiffened as Abby lunged and jumped up on her hind legs. Her nose touched the tea box on the kitchen counter. What was that about? Normally she didn't get so aggressive about smelling the—

Glass shattered behind him. He spun around. Steaming tea ran across the floor. Karenna was seizing violently on the couch. Her wide eyes stared at the ceiling as her body convulsed.

"No!" Ray flung the leash down. "Stay!" He rushed forward and grabbed Karenna's shoulders, lifting her off the couch, and shifted, careful to avoid the area with the hot puddle. She needed to be somewhere flat where she could straighten if she was seizing.

He placed a hand underneath her head as he lowered her to the floor. Her eyes rolled back, and her eyelashes fluttered. Her lips turned blue. He knew the signs of fentanyl overdose as well as the alphabet. To have such a strong physical reaction, though...

"No! Stay with me, Karenna."

Abby's whine turned into a bark. Not only did she disobey his command to stay, which she never did, her left paw crossed over her right paw and she tripped, hitting her nose on the floor. "No, no, no, no." There was only one explanation for Abby's odd behavior. The box of tea was tainted. Abby had gotten too close when she had jumped up to smell the counter.

Lord, please!

Ray ignored the fluttering in his belly and chest. He flipped open the compartment on his belt, removed the nasal spray, and administered the naloxone to Karenna with shaky fingers. Training and policy required he always take care of victims before attending to his injured K-9, but Ray was certain he could do both. He had to save both.

He clicked the radio on his shoulder with one hand and demanded an ambulance. With the other hand, he grabbed a pre-filled syringe from his belt and lunged for Abby. She wouldn't recognize him in the drugged state and might bite. Thankfully, she wasn't a German shepherd and any bite she gave him, he figured he could handle.

She growled but didn't attack as he grabbed her. He plunged the needle into her hindquarters. He couldn't afford to wait to see if she responded well, though. He spun on his knees back to Karenna. "Come on, come on. Open your eyes."

The gurgling sounds from her throat silenced.

"No!" The response was the opposite of what he hoped. He was losing her. She'd stopped breathing.

He bent over to start administering mouth-to-mouth but stopped three inches from her lips. If he became exposed to fentanyl, as well, he'd be no use to her or to Abby. His arms vibrated with indecision until he remembered the flat plastic barriers in his belt. They were specifically for giving mouth-to-mouth resuscitation, but he didn't know if it'd be enough of a precaution to block him from the fentanyl. He had to take the risk. Karenna needed oxygen to reach her brain until the naloxone worked.

He placed the barrier on her lips and moved to breathe slowly but forcefully, counting and watching for her chest to rise. He forced himself to go through the motions even as his eyes stung, his breath turned hot and his gut twisted. Nothing was working.

"Breathe, Karenna! Breathe!"

Eighty percent of overdoses weren't overcome by a single dose of naloxone. Logically, he knew that, but he'd also never seen such a strong reaction in person, and he had never had to perform a second overdose medication himself.

Time seemed illusive. Ray didn't know whether two minutes or ten had passed. His hands fumbled for the spray again and administered the second dose. He clicked his radio and heard his voice cracking as he begged for an update on the ambulance.

He didn't chance even a look at Abby. He couldn't attend to her right now and it would break him if her cure wasn't working, either. He had no backup methods to help her.

He reached for Karenna's wrist to look for a pulse.

Please don't let them die. Please.

Karenna sucked in a rattling, deep breath. Her eyes flashed open so wide she looked to be in shock.

He folded over her, his own vision blurry. "Good. Breathe, honey. Breathe." He was a little afraid he was about to collapse in relief.

The door shook with harsh knocks. Ray jumped up on shaky legs, ran and flung open the door. "Hurry! I already gave her two doses of naloxone. Be careful to avoid the tea. Tainted with lethal amounts of fentanyl."

The paramedics nodded as if they'd seen attempted murder every day. In his peripheral vision, he saw two eyes tracking his movements around the apartment. Abby rested on the ground, breathing, but watching him. Ray put his hands on his knees for stability. *Thank You. I don't know why You listened this time, but thank You.*

Karenna sat straight up. "Ray? I… I was poisoned? They say I was—" Her voice sounded rough and she coughed a few times. "Ray? I feel so weird." Her hands moved to her stomach, her throat, her chest, as if hoping to find the explanation.

"You're feeling the naloxone in your veins right now. You'll feel unusually alert for a little longer, but you need to go with the EMTs, Karenna. You weren't breathing for so long…" He cleared his throat. "You need to let them take you. You're not out of the woods yet." His voice shook, against his will, at the last statement.

Ray had seen the scenario time and again. Addicts would overdose, get saved by a responder and then refuse to get checked out because the naloxone left them feeling wide-awake. He often wondered whether his father would've survived had responders had naloxone with them back then. No one had investigated his dad's death, though, so he'd never know just how much oxycodone had been in his system.

Her wide eyes shifted from his face to the puddle of tea a foot away. She was still trying to make sense of what had happened. There was no use explaining any more right now. She had two high doses of warring chemicals pulsing through her veins. She finally blinked for the first time, and her eyes drooped a bit.

Abby's tail began to wag. Not in full happy mode,

but at least the injection had worked. He needed to get her to Dr. Gina Mazelli, the team's veterinarian, before she left the K-9 training center for the night. He leaned over, patting Abby's head in the hope she wouldn't attempt to stand, then turned to Karenna. "I'm going to get a team to sweep this apartment and I'll meet you at the hospital, okay?"

Karenna didn't answer but her eyes met his for half a second before the paramedics rushed her out of the apartment. Ray needed to get out fast, as well, to avoid any more exposure. He picked Abby up with both arms, not wanting to risk her stepping in anything. The spaniel tucked her head in the crook of his neck.

The light reflected off the edge of Karenna's phone on the desk. He scooped it and her purse up with one hand and rushed Abby out the door.

His partner was more compliant than usual and that worried him. Abby loved belly rubs and pats but she wasn't the type of dog that liked to snuggle like a normal pet. She was a working dog who didn't seem to want that type of affection, so maybe she was worse off than he'd first thought. He clenched his jaw and ran toward his vehicle. "It's okay, girl." She let him place her in the SUV and didn't so much as lift her head.

He flipped on the siren and sped back to the center.

He would find Marcus Willington and make him pay if it was the last thing he did.

First, though, he had to make a call to the person he hoped he'd never speak to again. Even if the conversation was uncomfortable, a father should know if a murderer was determined to kill his daughter.

SIX

Karenna tried to nod along as the doctor spoke about oxygen saturation rates and respiratory rates, but he spoke so quickly she didn't retain much. Maybe she should call someone to sit with her. But who?

Ironic, really. She'd felt sheltered in her father's world and wanted out, but once she was free, she'd built her own insulated world where she was safe in every way. Until now. Perhaps the feeling of safety was only an illusion anyway, especially since she was at the hospital alone. Either way, the comfort and security of the life she'd made had shattered.

If she wanted to call on someone, she'd have to share so much she wasn't ready to divulge. Not that it mattered. Her phone was still in her apartment, along with everything else that might be useful. She glanced at her cold, bare feet. Shoes, for instance, would be nice, as well as a toothbrush to get the horrible chemical taste out of her mouth.

"—the bottom line being we're going to move you out of emergency and admit you overnight until those levels get back to where we want," the doctor said. "We'll add some noninvasive, positive-pressure ventilation just to be on the safe side. Okay?"

Except, he didn't wait for her to answer and strode out of the room.

The nurse looked at her, amused. "Looks like you might have questions."

"Honestly, I wouldn't know where to start."

The nurse's tight curls bounced when she chuckled. She gestured to a wheelchair with a tank of oxygen on the back. "Your breathing was depressed for so long we need to keep an eye on you. You'll wear something like a CPAP mask—one you can take off and on yourself—to help get your oxygen levels to rise a tick or two higher before we feel like you're out of the danger zone."

She was still in the danger zone? Goose bumps erupted over her arms. Her teeth chattered as her entire body started to tremble. The heart rate monitor gave a warning beep.

The nurse took one glance and stepped out of the room. What did that mean? She returned a second later with a heavy blanket. "The shivering is a side effect from the overdose medication. It'll wear off in another hour and then you'll feel more like yourself."

"Yourself, maybe, after a truck has rammed into you at sixty miles an hour," an orderly said as he pulled back the curtain, the only thing providing privacy in the crowded ER. He winked at Karenna. "I hear you get to take a ride to the good part of the hospital."

"Ignore him." The nurse smiled, attached a continuous positive airway pressure mask to the tank and monitors, and slipped it over Karenna's head. "I know this feels odd, but it's only for a little while." She bent over and adjusted the straps around her face.

When Karenna inhaled, the machine somehow sensed her breath and air rushed into her lungs. Uncomfortably so, but her headache faded a tad, so maybe it wasn't entirely bad.

"Let's go on a ride." As the man pushed her out of the exam room and through a maze of hallways, she focused on breathing in and out, trying not to fight the machine. She closed her eyes. Her mind raced ahead, allowing the thoughts and feelings she'd been pushing away to demand attention.

Maybe Sarah was somewhere in the hospital and she could finally see her. She didn't want to be the one to share the sad news about Zoe, though. A loud sound beeped from the monitor attached to the chair and the orderly stopped pushing.

"Hey. Your heart rate just spiked. You okay?"

Karenna nodded, unable to answer without taking the mask off. She wanted to be home, to be allowed to fall apart without an audience, but she didn't want to be alone, either.

"Where is my daughter?" A man's raging voice could be heard echoing down the hallway, likely around the corner since she couldn't see anyone. The voice sounded remarkably like her father's but she hadn't spoken to him since her short visit around Christmas. Dad wasn't listed as her emergency medical contact, either—Sarah was, actually—so his appearance didn't seem likely unless she decided to bother him. He was probably out of town, anyway.

"Sir," a man's deep voice answered. "You can lower your voice. The attendant informed us to wait here. She's being moved—"

Ray's voice. She was almost certain. He wouldn't have called her dad, would he? The sound on her monitor beeped again. Like clockwork, the orderly slowed to a stop, but Karenna waved her hand in a circular motion, encouraging him to keep going. She wanted to see who was talking around the corner.

"I think maybe I should check with the doctor first," the orderly said.

She pulled off her mask, really wanting to hurry up and get down the hall. "I'm sure I'll be fine once we get to the room. I just have a lot of stressful things to process. That's all."

"Well…the doc is just in that room, two doors down. Stay here."

"How could you let this happen?" Dad's voice railed. "I knew something like this would happen if she stayed with you."

"Sir, if he hadn't been there, your daughter would be dead," a gruff voice Karenna didn't recognize interjected.

"And you are?" Dad barked.

"Sergeant Gavin Sutherland, Officer Morrow's superior," he answered. "And I can tell you that—"

"Okay." The orderly returned. "The doctor is going to come check on you in your room in a second. Make sure that heart rate isn't a problem. I'll just turn this beeping down a tad so it stops scaring us. Let's go."

Karenna almost groaned in frustration. Between the orderly and Gavin lowering his voice, she missed hearing half of what was being said up ahead. The orderly moved her along in the wheelchair at a much faster clip, likely eager to get a high-risk patient off his hands, lest she die on him.

"Sir, I promise you I will get the guy." Ray's voice could be heard again, infused with passion.

"I have no doubt you will. Catching dealers is obviously your life, but I'm not so sure you'll treat my daughter's safety with the same diligence."

The orderly pushed her around the corner. She could see Ray and her father facing off in the hallway, in front of the entrance to a waiting room. Ray still wore his police uniform. Her dad's salt-and-pepper hair complemented the medium blue suit and silver shirt he wore.

Ray reared back. "If this is about the past, I can assure you that I'm not dating your daughter. There's no need to threaten to disown her again. I'm keeping my distance."

Her stomach flipped. Dad had threatened to disown her before—always to her boyfriends, never to her. He'd claimed it was a good test to weed out the men who were only interested in her because of his money and career influence. Whether she liked it or not, her father's wealth and success brought a fair amount of power to his fingertips. He'd reasoned that if a man truly loved her, he wouldn't care whether she lost an inheritance or not.

Karenna pulled her mask off. "Oh, Dad, you didn't. Not again." She had no idea he'd made the threat to Ray, though. They'd already been dating almost a year before she'd introduced them. She hadn't thought such tactics would've been necessary after such a long time.

The men turned to her, expressions of surprise at her appearance evident.

"Well, can you blame me?" Dad asked. "Remember Brandon?"

She fought against rolling her eyes. Bad boyfriends from back in college shouldn't count and should never be brought up in front of other ex-boyfriends. Her father's threat hadn't made a difference in her relationship with Ray, had it? That couldn't have been the reason he'd broken up with her. Ray had never cared about money. If anything, she'd felt he looked down on those who had more than enough. No, the more likely scenario was that he'd seen through her dad's charade but was irritated enough to bring it up again all these years later.

Dad's chagrined face morphed into a concerned smile as he crossed the divide between them. "Hi, sweetie." He approached her and picked up her hand. "You okay?"

"I will be. Thanks to Ray," she emphasized. Ray had saved her life. She didn't need the added stress of hearing them fight. "It's a long story, Dad." A set of involuntary coughs racked her lungs. The warning beep, even though not as loud, sounded.

A nurse appeared in the hallway behind them. "Please lower your voices. We have patients sleeping."

"Of course, we're sorry," Dad said as the frowning nurse disappeared.

"You need to put the mask back on," the orderly insisted.

Karenna slipped the apparatus on with a nod. Ray stared at her, his face pale, as if he'd been punched in the gut. His sergeant stared at him with concern, glancing between them. He placed a hand on Ray's shoulder. "I'll meet you at Miss Mayfair's room."

Ray blinked a couple of times. "Sure. Thanks, Sarge."

Sarah's room? This was the absolute worst time to have to wear the CPAP mask. She had so many questions.

Ray stepped closer to Karenna and took a knee. "Sarah's parents are here. She's on the third floor." As if he understood the questions in her eyes, he shook his head. "She's not awake yet, but we're hoping her parents know something."

"Sarah's involved? Sarah Mayfair?" Dad's eyes bugged. "She's from a good family. We've known them forever. She wouldn't be mixed up in—"

"Sir, I'll explain everything once Karenna gets settled." Ray looked over his shoulder at an approaching man, hefty, wearing a dark blazer and light gray pants. "The hospital has agreed to provide a security guard for your room."

Dad stiffened. "I'll see about his credentials."

As soon as her father stepped away, the orderly took advantage of the space in the hallway and rolled her to the room three doors down. "I'll go let your nurse know you're here." He acted as if he couldn't get away fast enough from the drama surrounding her. She didn't blame him.

As soon as they were alone, Karenna realized Ray didn't have his partner with him. She'd have thought K-9s were allowed in hospitals, but maybe not. "Where's Abby?"

He tensed. "She got a little too close to the fentanyl."

Her hand covered her mouth. "Oh, Ray. I'm so sorry. Is she okay?"

"The vet thinks she will be." His hands fisted. "And don't go blaming yourself. You didn't do it to her." He cleared his throat, as if putting aside all emotions, and handed her the phone she'd left behind. "I thought you might want this. Since you gave me permission earlier, I went ahead and checked your privacy settings. You did a good job, but…" His hesitation was enough to fill her with dread. "You must have shared your location with Sarah through the Now You See app."

She pulled the mask down to answer. "No, I didn't…" Her voice faltered as her memory cleared. "I did once. It was months ago when she never showed on St. Patrick's Day. We were supposed to meet for the parade. I sent her my location in case she couldn't find me. Turned out she'd bailed on me and forgot to let me know. But I've checked my settings since then. I know I haven't been sharing my location with anyone."

"Apparently there's a glitch. Your phone continues to share the location through the app once you've done it once, despite your general phone settings."

The shivering returned, though this time she had a feeling it wasn't because of the drugs coursing through her veins. "So he… Marcus knew my every move since he tried to kill me."

Ray's frown deepened, confirming her theory. "Since he likely had Sarah's phone, yes. Well, at least enough to know where you live and plan the…" He exhaled. "The close call. He obviously got all the information he wanted because he left Sarah's phone at Zoe's house, as you know. I took the liberty of deleting the app on your phone and asked our resident tech guru to do me a personal favor and double-check my work. Your phone is safe now. I hope I didn't overstep. I thought you might want to call someone from the hospital."

"Thank you." She glanced at her phone, simultaneously glad for it and wanting to hurl it across the room. Betrayal wasn't a feeling she normally associated with inanimate objects. Nonetheless, frustration built that she couldn't have heated words with the device.

"I'm afraid I left your purse in my SUV, which is back at the station."

"You didn't drive." She tilted her head, trying to make sense of the last few hours. "Why'd your boss bring you here, anyway?"

Ray shifted, avoiding eye contact. "He thought it would be best to come along to interview Sarah's parents." He finally met her eyes. "And because I was pretty upset after you…" He cleared his throat. "Well… and Abby."

"Because of your father." Pieces fit together about his history with his dad overdosing and understanding dawned. Since his father's death, seeing someone go through the same thing had to be awful. "I'm sure it's hard to see anyone overdose—"

He groaned. "*You're* not anyone, Karenna. I thought—"

"Sounds like we have a high heart rate?" A nurse stepped in, the orderly behind her. "The doctor said we should get you settled before he comes in to have a second look."

Ray dropped his head, looking spent and defeated in a way Karenna had never seen him before. She almost wanted to reach out and comfort him even though she was the one in the wheelchair. His words to her father about not being in a relationship stopped her from acting on the impulse.

Her father stepped into the room but didn't come any closer, shooting Ray daggers with his eyes.

Ray didn't acknowledge him but touched her shoulder. "I should go. I'll be back in the morning. Get some rest and don't go anywhere without me, okay?" He smiled and walked out the door.

She stared after him, so much unasked and unsaid. Why did she feel like her heart was in danger in more ways than one?

Ray dragged himself to work at six in the morning so he would have time to stop by the veterinarian's at the training center to check on Abby.

Dr. Mazelli must've known he would stop by early because there was a message for him at the front desk. As long as no complications arose, he could pick Abby up for the remainder of their shift later in the day.

He walked to the kennel where the spaniel was resting. She lifted her head and rose to attention as if ready to work. "Sorry, girl. Not yet." He stuck his fingers through the kennel bars. "Looks like we get to be back together after lunch, so follow doctor's orders, okay?" Abby nuzzled the side of her snout against the backs of his fingers before she returned to her bed.

He stood there, watching her while she got comfortable and fell back to sleep. She'd never been much of a morning person—well, dog—anyway. At least he knew Abby was comfortable.

He would do anything for her, with plans to adopt her once she reached retirement. To the city, Abby was a vital, valuable part of the NYPD. Only the best food, the most comfortable temperatures, and the best medical treatments were allowed. It was also why each handler—even the ones who didn't work in narcotics—carried a syringe of naloxone. He'd never been so thankful for policies that made them carry so much in their belts.

Once Abby's breathing turned to light snoring with the occasional moving paws, he knew she was fine. She had to be dreaming about that squirrel that taunted her behind his apartment. Ray quietly slipped out of the area reserved for recovering dogs and walked next door to the police station.

His boss stood at the coffee maker, filling a tumbler. Gavin caught sight of Ray and gestured to the meeting room with his chin.

Gavin had said the bare minimum last night, even driving back from the hospital in silence, but Ray knew a debriefing conversation was overdue. Maybe it was because Gavin's partner was a springer spaniel, as well, but Ray respected and related to the man more than he imagined he could with a superior.

Ray followed him inside the room. Since the unit meeting wasn't due to start for half an hour, they had some privacy. So he didn't wait for Gavin to ask questions. "I want to thank you for standing up for me with Mr. Pressley last night. It wasn't necessary, but I still appreciate it."

Gavin shrugged as he took his seat. "I could tell you intended to remain silent while he ranted, but I don't take kindly to false accusations, as you know. Especially when he's your ex-girlfriend's father and didn't have all the facts." He chuckled, shaking his head. "What was all that about disowning her?"

Ray's gut sank again at the mention. When Karenna hadn't seemed surprised by her dad's admission, Ray had felt as if he'd failed an exam he didn't know he should've studied for, even though it had happened years ago. "I shouldn't have opened my mouth and dragged the past into the conversation, but his insinuation that I wouldn't consider Karenna's safety rubbed me the wrong way." He shook his head and sank into the closest chair.

Gavin nodded with an understanding he couldn't possibly have. "You didn't break up with her because of that disowning threat, did you?" His eyes narrowed but then he pulled back and held up his hands. "Sorry. None of my business."

If Gavin hadn't admitted that it wasn't his business, Ray would've stayed silent based on principle. But he realized he really needed to talk about it. "The short answer is no. I can't honestly say his threat didn't play a part, though. I don't have a dad anymore." He slipped the challenge coin out of his pocket, as was his habit whenever he thought of his father, and started rolling and flipping it over his knuckles. "And Karenna *only* has her dad. So even as messed up as the threat seemed, I wasn't about to stand in the way of a relationship between father and daughter."

Gavin's brow furrowed. "I'm guessing you didn't give her the chance to weigh in on that decision."

Like finally finding the last piece to the puzzle, Ray's emotions clicked together, distracting him. The coin slipped from between the third and fourth finger and fell to the ground, spinning. His decision to call it quits the way he had seemed so wrong now but had seemed so right back then. Was the difference maturity or something else? He grabbed the coin and sat back up.

Gavin tapped his pen against the yellow notepad on the table. "So, back to the case. I need to know if you have your head in the game. We can assign this case to someone else."

Adrenaline coursed through his veins. He *had* to get

Marcus. Surely, Gavin understood that, as well. And if not, he had to make him see it.

Ray leaned forward, placing his elbows on the table. "We know Marcus used to work for a pharmaceutical company as a scientist or a chemist. The drugs that were in Sarah's apartment and in Karenna's tea were a composition of fentanyl our lab had never encountered. I think he's making his own formula and targeting the upper class in the area. My gut says Marcus is working on his own, for now, trying to start his own enterprise. I can take him down before he builds it." Ray leaned back, hoping he'd just proved how deeply his head was in the game.

Gavin folded his arms across his chest, studied him for a second, and nodded. He looked up as Eden entered the room. In her late twenties, Eden wore all black, her long, dark hair in a low ponytail.

"Glad I caught you both before the meeting." Eden pointed at Ray. "I contacted the geneticist—she prefers we call her a DNA detective, though. I can't blame her since it carries that little bit of street cred with it, you know?"

He'd never thought of a geneticist carrying street cred, but Ray nodded all the same, encouraging Eden to continue.

"She's very interested in tackling the McGregor cold case, especially since she knows Bradley and Penny work here. So she agreed to officially bump it to the top of her stack. She'll take a look at the DNA sample as soon as we get through the red tape of contracting her." She offered a thumbs-up as she left the meeting room. "Good idea, Morrow."

Ray didn't feel like congratulations were earned yet.

"Let's hold the applause until we see if we get any-where."

"The idea brings hope and, right now, our team needs help with morale." Gavin didn't need to explain why. The murder of Bradley and Penny's parents may have been twenty years ago, but that kind of wound remained fresh.

Ray had been reminded of that last night. His dad's death from oxycodone was almost fifteen years ago. He never wanted to see someone overdose again, but he also wanted to stop it from ever happening. Knowing the same murderer, or a copycat, had killed someone else's parents in the same way had to be gut-wrenching for Bradley. Particularly when Officer Nate Slater would be adopting the orphaned little girl, Lucy Emery. Nate's fiancé, Willow, was Lucy's aunt. Ray looked around for Nate but didn't see him among the officers coming in.

Most of the team was there, so Gavin changed gears and rattled off news from the boroughs. Ten minutes into the briefing, Nate Slater stepped inside, carrying a tablet.

"Being engaged is no excuse for being late, Detective," Gavin quipped, his voice light but his face serious.

Ray cracked a smile as many laughed, but Nate's somber expression didn't waver. "It's relevant, sir," he said. "I've been following a new lead."

Gavin waved at the empty chair. "You have the floor."

"It's going to sound ridiculous. I offered to watch some cartoons with Lucy while Willow cooked dinner. Ten minutes into the show Lucy got scared and said, 'He sounds like bad man.'" Nate took a deep breath, his face paler than usual. "I tried to shake it off as a comment on the character, but she looked at me. She asked me if he killed Mommy and Daddy."

A chill went up Ray's spine. What a horrible thing for a three-year-old to have to wonder.

"So I came in early and traced the actor. Lives in LA. The guy apparently has steady work and, as such, has an alibi for both twenty years ago and now. So another dead end." Nate sighed and sank into a chair. "But…on the odd chance it might help, I'd like to play the audio clip that caused Lucy's reaction."

Gavin pursed his lips, considering. If Ray hadn't been watching, he wouldn't have seen the quick side glance his boss made in Bradley's direction. Bradley had his arms across his chest, so still that he looked like a statue. Gavin finally nodded his approval, and Nate pressed Play.

A rich, comforting voice with firm, bass notes reverberated through the room. Such a laid-back baritone would be the go-to choice as an emcee for events.

Nate paused the recording and leaned back, surveying the team. "Look, I know a three-year-old isn't the most reliable witness, but I think you'd agree this voice is very distinct."

"We'll keep it in mind," Gavin said, effectively closing the matter.

Such a small clue and yet Ray found himself slightly envious. At least Nate had a lead on a case.

The meeting was excused, but Penny McGregor waved him over to the front desk before he left the building. "CSI just finished cleaning Karenna Pressley's apartment. They found fentanyl in everything."

Belle Montera stopped behind him and leaned forward. "What do you mean 'everything'?"

Penny shoved a piece of paper across the counter. "Seriously, whoever did this went overboard. More than a dozen items in her pantry and refrigerator all contained the stuff in lethal amounts. All the staples had the stuff. Would've been unavoidable." She smiled sympathetically. "On the bright side, the place is fully cleaned and sanitized now. She can go home without worrying."

Ray's head swam. More than a dozen items? To taint that many things with lethal amounts… There was no way she would go home without worrying because one thing had become evident. Marcus was never going to stop until Karenna was dead.

Unless Ray got to him first.

SEVEN

Karenna opened her eyes to find her father sitting up-right in a chair, in the same suit he'd worn last night. "Did you even sleep?"

"You're more important than sleep." He shrugged. "Your mother spent many sleepless nights with you in your early years. It's about time I took a turn."

Talking about her mom rarely happened except for holidays and birthdays. They'd likely never get over her passing, not that she'd want to. Sometimes the grief kept her memory closer.

"At least I don't need to give you a bottle now," Dad joked.

"No, but I would appreciate some coffee."

He clapped his hands and stood. "That I can do. Coming right up."

Thankfully, the doctor had given the all clear to be done with the oxygen machine sometime after one in the morning. She was finally able to drift off to sleep a couple of hours later. The orderly had been right, though. Her entire body ached as if it'd been run over then forced to get up and attend a group fitness class.

A knock at the door drew her attention before the

security guard poked his head in. "A Mrs. Mayfair is here. Now a good time?"

"Oh, yes, please." Karenna pressed the bed controls until she was sitting upright. With her other hand she tried her best to brush her hair with her fingers.

Mrs. Mayfair, much like Sarah, wore fashions that made her look like the millions she had in the bank. The slight dark circles gave away the woman's exhaustion but otherwise nothing about the crisp clothes and glossy hair hinted that Mrs. Mayfair had also spent the night in the hospital. She took a seat next to Karenna's bed. "I wanted to stop by and say hi. I hear you get to leave soon."

Guilt washed over Karenna in waves. She was able to leave the hospital, but Sarah couldn't. "I was hoping I could go up to see Sarah first. Any change?"

Her lips tightened and she gave the slightest shake of the head. "I heard what happened to you." Mrs. Mayfair looked down and fidgeted with her smartwatch. "You know you have these roles, parent and child. And you get good at your role's expectations, but once your child is all grown up… Well, it's hard to know how to interact."

Mrs. Mayfair extended her fingers to inspect her painted nails, almost as if searching for excuses to avoid eye contact. "Sarah is a grown woman, so I know she doesn't need a mom anymore." She finally met Karenna's gaze. "But I didn't want to be relegated to girlfriend status, either. I wouldn't be able to keep my mouth shut if I spotted a train wreck coming with some of her decisions. So I thought it'd be best to give her space." Her eyes grew wet. "But then this happened… I didn't know a thing about this boyfriend, Karenna. I'm sorry. If I had, maybe this…" She gestured at the hospital bed and blinked rapidly while forcing a smile. "Well, the point is I'm sorry you got hurt."

Karenna opened her mouth to tell her she didn't blame her and didn't know anything about the boyfriend, either, but Mrs. Mayfair had already stood and the tough, no-nonsense woman Karenna had found intimidating throughout her childhood returned.

"Well, your father has managed the transition of your adulthood wonderfully. Maybe you two can give Sarah and me pointers when she wakes up."

Karenna's mouth dropped open, speechless for a second. Barely talking for the past five years wasn't her idea of a wonderful transition. "You know I no longer work for my father's company?"

"Yes, of course. Years ago. Your dad couldn't stop bragging about how you're changing the world."

Karenna's throat tightened. Was that true?

"Well, I should go back. Stay safe and be picky about your boyfriends, okay?" Mrs. Mayfair threw her hands up. "See? I can't help myself even with other people's grown daughters." She offered a wry smile, shook her head and strolled out of the room just as her father filled the doorway with two cups of coffee.

He set her foam cup on the stand by her bed and took his seat again. "You look as if you've received shocking news. Any change with Sarah?"

She shook her head. "Do you really brag about me?"

His eyes widened. "Of course I do." Frown lines deepened in his forehead as he stared at the floor. "I'm sorry you even need to wonder." He glanced up. "I've known for quite some time you don't need me anymore.

In fact, I wouldn't have given you that job or the company apartment if I thought you did."

"What?" Karenna's question was so unexpectedly loud she clamped a hand over her mouth before removing it.

"I wouldn't have left you on the street, either. I'm not going to lie, Karenna. I liked the idea of leaving the company to you, of having a legacy. I was hurt when you left."

She pressed her head back into the pillow, suddenly dizzy with how badly she'd interpreted his behavior. She'd built walls around herself. "I wanted to know I could stand on my own two feet." Although maybe she'd wanted to prove she didn't need anyone. The thought surprised her. Was that what she was actually doing?

"Well, I should've encouraged you instead of being distant." He sighed. "It might've taken me five years, but I realized I'm leaving a great legacy in you no matter what you do. And if you happen to ever want to come back to the company…"

"Dad…" She laughed. "I'll keep it in mind. No more telling others you might disown me, though, okay?"

He chuckled and patted her hand. "I think I can agree to that, as long as you understand that even though you're an independent adult who can take care of yourself, you will always be my daughter. I take your safety very seriously." His phone buzzed and he groaned. "With that said, are you sure you're okay on your own?"

"I'm fine, Dad. They're going to release me this morning. Singapore calling?" She remembered that some of the company's biggest business deals and clients were international.

He nodded. "It's the car service ready to pick me

up. Short business trip. You call me if you need any-thing, though."

"Go. I'm in good hands."

As if on cue, Ray filled the doorway, deep in con-versation with the security guard.

Her father looked back and forth between them. "I hope you're right about this decision, too, honey." He kissed her forehead and left.

Thankfully, he didn't wait for her to answer because she didn't know how to. She refused to believe that Ray had broken up with her because of her dad's idle threat. Ray would've talked to her first if that was the reason. Right? Despite wanting to leave the past in the past, she could feel the walls start to crumble. She needed to know. Even if that meant facing rejection and heart-break all over again.

If Sarah were awake, Karenna would probably ask her opinion. She smiled, easily able to imagine what her sage advice would be. *It depends. If he breaks your heart again, does The Chocolate Room have a rewards card yet?*

Her phone buzzed for the first time that morning. An unknown number flashed across the screen with a text message.

I found your number in the trash. Haley.

Karenna put a hand over her heart. Poor Haley. The memories of yesterday played on a loop and she couldn't help but wonder what she could've done differently. She was glad Haley had found the business card with the number on the back.

I'm so sorry about Zoe.

Haley's response was instantaneous.

Can you still contact that police guy?

Karenna stared at the screen. Haley knew something and probably had no idea Karenna was in the hospital at the moment.

Instead of explaining, she simply answered, Yes.

A grainy profile image appeared on the screen. Karenna flinched. Was it him? She zoomed the photo in and out, closed her eyes for a second, opened and repeated the same zooming. The phone buzzed again.

Please don't tell police where you got this. Just get him before he hurts someone else.

Karenna hesitated. Haley obviously could tell her more about Marcus, but she might be in just as much danger as Zoe was yesterday. That would explain the request not to tell the police the origins of the photo.

Ray said goodbye to the guard and stepped into the room. Ray's top priority was taking down drug dealers one by one. Was her father right that maybe he would choose that over her safety? What about Haley's safety? Would she end up just like Zoe?

Before she could second-guess her decision, Karenna texted the photo to Ray.

He strolled up to the foot of the bed. "How's the patient? Ready to get out?"

"Check your phone, please. I just texted you."

He tilted his head in confusion but pulled out his phone. His eyes widened. "Is this Marcus?"

"I think so." The photo taunted her. "I'm certain if I saw him straight on, I'd recognize him in a heartbeat, but this side view…"

"I agree it's a bad photo, but at least it's something to go on." He looked up. "Where'd you find it?"

She cringed. "Please don't ask me. At least not until we're sure he's the guy and you can get him."

He raised an eyebrow and stared. If it was a technique to get people to talk, she could see how it would be effective. "What about the pharmaceutical connection?" she asked instead.

"So far we've come up with nothing, but I've only scratched the surface."

She glanced back down at the image and shivered slightly. "I don't like looking at him."

"Understandable. Listen, CSI cleaned your apartment fully. I picked up some groceries to hold you over. They're in my SUV."

"Oh." She looked around for her purse. "I'll pay you back."

His expression looked pained. "No, I wanted to do it." He set down a plastic bag at the foot of the bed. "A female officer picked out some clothes and shoes for you since the clothes you were wearing were bagged for evidence. I'll step outside while you get dressed and then I'll take you home."

She moved through the motions. It wouldn't have been the outfit she would've chosen, but she was thankful for the fresh jeans, the soft blue T-shirt, pink cardigan and canvas shoes. Home, though, seemed like a foreign term. The idea of the apartment didn't sound like home anymore. Where else might Marcus have hidden his poisonous drug?

The crackle of Ray's radio sounded in the hallway followed by harsh rapping against the door. "Karenna? Are you dressed? We need to get you out of here now."

She grabbed the doorknob and pulled. "I'm ready. What's happened?"

His face paled. "There's been an incident. A supposed doctor tried to inject Sarah's IV with poison. Don't worry," he added hastily. "Her mother showed up and stopped him."

"What about the security guard?"

Ray glanced at the guard on duty at her room. "He thought it was a legitimate doctor, so he left the room."

The security guard shuffled his feet. "They chased him, but I'm afraid he got away."

"The place is filled with cameras, though, right? You caught him on a security camera?"

The guard looked as if he was going to be sick. "There was a volunteer who claimed he had a bad cough, so he rode the elevator to the floor in question with a germ mask on. He stepped into the bathroom but only a doctor in scrubs came out. He avoided the cameras in the hallway. When he ran out, he was wearing a surgical mask. We have no idea who he is."

Ray's eyes met hers just as Karenna felt like her knees might buckle. Now was the time for clear thinking. She couldn't let her emotions lead the way, but one thing was becoming crystal clear. "He's not going to stop until Sarah and I are dead."

"I'm not going to let that happen," Ray said. She flashed him a look but said nothing. His insides twisted.

He'd also never wanted to let her get hurt, but she had been poisoned to near death. "We have his picture now. We're going to get him, Karenna."

Color returned to her cheeks and her shoulders fell in visible relief. "Even though it's a horrible photo?"

"I'm asking the best people I know to help on this. Your safety is the most important thing to me."

She tilted her head and studied him before she nodded.

Ray knew his words sounded like he was just trying to prove her father wrong, but he meant them. "Come on, let's get out of here."

He reached for her hand out of habit. Except how could it be habit when five years had gone by?

Her fingers, soft and gentle, wrapped around his grip. She glanced down but didn't pull away. "You treat all your witnesses like this?"

The teasing lilt in her voice didn't mask the concern in her eyes. He didn't want anyone to ever hurt her, including him. Not again. "Just you." His eyes held hers for a second and her returning smile almost took his breath away.

"I notice I'm on your left side. Missing Abby?"

"I am, but that's not why. My right hand is closest to my gun."

She sobered. "Okay. Lead the way."

The security guard flanked her other side as they took the elevator to the first floor. Half a dozen cops were inside the main entrance. The automatic doors slid open and Nate and his K-9, a yellow Lab named Murphy, walked inside. Ray reluctantly let go of her hand and approached him. "They have any scent for you to go on?"

"Not that I know of," Nate said. "Gavin wanted me here in hopes they find something quick, though."

Ray texted him the photo of Marcus. "I've already sent this in to the station to see what turns up. Can you make sure everyone here has his photo to help with the search? He might be hiding in plain sight somewhere on the grounds."

"I'll take care of it." Nate nodded toward Karenna. "Want some cover while getting her to the car?"

It didn't seem necessary, but Karenna might feel safer and Nate's partner, Murphy, seemed eager to work. "Sure."

Once Karenna was secure in the front of his SUV, she visibly relaxed. She had to see how important his job was now, after experiencing it firsthand. If they were to try to give it a go again, things would be different. They'd both changed and her father wouldn't try to pull any stunts, especially after Ray had saved her life.

Despite their deepening connection, he needed to proceed cautiously because he couldn't bear to see her cry again, like she had when he'd first broken up with her. Her eyes held all the emotion even when she fought to keep everything else still and controlled. He'd been troubled by that look for months. He couldn't hurt her again. He had to be sure, and he couldn't do that until Marcus Willington was behind bars. So the instinct to hold her hand, to hold her, needed to be buried fast.

"How *is* Abby, by the way? I was surprised she wasn't in here."

"Ready to go back to work as long as nothing changes. I'm actually going to get her a little bit later today."

He pulled into traffic and took his first left turn.

She looked over her shoulder. "Getting to my place is faster if—"

"You're right, but I'm making sure no one is following us."

"Oh." The color drained from her face. "What's the point if he already knows where I live?"

"First, he doesn't know that we're taking you back home. Second, we're going to make sure your place is safe. I bought new locks for your door. I'll make sure your landlord approves it," he added hastily as he took another left turn. "And I've arranged for someone to be guarding you wherever you are until Marcus is out of the picture."

Her mouth opened in surprise. "Don't you need a court order to offer protection like that?"

"Well, there are *some* benefits to being friends with me."

"I—"

A streak of dog fur on his right caught his eye. Skinny German shepherd mix. "Brooke." He didn't need to check the photo this time. He turned right to follow her. "Sorry. I just need to find someone in the area who can take over following this dog."

"Ray, I'm in no hurry to get back home. I don't mind if you're the one to follow Brooke."

He glanced at her. "Are you sure? If we did find the puppies, I could actually transport them back to the vet since I don't have Abby in the back."

"Absolutely. I felt horrible that I was the reason we lost her in the first place. I want to make sure those puppies are okay as much as you do." She peered through the window as he slowed to a crawl. "She really is a skinny thing. How can she possibly have enough milk to feed her puppies?"

"The health of them all is definitely in question."

They followed Brooke through the maze of Brooklyn. Occasionally, she looked back as if she knew she was being followed. A couple of times she darted into an alley and Ray thought they might have reached the location of the puppies, but instead, Brooke was making stops at various Dumpsters.

"She must be so hungry."

"All the more reason to have her lead us to the puppies so we get them all some proper nutrition. She's really covering a lot of ground so they could be anywhere. We're getting closer to our station in Bay Ridge."

Karenna smiled, the most peaceful and genuine smile he'd seen all week. "This must be the good part of the job, right? Finding puppies? How, uh…" She shifted, growing more uncomfortable. "How has work been going for you lately?" she finally asked.

He glanced in the rearview mirror, ever mindful to watch for familiar vehicles. If he spotted one, then there would be cause for concern since no one else would take so many random turns. "Never a dull moment. Did you hear about the double homicide a few weeks ago? The possible copycat murder?"

She cringed. "The one where two parents were shot by some guy in a clown mask?"

Ray nodded. "My K-9 Unit colleague, the one I was talking to at the hospital—Officer Nate Slater—is adopting the little girl left orphaned in that case. He's marrying her aunt. They actually met when he was a first responder to the scene."

"Oh, wow," she said, taking that all in for a moment. "Are you getting close to solving it?"

"We don't have much to go on at this point. But both cases are personal for the team. The victims from twenty years ago were the mom and dad of two of our K-9 Unit members—Bradley McGregor and his sister, Penny."

Her mouth dropped open. "So it's very personal."

He had a feeling she would understand. "A little of the DNA we found from the first murders has been run countless times through our systems and nothing turned up. I got to thinking about some of the true crime shows I'd watched and had the idea to approach it from a genealogical standpoint."

Her mouth dropped open. "I know which one you're talking about. They found the family tree and went from there."

Ray pulled back in surprise, careful not to glance at Karenna in case he lost Brooke again. They'd watched those shows together back when they were dating, but he was pretty sure the one that gave him the idea was more recent. "You, uh, you still watch those?"

"Sometimes," she answered.

Brooke rushed up a yard and disappeared at a run-down two-family house. The windows and doors were boarded up with wood. Abandoned. A shame. The front stairs led to what must have been a beautiful wraparound porch at one point. He checked his mirrors again.

No one was visible on the street. He pulled into the driveway as far as he could until his vehicle was parallel to the latticed sections covering the underside of the porch.

"Ray, look." She pointed across him. "That's a huge hole."

He grabbed his flashlight and rolled his window down just enough to shine it inside.

Brooke, prostrate on the ground, had five little black bundles of fur curled up against her belly. "And there they are," he said softly. "Looks like lunchtime." The light reflected off the fur and Brooke's eyes as she lifted her head to meet the beam.

Karenna leaned over as far as possible, craning her neck to see. "Oh, they're so cute. But they've all got black fur, well except those sideburns of brown, and—" she squinted as he tried to keep the beam steady "—tiny little ears. Are they full-bred German shepherd puppies?"

He turned off the beam, not wanting to agitate the mom anymore. "Well, they're likely a mixed breed, but if they're only a few weeks old, they actually look like textbook shepherd puppies. They'll change their appearance week by week." He cast her an apologetic glance. "I'm afraid you need to stay in the vehicle."

She leaned back and sighed. "I had a feeling you were going to say that. Go get those puppies, Officer!"

He laughed, rolled up the window and stepped out of the SUV. A warning growl reverberated from underneath the porch. He clicked the radio on his shoulder and reported his location as he retrieved a small handful of dog food from the trunk. He approached the hole in the lattice slowly. "It's okay, Mama. I'm not here to hurt your puppies. How about you enjoy some nutritious food while I take a look?"

He squinted into the darkness, trying to get his eyes to adjust before resorting to having to use the flashlight again. He ducked down, trying to get a better look, when Brooke's head lunged out of the darkness through the hole, mere inches from his face, baring her teeth.

EIGHT

The growl sent chills up Karenna's spine. Ray popped back into view. "It's okay, girl." He stepped backward and slipped inside the vehicle, his cheeks coloring. "Guess I'm not getting those puppies today."

"Do you think she'd bite you? She could have rabies."

"Possible, but I didn't see signs. I think she was issuing me a warning. Definitely more growl than bark, which tells me she's a confident dog, probably as intelligent as Nate and Lani assumed. If she had wanted to bite me, she would've kept coming."

Brooke's watchful gaze on the pair of them broke and she slowly retreated, pulling her head out of the light and back underneath the porch.

"I'm glad you're okay," she said. Their gaze seemed to crackle with the electricity of the past. She realized she was still leaning over the console, close to him. She straightened, pressing her back into her seat. "I... I never came right out and thanked you for saving my life. I meant to but—"

"I know. The hospital was a bit crowded right after."

He had to be referring to the conversation with her father. The opportunity to ask him about the breakup couldn't have been set up any easier, but still she hesitated. Maybe there was good reason to keep up some walls.

The idea that she feared what he might say after she'd faced death and excruciating pain twice in the past couple of days seemed ridiculous. She felt certain that he still cared about her after the gentle way he held her hand and led her out of the hospital.

She also loved seeing firsthand how he interacted with the rest of the K-9 Unit, like a real team. And, he wasn't only focused on drug dealers. Maybe that's what he'd meant earlier about having some growing up to do.

He grabbed his radio as he looked behind and backed out of the driveway, and she knew her chance to bring up the topic was gone.

"Puppies are no more than a few weeks old and look in healthy condition on first glance, but given the lattice covering I mentioned, retrieving them will be a challenge without causing this mama bear undue stress," he said into the radio. "I recommend providing food and water and gradually getting her to trust us. Looks like the house is facing demolition in the near future, though, so we've got a time crunch. Signing off so I can get my witness somewhere secure."

The radio crackled a response from a female officer named Belle Montera. "Copy that. I'll track down the owner and get permission to remove the lattice barrier. We'll proceed from there."

Ray slipped back onto the roads of Bay Ridge, weaving his way to Park Slope. He secured a spot right in front of her building. "Let's get you inside and, once I know you're safe, I'll bring in the groceries I picked up for you and get your lock changed."

Seeing the apartment building overwhelmed her with

a vulnerability she hadn't expected, coupled with Ray's thoughtfulness… Her eyes stung with hot tears trying to escape.

"Hey." His voice lowered and he reached for her hand. "I get it. Robbery victims struggle with it, too. I know it doesn't feel safe anymore, at least right now, but it'll feel like home again soon."

She nodded, relieved. She wasn't weak. She was normal. "Any hits on that photo? Do we know if the guy is Marcus?"

He checked his phone. "Nothing yet, but the photo is a high priority so I expect to hear back soon." He studied her for a second. "You ready?"

"Yes."

He opened the passenger door for her and they walked around the side of the stairs to her garden-level apartment. He placed one hand on her back, walking beside yet slightly ahead of her.

He spun on his heel and grabbed her arms, picking her off the ground and spinning them in between the trees at the side of her building. The tree was at her back and he stood in a way that shielded her from every angle.

"What? What happened?" Her heart raced. "What'd you see?"

Ray put his left finger on his lips. His right hand was firmly on the gun holster. He shifted to the right, a small look around the bark of the tree. He pulled back, a soft laugh escaping. He leaned forward, shaking his head, relief on his features as his forehead gently brushed against hers. "I saw men inside, but it looks like a security team installing a system in your apartment."

While that statement triggered many questions on how he'd pulled it off so fast, she should've known he wouldn't leave her safety in question. "My dad," she said softly.

He straightened and grinned. "That'd be my guess, but we'll confirm it before moving on."

She closed her eyes. "For once, I don't mind him overstepping."

"Same. Whatever keeps you safe. I would've liked if he'd given us a heads-up."

She sighed. "I think he didn't want to give me a chance to refuse." She opened her eyes and found Ray was still only mere inches from her face. The laugh had disappeared. She knew those eyes. She remembered swimming in the warmth and comfort of that gaze.

His hands reached up and cradled her face. He searched her eyes for objection, but she couldn't offer one, despite all the fear minutes ago. Would his kiss feel the same as the tender ones they used to share?

"Karenna." He said her name softly. "I—"

Whistling and fast-approaching footsteps interrupted whatever he was about to say. Like a switch had been flipped, his hands returned to his belt and he pointed to the sidewalk. "Your landlord is back. I think we should ask him some questions."

He was right that they should, but at the moment she only had questions for him. Had he been about to kiss her? What was he going to say?

Adrenaline rushed through her veins. Ray may have made the decision to break off their relationship unilaterally, but if he thought he was making the call to get back together by himself, he was sorely mistaken. In fact, *she* should be the one to ask the landlord questions. After all, if her dad could bribe his way inside, maybe that's how Marcus got in, as well. Her gut twisted at the thought.

"Mr. Northrup," she called out before he'd reached them. "I'd like an explanation of why there are strange men inside my place without prior approval?"

He blanched but quickened his steps toward them. "I can explain. We have a new owner. As of yesterday. He kept me on as property manager." He beamed in a way that made Karenna sure the salary had to be more than Mr. Northrup was used to making as an owner. "As part of the deal, he insisted the garden level have more security."

"A new owner? That doesn't justify the lack of proper advance notice that you were going to enter my apartment."

"Well, Miss Pressley, sometimes an offer is too good to refuse."

Raymond crossed his arms across his chest, all traces of humor gone. "Has anyone else made you an offer to get in her apartment before?"

Mr. Northrup noticed the action and held his hands up. "No, of course not. What I mean is…sometimes these owners have big pockets and lawyers who find loopholes. Everything was done aboveboard. There was some fine print that lets me make security upgrades like this."

She wanted to push but instead said, "Does this new owner have a name?"

Mr. Northrup flashed all of his teeth this time. "He does, but he said, and please remember this isn't me talking, that if you insist on knowing, we might have to raise your rent."

Oh, that was so like her dad. She smiled and shook

her head. "No insisting on a name here as long as you don't deny my father orchestrated this."

Mr. Northrup winked and placed an index finger on his nose before he twisted toward the short walkway to her door. "May I?"

She nodded to let him lead the way.

Ray quirked an eyebrow. "You're okay with this?"

"If my father had pulled a stunt like this before the first time Marcus tried to kill me, I would've been furious, but my life hasn't been in danger like this before. At least he's respected my decisions for the past five years." Even saying the words aloud made her realize there was no reason to fight with insecurity. She was good at her work and could even admit she'd probably inherited some of those skills from her father. For some reason, leaving the insecurity behind put his actions in a new light. "After our talk this morning, his help doesn't bother me."

Something had shifted. She no longer felt the need to prove anything to her father. She could be herself around him now and, for some reason, it made it easier to accept his help. She didn't fully understand why, though. There hadn't exactly been lots of time for reflection. "I guess I'm choosing to be thankful that he gave me something I didn't even know I needed yet." She shrugged. "You said it yourself. If you hadn't been there to save me, I'd be dead. And that man is still out there, knows where I live and how to get inside my apartment."

Ray watched the men as they ran through the instructions for her on how to hit the panic button and how to change the security code. Karenna seemed more relaxed than she had an hour ago. Was that because of the new system or because of their time together?

The men gathered their equipment and gave a nod as they exited. Ray brought in the bags of groceries and set them on the counter. "I didn't get much in the way of refrigerated products, but I got all your favorites." He froze for a second. "Well, they might not still be your favorites."

He was talking way too fast. His nerves never got in the way of taking down criminals, but almost kissing Karenna had him flustered. If the landlord hadn't interrupted them...

"Ray, I think it's time we talked." She sat on the corner of the couch with her hands intertwined, staring at the floor. "When this whole thing started, you offered to talk about the breakup. I think I'm ready for us to do that now."

She'd surprised him. While he'd fully expected her to discuss the little moment outside, he didn't think she'd wanted to discuss the past. He moved to sit on the opposite end of the couch. "What exactly?"

Her eyes widened. "Well, for starters, why."

He leaned back. Of all the questions, he hadn't expected that one. "Are you trying to tell me you didn't know why we broke up?"

"You're the one that ended things."

He frowned. "Because it was obvious we weren't working out. You didn't object, so I thought you agreed. You're telling me you didn't know why and it never occurred to you to ask for all these years?" For some reason he found that very insulting. She really must not have cared that much for him if she never knew why and hadn't bothered to ask.

Her eyes flashed. "Why would I want to object or go after you when you clearly didn't want anything to do with me?" She blinked rapidly and exhaled, her shoulders dropping. "At least, that was my thinking until this week. Either something big has changed for you given today…" She gave a side glance to the window. "Or… or… I'd just like to know what you're thinking."

"It was about my job. Pure and simple."

Her mouth dropped open. "Are you kidding me? Because I brought up my concerns over your safety? You said you'd take them into consideration. It was never a heated conversation."

"What I recall was that you didn't understand or support my job even though you knew how important it was to me. I've known since I was twelve years old that I was going to work as a cop in narcotics. I made no secret of that. And then, when I met your father and—"

"So that did play a part."

He ignored the shame building in his gut. "I couldn't come between you and your father. I mean you waited a full year before you even introduced us, as if you were scared of us meeting in the first place."

"I needed to be sure you liked me for me before you met. Too many times burned."

"I took the long wait plus your father's words as confirmation you weren't sure about me in the first place. That you didn't care as much about me as I did about you."

Karenna's eyes widened and she pulled back as if slapped. "I'm realizing that I've had a lot of walls built up around me. I thought it didn't happen until after we'd broken up, but I think it's been a pattern long before that. I'm sorry. I regret you didn't talk to me about that, because it definitely wasn't the case." She folded her arms across her chest. "And you thought I didn't

support your job choice? I *know* how important your
job is. Trust me, I never would've sat through so many
true crime shows as dates if I hadn't."

He laughed, though it was bittersweet. Maybe he
had taken her for granted and not made her a priority
back then. "I thought you said you watch them now."

A small grin played on her lips. "They grew on me."

He shook his head, the past washing over him all
over again. "If I'd been a little more mature, maybe
things would've been different. I made a lot of mistakes."

Her face softened. "I guess we both did."

He reached for her hand and she let him take it, staring at their fingers wrapped together. "Seems to me
we've both changed in only good ways."

Her eyes met his. "I'd like to think so."

His mouth went dry. Was there still a chance for
them? A bell rang, ripping them apart.

She clasped her hands together. "What was that?"

He stood and walked to the door. "Your new alarm
system." He peeked through the eyehole. "Ah. I didn't
realize so much time had passed. I asked someone to
meet us here."

She frowned. "Someone?"

"I need to pick up Abby, so I asked another officer to
come by." He opened the door to let her in. "Karenna,
this is Officer Noelle Orton and her K-9, Liberty. Since
I don't have Abby with me, she's here for reassurance.
She'll make sure our team got the place as clean as we'd
want and check your food for good measure."

Noelle and Liberty, a yellow Lab with a dark splotch
on one ear, stepped inside. Noelle was considered a
rookie K-9 officer within the team, but she had plenty

of experience, especially since she'd been a K-9 trainer first. And that was probably one of the reasons she'd been assigned Liberty, a gifted detection dog cross-trained in multiple areas but especially illegal guns.

Noelle offered her hand to Karenna. "Thanks for giving us an opportunity to get some fieldwork. Liberty has been itching to get out on the street—even for protection duty in an apartment. She needs a lot of time in the field to stay at the top of her game."

Karenna's polite smile dropped, and she looked at Ray for answers.

"Liberty is so good at her job that a gunrunner put a bounty on her head."

"We're only doing low-visibility assignments at the moment," Noelle said. "Evenings and indoor work are safest, anything that doesn't make it easy for people to notice the unique marking on Liberty's ear. Can we go ahead and take a look around?"

Karenna shrugged. "Sure. It's a studio apartment, so I doubt it'll take long. What you see is what you get."

Ray's phone buzzed with a call from the station. He nodded at Noelle to proceed before he answered.

"This is Ray."

"Do you want the good news or the bad news?" Eden asked.

Being presented those options always grated on his nerves. "Bad news." He wouldn't be able to celebrate anything good if he knew the bad followed on its heels.

"Fair enough. I just got done talking with the guys in forensics. They'll be emailing you, but I thought you should know right away. That photo you sent us? It's no good."

"The one we believe is Marcus Willington?"

Karenna's face, full of hope, turned in his direction.

"Well, we wouldn't know, would we?" Eden continued. "They've tried all their filters, but scanning recognition gets nothing. The resolution and the angle of the photo are just too bad. If you want to put me in direct contact with the person who took the photo, then I might be able to work with them to get a better quality original from their camera or phone. No guarantees, of course, since the angle still might be too bad, but I'm willing to try."

His stomach sank. He'd had it with all the dead ends. "Is the fact you're willing to try your good news?"

Eden hesitated. "Well, judging by your tone, I take it *you* don't think it's good."

"I'm not an optimist." Besides, he felt certain Karenna wouldn't change her mind about telling him where she got the photo. His gut told him that Haley or one of Sarah's other friends had sent it her way. Perhaps they were addicted to oxycodone themselves or feared for their own lives.

"Well, the other news is that the geneticist has started working on the DNA from the McGregor case. She says the sample is a little degraded."

"Sounds like more potential bad news." He sighed. "Thanks for letting me know, Eden."

"Sure. I'll let you go spread your sunshine around town now. Bye."

He grunted a goodbye and slipped the phone back in its holder. He didn't want to meet Karenna's eyes. He'd promised to keep her safe, and he was failing. He couldn't let another dealer kill someone he loved. If Marcus succeeded, Ray wouldn't be able to bear the guilt, and he wouldn't be able to forgive God for ignoring his prayers again.

Karenna stepped closer to him. "Let me guess. The photo was no good."

"You heard."

"Enough to know it wasn't helpful."

The sound of Liberty's sniffing stopped. "I'm happy to say that your place is clean," Noelle interjected. "Liberty isn't happy about it, but still."

The dog's back went rigid. Her yellow hair spiked in between her shoulder blades and her nose strained toward the door. Ray spun to see if he could see anything through the window, but the blinds were closed. The dogs could smell things both far away and underground, but in a cross-trained dog, what was the threat? Surely not a rat.

"Liberty?" Noelle asked, concern in her voice.

Liberty barked once.

The window exploded. Glass shards sprayed everywhere. Ray threw his arms up in instinct, hunching over Karenna. The sound of bullets peppered the walls around him. A siren erupted, blaring from the security devices.

Ray threw one hand around the back of Karenna's head as he dove into her, the momentum slamming them both to the ground. He peeked through the ambush of glass and drywall flying through the air. "Noelle," he yelled. Had she been hit? Had Liberty?

The bullets showed no signs of stopping, with no way of escape.

NINE

Karenna held her hands up over her face. The pinging didn't stop. She peeked through her fingers. The intense pressure of Raymond's weight on her lungs lifted. He rose up on one elbow. She grabbed a fistful of his shirt. "Don't!" She couldn't watch him get shot, especially if he was getting up for her comfort.

She squeezed her eyes closed as another round of bullets peppered her apartment. His hot breath hit her left ear. "Bullets mostly through window. Roll over. Stay down. Crawl to bathroom."

Her hands cupped her face, hoping to avoid flying debris as she opened her eyes. She focused on Ray's face above hers. His dark eyes looked her over and his hand reached for her forehead. His touch stung and she winced. He pulled his fingers back, now covered with blood, and only then did she feel the heated liquid pumping at the edge of her hairline. With bits of glass and drywall flying through the air, something had made contact.

He dropped his head again to her ear. "Can you move?"

She nodded, the side of her face brushing up against his. Her throat was so tight, she feared if she tried to talk she'd lose the battle against crying. Only when she started to turn over did he move away from her. The bullets had stopped for a second. She flipped over, as he'd said, and gingerly turned around until she faced the opposite direction.

He placed a hand on her back for half a second. "Go, go, go."

She squinted and looked up. The bullets started another round. Noelle peeked around the hallway edge. She squatted low, beckoning with her hand for Karenna to keep coming. The dog was nowhere in sight. Was Liberty okay?

Never before had Karenna understood the importance of planks and burpees as when forced to army-crawl underneath flying debris. She tried to stretch her arms as far as possible with each move, while doing her best to avoid the glass littering the floor. Her elbows stung with the tiny sharp grains that were impossible to miss. She'd moved maybe three feet, keeping her head down, when a hand grabbed her upper arm and pulled.

Noelle dragged her into the small hallway. "Keep going. Into the bathtub. Hurry!"

Karenna popped up onto her hands and knees and finally into a crouch. Judging by the floor debris, not as many bullets had made their way into the small area. She stepped into the bathtub only to find a companion waiting there for her. Liberty sat at attention, glancing up at her with a whine and a bark. The dog shifted forward, in an attempt to stand in front of her in the tub, as if to protect her. Only, given the little room in the bathtub, the movement forced Karenna to press her back hard against the shower wall. From this angle, she couldn't see anything in the hallway.

The bullets abruptly stopped. A minute of terror followed by silence, except for her heartbeat and Liberty's panting. Was the shooter reloading? Sirens from afar filtered through the walls. Help was on the way.

She exhaled and lifted her head up with a silent prayer of thanks. The sound of crunching glass preceded Ray as he jumped on the toilet and pulled up the blinds. With a flick of the lock, he shoved the window open.

"Wait, Ray!" Noelle stepped inside the bathroom with a huff.

Ray didn't so much as answer her before he kicked out the screen and disappeared through the window that led into the back courtyard. Was he just checking that the coast was clear in the back before offering them a hand?

Noelle put her hands on her hips and offered a weak smile that looked more like a grimace. She glanced at her dog. "Good, Liberty. Good protect." She gestured with her hand and the dog sat, giving Karenna room to move.

The radio attached to Noelle's shoulder went wild with bulletins that Karenna couldn't understand. Noelle seemed to understand, though, as she pressed the button down. "Backup needed on the east side fire exit." She offered Karenna a hand to help her from the bathtub.

"Why'd you tell Ray to wait?" She craned her head over Noelle's shoulder to look out the window. "Where did he go?" Deep down, she knew. He'd left her behind to go after Marcus, in the midst of a barrage of bullets, without backup.

Noelle shook her head.

What did that mean? That she didn't want to talk

about it or wasn't allowed? "I think it's time to get out of here," Noelle said instead.

Karenna clutched her throat, afraid she was about to be sick. The radio had gone off so much, surely Noelle knew where Ray was and could understand the police shorthand that Karenna couldn't. "Spell it out," she said. "Is he okay?"

"At the moment," came Noelle's terse reply.

Sirens became the only thing Karenna could hear but she watched the empty courtyard. A German shepherd came into view, running ahead of a female officer with dark hair pulled back in a bun. Several other officers ran behind her until they reached the window.

"Clear," the shepherd's handler shouted. One of the other officers reached a hand out for Noelle.

Instead Noelle took a step back. "You first, ma'am."

The toilet lid shifted precariously as the tread on Karenna's shoe slid on the porcelain. Noelle offered a steadying hand until she was able to put another foot on the tank. The officer grabbed her hand and pulled her the rest of the way out.

She stepped onto the grass as Liberty bounded out behind her and remained right beside her, not paying any attention to the other dog until Noelle picked her leash up and rubbed her behind her ears, making soothing noises.

A few parents and children, tenants of the higher floors, were in the process of running down the rear fire escapes. Police officers, firefighters and paramedics filled the small grass space to offer their assistance. With everything going on, the loudest noise was the beating of her own heart and the reoccurring thought, *Where is Ray?*

A blanket draped over her shoulders and gloved hands brushed her hair back, forcing her to be mindful. The paramedic ripped open a package and wiped the antiseptic on her forehead. "Looks like a surface cut."

"Where's Ray?" The dark-haired female K-9 handler asked Noelle. "I thought he was with you."

Noelle stepped closer to the officer, but Karenna was still able to overhear her say, "The second the bullets stopped, he ran after the shooter. I don't get why he didn't wait for backup. Or, you know, for the handler that has a gun-sniffing dog." She gestured at Liberty.

The other officer shrugged. "Ray has a history of doing *anything* to gets his guy. Gavin won't be happy, but I suppose it's understandable since this dealer has made it personal." She glanced at Karenna and her eyes widened as she realized their conversation could be overheard.

"Ma'am," the paramedic said. "Stay still."

Karenna shook her head and touched the bandage. "I'm fine. Check on the other people." The thought that any of those children could be hurt because of this man's vendetta against her made Karenna nauseous.

The officer, whose shirt read "Montera," flashed a wary glance at Noelle before addressing Karenna. "Ma'am, I'm sure Officer Morrow is safe."

Except no one had Ray's back out there. Maybe her father was right. Catching dealers was his life, his identity, and his number one priority over all things.

If that was the case, Karenna finally understood why he'd thought she wasn't supportive of his job years ago. It was also no wonder why he'd suddenly wanted to be with her. She could lead him to taking down a dealer.

But after that, would she be someone he could easily cast aside again? She wasn't about to let that happen.

"Can you at least tell me if he's okay?" she asked. "Has the shooter been arrested?"

The officers exchanged a glance that prepared her for the worst.

If only Abby were there. Her nose would surely lead him directly to Marcus. Judging by the trajectory of the bullets, the shooter had been on a higher floor of the apartment building on the opposite side of the street. Two occupants rushed out of the building and Ray caught the door. "Get back inside your apartment. It's safer to stay put. Did you see anything?"

"No, just heard bullets." The wide-eyed women rushed back into their apartments before he moved to go upstairs. Ray pressed his back against the stairwell, his hand on his weapon. Usually shooters avoided using the elevator, wanting a hasty, unnoticed escape. He rounded the second-floor landing and turned off his radio, lest the loud updates give away his location. A door opened and a teenager popped his head out.

"Get back inside," Ray ordered.

The boy, dressed in a hoodie and loose jeans, frowned. "The other cop said that, too, but the shooting has stopped, right? He had one of those ghost guns, a modified AR-15. That's what did it, right?" He eagerly nodded as if it was the coolest thing he'd ever seen before.

A shiver ran up Ray's spine. There was no way that anyone could've beaten him to the location unless an off-duty officer lived in the building, which was a possibility. "What'd the other cop look like?"

The boy folded his arms across his chest and smirked.

Ray didn't have time to deal with stubborn attitudes and games. He gestured at himself. "Did the cop have everything on him that I do?"

The boy's lips turned downward, surprised at the question. "Not the belt or the cam you got. Was it a fake cop?" He wavered between excited and upset in a heartbeat. "Am I on camera?" He stepped back inside. "Nah, man. I don't want to be on camera."

Ray stuck his foot in the doorway. "Why'd you say 'ghost gun'?"

"You could totally tell it was made by one of those digital printer things I've seen on television."

"Did you see his face?"

"Not really. He had his hat down and wore sunglasses."

"Stay inside for now." Ray didn't take the time to ask any more questions. He spun on his heel and ran toward the stairway. He turned his radio back on and pressed the button. "Suspect impersonating officer. On foot out of building. Possibly carrying ghost rifle."

Ever since a company released aluminum milling machines specifically designed to make the bodies of AR-15s, untraceable guns had become the bane of law enforcement. If Marcus had one of those guns and had gotten away, ballistics on the bullets wouldn't help them at all.

He launched himself down the stairwells and burst out the door that led to the alley. On a hunch, he sprinted away from the scene, even as he spotted officers running his way. He turned the corner and out of his peripheral spotted telltale navy sticking out of a Dumpster lid.

Ray grabbed his gun, knowing that sometimes desperate criminals hid in Dumpsters until the coast was clear. He cautiously lifted the lid, only to find a costume replica of his shirt and the hat of a patrol officer. Next to it was the ghost gun. Hopefully, the shooter's DNA would be in the system or Ray'd run into another dead end.

He kicked the metal garbage unit as hard as he could with a giant yell of frustration. Pain rushed up his foot and shin, but the discomfort was welcome compared to the feeling of failure.

"Hey!" Nate called out. His K-9, Murphy, had a long lead, sniffing ahead of him, ignoring Ray and working.

"You found a scent?"

Nate focused on Murphy and simply nodded. Hope blossomed in Ray's chest. Murphy reached the Dumpster, stood on his hind legs and touched his nose to the edge.

Ray stepped back. "Yeah, he dropped his shirt in there." Nate reached inside and pulled out the shirt, placing it for Murphy to take another sniff, but not before he groaned, having seen the gun.

"I know. Go get him, Murphy."

Nate nodded as the dog found another trail and took off.

Ray turned to follow.

"Ray!" a deep voice yelled. "A word."

Gavin Sutherland pointed at a few officers, who nodded and ran after Nate, serving as backup. He continued his advance toward Ray, his K-9 partner, Tommy, a springer spaniel, at his heels.

Down the alley, at the front of Karenna's building, Ray could see Belle and Noelle with their K-9s, thankfully standing with Karenna who sported another horrible emergency blanket. His blood pumped hotter. She shouldn't have been in danger with him.

The radio chirped. Murphy had lost the scent at a park.

Ray's hands balled into fists and Gavin noticed.

"Ray, I get it. But this isn't about you," the sergeant said gently.

Ray reared back. "Of course not." In fact, he resented the implication.

"We're a team, Ray. Not a bunch of vigilantes taking justice into our own hands. You're a great cop. But you do have a reputation—"

"Of getting results," he snapped. His former supervisor had said the same.

"Backup prevents mistakes, escapes, hostages, injuries to other officers," Gavin said. "Following procedure gives you more options, Ray. Greater chance of success, not less.

"I need my officers to count on each other. The Brooklyn K-9 Unit is a team, Ray. A smart team. If today had gone wrong, guess who would have to deliver the news of your passing? Think I'd be able to look into your mother's eyes and defend why you ignored active shooter protocol?"

The mention of his mother took the fight out of him, but the dressing down still stung, especially in front of other officers even if they were out of earshot. "Sir, you asked if my head was in the game."

"Not so you would go off foolishly trying to prove yourself."

Ray exhaled. "Marcus has been one step ahead of us this whole time. I couldn't stand by and miss the one chance to catch him. Not that I succeeded."

Gavin stood still for a moment, chewing his lip. "So he's smart. We've beat smarter. Utilize our resources. Two heads are better than one. I'm looping Belle in on this one."

Ray fought against arguing as Belle approached with her German shepherd partner, Justice. Noelle took it upon herself to follow, keeping Karenna between them both.

Gavin watched as they approached. "It's not a penalty. It's teamwork. I think it's obvious the safety of the public is in question, so we have grounds for court-ordered protection, around-the-clock, for Miss Pressley. No more unofficial favors from my officers," he said, a warning in his good-natured tone.

Grounds for a court order was good news. At least something had gone right. "I'm requesting assigned duty until the order is official, sir," Ray declared.

His sergeant nodded. "I thought you might. We're going to get this guy, Ray. Just like we're going to get whoever is behind these murders."

The encouragement was appreciated but did little to bolster his spirit. Belle, Noelle and Karenna reached them.

Belle nodded at Ray in greeting then turned to Gavin. "Sir?"

"I'd like you to tag team with Ray on this case," Gavin directed.

"Glad to help," Belle said.

Ray nodded. "What I've gathered so far is that our shooter was no sniper. Most bullets came through the window. The trajectory from the apartment on the third floor allowed him to skim over the trees. Thankfully, he started at a moment when there were no cars passing. The sound was loud enough that traffic stopped and no accidents or injuries were reported. He hit a lot of branches but otherwise the bullets were solely at the garden level."

Karenna shivered and Ray realized he needed to get her away from the conversation, but she leaned forward. "Did anyone else see him? Someone driving by in a car? If enough people can identify him maybe we can make it public knowledge and he'll stop going after us."

Ray held up a finger. "There was a teen boy in apartment 3-A who saw the shooter. He realizes now the shooter was impersonating a cop. I'd like someone to interview him."

"I've got the formula memorized," Noelle offered.

Ray knew there was a checklist of questions to ask witnesses to help them remember the size of a suspect's forehead, nose, mouth, et cetera. In his experience, only rookies used the checklist. The questions rarely helped to identify a suspect unless the witness had gotten a good enough look to sit down with a sketch artist. Given Marcus had been wearing big sunglasses, he doubted they'd get anywhere with the witness, but he was willing to try anything at this point.

Karenna kept her arms folded across her chest. "I wonder if it was Celia's apartment that Marcus was shooting from."

"Who?" Belle asked, her eyes widening.

"You said 3-A. I know a woman who lives in the apartment building across the street on the third floor. Celia Dunbar. She works in advertising. We met once at an association meeting when I worked for my father."

Gavin nodded. "Now we're getting somewhere. If the suspect is reaching out to other people to get to you, Miss Pressley, he must be getting desperate, and that's when mistakes happen." He shot Ray a meaningful glance, as if proving his point about backup. Ray didn't appreciate the move, but he didn't let himself react.

"Belle," Gavin said with a nod, "touch base with the officers collecting evidence in the apartment. Ray, pick up your partner and get Miss Pressley somewhere safe." He gave another nod and the group dispersed, leaving Ray and Karenna alone again.

Karenna crossed her arms against her chest and avoided eye contact. "Celia wouldn't shoot at me. I don't know her well, but I'm sure she wouldn't."

"The witness described a male with a rifle. It wasn't her. I think we're still after Marcus Willington."

"I'm starting to wonder if one guy could do all of this."

Ray stepped closer to her. "Are you okay?"

"Yes," she answered curtly. "I think I have a better handle on the reality of the situation now."

He brushed some fragments of glass off her sleeve, a little concerned by her tone, but he couldn't judge her reaction after a barrage of bullets had come at her. "Come on. I don't know if they'll let us reenter the apartment, but we can ask if you can pack a bag before we leave." He gestured toward the street, his mind swimming over the events of the last half hour.

Was there anywhere he could take her that would really be safe?

TEN

Karenna walked forward in a daze. Was it possible Celia had known Sarah? And if so, what if Marcus had used his connection to her to get into Celia's apartment? For a city, sometimes it seemed like a small world among certain circles.

"Karenna!" A shout came from the right.

Ray stepped forward in front of her, his left hand out, ready to block anything that came their way. She peeked over his shoulder, past the barrier set up on either side of the sidewalk in front of the apartment buildings. "It's Lindsey! From work."

He lowered his hand. "Do you want to see her?"

Weariness weighed down her bones. "Maybe just for a minute."

Ray beckoned with two fingers and the officer guarding the barrier let Lindsey through. Wearing a black-and-white-striped pantsuit, Lindsey rushed forward, holding a giant plastic container of what looked like soup.

"Karenna, are you okay?" With one arm she wrapped Karenna in a much-needed hug.

"I'll give you a moment while I ask if we can get in there to gather your things," Ray said.

They stepped apart as Ray moved to talk to an officer. Karenna gingerly touched her forehead. "Somehow I managed to only get a small cut."

"I'm so thankful. I heard the shots a couple blocks away." Lindsey's perceptive eyes moved between Karenna and Ray. "He wasn't at the office for a social visit."

"No. I might be able to identify a criminal, and I'd rather not say any more in case it puts you in danger. I couldn't stand that." Her chest hurt not only from the trauma of the last day but also from holding back all the things going on in her heart that wanted to burst.

"And spending time with him is making things even harder on you," Lindsey said.

"Is it that obvious?" Her gaze drifted to Ray's profile.

"Well, it might be partly the ugly yellow blanket's fault, but your face looks like you wanted to adopt a puppy you had your heart set on and your parents said no."

Lindsey could always explain things in the most expressive ways.

"It's a little more intense than that, but yeah."

Her friend offered a sad smile. "I had a feeling something bigger was going on, and when you called in sick for work, I thought I should bring you some soup." She handed Karenna the big plastic container of what looked like a tomato bisque, as well as disposable spoons and napkins. "And, in case it was a heart-related sickness, I brought some emotional support." Lindsey reached into her purse and pulled out a giant chocolate bar.

Karenna accepted the gift with a laugh. "Dark chocolate with almond toffee bits. Good call." Her stomach growled loudly as if agreeing. She hadn't had anything to eat at the hospital, having arrived after dinner and leaving before breakfast.

"Almonds have protein," Lindsey said with sincerity. Her gaze followed some of the officers to Karenna's apartment and the blown-out window. Lindsey's hands flew up to her mouth and her eyes instantly welled with tears. "Oh, Karenna. When you said—I mean I saw the barriers and heard the shots, but I had no idea. Your apartment!"

In that moment Karenna had no doubt that her dear friend loved her. So why had Karenna been so scared of opening up?

"You can stay with me tonight, Karenna."

"Absolutely not. I'm not putting anyone else I know in danger." For some reason she felt the need to get everything out in the open. "I've never told anyone at work, but my father is *the* Mr. Pressley."

She eyed her skeptically. "Your dad was Elvis?"

Karenna had no idea how healing laughter would feel. "No. Greg Pressley."

"Oh, the conglomerate. Wow. Okay." Lindsey's eyes widened. "Is the criminal you can identify from his company?"

"No, I…" She shrugged. "I've been trying to keep it a secret that I was related to him because I was worried people might judge me or try to use me to get to him. But not you. You've been a great friend to me." Her voice shook. "Sorry. I'm so tired. The point is, I think he'll be able to help me find a place to stay that won't put anyone else I know in danger."

Lindsey placed her hands over Karenna's, which were wrapped around the soup and the chocolate. "Well, if it doesn't work out, my apartment is still an option."

And just like the security system she didn't know she needed, the soup and the friendship warmed her chilled hands. "Please pray for me."

"Absolutely."

Karenna knew Lindsey would. So, if she had no problem asking for help with people who really knew her, who provided for needs she didn't even realize she had, then why couldn't she ask God for help? Didn't He know her and love her more than anyone else?

The realization rocked her back on her heels.

Ray's hand touched her elbow. She hadn't heard him approach. "We need to get going."

There was no time to really process, but she tried to play the thought in a loop, as if she'd forget the moment she finally got some rest.

She waved at Lindsey one last time before getting in Ray's SUV. He moved slowly through the maze of firetrucks, police cruisers and ambulances, until they opened a barrier for his car. "I'm sorry they didn't let us go into your apartment. We'll have to stop somewhere for you to pick up clothes for the night. I'm sure by tomorrow, after they've let the crime scene techs go over the place, they'll let someone gather you a bag worth."

Karenna nodded. At this point, the concerns over her appearance had all but disappeared.

Once on a clear road, he drove with one hand, silent, as his other hand flipped his dad's challenge coin back and forth over his knuckles. "I'm glad I at least went over and asked," he said. "If I hadn't, I wouldn't have seen my dad's coin on the side of the road. It must've fallen out of my pocket at some point." He shook his head. "I don't know what I would've done if I'd lost it."

Despite her exhaustion, the drive behind his actions

had never been clearer. And, while she was ready to open her heart more to family, friends and, finally, to God, she felt certain it wasn't safe to drop the walls for a man driven by vengeance. "Did I misunderstand or was your boss upset that you ran in before backup arrived?"

"You overheard that?" He flipped the challenge coin into his palm and clasped it. "Once you're in administration, you have to be concerned about red tape and bureaucratic stuff. It doesn't change the fact that I've had the most drug dealer collars of anyone within the NYPD. So they have to gripe at me, but they still want my results. The bottom line is he can't truly understand." He shrugged and pocketed the coin. "Just like you didn't used to understand, but you get it now."

She digested his words. "What if I told you that I understand but I don't agree?"

He frowned. "What are you saying?"

"You ran toward the bullets without backup, Ray. There—"

"I did my job."

"With unnecessary risk."

He exhaled and pulled out into traffic. "Maybe. But I had to try to get him. Risk is an inherent part of the job. If we'd stayed together, we'd probably always have disagreed on the appropriate level." Ray glanced over, the question in his eyes barely masking the anger in the rest of his face. The message seemed clear. If she wasn't going to agree with him, then they had no future. Fine. His eyes still made her heart pound faster, though, even if she was hurt, disappointed, and scared for his safety.

His phone rang and he clicked the speaker button with more force than necessary.

"It's Belle. We went through the apartment and found

a business card that seems to indicate Celia Dunbar works at an advertising agency in Sheepshead Bay."

"No she doesn't," Karenna said. "Not anymore, but I can get you in to see her at her office without a warrant, I'm sure of it."

"What if she was in on the plan to kill you?" Belle asked through the speaker.

She sighed. "I guess anything is possible, but I doubt it. I let her come over once when I found her in the rain, having lost her key. She waited at my place until the property manager was back. She seemed like a really nice person."

"Like you said, Miss Pressley, anything is possible. I'll see you back at the station, Ray," Belle added.

"Affirmative," Ray said. He clicked the phone off.

Karenna faced forward as a line of police SUVs lined up in front of a building came into view. The best thing she could do for herself was to help Ray catch the dealer as fast as possible so he could be out of her life forever.

Ray bit back the angry words rolling around in his head. Here he was, trying to do his best to catch the guy who wanted to kill her, and everyone wanted him to focus on protocol? Didn't anyone understand?

He gestured to the small waiting area in the K-9 training center, where Karenna could wait.

The veterinary tech at the front desk hitched a thumb over her shoulder. "The doc is giving Abby a final check. She should be ready in two minutes."

Ray nodded and approached the door to the kennels where Abby would be returned. A grown man's familiar holler in the distance drew him farther into the center.

A German shepherd Ray didn't recognize dragged

a suited officer out of a Jeep used for training pur-
poses. Ray knew the officer the moment his shiny head
emerged from the vehicle. Henry Roarke hollered again
as the dog's firm grasp on his arm wouldn't release. Ray
knew from his time in training that the hollering was
necessary so the dog would get used to it, but Henry's
sounded so real, Ray wondered if the padded suit had
seen better days.

The trainer yelled a command but the dog was having too much fun using Henry's suited arm as a play
toy. They clipped the leash onto the dog's harness and
she finally released. Henry caught sight of Ray watching and shook his head.

Another trainer helped unbuckle the suit. "He's got
the clamp down obviously, but he hesitated when he
jumped in the car and I yelled. We need to work on
that." The trainer nodded as Henry stepped fully out
of the suit in a navy T-shirt and pants, sweat dripping
down his neck.

"The perks of modified duty?" Ray asked. He knew
Henry hated not being allowed in the field while being
investigated by Internal Affairs over alleged excessive
force.

Henry chuckled. "Don't even start." He swung his
arms over his head and stretched. "As much as I never
wanted to wear the padded suit again, I forgot how
valuable it was to see the dog's point of view. The suit
though, man…"

"Still reeks?"

"The last person who wore it *had* to be taking daily
onion pills. It's killing me."

Ray smirked. "Yeah, keep thinking that's onions."

They both knew that part of the test for becoming

a K-9 officer was the ability to withstand the smell of bodily odors within the padded suit they all had to share. It was impossible not to sweat buckets in that suit, whether hiding in a box, a car or just withstanding the chomp of a Belgian Malinois. Though they joked, they knew the suit often kept the dogs from breaking skin even if the olfactory experience for the officer wasn't pleasant.

"You trying to earn a nickname like Lone Ranger?" Henry asked.

Ray groaned. "Not you, too."

"Pretty hard not to hear all about it." He waved at the officers going in and out between the center and the station. "I might complain because Internal Affairs is taking forever to get their act together, but I'm counting on the fact I followed protocol in order to prove my innocence. If I hadn't, and that punk had gotten my gun, I'm certain I wouldn't be alive right now." He pulled his chin back. "Not to mention my partner."

"I think this is a little different."

"Is it? If we all get to pick and choose what protocol we use, how can I trust that you've got my back?" Henry glanced purposefully at the security wall monitor dedicated to the waiting area where Karenna sat. "How can the people who care about us trust we'll make good decisions? All I'm saying is remember it's not all about you."

Why did people keep saying that? The whole reason Ray had run inside that building was the exact opposite of thinking about himself. He watched all those true crime shows to make sure he didn't mess up, that a case would never be thrown out because of a mistake, but he found his arguments faltering. He respected

Gavin and Henry. If they were spotting a weakness he was blind to…

"Looks like your partner is ready for you, Abby," came Dr. Mazelli's voice. Ray smiled at the sight of his K-9 partner. "We gave her a precautionary IV of fluid for supportive care last night. She's fully recovered. You did good, using your syringe right away. There's a new one waiting at the front for you."

"Thanks for outfitting us. I hope I never have to use it again." Ray turned to find Abby wagging her tail. "There's my girl." She flopped over at the phrase he used before he rewarded her with a belly rub.

Henry laughed. "Speaking of ready to work, Cody is ready for some more bomb training. Gotta stay at the top of our game. Later, man."

Ray grabbed Abby's gear and they fell in step as if nothing had ever happened. But nothing felt the same. He stepped in the waiting room to find Karenna halfway through her container of soup. She looked up with a guilty expression. "I was starving. There's another spoon here."

"I'm glad to see you eating. Are you ready to go?"

"Absolutely." She exhaled. "Celia's new job is with my father's company."

His mouth dropped open, despite himself. "No wonder you can get us in without a warrant."

"My dad might not be too pleased, but if it leads to catching Marcus, I'm sure he'll agree a little disruption is worth it. She's at the Prospect Heights branch of offices."

She rattled off the street intersection and Ray texted Belle to meet him there so the officer could stay in the loop. The last thing he needed was one more reason for another coworker to give him grief.

The four-story commercial building was brand-new, having replaced an older building that had been demolished a couple years back. Belle's SUV pulled up behind him and he waited for Justice to be at her side before he let Abby and Karenna out of his vehicle.

"Here's how this is going down," he told Karenna. "We'll accept your help to get us inside the building for a friendly chat with Miss Dunbar, but you will need to stay in a waiting room or meeting room or something."

She pursed her lips for a moment before nodding. "Fine."

The security guard behind the curved desk looked between the two officers and their K-9s, but his eyes lit up at the sight of Karenna. "Miss Pressley, glad to see you again. And are you officers with her or separate?"

"They're with me, Mike. We just have some news to deliver to Celia Dunbar. Is she in the office today?"

He checked his screen. "Yes. Fourth floor. Should I let her know you're on the way up?"

"No, there's no need to interrupt her if she's in the middle of something. We'll wait until she has a minute."

They got into the elevator, the back wall of which was clear glass. At the first floor, the view was of the older oak trees in the area but by the fourth floor, a significant part of Brooklyn could be seen. Even the dogs seemed transfixed.

They stepped out into the lobby. All the offices had glass doors and walls facing the carpeted hallway. Karenna pointed to the right. "I see her. Red blouse. She's in that third office."

Belle gestured to the padded leather bench against

the wall next to the elevator. "Why don't you wait here, Miss Pressley?" Karenna clearly decided not to argue as she sat down.

Ray knocked on the open door and Celia's eyes went wide. She stood, her eyes moving to the black leather futon on the side. Behind the far end, a duffel bag, a folded blanket and a pillow were stacked. Her office chair, now empty, held a lumbar support device.

Abby lifted her nose high in the air and strained forward, but without Ray giving her permission, she stayed at his side. Her feet began to move.

"Is there a problem?" Celia asked.

"I'm Officer Montera, and this is Officer Morrow," Belle said. "We just need to ask a few questions. Do you still live at…" Belle glanced at her phone and rattled off the address.

"Uh…" Celia glanced down at her desk and to the bookshelf behind the futon as if looking for an answer. "I guess. Yes."

"I've heard that back pillow is great. Wrestling with back pain?" Ray asked nonchalantly.

She blinked rapidly, flustered, and turned around to see what he was referring to. "Uh, yes. I slipped on the ice this past winter. My back hasn't quite recovered yet."

"Have you been sleeping here, Miss Dunbar?"

Her eyes flashed. "I don't see how that's any of your business."

"It's our business when someone uses your apartment as a vantage point to shoot up the building across the street, risking many lives," Belle said.

Celia blanched, her face pale. She sank down in her chair.

Abby strained a second time, her nose working overtime.

"Do we need to worry about what's in that duffel bag, Miss Dunbar?" Ray asked, nodding at the black futon.

"Of course not." Her voice shook. She clasped her twitching fingers into a fist on top of the desk and swallowed hard. "Are you here with a warrant?"

"No," Ray said softly. He took a step closer to the desk and held his hand down low so Abby knew to stay close to him instead of going for the duffel bag. "But I'm sure that will be the next step. It would help you in the long run if you worked with us to help find the shooter."

She reached for her water bottle and drank greedily before she set it down. "A…a friend asked if he could use it for one night. I thought—I had no idea. A shooter?" Her lip trembled.

"Check the news, ma'am," Belle offered.

Celia typed rapidly on her keyboard and the large computer monitor on her desk flashed to local news. Her mouth dropped open and her eyebrows rose as a tiny cry escaped. Ray leaned forward enough to see the photo of the blown-out window.

"Does your friend have a name?" he asked.

She blinked her eyes rapidly. "I…we…uh…"

"Celia?" Karenna asked.

Ray spun around. He couldn't believe she'd ignored him.

Celia stood, her fingers gripping the edge of the desk. "Was it your apartment?"

Karenna nodded.

Her head dropped and tears ran down her cheeks. "I had no idea. I promise. I had no idea. He said one night, just for a place to crash in exchange for more… It's just my back pain…"

Ah. So Celia was exchanging use of her apartment for drugs.

"I know," Karenna said soothingly. She walked past Ray and Belle and the dogs to reach the desk. Grabbing a pen off Celia's desktop, she wrote a name and number on a notepad.

"Is that the client you told me about?" Celia asked hesitantly.

Karenna nodded. "I promise she'll get you the help you need for your addiction. It's not going to be easy, but the people here will help."

The tears continued to roll down Celia's cheeks. "Stephen. The guy who asked to use my apartment. That's his name. I don't know a last name."

Ray exchanged a glance with Belle. Who was Stephen? Was there another dealer involved or had Marcus hired a shooter? He pulled out his phone and pulled up the image Karenna had sent him. He turned the screen to show Celia. "Is this your friend?"

Her eyes flickered to the photo and widened in recognition. She lost all color in her cheeks as her hands clasped her stomach. "I don't know anything. I need to ask you to leave."

Ray nodded and they all turned to leave. He and Abby brought up the rear of their caravan back to the elevator. One thing seemed obvious, though. Celia was a woman scared for her life.

ELEVEN

Karenna could barely keep her eyes open once they were back in the SUV. Dark clouds had moved into the area and raindrops sprinkled the windows. The sound of windshield wipers always made her sleepy.

"What was that stunt back there?" Ray asked as he turned on the engine. "You were supposed to stay out of the conversation."

His harsh tone pushed away her thoughts of a nap. "No stunt. Celia was being evasive, and I thought I could help. Besides, you seemed to indicate that protocol doesn't matter so much if you have a chance to get your guy." The moment she'd said the words, she realized it was the wrong time to make a point.

"Forget I said that, please," she said. "I wasn't trying to start a fight. Really, I just overheard you asking Celia about her back and I remembered she'd told me about how she'd slipped on the ice in her heels one early morning on her way to work last winter. I wondered if she was self-medicating then, but I didn't know her well enough to have that conversation."

"So she became an addict who's easily used by Marcus or Stephen or whatever his real name is," he snapped.

"It could've happened to anyone," she said softly. "It could've happened to me."

His eyes widened. "Do you think I don't have compassion? Believe me, I saw my dad in excruciating pain for years. I think I'm the first one to have compassion."

"I wasn't implying you didn't," she said sharply. "I'm explaining why I felt the need to go in there. I wanted to make sure she had a chance to get help."

He sighed. "And because you can't help but be kind to everyone you know."

"Is that a bad thing?"

"No. It's one of the things that I lo—" He shook his head and shifted into Drive. "So what was that number and name you gave her?"

Karenna blinked slowly, processing. Had he been about to say he loved that about her? Her mind fought to refocus on his question. "My biggest client is the Opioid Crisis Foundation, but the majority of their work lately is specifically helping people addicted to fentanyl and oxycodone. They are making leaps and bounds in harm reduction and are studying some new treatment pathways."

She always got excited when talking about the work. "It's actually what drew me to take them on as a client," she added. "I gave Celia the number of one of the counselors I've gotten to know. She's amazing. Helps so many people."

"You said it's your biggest client?"

"Yes. They need a lot of funding and they're constantly struggling to make ends meet because they don't want to turn anyone away."

For some reason she couldn't stop talking. Of all the people in the world, Ray had to understand her passion.

"Your job is super important, Ray, but you can't cure the opioid epidemic on your own. Even if you caught every drug dealer in town, more would pop up before you could turn around. As long as there's a demand, they'll just keep coming out of the woodwork." She lowered her voice. "And it won't bring your father back."

He reared back in his seat. "Oh, you're one to talk about fathers. You left a lucrative position just to prove something."

"To myself," she stressed. "And I can make a difference, too. I'd like to think I'm helping the same cause as you, just from a different angle. Prevention, recovery—" She ticked off her fingers. "It has to go hand in hand with catching the dealers or it'll never make a difference."

"Never make a difference? Wow. I think we better talk about something else."

She folded her arms across her chest. He seemed determined to twist the meaning of her words. "Fine. You know it's probably a good thing we aren't getting back together because I've changed a lot in the last five years and I'm not sure you'd like it. When someone isn't trying to kill me, I'm actually a pretty confident woman who has her own opinions and doesn't back down easily."

His eyes shifted to her in surprise then back to the road with a nod. "Some good came out of our visit with Celia," he said as if they'd never diverted into personal matters at all. "Belle will work with the other precinct on the shooting case and set up someone to trail Celia to see if she leads us to Marcus. Gavin is also working on getting you a court-ordered protection. Once that goes through, you won't be stuck with me the entire time."

"Ray…" She wasn't sure what to say but knew he always spoke rapidly in that tone when his feelings were hurt.

"It's actually a challenge to get a court order if we don't have the official identity of the threat," he added, "but given what happened on your street, Sarge thinks we have a good chance. So you can stay at my place and go back to work tomorrow."

The news shifted her thoughts drastically. "No. I'm not going anywhere with a lot of people. I'm not putting other tenants or coworkers in danger anymore. My dad has a new place in Bay Ridge. I already made arrangements through his secretary to stay there while you were getting Abby."

"He's not in Park Slope anymore?"

"No, he sold the brownstone right before Christmas. Apparently this place is more conducive to hosting clients, but my dad's out of town right now. I'll have the place to myself, although he's got a bodyguard manning the driveway and the housekeeper lives in the little cottage behind the pool. But other than that, it's kind of secluded. The whole place is gated with mature trees surrounding it."

"In Brooklyn?" He couldn't imagine a place of that magnitude in the vicinity.

"Well, it only cost him ten million," she said sarcastically. "It's a half-acre lot. Shore Road in Bay Ridge."

Ray whistled. "If the officers end up taking turns guarding you there, they'll be talking about the case for years."

Judging by his tone of voice, this wouldn't be a good thing.

He cleared his throat. "I'll sleep on the couch tonight, if you don't mind, so you won't be alone there, then. I imagine by tomorrow night, they'll have someone new assigned to you." The silence felt heavy within the vehicle for a minute. "Was it Haley who sent you that grainy photo of Marcus?" he asked.

She closed her eyes and shook her head. "I can't tell you. Please don't ask." She'd seen the fear in Celia's eyes. Whoever was behind the attacks had also struck fear in the heart of his customers.

"Whoever texted you that photo can probably lead us right to Marcus," Ray persisted.

"And if so, they'll be putting themselves in extreme danger. I can't have another death on my conscience!" Her imagination took her to Zoe's room, and her heart pounded so hard, her ribs began to ache again.

Abby grumbled in the backseat as if telling them to knock it off.

"And I can't have your death on mine," he snapped back. "My dad's is more than enough!"

She reeled back. "What? What are you talking about? You were a kid. You couldn't have stopped your dad from abusing—"

He pulled over and let his head drop, his eyes closed. "Karenna, my dad would've never been on painkillers if it hadn't been for me." His voice shook. "He was always telling me to put away my football gear. I had a bad habit of leaving it by the door."

He straightened and dragged his hand over his eyes and cleared his throat. "He, uh… He came in after work and tripped over it, tried to avoid the table we had by the door for keys and stuff, and wrenched his back. He'd had back issues for years, but it was like the last straw. He couldn't handle the pain anymore. Ruptured discs or something—I never asked Mom for the full details. But Dad wouldn't have been on pills and never would've gotten desperate enough to go to a dealer when the doc wouldn't prescribe him any more."

Her hand covered her mouth as she tried not to react. He'd never told her that before. He'd probably never told anyone. How long had he been carrying that burden? She dropped her hand. "That doesn't change that you were just a kid doing what kids do. Things like that happen all the time. If it hadn't been from your football gear, maybe it would've been your mom asking him to move some furniture, or your sister hugging him too tight. You wouldn't have blamed them, would you?"

"Of course not, but—"

"And your dad still had the choice of getting help instead of going to the dealers. There were other options. Maybe he couldn't see them at the time, but I'm sure he never would've wanted you to let this—"

"Well, we'll never know, will we?" he interjected, placing his hand on the front pocket that held the challenge coin.

So did his entire career revolve around revenge and guilt now? That didn't sound like the Ray she knew.

Even if that had been the initial reason he'd wanted to go into law enforcement, he'd been a man who'd genuinely wanted to serve his community. Had her concerns back then only grown worse with time, then?

He put his hands back on the wheel and pulled them back into traffic. "Whether we're together or not, Karenna, I still care about you too much to let this guy hurt you on my watch. I'll do anything—"

She held up a hand, not ready to dive into her feelings about him. And she certainly didn't want him to use her as an excuse to recklessly put himself in harm's way. "If I tell you who sent the photo, can you give that person court-ordered protection, too?"

He pondered her question for a moment. "Not immediately, but if she has enough information on him, then it's a possibility. Or, we might be able to get a warrant and tail her like we're setting up to do for Celia. I'd need to talk to Sarge about it."

"I'd like some time to think about it." Her gut, though, knew the answer. Haley had lost her sister already. Her parents were mourning. How could she ask Haley—when she was barely an adult—to jeopardize her life without guarantees? After all, even with police protection, Marcus or Stephen or whoever he was, had almost succeeded in killing Karenna twice.

The thought gave her chills. Was it inevitable that he'd succeed?

Ray pulled into the driveway on Shore Road, reeling from the events and emotions of the day. He'd like nothing more than to sit in front of the television and let his brain shut off. Although, not even his favorite reality crime shows appealed at the moment.

They reached a small gate with a speaker and camera. "Officer Ray Morrow here with Karenna Pressley."

A buzzer sounded and the gate slid back. Another twenty feet down, what looked like a brand-new security structure held a guard who tipped his hat in their direction. He pointed down the driveway. "There's a place to park at the end."

The rain had stopped for the moment, though thunder sounded in the distance. The driveway led them past the residence. It was a two-story house that would be considered mammoth in any area of the country but looked especially out of place in Brooklyn, despite being surrounded by trees. He stopped before reaching the garage, which he had no interest in parking inside lest he needed a reason to leave fast.

"It was one of the few properties handed down, generation to generation, that wasn't sold off during the Depression," Karenna explained. "They remodeled it about forty years ago and, for some reason, were ready to part with it last year."

He gawked at the grounds as he slid the vehicle into Park. "There's a solarium?" What looked like a gazebo, with glass walls and plants and furniture inside, sat next to the lap pool and was surrounded by immaculate gardens, paths and even… He couldn't believe his eyes. "Statues, too?" The one in the middle of the property looked like it was going to a toga party.

Her radiant smile returned, one he hadn't seen much at all in the last few days. "Yes. Dad likes to use the solarium for strategic planning meetings. Well, you've been warned. It's a bit much. They really liked marble."

Ray grabbed his pack of supplies for Abby before he opened the passenger doors. They made their way to the path that wound past hedges. Abby enjoyed sniffing everything but showed no sign of alerting, which was a relief given the last time.

In many ways, the property would serve as the perfect safe house. The high fence was actually a cement wall, painted in a way to resemble stucco. Mature evergreens lined the corners. A shooter couldn't possibly gain a good vantage point from outside the walls. His gaze traveled over the windows and roof and terrace on the second floor. "It's an Italian villa that didn't know when to stop growing."

"That doesn't sound like a compliment."

"If my mom were here, she would insist a real garden with grapevines and tomato plants be put here instead of box hedges."

Karenna opened the side door and wonderful smells enveloped them as they stepped into a kitchen that had to be five hundred square feet alone. The counter was lined with pans of quiche, a tray of brownies and a pan of lasagna. A woman in her late fifties closed the fridge, a smile on her face. "Karenna!"

"Mrs. Medina." Karenna held her arms out and exchanged a quick hug. "What is all this?"

"Your father told me you were coming and to prepare."

"How much do you think I can eat?"

Mrs. Medina gestured to Ray. "Well, he said you might have a cop friend coming here with you."

"Fair," Ray said, noticing that she referred to him as a friend. Maybe that meant Karenna's father didn't want anyone to know she was in danger. "I've been known to shovel in a fair amount of food."

The housekeeper narrowed her eyes. "He didn't mention a dog."

"She won't cause any damage," Karenna said. "She's highly trained."

"Mom?" The side door opened again, revealing a wiry man in his twenties, with a worn T-shirt, greasy hair, and pale face. He didn't look well. His eyes widened as he looked between the cop and Karenna. "You're here," he said as if in awe.

"Yes. She's here. Go back home. I'll be there in a second. I'm just finishing up," Mrs. Medina ordered.

Karenna offered a halfhearted wave as the man backed up and let the door close. "I didn't expect to see Colton here. How is he?"

The woman's smile faded. "Oh, he's had a rough year. Laid off. He'll get back on his feet, though. He's just not feeling very well this week." She grabbed the pans of food, well, all except the brownies, and shoved them in the refrigerator. "Heat up whatever you want. Your dad gave you a tour?" she asked.

"Yes. At Christmas."

"Good." She pointed to a notepad. "Security system code is here. I'll set it on when I leave."

"Mrs. Medina, does your place have its own security system, too?"

The woman looked as if that was a ridiculous question. "Yes, your father insisted, but I have nothing to steal." The rumble of thunder grew louder, causing them all to look up to the ceiling. "I think I'll stay in tonight. Catch up on my shows. Call me if you need anything. My number is on the notepad, as well." She wiggled her fingers as a goodbye and disappeared out the side door.

"So…you hungry?" Karenna asked.

"Not at the moment, but it's good to know we have options." Being alone together in the giant house suddenly felt awkward. "If you don't mind, Abby and I probably should search the place first."

She nodded rapidly. "Yes, of course. Does she…does she smell anything in here?"

He grinned. "No signs whatsoever, but we'll double-check before we eat."

Karenna picked up a brownie and started to hold it out toward Abby.

"No, she'll think you're offering her food to eat instead of asking her to work. And chocolate is toxic for dogs."

She pulled her hand away and put the brownie back on the tray. "Oh, sorry!"

"You didn't know. Best to keep it on the counter and we'll walk past it on our search to see if Abby alerts." He turned to the spaniel. "Time to go to work, girl."

Abby sniffed throughout the kitchen.

Karenna worried her hands together. "You could see how ashamed Celia was after realizing what she'd unwittingly been a part of. Sometimes it feels like everyone I meet might be on drugs. I know it's not true, but it feels that way."

"I'm sure that's partly because you're working with the opioid crisis client and have trained yourself to notice the signs." The news that she'd sought out the foundation to be her client had floored him. She clearly *did* care about the same things he did, and she had acknowledged how important his job was. He didn't understand what was holding him back from letting go of his pride and admitting that sometimes he went too far and allowed his anger at the situation to rule his decisions. He stopped at the threshold of the dining room. "So much of the time when Abby alerts, I can't do anything about it. Like if we're just on a walk in the neighborhood, and she strains for someone's porch. The latest stats from five years ago say that ten percent of our youth are addicted."

"I know. I've seen the statistics."

Maybe seeing the drug problem get worse instead of

better had contributed to the growing urgency and frustration he felt. Everyone in his life seemed to be shouting warning signs at him that he'd refused to notice, but whether they were right or not, he wasn't sure yet if he was ready to change his methods if they got results.

"You walked through my office. You were around all my coworkers…" She didn't outright ask, but the question was in her eyes. If Abby *had* alerted to anything, he wouldn't be able to tell her. Thankfully, for the first time that day, he could give her genuine good news— at least as far as the kitchen was concerned. "Nothing."

She beamed. "I thought so." And took a giant bite of the brownie. He'd forgotten how much she loved chocolate. He used to bring her specialty chocolates from various shops he'd passed during his time patrolling.

"We're going to check the rest of the house," he said.

"You can pick your bedroom, too, if you want. There are seven, each with its own bathroom."

"Thanks, but I'm going to stick to the couch." He looked out into the giant house where he could see a dining room in one direction and what looked like a living room in the other. "Unless there is more than one couch?"

She laughed. "There is a family room, a den and a study, but the one next to the front door is, in fact, the living room."

He stepped out onto the marble flooring. "Your dad was right about one thing. I definitely couldn't have provided you with anything like this."

"Ray." Her voice was so full of emotion, he looked over his shoulder to see if she was okay. She shook her head slightly. "I never asked you to."

The sky cracked with a giant thunderclap loud

enough to make Karenna jump and Abby's hairs stand on edge. The sudden deluge of rain, hitting sideways against the windows, followed.

Karenna gave an awkward laugh and peeked out the window. "Mrs. Medina must have made it to her cottage in time. Hopefully the storm moves through fast."

"We can hope."

By the time Ray and Abby had checked every nook and cranny of the ten-thousand-square-foot house, he was feeling the effects of the arduous day. The back of his neck prickled with a nagging feeling that his pride and anger had messed up what could've been the love of his life.

He took a moment in one of the restrooms to open his pack and change into his NYPD sweats. Night had fallen and still the rain pounded the house, echoing especially in the cavernous rooms with marble flooring, like the bathrooms and entryway. He moved to close the blinds in the last room they'd searched. The trees swayed with the wind and the lightning lit up the sky momentarily. The display of such power humbled him. He closed his eyes.

I don't know why You answer sometimes and ignore the others, but if You could show me the right path and keep Karenna safe, I'd appreciate it.

Abby touched her snout to his hand and he gave her a proper belly rub of thanks for a job well done before they headed downstairs. Thankfully, the main living room had plush carpet and four couches to choose from. The green one with nail-head trim looked like a wingback chair except it was a full-size couch with one giant cushion.

Karenna had already set some coasters and placemats down on the giant circular coffee table. She walked in with a tray of lime sparkling water and plates of steaming lasagna and broccoli.

"We're allowed to eat in the living room?"

"I am. This is the comfiest room in the house. You can do what you want."

He laughed. "I don't think you'd appreciate Abby doing the same, though." He placed her water dish, which he'd filled with bottled water, and her food bowl down on the marble entryway closest to them before finally sitting next to Karenna on the couch.

The thunder rumbled for what seemed like the hundredth time, though it sounded farther away. The rain seemed to be slowing down but the wind was still howling through nearby trees.

Ray's heart ached as he sat next to her, sharing a meal with her, knowing she was the woman for him. She leaned back in the couch and sighed. "I really want one night of blissful delusion. Like we're just two people who bumped into each other in this unusual hotel lobby and are sharing dinner."

"Can we be friends catching up in this delusion?"

She hesitated. "I guess so, but the number one rule is pretending there's not a drug dealer trying to kill me."

A loud crack of lightning punctuated her request just before the lights went out.

TWELVE

"**S**hould we panic?" Karenna asked, her eyes straining to adjust to the darkness. She twisted the fork clutched in her hand upright to be used as a potential weapon.

"Security systems have backup battery power and there's no alarm going off, so that's a good sign." Ray turned on his flashlight and cast it through the room. "Abby doesn't seem upset. Is your phone working?" He pointed the flashlight slightly in her direction. "Do you have a license to carry that fork?"

"In self-defense, you're taught to use anything and everything at your disposal."

"True, when you're not sitting with a police officer who still has his gun. The security guard has our numbers." He looked at his phone and glanced at hers. "So far, no texts." He took another bite of lasagna. "I'm sure the power will be back on soon."

The rain and tree branches slapping the side of the house sounded more ominous without the lights and hum of air-conditioning.

"I remember another time the lights went out," he said.

"Yes. Your mom and sister challenging us to an epic

game of charades. That was a fun night. You guys still
do that?"

"Nah," he said. "Timing is never right."

His words seemed to have double meaning and she
wasn't sure how to respond.

"You were wrong," he blurted.

"About what?"

"I already knew you'd changed a lot over the last
five years." He hesitated. "You've only gotten better
in every way—more confident, more secure. You had
every right to feel that way years ago, but now I'm glad
you finally know it."

"Ray." Her voice had a tinge of warning to it.

"Please, Karenna. If I don't say it now, I probably
never will… I worked so hard to become a cop, you
know that, and something clicked when I did. Like this
was my chance. My chance to make sure the dealers
didn't hurt anyone else. But everywhere I look, there're
more and more overdose deaths. So my drive and push
increases. The percentage rate has gone up instead of
down, no matter how hard I work."

He sighed. "I don't think I really understood what it
was doing to me. When we dated… Well, it was getting
serious, at least for me, but after you expressed your
concerns, about a week later I let a dealer slip through
my fingers. Because I'd played it safe and waited for
backup."

"So you blamed me," she said. "Even though you
were just following procedure?"

"I know it wasn't right, and with your dad's threat, it
was easy to make excuses, to believe I was making the
right decision. If I'm being honest with myself, I think
I was able to justify taking extra risks in my work be-

cause I seemed to be invincible, and if I didn't go right that moment, the bad guy might get away."

"And you've been alive to face another day time and time again," she countered. "It's not solely up to you to catch the bad guys."

"Which would mean trusting God more than I've been able to in recent years."

"And now?"

He laughed. "Now, I get knee pain and back pain after a hard day, and people keep telling me I'm not bulletproof. I'm trying to say that I want to change, Karenna. I'm weary of being driven by revenge and guilt, and at least this week, fear."

She was silent a moment. "We used to go to church together and even then I had a hard time praying for myself."

"Understandable."

"What do you mean?" she asked.

"Your mom still died, my dad still died. Sometimes I think if He's listening, He's ignoring."

She fidgeted with the fraying hem of her shirt. "I don't understand why He didn't answer that one, but I still believe He listens. I can't even see this house all at once, so I know better than to think I can see the big picture as well as God."

"Sometimes that's hard to do."

"I came to the conclusion today that I have an easier time asking for help if I know for certain the person loves me." She looked down, suddenly embarrassed. "I know in my head that God loves me, but sometimes… well, maybe for the reason you listed, it's hard." She held her hands out in a shrug. "I guess what I'm trying to say is I've been asking people to pray for me and others without doing it myself. I'd like to change that and start by…" She took in a deep breath. "Praying for you."

Her phone buzzed. "Sorry." She glanced down and felt a cold, clammy sensation start from the back of her neck and work its way down her shoulders and arms.

Ray leaned over her shoulder and read aloud the text from Haley. "'Keep your head down. Word is if someone shares your location, they can earn themselves a very big score.'"

"That's what I think it means, right?" She put her phone on the coffee table, giving it a little shove because, honestly, she didn't want to look at it anymore. "I'm never going to be safe, am I? I've heard so many stories since I met you, Ray. So much loss and desperation…the addiction made them do things they never in their wildest dreams thought they'd do. How can I ever have a life again? I can't hide from that much of the population. I wouldn't even know who to fear without borrowing your dog." She threw her hands up in frustration.

Ray clasped her left hand and brought it down gently to the cushion. "First of all, this guy doesn't service every addict. Second, you're going to ask for help."

She knew where this was going. He wanted her to contact Haley. "I told you I didn't want to put—"

"*You* didn't kill Zoe, Karenna. If we'd had any idea our visit would've put her in danger, we would've done our best to make sure he couldn't have gotten to her. You need to take your own advice."

She watched his face, lit only by the shadows of the flashlight he'd placed upright on the coffee table. "What do you mean?"

"Zoe made a choice. She *chose* not to talk to us. She

chose to be loyal to Marcus. Despite knowing what he'd done to you and…especially what he'd done to Sarah. It wasn't your fault."

She'd never thought of it that way. Zoe had to have known the truth about Sarah since she'd introduced them. And how could she justify feeling guilty when she'd insisted Ray shouldn't do the same about his father. She exhaled. "You're right," she finally said. "Doesn't mean it's easy to accept, though." Beating herself up with undeserved guilt almost seemed easier than accepting she had no control over Zoe's choices.

He grabbed her hand. "At least tell Haley about the attempts on your life."

"I never specifically said it was Haley who texted me the photo of Marcus," she answered halfheartedly, even though she refused to insult his intelligence or lie to him. "I'm trying to respect her request. She didn't want the police to know."

He pivoted on the couch so they were face-to-face, his hand still holding hers like a warm lifeline. "She's scared for good reason. I get that. But you also haven't told her the photo was a dead end, have you?"

She shook her head.

"My gut tells me this girl would want to help you, especially if doing so leads to the added bonus of getting justice for her sister's murder. I believe that's the second piece of advice you gave me. You need to request backup."

Karenna's eyes widened at the comparison. Asking someone for help and following protocol in his job by waiting for backup seemed an unfair comparison. "Well, those are completely different scenarios."

"Are they?"

She closed her eyes momentarily in defeat. "We're quite a pair."

The electricity in the air didn't seem to be from lightning anymore. "What about Haley?" she whispered. "You said you weren't sure you could get her court-ordered protection."

"I have an idea about that. But…" He took a long breath as if getting ready to lift a heavy weight. "It means asking a whole lot of people for help."

"You mean requesting backup?" Her heart felt lighter and more connected to him than it ever had during the time they'd been together.

He leaned forward. "I want us both to be able to live to fight another day, Karenna."

She reached for his neck and pressed her lips gently onto his. He wrapped his arm around the small of her back and pulled her closer. A warbling bark pulled them apart. "Was *that* Abby?"

Ray laughed. "She always makes her opinions known."

"What opinion was that?"

"I believe she was saying, 'You took long enough to realize what a horrible mistake you made in ever letting her go.'"

"She said all that, huh?"

"I'm pretty sure she did. Yes." His voice had the light, teasing lilt she adored. "And I think she was also saying it might be time to get an estimate on how long this outage will last."

A door closed in the distance, quiet and far away, nevertheless the sound sent shivers up Karenna's back. Abby's paws clicked and the shadow of her shape moved toward Ray.

"Something tells me Abby wasn't saying any of that, Ray," she whispered.

Abby made the guttural noise again. Ray placed a hand over Karenna's and encouraged her to stand as he grabbed his gun with the other. "She might've been trying to ask me if a stranger should be inside this house."

Ray reached and clicked off the flashlight, lest he give away their location. He studied the shadows, searching for any movement around the doorways at the far sides of the room, straining his ears to hear anything unusual. Lightning lit up the outside but only seeped inside through the edges of the closed curtains.

He'd spent a lot of time searching through the house, but it had proved so massive he couldn't claim to have memorized it.

"Maybe I didn't secure the swinging door in between the kitchen and the dining room very well," she whispered in his ear.

He held up a finger to his mouth even though he wasn't sure she could see him. He would like to believe an accidental door closing to be the most logical explanation since there had been no news from the security guard or alarms. But, given the power outage and Abby's unusual reaction, he couldn't take any risks.

In his sweatpants, hoodie and socks, he also felt unprepared without his radio and belt as he led Karenna to the stairway. Leaving and going outside was tempting, but the storm still raged, which would decrease visibility. There were two stairways to the upstairs, one on either side of the entryway, which was the size of a two-car garage. He chose the far right since it was the option that would avoid Abby's nails clicking on the marble.

Without Abby's leash or harness on, he had to trust that she would know to stay by his side. Karenna placed a hand on his back, twisting his hoodie slightly, as she stayed extremely close to him. They hustled up the carpeted stairs, tiptoeing, until they reached the farthest room down the hallway.

He closed the door with painstaking patience to make sure it didn't draw attention.

Ray clicked on his phone. Karenna let go of his hoodie and moved away from him. He texted rapidly a message to Bradley, knowing the night shift had just begun and he could be there within ten minutes. Ray asked for assistance with a possible intruder and listed the code that meant no sirens. His phone vibrated in his hand a second later with confirmation.

He looked up to see Karenna twisting the blinds in the room. Lightning flashed, this time farther in the distance. The rain still beat against the windows.

He crossed the room, careful to step lightly, until he reached her. "Help is on the way," he whispered.

Abby whined. Ray tried to control his frustration. "It's okay, girl," he whispered. "Quiet."

She knew that command, and the light from outside confirmed it when she lifted her face and looked him square in the eyes and defiantly barked. She strained her nose forward in an alert. If Abby disobeyed an order, it was only for one reason and one reason only. They were in danger.

"Ray…"

He knew what Karenna was wondering. Maybe it was a fire again or a drug dealer. Either way, someone was definitely in the house and Abby's barking was making sure that the intruder knew exactly where they were.

"Ray," she said again with more urgency. "Look." The lightning illuminated her wide eyes as she pointed far in the distance, squinting as she looked out the window. "Those houses have lights on."

His stomach dropped with the realization the power outage here was intentional. How long had Marcus been in the house?

"Do you know if the security guard has a gun?" he whispered. The last thing he wanted was to alert the man only for him to mistake Ray for an intruder.

"I... I'm not sure. Wouldn't he?"

He clicked on his phone again and texted the security guard.

Let the police in quietly. We have an intruder. Stand down.

He looked out the window. "Is there a way to get down from the terrace?"

She pointed to the door. "No, but at the end of the hallway there's another stairway that takes us directly to the kitchen."

He considered his options. His gut wanted to tell Karenna to stay put while he searched the house and took down Marcus before he could reach the room, but what if Marcus got to Karenna in those few minutes? He couldn't take that risk.

Abby whined again.

"Do you smell that?" Karenna asked.

He hesitated. *Please, not another fire.* He sniffed.

The faintest smell of rotten eggs reached him. The deeper he inhaled, the stronger the smell became.

"How many fireplaces are downstairs?"

"I don't know. I've only been here once at Christmas, right after he bought the place."

Ray glanced at the clock on his phone. They couldn't wait around any longer. Abby had to be reacting to the gas and if Marcus was still in the house, her barks would lead him right to them. "Okay. We're taking the stairs. Stay against the wall."

She nodded and followed him wordlessly. He looked both ways into the hallway and, seeing the coast was clear, they made their way down the rest of the hall and took the curved staircase that ended at the door of the kitchen.

The smell grew stronger with each step until his socks reached the cold floor of the tiled kitchen. The gas oven was wide open and a loud hiss accompanied the smell. He flipped the dials off as rapidly as he could. He reached down, picked Abby up and moved her to the welcome mat next to the door. The security alarm panel was lit with "Disarmed Ready."

How had Marcus known how to turn the security system off?

Karenna patted his back with urgency and stuck a shaking finger past his face.

From his vantage point he could see a bent shadow, close to a fireplace. Another hiss, at a different pitch, harmonized with the gas oven. He was trying to fill the house with as much natural gas as possible? On the dining room table, someone had lit a candle, the flame flickering.

Ray didn't wait for Marcus to see him. He couldn't

afford to point his weapon and risk Karenna getting shot. He opened the door in one smooth motion and shoved her and Abby out in front of him and into the deluge. He pulled the door closed against the wind. "Run to my car."

She didn't need to be told twice. Abby seemed to sense the urgency and kept up with Karenna. He did his best to run sideways, keeping his eyes on the side door in case Marcus tried to follow him. The puddles on the sidewalk splashed over his feet and shins, the moisture seeping through the fabric of his socks and chilling him to the bone.

They rounded a tree, Karenna and Abby still ahead of him, where he found his SUV sitting at an odd angle. Lightning flashed. His tires had been slashed.

"Stop." A dark figure just behind his SUV held out a gun pointed directly at Karenna.

She held her hands up. "Colton?"

It only took him half a second to realize that the shadow of the trees had worked in his favor. The man hadn't spotted Ray yet. Ray took a slight step backward and around the closest tree so he had a better shot at Colton. There was always risk that if he shot the guy, he might still be able to take a shot at her.

Karenna's eyes flicked his direction and she shook her head, as if trying to tell him to wait.

"We know each other, Colton. You don't have to do this."

Colton's gun trembled in his hand, making him all the more dangerous. "You were supposed to stay upstairs," he yelled through the rain. "It would've been painless that way," he cried. "You wouldn't have to die like this. Boom. It would be done and over."

"I can still go back inside, Colton," she offered as if it would be the easiest thing in the world. "It'd be so easy. Is that what you want?"

Smart. He almost smiled. If she headed back this way, Ray would be able to stop Colton without risking her or Abby's safety.

Colton dropped his head. "I need to stop the burning inside."

She nodded and took a step back, easing her way closer to him. "I can help with that."

"If you really understood, you'd know nothing can help. Only the stuff. I need the stuff. I can't keep worrying all the time, every time, about getting it. I need it forever. He promised I could have it forever now."

"If you kill me?" Her voice shook as she questioned him. "I don't want to die, though, Colton. Your mom wouldn't want you to do that, either. I'm sure of it. I can help you. You don't have to go off cold turkey."

"I can't let Mom be threatened!" He held one arm over his stomach, bending slightly as if in pain, his gun still pointed at Karenna. "I… I don't need to kill the dog."

She nodded slowly. "Okay—"

He waved his gun wildly. "Did you hear what I said? Get in the house!"

Flashing lights appeared behind Colton, catching his attention. The man spun around, giving Ray his chance.

Ray dove for him. "Get down," he shouted at Karenna.

Ray went to grab the man's gun, but Colton twisted and his elbow collided into Ray's torso with full force. Their bodies fell to the ground with teeth-jarring force.

Ray refused to relinquish his grip on the guy's wrist

as Colton grunted and thrashed. "Police. Drop your weapon!" Ray pried the gun from the man's hand.

Pounding feet ran up the driveway. Bradley and King, his Malinois partner, reached his side. King's guttural growl sent chills up Ray's spine as Bradley reached down with handcuffs and began issuing orders and delivering Colton his rights.

Ray sat up, completely drenched. With one look over his shoulder, he spotted Karenna on the ground, behind the tree, her hands over her head. Abby stood in front of her, refusing to budge from her protective position.

His shaking legs managed to finally work as he stood and reached for Karenna. "Are you okay?"

She let him pull her to standing, nodding rapidly. Her hands reached for his soaking wet hoodie, pulling him close. She pressed her face into his chest, still nodding.

He wrapped his arms around her trembling form. "Karenna, you were so brave. You did all the right things. Are you sure you're okay?"

She lifted her face to him, her wet eyelashes accentuating her deep blue eyes. "I'm ready to ask for help. What do I need to do?"

THIRTEEN

Karenna sat on the couch, in the well-lit living room, with Abby at her side. Thankfully her father had brought along her old trunks when he'd moved; she'd found her favorite college sweatshirt and some out-of-style jeans that, thankfully, still fit. The gas had dissipated after the firemen had opened all the windows and proclaimed it safe enough to return.

Colton's mother was in the dining room being interviewed by officers. The poor woman was sobbing, not realizing that her son hadn't really had the flu or had been laid off. She didn't know he'd known the security code for the alarm system but she'd written it down in so many places it was like handing him access. The security guard was in the den, apparently nursing his hangover from the hefty dose of Colton's mom's prescription sleeping pills that Colton had crushed up and put in the man's coffee.

Ray had changed back into his uniform and was conferring with other officers in the entryway. He spun on his heel and returned with a smile on his face.

"I think we have a plan. Are you ready to contact Haley?"

Karenna glanced at her phone.

"Maybe we should pray together about it?"

She looked at him in surprise.

"Well, if I'm going to start calling in backup, He's the best I can call, right?"

His smile emphasized the left dimple in his cheek.

She fought back a laugh, not wanting to draw attention to them, and grabbed his hand. "God, thank You for keeping us safe. Please help us to know how to best proceed in each of our own circumstances and give me wisdom as I reach out to Haley," she whispered.

Ray squeezed her hand as she finished the prayer. No one had ever told her that once you started praying about things on your heart, it might be hard to stop until everything was laid out. So she silently ran through the rest of the things on her mind: Colton and his mother, Sarah and her parents, her own father, Haley and her parents, Lindsey and the rest of her coworkers...

"Karenna," Ray asked, "why don't you start by seeing if she is available?"

She nodded and texted Haley. Can you talk?

A second later her phone rang and she held it to her left ear so Ray could hear, as well. "Are you okay?" Haley asked. "Did the police get him?"

"I'm afraid the quality of the photo was too poor. You already have enough grief on your plate but—"

"I want him behind bars. I'll do anything."

Karenna met Ray's gaze. He nodded encouragingly and moved his index finger like a wheel that should keep going.

"Haley," she said slowly, trying to remember what Ray had coached her earlier. "Do you know how he meets up with people to sell them drugs?"

"I don't do drugs anymore." Her voice wobbled. "But yeah. He gives clients free scores if they bring him new clients. Price sometimes goes up if you don't, too."

"Does he think you're still a client?"

"Yes," she said, her voice cracking. "He knows I know he killed Zoe, too. He thinks I'm scared enough to keep in line."

Something about the way Haley was phrasing her words caused Karenna concern. "Haley, honey, when did you stop using?"

Heavy breathing, just short of panting, filled the line for several seconds. "When Zoe died," she whispered, and a cry escaped.

Karenna's heart broke hearing the girl's pain, but she knew that soon Haley wouldn't be herself. If they put their trust in her while she was in the grips of withdrawal, she'd be like a ticking time bomb. Karenna had known Colton before addiction and, like him, she knew Haley's brain would betray the best intentions and the need for another hit would put them all in danger.

Ray had a deep frown. Their eyes met and she could see he was imagining the same scenario.

"Haley, we think we have a plan to take him down," Karenna finally said. "But I'm worried about you. You can't do this alone."

Quiet sobs filled the air. "I know. But I can't go anywhere for help or he'll know. He always knows where I am. The other times I've tried to wean off, he's suddenly rounding the corner. He's very nice when he wants to be."

Her last statement was very worrying indeed, given the man had murdered her sister. "Haley, how do you get in touch with him?"

"Do you have the Now You See app?"

"Yes." The puzzle pieces started to snap together in her head. No wonder his clients were scared. "Did you ever share your location with him?" Karenna asked.

"You have to when you're at the next location. But it's just a ping. I have strict privacy settings. That can't be how he knows."

"It is. There's a glitch with the app that makes it so your location sharing with him never stops." Karenna placed a hand over the mouthpiece and turned to Ray. "Did you hear that? That's why everyone is so scared. He knows where they live."

His eyes widened and he gestured for the phone.

"Haley, I'd like you to talk to my friend Ray for a second."

"It's Officer Raymond Morrow," he stated in the phone. "I hear you're willing to help, and I want to help you. If you can help us set up a meet with Marcus, would you let me send someone in an unmarked car to pick you up and take you to the hospital? That person will be a female from our station, not a cop, but a tech guru named Eden Chang. She will fix your phone so he won't be able to follow you anymore."

"But he already knows where I live. He knows my parents came back after Zoe—" Haley's voice broke off.

"It's okay, it's okay," he soothed. His eyebrows were set low in deep concentration. "New plan. You set up the meet, an officer comes to get you, and you leave your phone at home so he doesn't suspect anything until after we arrest him. This will all be over soon, and we'll help you clean your phone."

"I… I don't know."

Karenna beckoned for the phone back. "Haley, I'm

calling my friend with the Opioid Crisis Foundation to ask her for a personal favor. She'll make sure someone will meet you at the hospital and will hold your hand through the process. I'll stop by to see you as soon as it's safe for me to do so without putting you in danger, okay? You're not alone."

"Yeah, okay. I guess I'm willing to try. One second." The line went quiet for a few seconds. "Okay. I messaged Marcus and said I have a friend who wants a score. He can meet tomorrow, but I forgot to tell you, he doesn't sell to anyone he doesn't know."

"Wait. What does that mean? You don't have to be at the meet, do you?"

"No, but the first time you meet, he won't have any drugs with him. In case you're a cop."

"Smart," Ray muttered.

"Thank you, Haley. Where's the meet?"

"Usually somewhere in Prospect Park. He'll text you the exact place ten minutes before and then you share your location when you're there."

"On the Now You See app?"

"Yes."

"Okay. What's his username and we'll message him."

"The Feel Good Chemist."

Ray rolled his eyes and shook his head.

"You have to mention my name," Haley added. "Don't say anything about drugs," she warned. "Tell him I said you had a lot in common and we should get together."

Ray took notes on his phone, documenting everything relevant. He looked up. "Tell her Officer Vivienne Armstrong and her border collie, Hank, will be over to pick her up in an hour. It's important Haley leaves her cell phone at home. Vivienne will give us updates and, once your counselor friend is with her, we'll make contact with Marcus."

Karenna relayed everything to Haley and just before they said their goodbyes, promising to talk soon, Haley sniffled. "You'd have been a good big sister."

The statement broke Karenna's heart and she prayed that someday she would be an honorary sister for Haley.

She ended the call and Ray smiled encouragingly. "You make a good partner," he said. Abby sat up from her position on the floor next to Karenna, as if to remind him that he already had a partner.

Karenna laughed and patted her head. "Don't worry, I could never fill your shoes, Abby."

Ray sighed. "I'm afraid we can't stay here."

"Because Marcus knows where I am."

"We'll go to my place. You can stay in my sister's room. Sarge is working on securing a safe place for you to stay after tonight."

"But—"

"We'll take every precaution. Keeping my sister safe is a priority, and I wouldn't suggest it if I didn't think it was the best option. I'm on the garden floor and we'll sneak you in the back." He reached over and squeezed her hand. "Another cop will sleep on the couch. My neighbors are used to cop cars out front. It won't look suspicious."

She exhaled. He'd taken down all her excuses, and not just for staying at his apartment. Her heart was more vulnerable than ever. She squeezed his hand back so it'd seem natural to let go.

He glanced down at her hand and back up at her face with a soft smile, as if he understood she needed more time. "I'll wrap up with the other officers and as soon as we have a vehicle, we'll go get some rest."

She dialed her friend at the foundation while Ray made sure Vivienne Armstrong was en route to help Haley. So far, Marcus had been a step ahead of them every step of the way. A nagging fear in the back of her mind made her wonder if he'd succeed again.

Ray stared at the digital clock next to his bed. Morning had come too quickly. He shouldn't complain, though. An officer was guarding the apartment building, and after Vivienne had taken Haley to the hospital, she offered to sleep on his couch as an extra layer of protection for Karenna. The extra help had given him enough peace to catch a few hours of sleep.

Abby's head lifted from her bed in the open crate in his room and she flopped back down, placing a paw over her snout. "I feel you," he said. "I want to stay in bed, too." The week's events were catching up to him, despite being able to sleep in his own bed. "But today's the day we lock up a very bad man."

Abby's ears perked and she sat up, but it wasn't from his words. Ray had also heard the lock open on his front door.

He stepped out into the living room in time to see his sister, Greta, open the door for his mother. His mother only had a few silver strands in her curly black hair, and Greta's features were so similar they could almost be mistaken as sisters if not for the huge age gap.

Greta looked back at him with a shrug. "She's the only person I told about Karenna being here, and I made her promise not to tell the rest of the family. Besides that cop—"

"Her name is Vivienne."

"Yeah, yeah. Well, she and her dog left just a couple minutes ago. She said to kick you out of bed so you wouldn't be late to your staff meeting."

"Of course she did." Ray shrugged it off.

His mother stepped inside, holding three steaming casserole dishes. "Mom, Karenna weighs less than me." He waved his hand up and down. "This is enough to feed an army."

"Well, you have an army coming for your stakeout, right?"

"It's not a stakeout." He flashed his sister an annoyed frown for bringing their mom into the situation. "This is how operations go south."

"I didn't say a word," his mother said, clearly offended. "I don't understand why you don't ask the family to help, though. Your uncles and cousins would gladly take turns watching her."

"Mom, thank you for the offer, but this matter is for the police." He didn't want to explain the extent of danger Karenna had been in thus far, or she'd worry even more. "Is Karenna still sleeping?" he asked Greta.

"Dead to the world," Greta said.

"Don't say that, please." He lost his appetite thinking about how close she'd come so many times.

"Sorry. I mean she's a deep sleeper. She said your name once, though. With a smile," Greta made a kissy face and jumped out of his reach with a soft squeal.

"Let her sleep, okay? We have a big day ahead of us."

"Oh, by the way, I'm supposed to tell you Officer Max Santelli was already downstairs taking a security shift when Vivienne left. She said Max will stay there until Belle Montera's shift."

"Thanks." His sister had been around the team enough that she knew almost all of his coworkers. Ray grabbed a biscotti from one of the zipped bags on top off the casserole dishes. "I need to get ready to go."

He could feel his mother's eyes on him as he slipped out the back door of the garden-level apartment to let Abby do her morning stretch and yard loop before bringing her back inside. He gave Abby water and food, and still his mom stood there, her arms crossed, watching him.

"What's going on with you and Karenna anyway?" she asked.

His gaze automatically went to his sister's closed door, where Karenna currently slept. "I don't know." He enjoyed spending time with her, but he couldn't really ask her to commit to him, to truly give him another chance, until the case was over. Even if she had been the one to kiss him last. "You'll be the first to know when I do, though," he added.

Thirty minutes later he was ready and left his room to find Karenna, already dressed in his sister's clothes—a coral, long-sleeved top and white pants— in the kitchen. His mother and Greta were regaling her with stories of his relatives.

His heart warmed at the picture. Karenna was as introverted as his mom and sister were extroverted. They didn't seem to mind doing all the talking, though. In fact, they seemed to enjoy the captive audience.

Ray touched his front pocket, where he kept his dad's coin, out of habit. He stopped for a second. If he was really going to change his attitude…

He turned on his heel and headed back to his room, Abby at his side. His mother jumped up and followed him, closing the bedroom door behind them. "You seem different. Something is on your mind that's bigger than work. What's going on? Is this because of what's happening with Karenna?"

"No. Well, not entirely." He hesitated, not sure he was ready to share with his mom. "She's helped me realize I've been on this downward slope of guilt and revenge the last few years."

"I always liked that girl."

He shook his head. "If you thought so, too, you could've said something, Mom."

"Would you have listened to me?"

He smirked, shaking his head. "Probably not. But I know I need a clear head today so I can make smart decisions. It's hard letting go of the anger when it's the reason I became a cop."

"Raymond, that's not why you became a cop." She crossed the room and perched at the edge of his bed.

He fought against rolling his eyes. Even despite being a grown man, his mother wouldn't let any sign of disrespect slide. "Mom, I think I know why I became a cop."

She watched him for a long moment. "From the time you were in kindergarten, I always knew you'd be a cop." She held up her index finger and waved it. "You were always concerned with justice, with taking care of everyone's needs. You organized your first sting in first grade, Raymond. Caught the fourth graders who were stealing the chocolate milk. You remember that?"

"Mom, I was six and I asked my cousins. I would hardly call that—"

"I never had to ask you to help me with my rent when I needed it. You always just brought home your wages after…" She stood and put a hand on the side of his face. "Even your father knew."

She removed her hand with sad eyes. "He was in one of his moods, talking about becoming a dealer and getting free product made more sense than being a customer. He said that one day you'd probably be forced to choose between arresting him or looking the other way."

Her voice had a hard edge as she clasped her hands and looked down. "He said it as if he'd already decided to give up. That was the day I told him to leave and not come back unless he was ready to get help. He made his choice."

The silence between them hovered in the air for a moment. He *had* always wanted to be a cop, hadn't he? It hadn't always been about revenge. Maybe he'd just refused to remember, refused to let go… "I still miss him."

"Of course you do."

"I think I wanted his death to mean something."

She reached out and patted his chest pocket, where he kept the coin. "Your father's *life* had meaning. There were good times. I choose to focus on those. Focus on love, Raymond." She kissed his cheek and left his room.

Ray pulled out the challenge coin from his pocket and rubbed it between his thumb and forefinger, the texture reminding him of all the anger he'd been focused on the past few years. He was ready to let it all go. He placed the coin in his drawer. A peace he hadn't expected draped across his shoulders. The pain still lingered but it'd lost its sting.

He turned to Abby, who waited on her bed in the corner. "Time to get to work."

By the time he'd said his goodbyes, made sure Max

was scheduled to keep watch for the next hour, and returned to the unit, he was a full minute late for the scheduled meeting. The table had more officers than usual as half of the night shift had been requested to stay.

Gavin raised his eyebrow at Ray's tardiness but said nothing.

Noelle apparently had the floor. "I think my predicament affects the entire team. If Liberty and I don't get to work because of a threat then doesn't that set a precedent? If word gets out, wouldn't every criminal enterprise follow their example? Our entire team would be ineffective. We don't bargain with terrorists, so why should we allow some gunrunner's bounty threat to affect—"

"You're still working," Gavin replied. "You're just in low-visibility assignments."

"Sarge, with all due respect, aside from doing Ray a favor this week, Liberty—one of our best detection dogs—has basically been out of commission."

"I understand your frustration," Henry said with a nod to Noelle. "Since I'm in the same boat with Cody." He glanced at Gavin. "Speaking of being out of commission, any news on the Internal Affairs investigation?"

Gavin shook his head. "The mayor thought Brooklyn needed its own K-9 Unit, so the last thing I want to do is have Liberty and Cody on the sidelines, messing up our stats. Trust me, you two will be the first to know when something changes," Gavin said. "Now, everyone listen up. You're all familiar with Ray's case. We've had a development. Tonight, we hope to apprehend the suspect. Ray?" He nodded to give him the floor.

Ray held out his hands, unsure of how to begin. He floundered for a second before he finally said, "I'd like to enlist your help."

Henry's mouth dropped and he did a double take between Gavin and Ray. Henry leaned back. "Do continue, Ray. We're all ears."

"We've arranged a meet with the suspect in Prospect Park." He gestured toward Lani Jameson. "Lani, if you're willing, I'd like you to go undercover as Haley's friend. Sarge said you have a dancing background. We'd like you to go with that. Say you've been practicing a lot and got injured. Since you're getting on up there in age, it's your last chance to break into a starring role in a ballet, but you have pain and the doctor stopped prescribing."

"Hey," Lani said, tapping the table with her index finger. "Let the record show that I'm not old. But yeah, I can do that."

"We'll have a surveillance camera on you so my witness can be watching at a safe distance." Ray turned to the other side of the table. "Nate and Bradley, I'd like you on standby to make the arrest."

Henry's eyebrows almost jumped off his forehead but Ray ignored him, even though he knew Henry was surprised Ray was giving the collar to other officers. "Noelle and Vivenne will be stationed around whatever perimeter is left unguarded. We'll have a truck ready to set up barricades on paths once the meet is underway so the public won't wander into the middle of it."

Ray noticed the exchanged glances of apprehension. It was a lot of moving parts to keep track of without any rehearsal. "I know. The logistics will be tough," he added. "We know the meet will happen roughly around or just after sunset. We won't know the exact location of the meet in the park until Lani receives a message through the Now You See app."

"K-9 patrolling is at least pretty common in Prospect Park," Noelle said. "We shouldn't stand out too much."

"Let's hope so," Ray said. "We'll just have to be ready and be flexible. Once we have the location, Lani will go there and send our suspect a location share."

"Bradley and Lani will be in plain clothes. The rest of you will remain uniformed," Gavin added.

"Where will you be?" Lani asked Ray.

"With Belle and Vivienne at a safe distance, guarding the witness—Karenna. As soon as Karenna confirms visual that he's our guy, I'll issue the call to go in for the arrest. Sarge has secured tactical earpieces for communication."

"We'll use a private channel," Gavin said with a nod. "Depending on where the meet will be within the park, I'll notify the corresponding precinct to assist if needed."

"That's a lot of unknowns," Bradley commented. As a detective, Bradley had a lot of experience in dealing with unknowns.

Ray keenly felt the apprehension in the room. "Believe me, I know. This guy is smart, but he's also running scared. His desperation to kill my witness has endangered the public numerous times, not to mention my own K-9. I can't take him down on my own. I need the full force of the team."

This time no one laughed or teased him. Solemn expressions met his as they nodded. Ray felt the full weight of his request for help.

Tonight, they'd all be in danger.

FOURTEEN

"Ouch." Karenna flinched as the bobby pin dug into her skull.

"Sorry. This needs to look real, though." Ray's sister was doing her best to attach the dark brunette wig onto Karenna's head. Greta had already styled it into a braid since she'd apparently used it for a costume party the previous year. She adjusted the bangs and Karenna had to fight against blowing them off her forehead.

Officer Belle Montera supervised and glanced at her watch for the fifth time in a row. Everyone involved in this operation was anxious. "Looks good," Belle said, her gaze on the wig. "Ray should be here soon. We need to be ready to go when he arrives, okay?"

Karenna's stomach vibrated with energy as she nodded. The whole day had moved so fast.

Greta leaned over. "Almost done," she told Belle. "Close your eyes," she said to Karenna.

She obeyed as she felt something smeared on her eyelids. "Is this really necessary? I don't normally wear much makeup."

"My brother takes your safety very seriously. And I talked him into letting me give you a little disguise.

You're now in my very capable hands. I've watched all the YouTube videos of interviews from this former chief-of-disguise lady in the CIA. Subtle doesn't get the job done unless you're Clark Kent, so you need to look like a different person. Besides, this only makes your blue eyes more beautiful."

Karenna had missed Greta's vibrant personality, even if she pushed Karenna out of her comfort zone occasionally.

"A disguise can't hurt." Belle leaned over to examine Karenna's new appearance and nodded. "And she's right. Your eyes look amazing, but just in case the hair doesn't get the job done, you're going to keep those peepers hidden with these." She opened a plastic bag to reveal a black cap with "Brooklyn" embroidered in all caps, aviator sunglasses and a beige spring jacket.

Belle's phone rang. "Good to know," she told the caller. "Okay. Meet you there." She hung up. "We have a safe house—well, a hotel room—secured for you for after tonight, but hopefully you're not going to need it, because it's go time. We'll meet Ray at the park."

Greta practically attacked Karenna with lipstick before she hugged her. "I've missed spending time with you. Hope from now on it's without a death threat on your head."

"You and me both." Though she didn't know. Everything had happened so fast Karenna wasn't sure if she and Ray really had a future or not. She desperately wanted one, but how did they know if they were really ready for another shot? She couldn't handle opening her heart up once again only to have him drop her in a heartbeat.

She rode silently as Belle's passenger until they

reached the south side of the park. The day had gone by in a blur, but the clock was nearing eight at night. The sun's rays dipped enough to light up the tall trees, reflecting off some of the leaves waving in the breeze. Belle found a spot in an alley and let the car run. Justice whined in the backseat.

"He's anxious to get to work," Belle said with a smile. "Aren't you, boy?"

The dog barked in response.

"Sorry. I forget how loud he can be sometimes." Her phone buzzed with a message from Ray. She looked in her rearview mirror for confirmation that he'd arrived. "Okay. We're making the switch to Ray's car."

As Belle let her out, Ray exited his vehicle only to open the door for her. They didn't speak until they were both back inside.

"I almost didn't recognize you," he said. He backed out of the alley as Belle drove forward and around a distant corner.

"Your sister outdid herself."

"She would love to be contracted out by the police for undercover disguises. Too bad that's not an official thing. There might be something to using her skills." Ray attached an earpiece to his ear. "Ray here. Out."

He listened for a while, touched the earpiece, presumably to mute his voice, and then weaved around cars, heading west. "Okay, the sting is in play. Officer Jameson says the suspect just texted and wants to meet at the panthers." Ray frowned. "The panthers?"

"Oh, you know, those two statues on top of the limestone pillars. They're like fifteen feet tall or so. They look like they're surveying their kingdom." She pointed ahead. "You'll need to swing around. Third Street entrance to the park," she blurted. "Park Slope side of Prospect. Anybody who grew up in Park Slope would know."

Ray grinned. "Eden was relaying to the team the same thing. Now we have to secure a place to watch and wait."

"There are two sets of walkways." She held her hands out in a diagonal. "But from there they just keep splitting almost immediately. If an officer chooses the southernmost path to wait, there's a hill in between, covered with trees."

Ray smiled. "The perfect vantage point." He drove past the panthers, despite the roadway only being for pedestrians, and found a place to park. "Belle is parking on the other side, and Vivienne is closing the playground, placing park maintenance signs. They'll go in on foot and find a place to hide at the top of the hill. We'll stay in the car, keeping you out of sight, watching the tablet."

He pulled out the tablet and touched his ear again. "In place, Lani?" The screen Ray held showed black wavy lines but no picture. "Turn on the camera."

He frowned. "No, it can't be on because I don't have any visual. Try again." He grunted in frustration. "Understood. Over." He touched his ear and turned to Karenna. "The unit we borrowed from another precinct is on the fritz." He hesitated. "We're trying to figure out another solution. Maybe we can get him on intent to sell drugs and, once we get him to the station, you can identify him."

The statement sent shivers up her spine. She knew as well as he did that Haley had warned that Marcus would be on guard for undercover officers. "I've watched enough crime shows to know you don't have enough evidence to bring him in. It's weak and, even if you match his DNA after the fact, the arrest could be torn apart in court."

If Lani didn't convince Marcus to take a second meeting, they would lose him. Marcus would know Haley had betrayed him and they would never get another chance to draw him out into the open.

"Who knows how long I'll be in hiding while all his clientele are on the hunt for me." Karenna's voice shook as she imagined coming this close to ending the nightmare only for it to continue indefinitely. "And what about Sarah? The longer we take to get him, the greater chance he has in murdering her." She shook her head. "You need me to identify him. I've seen his face. You have tons of officers here. I know you'll have my back."

His face paled. "I agree with you, but I also need to make this decision for the right reasons. Your safety is my priority."

Karenna pressed forward, encouraged. "Let me go up on the hill. You said yourself those officers are hiding. Look how thick the trees and weeds are. If we go now, we can hide, too. It'll be easy."

He stared at her, his expression wavering.

"Ray, you know it's the best option."

"It doesn't mean I like it." He spoke to the rest of the team and listened for a while. Half a minute later, Officer Vivienne Armstrong and her K-9 partner, a border collie named Hank, appeared at the passenger side door.

"We need to get in position fast," he said, getting Abby from the back.

They hustled through the wooded area, hiking up

the hill. Ray let Abby lead the way, sniffing, working. "She'll give us a heads-up if he's in the area."

"But Haley said he wouldn't have drugs on him."

"If he's the chemist of this fentanyl, like I think he is, there'll be enough traces on him that she'll alert. If he did any dealing at all today, she'll alert. Besides, after her near-death experience, if this is the guy who put fentanyl in your apartment, I think she'll be highly attuned to his smell."

They reached the top of the hill and found a spot the officers all agreed would provide plenty of cover. Karenna bent over to remove the bits of twigs and leaves stuck to her canvas shoes. Some of the weeds in front of the bushes and trees were chest deep. They really were hidden well from view, but there were enough spots in between the vegetation to see below.

Ray tapped her shoulder and pointed to the opposite side of the hill. Belle stood guard with her German shepherd. Vivienne had moved and taken her station at the other end of the hill with the border collie at her side. Ray picked a spot behind some trees, holding a set of binoculars. "I've got visual of Lani and the entire area." He handed Karenna her own set of military-grade binoculars.

"If you see him and he's the guy, then we take him in. He left behind enough evidence these past few days that if his DNA is a match, we know he's our guy."

"Are you worried that if you take him down now, he won't lead you back to his operation?"

"Karenna, getting a criminal who tried to kill you off the street is enough for me."

"Is it?" She searched his eyes for signs of future resentment. The old Ray wouldn't be satisfied with one guy behind bars. He'd want to make sure an entire drug operation was eliminated.

"You've helped me remember the purpose of this job. It's to keep the streets safe so people can enjoy their lives. No guilt or revenge needed." He flashed the same shy smile that had made her fall for him all those years ago.

She believed him, but she was too scared to say it aloud. He pointed down the hill. She experimented with the dials on the binoculars, zooming onto the cement path designed to look like cobblestone. She found the leather flats of the officer Ray called Lani.

Lani wore a fashionable green spring jacket that cinched just below the waist and a loose silk scarf around her neck. An elaborate jeweled clasp held her long blond hair up. She really looked the part of a dancer.

Ray put a hand on Karenna's back. "Noelle just spotted someone matching his description approaching from the east."

Karenna swung her binoculars to the left, searching the path for Noelle and her partner, Liberty, the yellow Lab with the dark patch on her ear. "What about people? Park-goers? Will they wander in?"

"It's our job to consider all those angles, Karenna. We've got it covered. Our other officers are closing off the area behind him. Marcus will have no idea. Can you see up the path through the trees and bushes?"

She ducked slightly so she could peek through two groupings of tree branches. Expensive leather shoes came into view. She couldn't claim he was the guy based on the shoes, though. If she could zoom in a little further she might see scratch marks on the leather from when she'd tried to fight his foot off her chest, but then again, he could be wearing different shoes.

Her neck tightened, remembering all too well what it felt like to be suffocating under water. She moved the binoculars up to see the man's face. Then she'd know for sure. Something blocked her view. She dropped the binoculars.

Ray whispered into her ear. "Bradley jogged past him to get in place and to lessen suspicion that the pathways have been blocked. We've got confirmation the playground is empty. No civilians in the area. Officers from the 68th Precinct are on their way to assist with booking after we make the arrest." His finger remained on the earpiece as he narrated the news he was receiving. He dropped his hand. "Karenna, can you see him? Is it the guy?"

"I haven't had a chance yet." She adjusted the dial to lessen the zoom. This time, she captured a bird's-eye view of the park below. Three officers with their K-9s were hiding behind trees and shrubbery in various locations, but even though she could spot them from the high vantage point, she felt certain they'd be invisible to Lani and the approaching suspect. She found Noelle and her dog Liberty on a different path, but the other two were unknown officers. The strategic positions suddenly made sense. If Marcus decided to run, they had all three pathways blocked.

Detective Nate Slater, the one she'd met at the hospital, kicked his foot up on a bench around the corner from Lani. He wore gray sweatpants and stretched the back of his leg as if he were about to take a run. His yellow Lab, Murphy, waited patiently.

Karenna brought the binoculars back down to Lani

and was finally able to zoom in on the man. He was already talking to Lani.

Ray stepped closer to Karenna. "He's asking how she knows Haley, and she's telling him about hurting her Achilles tendon," he whispered. "Anything yet?"

With a shaky breath, she fixed the focus dial on the man's face. The same sunglasses covered his eyes.

"Can she get him to take his sunglasses off?"

Ray relayed the request. "Make him think you can't trust him without seeing his eyes."

However Lani phrased the request had made Marcus straighten. The hair and the build and... He relaxed and smiled at whatever Officer Jameson had just said, his teeth flashing. He lowered his sunglasses just for a second to gaze at Lani before putting them back in place.

Karenna dropped the binoculars, letting them hit her chest with a thud. It was as if he'd just bared his teeth and was coming for her again. "It's him. It's him."

"I thought so. Abby's been doing a passive alert for the past thirty seconds, but I didn't want any wiggle room in court." Ray's eyes hardened, and he lifted his finger to his ear. "Suspect's identity confirmed. Take him down."

Abby stood with her nose in a point as if she'd like nothing more than to arrest the man herself. But she remained still and quiet. Belle stood stock-still with Justice on the far side of the plateau they were on top of, while Vivienne offered a thumbs-up on the opposite side, the one closest to Third Street.

Ray watched her face. "Are you okay? They're going in for the arrest."

Karenna nodded and forced herself to lift the binoculars. While she didn't want to look at Marcus for another moment, she wanted to watch his arrest. Finally, she could get her life back without worrying the next breath would be her last. She could visit Sarah at the hospital and tell her of this moment every day until she woke up. She wouldn't have to worry that he'd target people she knew…

Two of the plainclothes detectives, Nate Slater and Bradley McGregor, began jogging in the direction of Marcus and Lani Jameson.

"Marcus is busy explaining to Lani his rules for drug drops. He's not suspicious," Ray told her.

Like a carefully choreographed routine, Nate ran on the path covered in wood chips while Bradley approached on the paved pathway. Without the binoculars, she never would've caught the way Nate moved his right hand to his back. Bradley mirrored the movement. Either going for their gun or handcuffs, she wasn't sure. The other officers remained crouched and ready in their hiding spots.

"They're really going to get him. It's almost over," she whispered.

"It really is," Ray answered.

The bush and ground next to Noelle's position exploded as the sound of a bullet echoed through the path. Noelle screamed and her dog, Liberty barked. Branches and leaves went everywhere.

The binoculars fell from Karenna's face as Ray's heavy weight plowed into her. They hit the ground, soggy old leaves barely cushioning their fall.

Ray covered her head with his arms. "Stay down."

Ray's elbows and right knee took the brunt of the landing, as he tried not to let his full weight crash on Karenna. His earpiece blasted with constant updates.

"Shooter! Active shooter!"

"Get Noelle to safety! Do we have Noelle?"

"I'll secure the east path."

Ray struggled to get his bearings. He wasn't sure who was talking to him. Belle and Justice were sprinting down the far side of the hill, toward the playground. Ray looked over his shoulder. Vivienne ran toward them, Hank by her side. She slid into a one-kneed crouch. "Everyone okay?"

Ray rolled off Karenna who, other than looking stunned, didn't seem to exhibit any gunshot wounds.

"Tell me we got him," he said.

Vivienne held her finger on her ear and looked out over the park expanse. Not a single person was in sight anymore.

Ray raised the binoculars. "Where's Lani? Bradley?"

Gavin's distinct gruff voice came through the earpiece. "Gunshots seemed to be targeted at Noelle and Liberty. Trying to locate shooter. Stay secure until notified. Switch to radios. Over."

"No." Ray groaned. "No." He zoomed the binoculars. In the farthest distance he finally spotted the majority of his team, including Noelle and Liberty. The hair on the back of Abby's neck stood straight and she pointed to the opposite side of the hill.

Karenna sat up and searched his face. "I'm fine. Go get him. Just call for backup. Please!"

He hesitated. He couldn't leave Karenna when Marcus and a shooter were out there.

"I've got her, Ray. I'll get her to safety," Vivienne said. "She's right. Go end this while Abby still has a scent."

He stood and looked between the officer and Karenna.

Adrenaline rushed through his veins but this time it felt different. He wanted to be smart and get the guy instead of rushing off without a plan. "I'll be back. Get to safety."

Ray ran down the backside of the hill, half sliding, half jogging to keep up with Abby on the incline. She had her nose pointed toward a grove of trees ahead. The park may be a city treasure, but over thirty thousand trees made it easy to hide.

He almost passed by his SUV parked on the side of the road. He warred with an inner desire to dive right into the trees and stop at nothing to get Marcus. But even though there was a shooter at the southwest end, there were still park-goers throughout. He couldn't risk their safety. He stopped, lifted a silent prayer that Abby would still find Marcus's scent, and grabbed the bean-bag rifle from his trunk.

All K-9 handlers kept such a rifle in the car to momentarily stun suspects that refused to surrender before the dog was sent in. It lessened the risk that the suspects would hurt the dog.

He swung the strap over his neck, the rifle at his back, and slammed the door. He'd just have to run faster and harder. "Time to go to work," he said again.

Abby didn't hesitate and bounded back onto a bark path across the street. They ran into the woods, off the main path. His lungs ached from the outright sprinting. Abby ran slightly ahead of him, with a loose leash, her white tail bouncing whenever there was a tree root or large rock Ray should jump over, too. The split-second warning was all he needed. They rounded a corner and Abby slid to a stop. Her nose strained toward a grouping of trees and bushes. She sat and did her front paw dance.

Ray struggled to gather his bearings and reached back for the beanbag rifle. He positioned it in front of his torso and pressed his shoulder radio. "I need backup at the most diagonal trail closest to West Drive."

The radio squawked back that all available officers were in the process of locking down the park.

His phone buzzed and he read the text: Share location—Belle.

Ray didn't hesitate to send her the coordinates, finding it ironic that the phone location feature Marcus used to scare and hurt his victims, Ray could use to make sure he didn't get away.

We're coming. Stay put, Belle texted back.

The seconds proved torturous, waiting, wondering if he was making the right decision. Would Karenna need to be locked up in some safe house without contact for months until they were able to set up another sting? By then Marcus would surely have other safeguards put into place.

He watched Abby to make sure she didn't relax. She glanced up at him, strained her nose, and did the same little dance. Marcus had to be hiding in there. The thick section of trees and bushes led to West Drive. If Marcus reached the road, there was a large expanse of grass to cross before reaching another hiding area. He'd be out in the open and sunk.

So it might be beneficial to run in after him. That way he'd force the guy out into the open. His gut didn't agree with the instinct that two days ago would've disregarded protocol to catch him. He took a deep breath and the peace from this morning returned.

The sound of footsteps ahead caught his attention.

He spotted Gavin and Belle. He texted them, lest Marcus overhear their plans.

I'll issue a warning that a dog is coming. If no surrender, I'm going in. The moment I spot Marcus, I'll deploy the beanbag to stun and you send Justice to get him. Sarge, can we get cover on the green expanse?

The phone buzzed immediately. Affirmative.

He nodded and belted out, "This is the Brooklyn K-9 Unit, NYPD. Come out with your hands up or we'll send the dog in and he *will* bite you."

Abby looked up with a pronounced tilt of her face as if saying, "Who, me? You know I don't bite." Her tongue flopped to the side as she panted. Her nose wriggled then she pointed again, this time with a slight diagonal. So, Marcus was on the move.

Ray spotted Belle at the end of the path. He aimed the barrel of his rifle up in the air. She gave him a nod to pursue the plan.

Ray positioned the beanbag rifle and readied his finger on the outside of the trigger. "Stay," he whispered and removed Abby's leash. She still pointed but remained on the spot. He couldn't risk her getting caught in the crosshairs. He stepped through the space between two hedges. The branches scratched against his belt, catching slightly, but bending to his will until he broke through a group of weeds surrounding the trees.

The last weak rays of sunlight fell on a pair of shoes moving. "Freeze! Police!"

Marcus burst out of his hiding place, heading in Gavin's direction.

"On the run!" Ray yelled. "Heads up!"

He lifted the rifle, aimed and pressed the trigger. The beanbag pellets, outfitted inside a clear shotgun shell, deployed and hit Marcus's lower back. He hollered, his arms flying up in the air as he tripped over a branch and fell to all fours.

"Clear!" Ray yelled.

"Seek!" Belle shouted. "Hold!"

The beanbag pellet had done the job of buying Justice time. The German shepherd burst through the far group of bushes.

Marcus was already up on one knee, clearly not ready to surrender. He raised an arm and Ray gasped. Marcus had a gun.

Ray dropped the beanbag rifle and moved to grab his weapon. Justice was already soaring in mid-jump. His jaws clamped on the man's arm and whipped it around like a chew toy. Marcus hollered and the gun dropped to the ground.

Belle followed behind Justice. "Good dog." She bent over and kicked the gun far away. Sarge stepped into the light from another set of shrubs and retrieved the handgun.

"Release," Belle said and Justice sat, panting and happy as if that was the best game ever. Belle recited the Miranda rights as she secured Marcus with a set of handcuffs. She clipped the leash back on Justice and gave the nod to Ray that it was safe to approach. Marcus groaned but said nothing.

"Come," Ray said. Abby bounded through the brush and appeared at his side. He attached her leash and crossed the distance to Marcus.

His insides shook a little, though, as he spotted the

shine of the guy's handgun in Gavin's possession. If Ray hadn't waited for backup and had entered through the bushes alone, would Marcus have shot him? Would he have shot Abby like he'd seemed intent to do to Justice?

A new sense of humility and thankfulness washed over him like never before. He wasn't some super cop that knew every criminal's move. He *needed* his teammates, and they needed him.

Sarge and Belle both kept watch until Marcus was secure in handcuffs. Ray took a second to investigate the man's forearm. Justice had been gentle. There were minor scratches but Belle's command to "hold" was a signal for Justice to use less teeth in her grab. Ray had worse bite marks from his time training the dogs, so this guy would be fine.

"They've found the park shooter," Gavin said. "It wasn't Marcus. It was someone after the bounty that gunrunner has out for Liberty. Word is he's not talking, though. Too scared."

Ray shook his head at what Noelle was going through with her partner. Gavin had thought the time of day and the location would make for a low-risk job for the top-notch tracker, but the bounty meant Liberty—and Noelle—would constantly be at risk. "I'm just thankful for the team. Couldn't have made this arrest without you."

Gavin took Marcus's elbow. "I'll deliver this package to the 68th Precinct to process. I believe you have a witness to thank, Ray."

Ray nodded. One of his favorite perks of being a K-9 officer was that the presence of the high-tech kennel meant his vehicle had no way to transport criminals. He spun on his heel and rushed back to the trail. The exhaustion of the past few days hit him in waves. He exhaled. He couldn't fully rest quite yet, though.

Now he *really* needed to lay his future on the line.

FIFTEEN

Karenna held her breath but kept the binoculars glued to her eyes.

"The shooter has been apprehended, Miss Pressley. We can move you safely to my vehicle now."

"Just one more minute, please." Karenna looked up at Officer Vivienne Armstrong who rested against the bark of a tree.

After Ray had run down the hill, Vivienne had listened to the radio and updated the surrounding officers on their position. Sarge had decided it was safer for them to stay put within the safety of the hill and trees until the shooter had been apprehended. Thankfully, despite Vivienne's halfhearted objections, she'd agreed to let Karenna use the binoculars to watch Ray go after Marcus.

Karenna hadn't been able to see what had happened in the middle of the trees and bushes to the north, but her heart finally started beating again when Ray emerged with Abby at his side and the rifle returned to his back. They were alive. And not only that, they were smiling.

The radio burst again with a gruff voice announcing, "K-9 Unit, suspect apprehended."

"That's what I like to hear." Vivienne patted her side leg and her border collie instantly sat up, alert.

"They're referring to Marcus, right?"

She nodded. "They got him. Come to think of it, I'd like to walk down *this* side of the hill instead and take the long way back to our vehicle. Hank and I haven't had enough steps for the day yet. As a search-and-rescue dog, he needs lots of varying topography to stay at the top of his game." Vivienne's eyes twinkled with her smile.

Karenna scrambled to standing, understanding the route choice would be her chance to see Ray right away. "Thank you."

The terrain proved harder to go down than it was going up, as they zigzagged through the weeds and bushes, forging their own path to the closed-off road. Karenna had to keep her focus on her footing when she really wanted to be monitoring Ray's progress.

The moment she reached flat ground, she looked up to find Ray already in front of her, beaming. He glanced at Vivienne. "Thank you."

The dogs, Hank and Abby, examined each other but didn't move away from their partners. They both displayed an exaggerated nod with a loud sniff. Karenna liked to think they were acknowledging and congratulating each other on a job well done, but she didn't voice her thoughts aloud.

"See you back at the station," Vivienne said and continued on toward the path that would weave around the hill and back to the playground, presumably to remove the signs she'd placed to keep park-goers away.

Karenna's attention shifted to Ray. He appeared uninjured. Aside from some leaves in his hair, he looked wonderful. In fact, his cute dimple had returned.

"Your, uh…" He lifted the cap off her head. "I think we better get this wig off you." He helped her remove the bobby pins and the fake bundle of hair. She understood why instantly. The braid was so full of twigs and weeds, she was probably at risk of poison ivy exposure.

"Apologize to your sister for me for ruining her wig."

He laughed. "Are you kidding? She's going to insist it's proof the NYPD needs her services. She'll be crowing about keeping you safe for weeks. I won't hear the end of it." He placed the wig and his rifle in the back of his SUV before turning back to face her.

She hesitated and finally, awkwardly, reached up to give him a hug, the binoculars around her neck bouncing against his gear. "Thank you," she whispered.

They parted and she bent over to pet Abby. Her fur was soft but also needed a good grooming to get rid of the weeds she'd collected from the woods. "I hope you like baths."

The dog instantly sat, rolled over and presented her belly. Karenna laughed and obliged with a belly rub.

"Hey, she never does that for anyone but me."

"You told me once before I'm not just anyone," she answered softly.

Ray offered his hand and Karenna accepted, the warmth rushing up her arms as he gently helped her return to stand in front of him. "That I did," he said.

His phone buzzed. He frowned and picked it up. She didn't mean to snoop but she could see the text from her vantage point.

Urgent meeting at station. Return ASAP.

"That's a first." He blinked rapidly. "I'm… I'm sorry. I need to go. You can either wait at the station or I can see if another officer is available to take you to the safe location—it's a hotel."

Her bones suddenly felt heavy. "I still need to be under protection?"

He moved to open the door for Abby, frowning. She jumped right inside and went straight for her water bowl. "Just until we confirm Marcus was the one who tainted the drugs and shot up your apartment. There's plenty of evidence, so if it's him, we'll find out."

"Yes, but—"

He closed the door. "I'm sorry, Karenna. It's not what I want, either. Given the threat he made through his clients, we need to make sure you aren't walking into an ambush. I'm trying to follow the wisest path instead of full-steam ahead."

As much as she wanted to argue, she couldn't. He really had changed. She could see it in his entire demeanor, like the weight on his shoulders had vanished. "I understand. But, given the shooting incident, these officers have enough to deal with right now. I don't mind waiting awhile at the station. I'd like to stay with you."

His eyebrows rose and he opened his mouth to say something before closing it and nodding with finality.

"Were you going to say something?"

He grimaced. "Not the right time."

She practically stomped to her side of the vehicle. Just this morning she'd prayed for clear wisdom about a possible relationship with Ray. She'd wanted to pour out her feelings just now. If she made the first move when Ray had been the one who had broken up with her, wouldn't she always question if she loved him more than he loved her?

He opened the door for her. She took a seat and forced a smile on her face. She was so thankful Marcus Willington had been caught. That should be enough. But she wanted an answer about Ray.

Wait wasn't the response she'd prepared to get from the Lord. Wasn't five years long enough to wait for a clear yes or no? But, if she wanted the Lord's help, she needed to be prepared for the answer to be no. She'd have to say goodbye to Ray. Again.

The station was bustling with activity when he arrived. Gavin was still in full gear, his K-9, Tommy, by his side, having obviously arrived mere minutes before him. He was standing in the doorway of his office in heated discussion with Eden and another tech Ray didn't recognize.

Henry slapped him on the back. "Sounds like you did good. No more Lone Ranger, eh?"

Ray bit back a snarky retort and instead nodded. "You're looking at a team player."

"Glad to hear it," Gavin said, having approached from behind. "You've always been a good cop. About time you became a great one. Meeting room in five."

After making sure Karenna was settled, waiting in the office cubicle he often used, he filled his cup of coffee. The team gradually returned, looking a bit ragged. But before Ray could hear each of their individual tales of the sting, Gavin sauntered in.

"Everyone okay and accounted for?"

Thumbs-up from all around, even from Noelle who,

despite looking shaken, seemed eager to hear whatever Gavin had called them back for.

Gavin was the only one who didn't take a seat. "Big day. Successful day." He placed his hands on the back of his chair. "I've called this meeting because we've had news from the geneticist we've contracted."

Ray leaned forward. In fact, the whole team seemed to be holding their breath.

"The DNA collected at the McGregor crime scene twenty years ago was degraded—"

Groans from half the team cut Gavin off. He held up his hands and continued. "But we had been prepared for that. The geneticist was able to work past that and found a match on CODIS."

Detective Bradley McGregor leaned forward. "You found him?" His eagerness was understandable. The DNA was from whoever had likely murdered his parents.

Gavin watched him with concern. "No, but we found his family tree. Once we had a match, there was a warrant made to the corresponding DNA sequencing firm." He grinned. "We've found the closest relative and…"

"Gavin, you're killing us with suspense," Nate protested.

Their sergeant beamed. "The relative lives in Brooklyn. We've officially got a solid lead."

The whoops, hollers and claps echoed off the wall. You would've thought the New York Giants had won the Super Bowl. Gavin didn't lose his smile but raised his hands for the team to quiet.

"The relative has an apartment in Dumbo." He used the Brooklyn neighborhood nickname for Down Under the Manhattan Bridge Overpass. "There's just one small fly in the ointment. He's currently undercover."

"He's a cop?" Bradley asked, his forehead in a frown.

"U.S. Deputy Marshal in fact," Eden interjected. She glanced at Gavin and realized she was stealing his thunder, so took a step back.

"Yes. His name is Emmett Gage, and he is a deputy marshal. Belle, I'm assigning you to interview Deputy Gage as soon as it's feasible given his undercover status. The Marshal's office said they'll have him contact you as soon as possible."

Belle seemed to sit taller, a smile on her face. "Yes, sir."

"Given the events of the day," Gavin continued, "Penny will be calling Sal's Pizza to give them fair warning that I'm treating the team to a late dinner. Dismissed!"

The group stood, the morale the highest Ray had seen in a while.

"Ray, a word," Gavin said, a finger up in the air.

Bradley also seemed to hang back.

"I don't want to get Penny's hopes up," Bradley was saying. "We found the family tree. It doesn't mean we'll find the murderer."

Gavin placed a hand on his shoulder. "You're right, but we need to celebrate the little victories, Bradley. Cling to hope. It's what keeps us going on long days."

Such a strong lead to the McGregors' killer might also answer questions about last month's double homicide of Lucy Emery's parents. Perhaps the Brooklyn K-9 Unit would know once and for all if they were dealing with the same killer or a copycat.

The moment Bradley exited the room, Gavin took

out his phone. "The protection order is lifted. The 68th Precinct took his fingerprints and finally got this Marcus guy's real name—Brice Angelo. He's a chemist fired by a pharmaceutical corporation for some illegal dealings in Florida. Gave the silent treatment until he heard we knew about the app and had a positive identification, the police shirt and gun you found in the Dumpster after the shooting. With so much evidence against him, he confessed to everything. Now that his drugs are off the market, no one will be looking for Karenna."

"That's great news."

Gavin nodded. "Take the rest of the day off, Ray. That's an order. And tomorrow, while you're at it."

Ray had never been so happy to follow orders. He rushed straight to the locker room to change into a pair of jeans and a shirt he kept there just in case. He had one last thing to do before he could relax.

Karenna fingered the family photo of Ray with his mom and sister with a smile. If she was going to have to say goodbye, at least she felt like she would have closure this time, even though the thought made her throat tighten with held-back tears.

Ray appeared at the cubicle in a navy polo and jeans. Once again, he looked like a million bucks while her hair, despite the thorough finger-styling, probably resembled tumbleweed.

He smiled. "Ready?"

They walked shoulder to shoulder next door to the training center and picked up Abby. On their way back to the SUV, he stopped at the bench underneath one of the trees. "I didn't want to tell you in front of everyone else, but the threat is over."

She gasped, her heart lifting. "What are you saying? Completely?"

"It's done." His smile took her breath away, and the tears she'd fought back for days finally won. He reached for her and pulled her close.

Karenna stepped back, wiping the moisture away from her eyes. "I'm just so happy." She exhaled. "But why did you wait to tell me?"

His smile vanished. "I need to tell you something and I wanted you to know without a doubt that it has nothing to do with duty or dedication to my job. I'm off work now." His hands dropped from her shoulders down to her elbows and his eyes searched hers. "More than ever, I've seen how much growing up I had to do to appreciate you. You don't owe me anything, but I can't say goodbye without telling you…" He pulled in a breath and looked at the trees. "Karenna, I love you and if there's any chance—"

"Ray," she said. His eyes met hers again. "You don't need to convince me to give a statement. I'll happily offer my confession. I love you, too."

He dropped his hands to her waist and pulled her closer until their lips were only inches apart. "You really have kept watching those true crime shows, haven't you? You're speaking the lingo now?"

"Ten-four," she whispered. He closed his eyes and gently pressed his lips on hers.

EPILOGUE

"You sure you want to do this?" Ray stood in the pedal boat, reaching for her hand as she waited on the dock at LeFrak Center.

She hesitated, her heart racing as she glanced at the water. "Yes. I love Prospect Park and the lake. I don't want to be scared of it the rest of my life." She nodded and grabbed his hand. He helped her into the rocking boat and gently tugged until she was safely to her seat.

"You okay?" he asked.

"Yes. New, happy memories in the making. Full-speed ahead."

"Aye, aye, captain," he said.

Only there was no dramatic motor to start. Karenna concentrated for a few seconds. "These things are harder to pedal than I thought. Too bad I already worked out for the day." Exercising was one of the many changes she'd made in the last couple of weeks. If anyone ever shot at her again, she'd be ready for the army crawl, though she prayed that would never, ever happen. "Where should we go?"

"If you don't mind me choosing, I have a spot in mind I think you'll enjoy. How was today's hospital visit?"

"Oh, wonderful! Sarah thinks she'll get to go home tomorrow." Karenna grinned. Her friend had finally emerged from her coma after a couple weeks. "She'll live with her parents until her apartment is remodeled."

He raised an eyebrow. "Think she'll be okay?"

"Yeah. She'd thought Marcus—I mean Brice—was cheating on her and followed him only to discover what his real day job was. She confronted him in the park right before I arrived. He force-fed the pills down her and was trying to finish her off when I showed up." She shivered at the thought. "She's trying to reevaluate the choices she made, but it's going to be a long road."

Ray squeezed her hand. "Sarge said the lead she gave Detective Slater panned out. They found his chemical lab and CSI is working at cleaning the whole thing out."

"What a relief."

"And once Celia Dunbar heard Marcus—or 'Stephen' as she knew him—was in jail, she was happy to agree to testify against him."

"How is that cold case you were working on going?" she asked.

"Well, I can't say much, but Belle is scheduled to interview our new lead tomorrow." He grinned. "And now I'll stop talking about work." He winked and they enjoyed the quiet lapping of the water against the hull as Ray steered around an inlet with his right hand. With his left, Ray wrapped his fingers around her hand, but changed his grip every few seconds, wrapping it in such a way that his knuckles made the same move they would have had he been flipping the coin across his hand.

She laughed. "You're missing the challenge coin, aren't you?" He'd told her recently how he'd stopped carrying it.

He flashed a bashful grin. "I never realized how much I fidget without it."

"Are you going to get a different coin then?"

He steered the boat to a nearby dock. She squinted ahead. There was a giant group of people waiting in the distance. It might've been her imagination, but they seemed to be scattering, as if they didn't want to be seen. Ray's face morphed into a mischievous grin as he gave her a side glance. "Nah, I don't think I want another coin. I've seen guys do the same roll-over-the-knuckles move with a ring."

Karenna's suspicions mounted and she couldn't stop the smile growing on her face. He was teasing her, on purpose. "Raymond Morrow," she said. "I'm telling you right now, if we ever get married, that ring better stay on your finger."

His head tipped back as he laughed deeply. She couldn't help but join him. "Yes, ma'am," he finally said. "I think that's probably fair."

"Glad we're on the same page."

He pulled up to the dock, the laughter suddenly gone. He tied the boat and helped her to standing. "There's something else I'd like to make sure we're on the same page about."

"Oh?" She looked over his shoulder. "Ray, was that your family back there? Your aunts and uncles? And my dad?" She squinted. "Did I see some of my coworkers and your cop friends?"

His eyes met hers. "Well, I hope we can say it will be *our* family and friends someday." He got down on one knee and, despite her earlier suspicions, her stomach still fluttered. She placed a hand on her chest and heard a bark in the distance. Abby came bounding down the dock, sliding to a stop at their feet.

"Sorry!" Greta's voice hollered from around the corner. "She didn't want to miss it!"

They were both laughing now, despite Ray shaking his head. He looked up. "Karenna, would you please do me the honor of being my wife?"

"Well, has he asked her yet?" Her dad's voice carried through the wind.

Karenna pulled him up to standing, filled with joy. "Yes," she whispered. "I would love to because I love you." His mouth found hers and she melted at his soft kisses.

Then she leaned back and yelled, for the sake of those hiding, "Yes!"

Cheers and the sound of running feet accompanied Abby's bark of approval.

Ray wrapped his arms around her shoulders as they turned to greet their family and friends. Karenna had never felt so safe and so loved.

* * * * *

SPECIAL EXCERPT FROM

LOVE INSPIRED SUSPENSE
INSPIRATIONAL ROMANCE

*Out horseback riding, Dr. Katherine Gilroy
accidentally stumbles into a deadly shoot-out and
comes to US marshal Dominic O'Ryan's aid. Now with
Dominic injured and under her care, she's determined to
help him find the fugitive who killed his partner...before
they both end up dead.*

Read on for a sneak preview of
Mountain Fugitive *by Lynette Eason,*
available October 2021 from Love Inspired Suspense.

Katherine placed a hand on his shoulder. "Don't move,"
she said.

He blinked and she caught a glimpse of sapphire-blue
eyes. He let out another groan.

"Just stay still and let me look at your head."

"I'm fine." He rolled to his side and he squinted up at
her. "Who're you?"

"I'm Dr. Katherine Gilroy, so I think I'm the better
judge of whether or not you're fine. You have a head
wound, which means possible concussion." She reached
for him. "What's your name?"

He pushed her hand away. "Dominic O'Ryan. A
branch caught me. Knocked me loopy for a few seconds,
but not out. We were running from the shooter." His eyes
sharpened. "He's still out there." His hand went to his
right hip, gripping the empty holster next to the badge

on his belt. A star within a circle. "Where's my gun? Where's Carl? My partner, Carl Manning. We need to get out of here."

"I'm sorry," Katherine said, her voice soft. "He didn't make it."

He froze. Then horror sent his eyes wide—and searching. They found the man behind her and Dominic shuddered.

After a few seconds, he let out a low cry, then sucked in another deep breath and composed his features. The intense moment lasted only a few seconds, but Katherine knew he was compartmentalizing, stuffing his emotions into a place he could hold them and deal with them later.

She knew because she'd often done the same thing. Still did on occasion.

In spite of that, his grief was palpable, and Katherine's heart thudded with sympathy for him. She moved back to give him some privacy, her eyes sweeping the hills around them once more. Again, she saw nothing, but the hairs on the back of her neck were standing straight up. "I think we need to find some better cover."

As if to prove her point, another crack sounded. Katherine grabbed the first-aid kit with one hand and pulled Dominic to his feet with the other. "Run!"

Don't miss
Mountain Fugitive *by Lynette Eason,*
available October 2021 wherever
Love Inspired Suspense books and ebooks are sold.

LoveInspired.com

LOVE INSPIRED
INSPIRATIONAL ROMANCE

UPLIFTING STORIES OF FAITH, FORGIVENESS AND HOPE.

Join our social communities to connect with other readers who share your love!

Sign up for the Love Inspired newsletter at **LoveInspired.com** to be the first to find out about upcoming titles, special promotions and exclusive content.

CONNECT WITH US AT:

 Facebook.com/LoveInspiredBooks

 Twitter.com/LoveInspiredBks

Facebook.com/groups/HarlequinConnection